The
BURNINGS

Naomi Kelsey

Harper
North

HarperNorth
Windmill Green
24 Mount Street
Manchester M2 3NX

A division of
HarperCollins*Publishers*
1 London Bridge Street
London SE1 9GF

www.harpercollins.co.uk

HarperCollins*Publishers*
Macken House
39/40 Mayor Street Upper
Dublin 1
D01 C9W8

First published by HarperNorth in 2023

1 3 5 7 9 10 8 6 4 2

A catalogue record for this book
is available from the British Library

Hardback ISBN: 9780008534769
Trade paperback ISBN: 9780008541934

Printed and bound in Great Britain by
CPI Group (UK) Ltd, Croydon

To my mum, who taught me not only to love stories,
but also that I could write them.

Now o'er the one-half world
Nature seems dead, and wicked dreams abuse
The curtain'd sleep; now witchcraft celebrates
Pale Hecate's offerings
'Macbeth'

Prologue

Denmark
1578

The walls loomed up before him, stark against a starless sky. As he approached, the noises of men drowned out the gulls' screams: groans of those too weak for more, shrieks of those who had long ago forgotten sanity, the cries of a few who still hoped to be freed. The man Bothwell sought had been in Dragsholm Castle almost ten years; Bothwell doubted he'd ever been blinded by hope. His uncle had been blind in other ways.

Coins rattled from his purse to the guards' hands; it took far less than he'd expected for the keys to start jangling. Were they so poorly paid? But he wasn't a man who wasted time on sympathy, and he gave them nothing else save an impatient glare.

They led him inside, through corridors where draughts bent torch flames backwards and an unseasonal chill wrung damp from stone walls. As their footsteps knelled past cell doors, men flung themselves against narrow grilles, gibbering, pleading innocence, snarling vengeance. A lesser man might have flinched; Bothwell eyed them thoughtfully. Had they once been warriors? Councillors? Churchmen?

One prisoner had dreamed of being a king.

They were moving upwards, towards the highest tower, and he felt a thrill of familial pride: of course a Hepburn would have to be confined in the most secure of cells. The further they ascended, the quieter the chambers became. These were men who'd had dignity drilled into them like sword-fighting, who wouldn't have screamed if the devil himself had appeared in their cell, but struck a bargain with him. Some said his uncle already had. Though, if so, the devil had failed to keep his side.

The guards stopped outside a cell so high the shutters trembled in the winds off Nekselø Bay. Bothwell glanced back at the spiral stairs: a long way to fall, should someone need to fall.

He turned back to the guards. Was it the barely past Danish winter making them so whey-faced, or could they see his thoughts in his eyes? The latter, he hoped: high time a Hepburn instilled fear instead of provoking scorn.

'You will leave me alone with him.'

Defying him didn't occur to them.

Once alone, he turned the key; it creaked, stiff with disuse. Good. No one else had been here.

The stench hit him like a flintlock, and it took every ounce of his obstinacy not to gag. The last thing he wanted was to appear weak in front of his uncle. Clenching his teeth, Bothwell stepped into the cell.

Seven paces by seven, no more. Just high enough for him to stand – but the prisoner couldn't. Hunched beside a wooden pillar was his uncle's wretched figure. Chains had chafed his wrists raw: a reek of rotting flesh and pus spread every time he shifted position. They'd been pinned at ankle height, forcing him to stoop or crawl; Bothwell rolled his own broadening shoulders with grim satisfaction.

'Who are you?'

The voice was harsh as a crow's, the mouth that hurled the demand a mess of black stumps and gaps, half-hidden beneath a beard once as dark and oiled as Bothwell's own, now tangled and crusted yellow with vomit. A man who no longer cared, who knew there were few things worth caring about.

Bothwell circled the prisoner. Best to check for concealed weapons – you never knew with a Hepburn, even one imprisoned for years, and besides, he rather liked making people wait. Beneath his boots a smooth circle had been worn, its edges exactly where Bothwell's feet fell. He liked that too: his stride was just like his uncle's, a man who might have fallen far but who'd had the furthest of distances to fall.

He crouched down to look the prisoner in the eye. 'I'm the Earl of Bothwell.'

A watery croak – and a pellet of spit landed on the stones. 'Pox on that. If you're here to mock me, be warned: no one emerges from a flyting with me pleased with themselves.'

'My name is Francis Stewart, grandson of King James the Fifth of Scotland, son of John Stewart, Prior of Coldingham, and Lady Janet Hepburn.'

'Jenny's brat!' The prisoner shifted, groaned with the new pain, and peered closely at Bothwell. 'So you've usurped my title.'

'You forfeited it. They belted me earl as soon as I turned sixteen.'

'Which was what – yesterday? You're a whelp.'

A flash of steel. The prisoner swallowed delicately as a blade pressed against his throat. 'I believe you've cut my beard. And there I was, taking such pride in it.'

Bothwell pressed the blade closer. 'They told me you were mad.'

Dark eyes glinted. 'Perhaps the world is mad.'

'Perhaps you're an arrogant fool.'

The prisoner laughed, the barked scorn of a man who'd lived a life where blades bit flesh more often than teeth bit bread. 'Hark at you. So young, so free with knives – and strolling into Dragsholm as if no one would ever dream of locking you in here. I'd say you've been called an arrogant fool all your life.'

Bothwell's smile glittered as mirthlessly as his uncle's. 'Half right. No one calls me a fool – but my so-called arrogance is no more than justified pride.'

'Apparently you've taken my words along with my title.' He arched an eyebrow. 'What else would you have? As you see, I'm excessively endowed with riches.'

'Your plan.'

'Then lower the knife.'

'You'd bargain with me?'

'Why not? I have something you want. Besides, words wrung at knifepoint rarely offer good sense.'

Bothwell regarded him thoughtfully – then tossed the knife up, caught it by the hilt and sheathed it. 'Then let's have your good sense. Your plan?'

The prisoner rubbed his throat; his chains scraped stone. 'My plan is locked in an English castle.'

Bothwell arched his own eyebrows, a darker, sharper version of his uncle's cynicism. 'She was never your plan. You, me, our family – *that* was always your scheme.'

A hint of a smile. 'Perhaps you aren't a fool after all.'

'How would you have done it?'

The prisoner leaned forward. 'Firstly, never trust the earls. They'll stab you in the back before you hear the daggers slide from their sheaths.'

'I don't trust anyone.'

'But you will need help.'

'To do what? Tell me what your plan was.'

Now the smile spread: thin malevolence. 'To raise the Hepburns to the throne of course. Why else did I have Jenny marry your father? You're a king's grandson – if I can't be king, you should be.'

'King James's father wasn't a bastard. I'm the presumed heir, true. But James is four years younger than me, and he'll marry before long.'

'The Stuarts have a habit of dying violently.'

'Bloodshed begets bloodshed. I want to keep the throne, not keep it warm for my assassin. It must be won legitimately. But without King James's mother – without our claim through marriage, how can it be done?'

'In truth she'd probably have proved more hindrance than help.' The prisoner narrowed his eyes in remembrance. 'If only she were more like her cousin. Elizabeth knows how to win. How to survive. She understands the easiest way to conquer an enemy is when they're already wounded. And if their own hands appear to wield the axe, so much the better.'

'So I should let James destroy himself?'

'You should make sure he does. What's he now, twelve? You have years to make him the worst king Scotland has ever seen. And when he's ruined himself, then all of Scotland will turn away from the Stuarts and towards their greatest lord. You.'

'How would you destroy James? As you did his father?'

'No one knows who murdered Darnley.' His eyes were unreadable. 'Though the explosion didn't kill him, so I wouldn't rely on gunpowder.'

'Darnley was already ruined before Kirk o' Field. I could bring James whores ridden with French pox.'

'Ah, but then he'd be truly mad, and madmen are dangerous. Moreover, he wouldn't know he was weak, and that's crucial.' The prisoner leaned forward again. 'You need to make him, and everyone else, see he's a pathetic, craven sliver of a man. Make him afraid. Terrified of his own shadow. Your greatest weapon will be that boy's fear.'

'*Fear.*' Bothwell rocked back on his heels, relishing the word. 'And how to frighten him?'

The prisoner's face lurched towards Bothwell's. 'I can help you! Set me free and I'll help.'

A slow smile played across Bothwell's lips. 'I will set you free.'

His hand closed around the chain, caressing its iron links as if they were sacred rosary beads.

The air around the tower was serrated with gull shrieks and human screams, stretched thin by the yank of sea winds. How easy it was for the guards to pretend they heard nothing.

PART I

Fair is foul, and foul is fair:
Hover through the fog and filthy air.
'Macbeth'

1

Denmark
June 1589

They were burning a witch in Helsingør.

Margareta could smell the smoke from the wharf, no matter how close to the oyster sellers she stepped; caught by the dawn boats, the shellfish were now drying into brackish dullness, but even salted rot was better than the smell of a burning. Only wood so far, but Margareta knew what would follow. She'd be smelling it for hours, if not days; every time she brushed her hair or smoothed her skirts she'd gag at the stench of seared meat. Dear God, if there were suckling pigs roasting on spits in Kronborg Castle's great hall, she'd be sick.

Others clearly weren't so squeamish: a gang of boys dashed past, nearly knocking Margareta and the oyster stall into the sea. Youthful ghoulishness, or the chance to cut a few purses loose in the crowd? Judging from their bare feet and the elbows poking through worn woollen tunics, Margareta suspected the latter. Behind them, knots of women drifted towards the square, half-filled baskets revealing they weren't truly ready to leave the fish market, while the men in sober black cloaks with piously stern faces didn't fool Margareta. They were all going to watch.

She'd never find Ilsa in this crowd. She might as well give up and go back to the castle before she was missed by the dowager queen. Any longer than an hour's absence from the princess's side and Queen Sophia would observe, judge, and punish. Wincing at the thought, Margareta hunched deeper into her black velvet hood and turned back towards Kronborg.

'Greta!'

The glee in her milk-sister's hiss – echoing so many triumphs in hide-and-seek, so many discoveries of Margareta's torn stockings – told her it was Ilsa, along with the childish nickname only Ilsa remembered.

Margareta drew a smile across her face and turned around. 'Ilsa.'

The fair-haired girl leaning against the whitewashed wall of a shipwright's building was everything Margareta wasn't: small bones as delicate as bluebirds' eggs, red lips sharpened in amusement, like a *havfrue* just emerged from the sea; it was far too easy to imagine Ilsa bringing down storms on a hapless fisherman. Next to her, Margareta felt like a sprite's capricious trick. She, who never quite knew what to do with her face or overlong limbs, should have been the one apprenticed to a midwife, elbow-deep in sweat and blood each day, not serving a princess in the Danish court.

Folding her arms, Ilsa said, 'We weren't supposed to meet here.'

Margareta tensed, ready to scrap. But they were no longer seven years old; they sparred with words now, and Ilsa's had all the reach her short arms had lacked. 'It's crowded.'

'So much the better. Come on, Greta.'

Ilsa spun on her heel and strode away, knowing Margareta would follow. Margareta grimaced and trailed after her, whisking her brocade skirts around the cats snarling over a cod carcass and away from the fish scales forming tiny, treacherous cobbles underfoot. Instead of joining the crowds, Ilsa led Margareta through crooked alleys where their pattens barely kept their feet above food scraps and other, less recognizable detritus; past houses with glassless windows where Margareta glimpsed stark-eyed children, heads too big for their thin bodies. A world she would never have seen, if not for Ilsa. Kronborg's walls were so high you could look at puffed-dandelion clouds and the sapphire silk of the sea all day and pretend all Denmark was wonderful.

But nothing in the alleys turned her stomach so much as the sight awaiting them in the square.

The wood had caught properly now: flames speared the air, rising in a red mockery of the church's spires behind them. Stray gusts from the harbour buffeted smoke into the crowd, but they barely flinched, too busy baying at the spectacle.

'Witch!'

'Burn in hell!'

It was a woman. Margareta couldn't remember a burning that wasn't. This one was young, and her shaved hair had either once been as black as Margareta's, or else her scalp was bruised with soot and filth. Pitch-soaked ropes pinned her greyed shift tight against her body, outlining small breasts, and Margareta wanted to look away, as if averting her gaze would salvage the woman's dignity. Her body convulsed with shredded coughs as smoke writhed into her skin, her lungs.

'They haven't granted her mercy.'

Margareta turned at the venom in Ilsa's voice. 'What mercy? You know they never let them go – no matter who asks.'

Ilsa shook her head grimly. 'Some are given gunpowder pouches. A kindness.'

Kindness, in Kronborg, was a courtier ensuring even the most ungainly girls didn't sit out every dance. Margareta tried to crush her shameful yearning to run back to the castle.

'Is this why you wanted to meet me? To make me watch?'

Ilsa threw her a scornful glance. 'You can't pretend this doesn't happen, Greta.'

'I know it happens! I was there when—'

'Besides' – she tossed her head – 'if they ever put me on a pyre, I'd want you to bear witness.'

'Why?'

'So I'd know not everyone watching despised me.'

'Child killer!'

'Evil hag!'

Margareta winced at the crowd's insults, and her sister's words: she didn't deserve Ilsa's faith. Not after what she'd failed to do – what Ilsa had never forgiven her for. 'But you won't ever end up like her.'

'How do you know? She was a midwife, like me. The last mother she attended had lost three babes and died losing the fourth – and, instead of blaming her husband's drunken fists, they insisted Dorthea had cursed her.' Ilsa blinked rapidly; it might have been the ever-blackening smoke, but Margareta knew better. Quietly, she slipped an arm through her milk-sister's, and wondered if any words could be good enough.

'I've been to Scotland,' Ilsa said suddenly.

Scotland. The word had been on everyone's lips at court lately: *The King of Scotland seeks a wife! The Scottish ambassadors bring jewels and horses for Princess Anna!* But Margareta hadn't expected it to be on Ilsa's. 'What? How?'

'A boat,' Ilsa said dryly. 'Did you think I'd sailed in a sieve?'

'But how did you afford passage?'

Resentment seethed in Ilsa's eyes. 'I didn't have to pay.'

That note in her voice. Margareta yanked their linked arms, forcing Ilsa to face her. 'Who did? Why did they need a Danish midwife in Scotland? What are you up to now?'

Ilsa met her stare defiantly. 'Something that might make me as rich and powerful as you.'

'Oh, Ilsa, I'm hardly rich or powerful—'

Ilsa snorted. 'How many courses did you feast on yesterday? Just seven? I've been eking out a pottage for three days now. Don't pretend you know what it's like to be poor.'

'But I care about those who are.'

'Then prove it.'

Margareta fumbled for her purse. 'I haven't much coin here, but—'

'I don't want money, Greta. I want your help.'

Again, that grim obstinacy. 'To do what?'

'A mere trifle.'

'Ilsa, don't pretend, not to me.'

'Fine!' Ilsa shrugged ash from her shoulders with contrived nonchalance. 'The Scottish embassy will be here soon, won't they?'

'Within the week. What's that to do with—'

'Someone like me?' Ilsa laughed tersely. 'You'll see. When the princess marries King James, you'll go with her, won't you?'

'It hasn't been decided – either the marriage or her ladies.'

Ilsa raised her eyebrows. 'We both know you'll be at Anna's side. And I need you in Scotland, Greta.'

'To do what?' Margareta demanded again. 'Ilsa, what do you want?'

'For you to meet with Geillis Duncan.'

'Who?'

'A midwife's apprentice, like me.'

A scream grabbed Margareta's attention: the flames had seized flesh. She almost covered her mouth, dreading the stench, but the thought of Ilsa's scorn kept her fingers clamped around her purse, brocade carving roses into her palm.

'A midwife's apprentice?' she pressed. 'Is that all she is?'

That infuriating shrug. 'What else would she be?'

'You know what!' Margareta jerked her head towards the pyre. 'If you think I'll help you do anything that might send either of us to the stake, you must be mad.'

'No, Greta!' Ilsa clutched her sleeve, a wild gleam in her eyes. 'Don't you see? If people like you help, then we'll be safe!'

'People who dabble in – in *that*,' Margareta hissed, 'will never be safe!'

'This time they will.'

'How can you think that?'

'Because we have powerful men on our side.'

Margareta shook her head. 'Powerful men don't keep poor women safe. They use you to keep themselves safe.'

'Oh, don't be so selfish, Greta!' Ilsa bared her teeth in a furious snarl. 'I know you'd hate to believe a scheme of mine might succeed, but this one will if you'd only help us. We shared my mother's breast, Greta. We shared *everything*. Now I want a chance to share in what makes your world so good. Is that so much to ask?'

Margareta had bitten the inside of her cheek; she tasted blood as she whispered, '*Yes.* If it's witchcraft, of course it's too much to ask. I don't want any part of it. You know that!'

Ilsa set her jaw. 'You took it with my mother's milk. It's made you what you are.'

'No more than herring and berries!' Margareta protested. 'Just knowing about healing and herbs doesn't give anyone magical gifts, no matter what you wish to believe!'

'Deny it all you want. Witchcraft is in your blood, Greta. You can never be rid of it.' Ilsa pressed her face close. 'Geillis Duncan. Remember the name.'

Margareta ripped herself away. 'Enough, Ilsa! I'm going back.'

'To your feather bed?' Ilsa sneered. 'If you ever want to sleep soundly again, you'd better help me.'

'You cursed me a dozen times when we were girls, Ilsa – it's all spite and bluster.'

'Then why are you so afraid? If curses are just words and witches just women, why won't you help me?'

'Because I'm not a fool!' Margareta spun on her heel and stormed away, jostling a path through the crowd.

'Oh, but you are!' Ilsa called, her voice piercing despite the screams and jeers. 'You just don't know how foolish yet!'

The words would echo, Margareta knew, fighting back tears as she broke free of the onlookers. Ilsa's always did, needling her like a nettle rash. But this was more than mere squabbles and name-calling. This was witchcraft. This was terrifying, no matter who was involved – and with Ilsa, the fear was as close as bone.

When Margareta stepped through Kronborg's gatehouse, the sounds of Helsingør ceased. Instead of street preachers shouting and fishwives hawking herring and mackerel, she could hear gardeners pruning roses, fountains tossing silver water at their own surfaces, peacocks flourishing their deep calls.

Her castle life and her Helsingør life could not connect. One had hundreds of white beeswax candles in golden candlesticks; the other had grey tallow slumped in its own wax, belching rancid fumes. Glass glimmered in Kronborg's windows, while oil-soaked linen pinned to wooden frames struggled against Helsingør's rain. In Ilsa's home, sunlight left misshapen pale patches on the cloth, as if a cluster of tiny ghosts were trying to get in. Perhaps they were: Ilsa's mother

Johanna had suckled five of her own children as well as Margareta, and only Ilsa and Margareta remained. When she was small, Margareta had had nightmares about the dead siblings she'd never met, sharpened teeth gnawing through the linen windows, demanding she give their mother back, like vengeful *mylingar*. But, when she and Ilsa were seven, it had been Margareta's father who'd come to take her back.

She hadn't known him. A black-haired man whose moustache was oiled sharper than most knives, Gabriel Vinstar had brought a skirmish of snow into Johanna's home, and the loudest voice she'd ever heard. His words cut Johanna's song short: 'I'm here for the girl.'

'But she's ready for bed,' Johanna had pointed out, hugging both girls closer. Years later, Margareta could still feel the flour-dusted softness of her lap, her round shoulders warm beneath Margareta's cheek.

Gabriel had tossed several coins at them; one disappeared among the rushes on the floor. 'She's coming to Kronborg with me.'

Ilsa and Margareta had exchanged bewildered glances; neither had known which of them this velvet-clad stranger was barking about. As far as they understood life, they were blood-sisters, not just milk.

'I've a new wife,' Gabriel had continued, 'and this one ought to be there when her baby brother arrives.'

'I see,' Johanna had said, with meaning beneath her words that Margareta couldn't grasp. 'As it please you then, Master Vinstar.' She'd risen, tipping Ilsa and Margareta off her lap and dispatching the former to bed with a kiss, then crouching down to face Margareta. 'Listen, sweeting. This is your father.'

Margareta had frowned. Hadn't they buried her father last January after he fell on the icy harbour steps?

'He's taking you to court. You'll have ever so many pretty gowns and delicious things to eat – perhaps even your very own sleigh!'

Gabriel had snorted. 'Don't give the girl ideas.'

Johanna had cast her frustration down at the floor, which she only ever did when the men deserving it were richly dressed. 'You'll be a good girl, won't you, Margareta?'

'Can Ilsa come too?'

Johanna had bitten her lip. 'No, my lovely. Ilsa and I … we don't belong in Kronborg.'

'But I belong with you!'

'I wish you did. But perhaps it's for the best that you don't.'

Margareta had burst into tears, and Ilsa, crouching behind the bedchamber door, had copied her immediately, so the house strained with shrieks and the following moments were streaked with salt. There might have been kisses, embraces, squeezed hands, but the next thing Margareta remembered was hurrying after Gabriel through the snow, making three footprints for each of his, and gasping as she realized she'd only put on one stocking.

That night was the last time Johanna ever embraced her. At first, Margareta hadn't known how to leave Kronborg. Later, Ilsa had told her Johanna couldn't bear to see the girl she'd sent away, and Margareta didn't dare venture close to see that rejection in her foster mother's eyes.

Retracing the path Gabriel had led her on, Margareta winced at the memory of her father. His rekindled paternal instincts hadn't lasted long. When her stepmother died giving birth to a blue-grey boy, Gabriel had drunk so much wine he'd passed out and choked on his own vomit. The next day, Margareta had been summoned to the queen's chambers and Sophia had held out a hand glittering with diamonds and cool as snowmelt. 'Child,' she'd said, 'your father has died of a broken heart. As my kin, you are now my ward, and I shall take care of you.'

Margareta had wanted to ask if she could go back to Johanna and Ilsa instead. But one look at Queen Sophia's silvery eyes had frozen the question behind her lips. For months afterwards, she'd wondered if a little bravery would have freed her to go home – until she grew to know the queen better. By then she also knew her distant kinship with Sophia would only ever bring obligation.

'I have two little girls for you to befriend.' Sophia had offered her children like an array of sweetmeats. 'From now on, you are Princess Anna's maid of honour. Shall you like that?'

'Very much, Your Highness,' Margareta had lied, and she'd spent the next ten years wondering if it were still a lie.

Some days it was easier to pretend than others. The ones when they rode white palfreys along the Øresund, or when they were allowed to teach their spaniels tricks.

But on days like this one, when smoke rose over Helsingør's red roofs, Margareta's smile trembled like a mirror on the verge of shattering.

Before entering the royal apartments, Margareta steeled herself, inspecting her reflection in a polished suit of armour for soot flecks on her cheeks. She pressed her wrists to her nose; only bergamot scented her skin. A swift twirl assured her that her skirts smelled of nothing but the lavender bushes she'd deliberately brushed against. A little smile she'd borrowed from Anna was tossed at the guards, as if to say, 'What a silly girl I am! But I simply cannot help it!', and a nod to tell them she was ready. Then Lady Margareta Vinstar returned to the service of Princess Anna of Denmark.

The chambers were awash with cloth: velvets murmuring against admiring fingertips, damask spilling from arms like gossip, silks draped languidly over chairs. Seamstresses knelt before the four princesses, cajoling Hedwig to stand still, pinning Augusta's hem, holding up samples of lace against Anna, pinning ribbons onto Elisabeth's bodice. Marshalling everyone was Queen Sophia; behind her clustered the princesses' ladies, awaiting instructions.

'The ivory,' Sophia declared. 'A spill at each cuff – no – there, just so. And a ruff to match.'

'Then the peony ribbons,' Anna suggested. 'They'd be so becoming, don't you think?'

Her mother's lips thinned.

'Besides, the rose makes me look like I'm blushing.'

'As you should. A blushing bride is a modest bride.'

Anna's eyebrows pinched together; as her gaze darted away from her mother's, it alighted on Margareta. 'There you are! Margareta, what say you? Peony or rose?'

It never did to disagree with the dowager queen – but Margareta was Anna's maid of honour and would be until death or marriage took her away. Once, Margareta would have floundered, but she'd learned to navigate the currents of the royal chamber, gliding between eddies with a serenity belying the ferocity of her kicking below the surface.

'Both are beautiful,' she said, coming to stand between Anna and Sophia. 'Though I'd suggest the rose makes you look joyful rather than flustered. Perhaps you could match the peony with the ivory taffeta instead, for it doesn't stand out so strongly against the silver.'

'I hadn't thought about my ivory taffeta!' Anna exclaimed, twisting to see the other gowns, which were collapsed over chairs behind her. Cream, pearl, dove-grey: Anna favoured colours that turned her into a confection of spun sugar, colours that made black-haired girls like Margareta look like corpses.

As Anna chattered to the seamstress, Sophia gave Margareta the minutest nod of approval before turning away to discuss Elisabeth's sleeves.

The dowager queen wouldn't be so approving if she knew where Margareta had been. Margareta stooped to pick up a length of lace and began winding it, using her fingers as a reel, watching her flesh disappear behind smoke-white loops.

Witchcraft is in your blood. You can never be rid of it.

Was it fear or the wind that brought, through the window and into the soft opulence of the royal chambers, a smell that scratched against skin, snagged on silk: the roast-pork-wrongness of burning flesh?

2

'Geillis Duncan.'

Geillis stumbled back from the door she'd been hammering on, where a fist-shaped smoothness in the wood reminded her that dozens, if not hundreds, of frantic people had done so before – though, judging by the size of the dent, it was usually husbands that came, not daughters. But the husband in this case had gone out to sea one November morning and all that returned was his salt-stiffened woollen cap and a boat with her hull staved in. And so it was Geillis who beat on the midwife's door in the middle of the night.

Now, the open door revealed a tall woman with iron-shot hair and shoulders so straight they might have been riveted together. Agnes Sampson, the best midwife for miles. Even the rich wives of Edinburgh and Leith summoned her for their lying-in, paying her handsomely in wine, bolts of wool, and occasionally coin. She was already fastening what must have been one such reward: the silver horsehead buckle on a black cloak.

'Oh.' Geillis gaped in defeat. 'Have you been called out already?'

By someone able to pay.

Agnes paused. 'Did you have another reason for trying to break my door down? You're Bridget's lass, aren't you? I hadn't expected you for a month yet.'

'It's coming early!'

'I thought as much – either that or she'd birthed a litter of kittens to have you out at this hour.'

Geillis flinched – to utter such things was dangerous; they said the devil's hearing was keenest after dark, and he preyed first on frightened girls. 'Don't say that.'

Agnes gave her a stern look. 'It's only ill-wishing if the wish is ill. Now, let's be off. You walked?'

She'd sold the horse in February; it still hadn't raised enough to stop David Seton evicting them. 'Yes. Well, ran.'

'Course you did. My Blossom will bear us both. Best get going if we're to make it back before the babes.'

'Babes?'

'Aye. It's twins – didn't you know?' Agnes tossed this over her shoulder as she strode towards a small apple orchard where a sturdy grey mare had been hobbled.

Geillis stared after Agnes. Was there any point closing her mouth? Surely in moments the midwife would startle her again.

But she couldn't dawdle. They had to get back to the cottage before it was too late – and Geillis had to find a way of paying for Agnes's services.

They heard her mother's moaning as they crossed the burn – raw, animal noises, both piercing loud and oddly muffled, as if she were biting down on something but couldn't bite hard enough to silence her pain. Geillis wondered who she was trying to keep quiet for; the hut clung to a rocky, heather-knuckled slope several miles from Nether Keith, which even the sheep had long ago abandoned. No one knew when the last shepherd had left, but when Geillis and her mother had staggered up the hill after losing their home in Prestonpans, the door hadn't been locked and there were enough bird droppings on the threshold to make them feel safe in assuming no one would evict them.

'Around twelve hours, you said?' Agnes queried as she dismounted.

'I think so. Maybe longer. I was …' Geillis hesitated. Now wasn't the time to tell Agnes she'd been trying to sell posies of snowdrops to the fishermen down at Prestonpans: *Flowers for your sweetheart, sir?* Their mocking laughter still stung; the shame of her own desperation hurt more. 'I was out just after sun-up.'

Agnes grunted thoughtfully, wedging her herb chest on one bony hip and heading for the door. 'It's what, her sixth?'

Did the formless clots on napkins they'd had to burn count, or just the little mounds of earth outside their old cottage in Prestonpans? 'Six full term.'

'And you all that's left. About five years since the last?'

'Yes.' But three had burned since then.

'Right then.' Agnes gave the door three sharp knocks for warning and marched inside.

Her mother was staggering around the room, one hand braced against rickety walls, the other flailing between kneading her back and cradling the spasms of agony in her belly. Her steps dragged, catching on loose floorboards and the stool she'd knocked over, as if she hadn't the strength for anything except fighting to bring these babies into the world. As Agnes and Geillis entered, Bridget raised her sweat-sheened face and blinked, first unseeing – and then, on recognizing Agnes, aghast.

'No,' she groaned, slumping against the wall. 'Geillis, you silly girl. We can't—'

'Agnes is here to help. Everything will be fine, I promise.'

'Let's take a look at you,' Agnes said. She crossed the chamber and lifted Bridget's stained nightgown with one practised hand as the other quested between her legs.

Over the midwife's head, Bridget's eyes sought her daughter's – fear grappled with shame and resignation. Geillis shook her head: *Don't speak of it. Not yet.*

Agnes straightened up. 'Best get you onto the bed, Bridget.' She half-led, half-wrestled her over to the tick mattress. 'Geillis, boil water.'

'But we've no other sheets,' her mother gasped. 'I can walk, I can!'

Agnes threw questions at Geillis. 'Is there a horse blanket? Any other linen?'

'Only what's in the windows.'

'Well then, tear it down and lay it out for your mother.'

Geillis hurried to the windows. Unsheathing her belt knife, she pried out the rust-gnarled nails pinning the linen across the frames. The wood was little more than splinters and they came out easily. Spread on the mattress, there was barely enough cloth for her mother to kneel on – but it would have to do. Bridget no longer seemed to care; pain had driven her gaze somewhere far off, and she sank gratefully down.

'Right then,' Agnes said. 'Between you, me, and your body, we know what to do, don't we? Let's get these babes born.'

She spoke so calmly, as if her words could make the world whatever she wished, and Geillis longed to believe it. But several hours passed and Geillis's hands were crabbed from rubbing her mother's back, the air sharp with scents of valerian and hellebore, and her mother's keening. Agnes had stripped Bridget's ruined nightgown away and laid it beneath her; another time Geillis might have been embarrassed by her mother's moon-white flesh, but not now. She couldn't care about anything but the screams.

Agnes rocked back on her heels, lips thin. 'Geillis,' she said, so softly Bridget wouldn't hear, 'you need to make a choice.'

Geillis crouched beside her, a half-wrapped poultice shedding mulch in her hand. 'What do you mean?'

'The babies haven't turned. Nor come any closer to being born – I think they're tangled together.'

'Can't you untangle them?'

Agnes shook her head: that wasn't the whole problem. 'One's distressed – I can feel it. The other I suspect is already dead.'

Geillis stared at her mother's belly in horror; how could something so round with life secretly be a coffin? 'Can you save the other?'

'I can.' Agnes met Geillis's eyes, silver cool against hazel. 'Or I can save your mother. The only way to save the baby is to cut her – and then she will almost certainly die. Or I can use a needle to scrape the babies out – and then they will certainly die and your mother may not.'

'You mean she still might not survive?'

'Nothing's certain in a birthing chamber.'

'But you're the best!'

Agnes touched her hand; her fingers were cool despite the sweat-hot room. 'Even I cannot save everyone. You must choose, Geillis.'

'I can't!'

'You must. It ought to be the husband's choice, but now you must do it in your father's stead. Which will you save, Geillis: your mother or your sister?'

Geillis shook her head, aghast – how could she make such a decision? An unborn, innocent baby, or her mother? What would Bridget choose?

She knew the answer, but she couldn't bear it. 'Save my mother. Please.'

Agnes nodded, impossibly calm. From her box she withdrew a bone needle as long as Geillis's forearm and tested its point against her thumb. 'You're certain?'

She would never be certain. Closing her eyes at her betrayal of Bridget, Geillis nodded.

'Bridget,' Agnes said, clear and gentle now, 'I'm going to have to hurt you a little. But it will all be better afterwards. Are you ready?'

Bridget answered with a blood-shuddering, animal wail, and Geillis thought: She knows. She knows, and she's furious.

Agnes thrust the needle into Bridget. This time the howl was raw as flayed skin. Bridget arched her back, thrashed her head madly from side to side, her fists clenched in the bloodied linen. There was a gush of blood and then another, too dark, thick, furious – and then a gleam of white. A fragment of skull. And then the babies came out, slippery-skinned as eels, their palm-sized heads a jagged mess of bone and gore.

Numbly, Geillis looked about for somewhere to put them – she couldn't let Bridget see what they'd done to her children. But there was only an old flour sack, and it seemed horribly cruel to kill her own siblings and then bundle them away in coarse hessian like weevil-infested grain.

'Geillis, get me moss!'

Agnes's hiss yanked her back to Bridget. Geillis hurriedly wrapped the babies and rummaged through Agnes's chest. 'Here.'

Agnes grabbed it and began packing it against Bridget's flesh. But blood was seeping through, suddenly bright scarlet, spilling between Agnes's knuckles, snaking down her wrists.

Another handful, and another. Still the blood came in floods, and Geillis thought it would never stop – until the tide suddenly ebbed, and then ceased to flow at all.

Cuckoo flowers were nudging through the heather, crawling between brittle stems towards the dawn light. Was it really only yesterday morning Bridget had pointed them out? *Will you pick some for me? I can't bend that low anymore!* But Geillis had been hurrying out, calling *Later* over her shoulder, and now she couldn't bear to touch the pale pink petals.

Geillis dug her chin deeper into the jutting bones on her chest and took the cup of camomile tea Agnes held out, letting steam writhe around her face.

Agnes, leaning on the drystone wall beside her, said, 'It wouldn't have made a difference, you know. You could have fetched me as soon as her pains started, and I still wouldn't have been able to save her.'

Geillis kept her eyes fixed on nothing. 'I thought you were supposed to be the best.'

'I am the best,' Agnes said. 'If a child's breeched, or early, or late, if a mother's hips are narrow or the cord's tangled, I can help. I've more knowledge of herbs than the rest of Scotland put together – but I'm not God. Some babies aren't meant to be born, and some mothers aren't meant to survive the birth. That's the world's way.'

'But—' Geillis gripped her cup. 'How can you stand it? Losing anyone – when you were supposed to save them?'

'At first, I couldn't,' Agnes said, with surprising candour; Geillis hadn't expected vulnerability from her, even long-gone vulnerability. 'I threw things, railed at God and men – and that didn't help. Only thing that does is learning from it. And making certain I do my best to save those who can be saved – and treating the others as if I still might, just in case I'm wrong and so the last thing they see isn't fear, but a level-headed woman doing everything the way it should be done.'

Agnes had found a way to turn anger and grief into hope. Into power. The steam had cleared; Geillis was staring at Agnes. 'Could I do it?'
Agnes gave her an assessing look. 'Verbena?'
Geillis blinked, confused. 'Ah – a sore throat.'
'Feverfew?'
'Headache. Or insect bites. Or fevers, hence the name.'
'Chickweed?'
'For a rash. And rheum in the bones.'
'Hmm.' Agnes considered her again. 'You've some knowledge. And you've steady hands. But you panic too much – and you show your fear.'
Geillis bridled. 'Of course I was afraid! My mother was dying!'
Agnes shook her head. 'You cannot do that as a midwife. You must forget who they are, whether you love them or despise them. And you must be the brave one, or else how can they trust you? You can never be tired, no matter how long the labour – because who are you to be weary when the mother's bringing life into the world? You must be willing to put your own life second – to know that no demand on your time, be it housework, or a lover, or your own family, is as impor-tant as a new life.'
Geillis glanced back at the cuckoo flowers. Yesterday morning she'd had Bridget, and a frail hope of snowdrops putting bread on the table. Now? 'I've nothing left to put first.'
Agnes sighed. 'Then I suppose I could teach you.'
Geillis didn't dare show her desperation. 'So can I ... will I come and stay with you now?'
'No!'
The barked word sent Geillis's tea slopping over her fingers. 'But – I thought you had room.'
'That room isn't spare. It belongs—' Agnes's face closed, abrupt and final as a coffin lid. 'Besides, you'll need money from elsewhere. I can't pay you, and no one else will until you've learned your trade.'
'But where? There's no work to be had.'
'There is if you ask the right people.' Agnes tapped a nail against her cup. 'A friend – a customer of mine, Euphame MacCalzean – has a sister-in-law needs a servant. Mistress Seton of Tranent.'

'The bailie's wife?' Geillis blanched. 'So I should slave for the man who threw us out?'

'I thought you needed work.'

'I do!'

Agnes smiled. 'Dignity's a fine thing, my lass, but it never buttered any parsnips.'

'It's not that,' Geillis muttered, flushing. 'He ... looks at me.'

'Then let him look.'

Geillis lifted her head, startled by Agnes's low, cunning tone.

'David Seton looks at many lasses,' Agnes continued. 'And he's been known to talk while looking. So you let him look – and you listen. There's much to listen to in Seton's house – and I'd like to hear it.'

Talk of more than evicting bereaved women from their homes? What was Agnes so curious about? And did Geillis really want to hear it? She folded her arms, aiming for firmness and only achieving bluster. 'So I'm to be your spy?'

'Not at all,' Agnes said, with a smile. 'We're on the same side, aren't we?'

She had no one else to cling to. All Geillis could do was say, 'Of course we are.'

3

Denmark
June 1589

Denmark and Scotland: it should have been the ideal union. Lands rugged with white-capped mountains; islands rising out of wild seas like mermaids. Preachers stalking the towns, commanding repentance for sins you hadn't realized you'd committed. Summer days stretched wide as eagle wings; winter nights closing fast as strangling fingers.

Watching the ambassadors bowing before King Christian, Margareta noted another thing the two countries had in common: boy kings. Christian had been eleven when his father, King Frederick, died last spring; now, Queen Sophia instructed a regency council behind closed doors. Meanwhile King James of Scotland hadn't been able to walk when he was given his mother's crown; the Scots had deposed Mary twenty-two years ago, and the English queen had executed her two winters past.

And now they planned to send Anna to Scotland. Where queens could be put aside or killed. Despite the fires roaring in a dozen hearths around the great hall, Margareta shivered.

Ilsa. She hadn't dared let her thoughts tiptoe too close to her milk-sister's cryptic demands and cold threats. But now the ambassadors had arrived from Scotland, where Ilsa had been and wanted Margareta to go, where this Geillis Duncan dwelled. Wrestling her mind back from Ilsa, Margareta forced herself to pay attention.

There were ten Scotsmen, all dressed in sober hues: deepest black, midnight-blue. Margareta imagined Anna's despairing cry later: 'But where were all the colours? Are there no embroiderers in Scotland, no ribbons?'

'Dark colours signal wealth,' Margareta would point out. 'The Scots wish to impress you.'

As the Scots bowed for their introductions, Anna's expression was brightly polite, but a ripple of taffeta revealed the princess was tapping her feet impatiently. King Christian's eyes had glazed over; he'd already drifted into daydreams of horse riding. Meanwhile, Sophia welcomed the ambassadors with glacial serenity, everything about her saying, *We are pleased to have you here – but do not forget how powerful we are.*

'How much longer until the feasting?' Elline Skinkell moaned into Margareta's ear. 'My stomach's growling will soon drown out any negotiations.'

'They aren't negotiating yet,' Margareta pointed out. 'Just showing off.'

The Scots' leader George Keith, the Earl Marischal, gestured to his men who flung open several oak chests.

'Finest Highland wool,' he declared. 'Silver plate. And for Princess Anna, a set of gold-backed mirrors – the glass was blown by master craftsmen in Leith.'

'Who'd run away from Venice,' Vibeke Kroas mumbled, unable to resist reminding them of her cynical intelligence. 'Scotland's full of refugees who've fallen foul of Rome.'

'Then we Danes will fit in,' Margareta muttered back. 'That's one of the reasons King James seeks Anna for a bride – strengthening the alliance against Catholicism.'

'He'd have any bride who could bear children,' Vibeke said dryly. 'Soon as he has an heir and a spare, Queen Elizabeth will declare him her successor.'

'After she executed his mother?' Margareta arched an eyebrow. 'I'd have thought him more likely to wage war on England, not crawl for her favour.'

'But he's terrified of her,' Vibeke said. 'All of Scotland's afraid of the English queen. So is most of Christendom – especially after the Spanish Armada's defeat.'

'Don't talk about shipwrecks!' Elline gave a dramatic shiver.

'Perhaps Anna could use it to her advantage,' Vibeke said, ignoring Elline's performance. 'If queens can be feared on the other side of the North Sea, perhaps she could learn to instil fear too.'

The queen on this side was formidable enough, Margareta thought. But watching Anna smile at her gifts, twirling a mirror's golden stem between soft white fingers, Margareta couldn't imagine her being fearsome. To terrify, you had to know what it was to be afraid.

At last, the banquet: golden pies decorated with Danish lions and Scottish unicorns, and enough fish to have emptied the Øresund Strait – gravlax scattered with dill, whiting in apple sauce, baked carp swimming in butter. Margareta, dipping soft manchet bread in the sauce gleaming on her silver plate, tried to swallow the bitter taste of Ilsa's words: *How many courses did you feast on?* The smells of roasting meat and simmering stews had wafted through Kronborg all day, rendering the whole court ravenous. Now, around the hall, chins and fingers glistened, conversations tilted and hitched around mouthfuls, beards and ruffs harboured rogue crumbs. Only those on the royal table ate with restraint: no hunger could overrule Queen Sophia's standards of decorum.

Elline leaned close, bubbling with giggles. 'One of the Scots hasn't taken his eyes off you all evening.'

Margareta couldn't resist following Elline's gaze, even as she said darkly, 'Well, he'd better. If Queen Sophia notices, she'll be furious.'

Especially since the Scot was handsome: hair dark as ravens' wings and a close-cut beard that flattered his strong jaw. As Margareta watched, the Scot raised his glass to his lips; over its rim, green eyes sparked – and something in their glimmer made her certain it was a toast. But to what?

'You never know,' Elline mused. 'She might favour another Danish and Scottish alliance.'

Margareta hauled her gaze back to her food. 'When it concerns her daughters' ladies, I think we always know.'

But again and again, throughout the feast, she couldn't help but be drawn back to the Scottish lord and the unspoken vow in his eyes.

* * *

It wasn't as though she'd never danced with a man before. For all that
Queen Sophia kept her daughters' ladies on a tight leash, she couldn't
deny the necessity of them meeting prospective husbands – under
close supervision of course – and dancing was the prime opportunity
to do so: it was public, the steps couldn't be disobeyed, and no inter-
action could last longer than a few minutes. Even girls whose fathers
were too inept or poor or dead to arrange matches for them had to
dance when the prospective royal brides did, decorum demanding that
everyone pretend they were dancing for joy, not possible marriages.

And yet, when the green-eyed Scottish lord bowed low before her
and asked if she would honour him with a dance, Margareta could
scarcely remember how to talk.

'Ah – it would be a pleasure,' she managed, fumbling for her French:
the Scots didn't speak Danish and the Danes didn't speak Scots,
making French a convenient, if random meeting point.

'Excellent,' he said. 'I'm John Wemyss, heir to the Laird of Logie,
and you, if I'm not mistaken, are Margareta Vinstar.'

She blinked in surprise. 'You know my name?'

'Knowledge is my coin of choice,' he said, holding out his hand,
'and I spend it wisely.'

'You think to buy me?' The retort slipped out before she could
marshal her thoughts, years of training her tongue into docile polite-
ness as much use now as snapped jesses. She blamed Ilsa for this: she
was never more brittle than when she'd seen her milk-sister.

Wemyss looked neither offended nor apologetic. 'Your price would
be beyond my purse. But perhaps I can afford to entertain you during
a dance.'

'Perhaps indeed.' She accepted his hand – and a challenge with it.

The dance was an almain: stately, sophisticated, and with many
opportunities for holding hands – or not releasing them. The ominous
twist in her thoughts startled her. Was she afraid of Wemyss? Should
she be?

He bowed, and the music coiled into silken ropes. She had to
curtsey and let her feet recall what her mind couldn't. As they moved

forward, his hands warm and firm around hers, she searched for a safe topic of conversation. 'Did you enjoy the feast?'

Those green eyes danced with quiet amusement to a rhythm of their own. 'Very much.'

He'd spent most of it watching her. She didn't dare dwell on that. 'Was our food very different from yours?'

His lips quirked as if suppressing laughter. 'Indeed. In Scotland we subsist entirely on oats and haggis.'

'Haggis?'

He did laugh then, and how could she be afraid of a man with a laugh so gentle? 'Well, it's also oats. Mainly.'

'You're teasing me.'

'You dislike being teased?'

She hesitated. Had anyone ever teased her except Ilsa, whose gibes had grown increasingly barbed over the years? Vibeke flaunted her superior intelligence and Elline her expertise in face paint, but warm teasing? 'I don't know enough about it to decide yet.'

'Perhaps I can aid your discovery.' He spun her in a circle. 'Did Ilsa never tease you?'

She gasped, thrown off balance. 'How do you know Ilsa?'

'I told you,' he said. 'Knowledge is my currency, and I intend to grow very rich.'

'Did you meet her in Scotland?' He made her turn again; she couldn't see his face. 'How? Why?'

'She met with some … associates of my associates.'

She couldn't break free. The last thing she wanted was to reveal how much he'd unsettled her. If he knew Ilsa – or what Ilsa was scheming …

'Stumble.'

'What?'

'The dance is drawing to a close, and I don't wish to end our conversation yet. I need you to stumble so I can escort you to a comfortable chair and play page as apology for causing you injury.'

'I—'

'Trust me, Margareta.'

The intimacy of her first name, the certainty in his voice – and the greedy, girlish part of her that wanted to cling to a handsome man: all that made her breathe, 'I trust you.'

She didn't yet know if she was lying.

Lutes plucked a crescendo, viols spun into a climax, dancers twirled their final twirls.

'*Now.*'

Her feet tangled in her skirts; polished wood cracked against her kneecap and she cried out in genuine pain. Dancers eager for more threw her looks of impatient sympathy. She saw Anna, hands fluttering to her mouth, urging her partner the Earl Marischal to help. But this was a celebration of Anna's betrothal; Margareta couldn't draw her attention – or Queen Sophia's.

But the Earl Marischal was patting Anna's hand reassuringly and leading her away. Did a look pass between him and Wemyss? She didn't know what to think: the pain and the whole evening were mazing her.

'I didn't expect quite such dedication to your performance,' Wemyss said at her ear. He crouched down, slipping her arm around his shoulders – rather pleasingly broad shoulders, she couldn't help noticing – and swooping her up as if this were merely another dance step. Before she could blush at the whispers rustling in their wake, he'd deposited her in a quiet corner, whisked a footstool beneath her injured leg and inserted a glass of wine into one hand and a marchpane rose into the other.

'Thank you,' she said, collapsing back into courtesy as if it were a cushion to break her fall.

Wemyss snorted. 'Since I bear half the blame for your injury, I hardly think gratitude's in order.'

'Why did I do that?'

He gave her an odd look. 'You chose to.'

'Because you said I should trust you – don't I deserve to know why?'

'Your bruises would earn you that right even if honour and good sense didn't compel me. You do deserve the truth – or some of it.'

'Some?'

'It isn't safe to know it all. Even I am not so rich as that.' He pulled his stool closer, lowering his voice still further. 'Two women you love are in danger.'

The wine tasted suddenly bitter; she might have been sipping blood. 'Who? How?'

His gaze was measured, as if deciding how much to conceal. 'Not all Scots favour this match. Some wish King James would never wed at all.'

'But kings must wed. Who wouldn't wish Scotland to have an heir?'

'Every Scot with his own claim to the throne. Our past kings sired enough bastards and legitimate heirs that half the nobles have enough royal blood to give them delusions of grandeur.'

'But—' Margareta stared across the hall at the princess whirling through candlelight. 'They wouldn't hurt Anna?'

Wemyss's reply was gentle – and yet anything but. 'There hasn't been a monarch in history whose hands weren't bloodstained. But the most dangerous enemies are those who make sure others' hands are stained darker. That's why your sister must be on her guard. And so must you.'

Pearls spat light like raindrops; heels clapped imperiously against the floor. Queen Sophia stood before them, a sullen Elline at her shoulder. 'Master Wemyss, I thank you for your attentions to my ward, but Mistress Skinkell will escort Mistress Vinstar to her chamber. I believe your fellow Scots will be desirous of your company.'

There was no gainsaying her. Margareta could only watch Wemyss bow and disappear into the throng, as she let Elline lead her away.

4

Scotland

David Seton was watching Geillis again.

She'd tried to ignore it at first, like a drip in the thatch that wakes you at night – intruding and icy – and yet, undealt with, it grows more insistent, bringing the promise of rot. Thus it was with the bailie's gaze, slithering down her back as Geillis draped wet sheets over rosemary bushes, seeping through her bodice as she reached up to oil the leather-panelled walls, running across her briefly bared wrists as she poured his wine at dinner.

What to be done? Nothing. He was the bailie. He had noble kin. Girls like Geillis, with no husbands or fathers or brothers, were expected to endure, endure, and endure again. She'd considered complaining to Mistress Katherine, but what wife wanted to be told about her husband's roving eye, still less asked for help restraining him? Besides, Seton's wife was no more approachable than a swan; she glided through the house, cutting conversations in two like water, the slightest arching of her neck a silent warning.

'She's a Moscrop,' Jeanie the kitchen maid had whispered below the spit of roasting pork, the day after Geillis arrived. 'He might have the nobler name, but it's her family the merchants will happily give credit to, and hers who've never been blemished by scandal.'

'What scandal?' Geillis had asked, shaping pastry leaves whose intricacies seemed a far greater waste of time than gossiping about their employers.

Jeanie eagerly held forth. 'The old Lord Seton helped Queen Mary escape to England after she had to abdicate. He stuck to her cause, even though he was exiled for it.'

Geillis began carving veins into the leaves. 'Does King James dislike the Setons for that?'

'Well, not that one – he's dead,' Jeanie said matter-of-factly. 'But our master's cousin, the current Lord Seton, has to work harder than anyone to convince the king he's loyal.'

'Why? Queen Mary's dead these two years – there's no one else to be loyal to.'

'Ah, but there is!' Jeanie's smile was sly. 'And with Lord Seton working hard to appear the most loyal of subjects, the rest of the clan can be secretly less loyal.'

Geillis's knife slipped; she almost sliced into her own flesh. Christ on the cross, what kind of household had Agnes thrust her into? Jeanie was talking of sedition, even treason – was the girl entirely addled to be babbling thus to a newcomer like Geillis, or to anyone?

Gripping her voice steady, Geillis said, 'Doesn't seem the sort of thing Mistress Katherine would approve of.'

Jeanie tossed a few scraps to the expectant kitchen cat. 'Ones like her are the worst for it. She might look all ice and marble, but beneath? Daggers and poison.' Lifting the herb basket, she moved towards the door. 'Can't imagine you need warning, but you should watch out for them both. Him you'll see coming, but her? The blade'll be in you before you know she's there.'

As Jeanie stepped out into the garden, Geillis contemplated the door. Running through it had never seemed so tempting.

But there was nowhere to run to.

If not for Agnes's lessons, Geillis might well have gone mad.

Every Sunday after kirk, Agnes would appear in the road back to Seton's house, sometimes mounted on Blossom, sometimes leaning on a stout hawthorn stick, usually with her arms folded impatiently. Geillis never saw her in kirk; Agnes must have attended some service closer to her cottage – if indeed she went at all, for it was difficult to imagine Agnes listening to a sermon's drone without interrupting to expose flaws in the minister's arguments.

When Geillis saw Agnes, she would mutter her goodbyes to Jeanie and the other servants, none of whom minded, and join her. And Seton would watch. The first time she'd thought he would command her to return to the house. Instead his eyes had shifted over to Agnes, and something passed between them: a challenge, perhaps. Then Seton's thin lips had hooked in irritation, and he'd ridden away as if Geillis and Agnes were of no more interest than goose-grass on the verge.

'Let's hope that sermon hasn't dulled your wits entirely,' Agnes would say, 'for you've much to learn today.'

Sometimes they tramped the fields rolling down to the clifftops, or tracked streams until they became rivers, until rivers became the sea. Agnes would stoop abruptly beside a plant and beckon Geillis across.

'What can you tell me?'

'That's yarrow,' Geillis might say. 'The soldier's herb. Good for colds and fevers.'

'For childbirth too. It's called the soldier's herb because it staunches heavy bleeding,' Agnes would remind her, chipping in whenever Geillis missed something out. Occasionally, Geillis had to bite her tongue: she couldn't afford to be sharp with the only person to show her kindness in months. But mostly she murmured the new fact over and over, inscribing it on her memory, vowing to carry yarrow to every childbed in future, so no one else had to suffer Bridget's fate.

On other days, Agnes directed Blossom to a dwelling, from the peat-roofed crofters' huts to the imposing gable-roofed houses in the heart of Haddington. Regardless of the patient's rank, Agnes insisted that Geillis smooth any stray hairs beneath her cap, wipe any smudges from her cheeks, and inspect her fingernails. 'How can they trust us to take care of their insides if we can't take care of our outsides?' A fair point, but not one that could hide the chafing on Geillis's wrists after laundry day.

Today the cottage was a small one in Prestonpans. Others might have flinched at the nearby saltpans' acrid smell of blood and ale, mixed with the tang of the sea and the less-than-fresh memory of the morning's catch. But to Geillis, the smells of the shore would always remind her of her father, while Agnes, who spent her days dealing with rotted teeth, suspect stools, and women in labour, noticed smells only to divine what could remedy them. Neither woman's nose so much as wrinkled as they approached; that is, until they neared the door.

Smoke inched fitfully out of the lopsided chimney. More wormed its way out of a window with a broken shutter; Geillis caught the whiff of a herring stew stretched over too many days. Beneath it all, stale sweat and rotting sweetness – the unmistakeable odours of sickness.

Geillis tried not to cough. But her throat was dry and her chest heaved, and she couldn't help it. She expected Agnes to upbraid her – it wasn't right to show sick people you found them disgusting – but Agnes's disapproval was directed elsewhere. Mouth pinched, Agnes rapped on the door. Without waiting for a response, she strode inside.

'Hey! You can't just barge—' But the gruff protest was hacked in half by a cough that bent its victim double on his stool.

He wasn't an old man, though he looked it: face crosshatched with lines from a life spent working outside and frowning all the while. Even huddled under a horsehair blanket, he was now clearly all bones beneath papery skin. A battered pot of that dismal stew simmered over the fire, and the man had pulled his stool as close to his cooking as possible without setting the blanket alight.

'If I'd waited for you to open the door, I'd have loitered outside until Judgement Day,' Agnes said brusquely, immediately setting things to rights: straightening bedding, pulling a cloth over cheese left out on a rickety table, swatting flies away. 'Now then, Robert Dixon. What have you to say for yourself?'

Dixon shuffled beneath his blanket; casting about for an excuse, his eyes latched onto Geillis. 'Who's that? Bad enough you march round like you own the place without some sharp-eyed shrew thinking she can follow suit.'

'My apprentice, Geillis Duncan,' Agnes said calmly. 'You're not fooling anyone, Robert Dixon. You're just making excuses to avoid admitting you've not done as I advised, aren't you?'

'Advised,' Dixon muttered, angrily stirring the fish. 'Commanded, more like. A woman's got no right ordering men about.'

Geillis shot a glance at Agnes. Would she still help him, despite his ingratitude?

'The roof,' Agnes chided. 'You've done nothing about it, have you?'

'Can't,' he said sullenly. 'My chest.' And he tossed out a juddering cough to prove his point.

'Your chest hasn't stopped you carousing until dawn with John Fian five of the last ten nights though, has it? Nor pawing Bessie Thomson's backside whenever she brings you curds from the dairy. And now look at you. House full of smoke and a chest filling up with it, and you summon me here saying my poultices haven't worked. Shame on you, Robert Dixon. Your Mary would be appalled to see the mire you've dragged her bairn into.'

Bairn? Geillis went rigid with horror. Where was it – he, she? That mound of bedclothes was far too small to be a child – you couldn't have hidden a brace of rabbits under there.

But then the bedclothes stirred and something pale trembled within them. A hand. At once, Geillis crossed the cramped chamber, barely noticing the rotting rushes as they slid beneath her boots, and dropped to her knees beside the child. Slipping her hand beneath his tiny one, she murmured, 'It's all right now,' knowing she lied. The boy was no more than three, or at least no bigger. Sweat glistened on the little boy's brow; his eyelids quivered with fever. Rummaging in the bag she now carried everywhere, Geillis found clean rags and began sponging his forehead. Cool water would help, but she doubted there was any in the cottage that hadn't gone stagnant long ago.

Behind her Agnes continued berating Dixon, her words flattening his bungled protests. 'I can give you a dozen poultices and tisanes, but they won't make you well unless you fix that roof and clean this hovel.'

'Can't,' Dixon muttered. 'Not with this chest. I keep telling you—'

'Your chest is entirely your own fault. Sit in smoke all day, puffing away on that pipe, and what do you expect? Air as clean as angel wings miraculously wafting into your lungs? You're a man, not a babe to be fooled with nonsense.'

'But—'

'Oh, enough!' Agnes broke the words like a stick over her knee. 'Do you want to choke to death? Do you want your boy to cough until he drowns in his own blood and phlegm? Because that's what will happen unless you pull yourself together. Fix that roof, or you'll both die before another winter's out. Understand?'

'Not stupid,' Dixon muttered into his horsehair.

'Then stop behaving like you are! I've seen cats with more sense – I've seen toads take better care of their young! You're a poor excuse for a man, and I'm utterly disgusted with you.'

The child whimpered; he tried to turn over but was too weak. Gently, Geillis adjusted his blankets, lifting him in one arm so she could beat the straw ticking into something less uncomfortable. He weighed almost nothing; his shoulder blades pricked her arm. She hadn't thought she could feel pity for another person again.

Perhaps it might have been better if Agnes had stormed out of the cottage; perhaps then Dixon might have been more inclined to heed her advice. But instead she glowered at the man until he looked away, only then turning to sift through her bag. When she next spoke, it was in her usual tones, unruffled statements as incontrovertible as the commandments. 'This poultice I'll place on your chest now, and I'll make up another for you to replace it with tomorrow. This tonic will loosen the phlegm. Fresh air would be best, of course, but this is better than nothing.'

They stayed for several hours, stuffing fresh straw into the mattress, airing the blankets. Geillis made a barley broth and the boy managed three mouthfuls. Agnes swept out the old rushes and scattered new. If you squinted, the place almost looked like a decent home.

On their way home, both astride Blossom, the wildflowers in the hedgerows pawing at their ankles, Agnes said, 'It'll make no difference in the end.'

Geillis flinched at her bluntness. 'How can you know that? He might—'

'He hasn't listened to anyone since his mother told him he was the bonniest of boys and a fine man he'd grow into. Perhaps if she hadn't said it so often it might have come true. As it is, Dixon's an obstinate, selfish wastrel. I've been giving him the same advice about his roof for two years, and if he ignores me much longer it'll be too late for the bairn.'

Still she spoke with that same flatness, not, Geillis hoped, out of cruelty, but out of weariness. You could only bang your head against a wall so many times before blood flowed.

'Is there nothing can be done?'

'Nothing,' Agnes said, and although her voice betrayed no emotion, she set her palm to Blossom's withers as if she needed to feel life pulsing warmly in her horse's flesh.

Geillis bit her lip. 'Then … why did we go? Why waste our time?'

'You call tending to the suffering a waste of time?' Agnes's challenge was dry, not angry.

'No! I just … there are so many people who are ill. So many hurt, who need help – and who might actually be grateful.'

'We don't do this for gratitude.'

'But shouldn't we help those who might help themselves?'

'If we only helped those, I'd be a beggar.'

'But we've made no difference! We can't save that little boy unless we get him away from that useless man.'

'What gives you the right to take children from their parents?' Agnes gave a reproving frown. 'Besides, what do you mean by difference? It might not seem much to you, but holding a dying woman's hand is worth more than jewels to the one going into the darkness. The simplest kindnesses – a cool cloth, a murmured word – can mean the world to the sick, reminding them they're human, they're cared for, even loved: that's why we do this. To help others. After all, we aren't here to heal their lives, just their ailments.'

'But you still try. With Dixon, you tried.'

'Aye, well.' Agnes clicked to Blossom as they turned towards Tranent. 'I'm an interfering old baggage.'

It wasn't only that. Bravado and practicality aside, Geillis was sure Agnes truly cared about her patients.

Or perhaps Geillis needed that certainty. Because if Agnes didn't care about them, why should she care about helping Geillis?

* * *

On a typical Sunday evening the Edinburgh road was so quiet you could hear the grasshoppers chirping in the fields. So when Geillis heard a distant thrumming, she dismissed it: deer catching a scent, or a beekeeper starting early with his hives. But as the beats grew closer, there was no denying what they were. Horses' hooves, fast approaching.

'That sounds—' Geillis didn't finish. *Like an army.*

Agnes glanced over her shoulder. Then her face darkened. 'Come on,' she said to Blossom, guiding the mare onto the verge.

Just in time. Several dozen riders rounded the bend. They bore no banners, no crests; not a single clan tartan could be seen. But their clothes told Geillis enough. Black leather gleaming in the lowering sun, black velvet softer than any shadows, even a few garments trimmed in black furs so thick and glossy they could only be sables. The men's hard-set mouths suggested they wouldn't think twice about trampling obstacles underfoot if necessary.

Geillis fought the urge to slip from Blossom's broad back and curtsey. As if these men would notice anyway. In front of her, Agnes kept her head high – but since they were pressed itchingly close against the cow parsley, Geillis wondered if even she was intimidated by this band.

Who were they? What business had them riding past Tranent? And without banners, as if seeking anonymity, yet with no attempt to disguise their power?

As if he'd heard her thoughts, the leading rider turned his head. His eyes locked onto Geillis. They were black and slippery as sealskin. He couldn't have been more than thirty – and yet the darkness of his eyes seemed ancient. As the riders drew level with the women, she thought fear would throttle her.

But then his gaze swung to Agnes – and he nodded.

Just once. But once was enough.

As the riders pressed on, leaving clouds of grit and dust in their wake, Geillis found her voice.

'Do you know him?'

Agnes watched the last black cloak vanish round the next bend. 'The likes of us never know such men.'

'But—'

'Oh, I know his name. I could reel off his titles and lineage and most famed exploits if you like. But as for knowing … Scottish noblemen trust no one, and if you want my advice, we ought to return the favour.'

'He looked as if he recognized you.'

'We've had dealings.'

'Who is he? Why was he here?'

'They've come from Tantallon Castle,' Agnes said grimly, nudging Blossom back onto the road. 'It's been their prison for the past three months, since their rebellion against King James failed. Looks like he's forgiven them. Proof enough, if you ask me, that he's a fool and they were right to rise against him.'

'Agnes!' Geillis didn't dare say what she knew she ought – *That's treason* – and part of her didn't wish to. She wanted to hear more about these men. 'Who … who was their leader?'

Agnes was silent, as if weighing up how much to tell. The implication of that choice rankled.

At last, Agnes said, 'Francis Stewart, the Earl of Bothwell. The man people call James's heir. Be on your guard, Geillis, for a more dangerous man will not be found in all Scotland. Avoid him as long as you can – and when you can avoid him no longer, better to bargain with the devil than risk Bothwell's wrath.'

5

Proxy marriages were strange things. After witnessing a bride say vows to a man who wasn't the groom, no one was ever quite sure how to celebrate. Margareta had attended other weddings of course, seen ladies leave court on the arms of men twice their age, or half. Sometimes the occasions had been truly joyous: a union between two people who not only shared rank and familial interests, but even a fondness for the same books or music. Those weddings had been as giddy as anything under Sophia's cool gaze could be: dancing until slippers were worn through, fireworks over the harbour, laughter spilling as easily as wine. But Margareta couldn't imagine Anna's proxy marriage being anything other than a stilted, stiff affair.

'She'll have to hold his hands,' Elline whispered as the seamstresses made final inspections of their gowns. 'Vibeke says he has a wart on his left – can you imagine?'

Margareta certainly could. She knew all about warts on flesh – and what they could be warped into by malicious tongues. They'd said Dorthea had one on her shoulder even the flames couldn't sear away. 'There are worse hands to hold than the Earl Marischal's.'

'And the bedding ceremony,' Elline continued, as if Margareta hadn't spoken. 'We'll have to watch as Anna and the Earl Marischal get put to bed and he puts his big hairy ankle over hers. I'd die of shame!'

People didn't die of shame, thought Margareta. They died because they choked on their own vomit, or their hips were too narrow for childbearing, or because too many tongues had said the wrong thing. Besides, Sophia's children would sooner cut their own throats than show they were ashamed.

'Anna knows her duty,' Margareta said. 'Anyway, this ceremony will be far easier to endure than when she finally meets King James.'

'Lord, yes! What if his hands have more warts than knuckles? What if he has them on his *face*?' Elline squealed with mirth – and again as a pin jabbed her ankle. Uninterested in the seamstress's hasty apology, Elline mused, 'Imagine kissing a warty man every night! How can the earl's wife stand it?'

'He's a very powerful man.'

'Plenty of powerful men aren't wart-covered. You don't have to choose between a handsome face and a strong name.'

She was wrong. Of course you did. And for girls like them, the decision would never be theirs.

If she could choose, what would it be? Handsome face, or strong name?

Stupid, Margareta told herself as she and Anna's ladies practised a new dance. What would a powerful man want with a drunkard's daughter? And, for all her distant kinship to Anna, if any man knew she was Ilsa's sister …

As for handsome men, didn't they always turn towards women who could match them? Delicate, slender girls whose hair glimmered like topaz, whose skirts never tangled around their feet. Even then, with their pick of the girls, handsome men always chose the one with the richest father.

He'd chosen her for a dance and a message. That was all. Only a fool would long for more.

What did she know of Wemyss anyway? Margareta missed her cue and, instead of taking Vibeke's hand, scraped her nails along it, earning a scornful glare. As they turned, stepped, skipped, Margareta counted the things she knew in time to the beat.

His father was Laird of Logie. Forward two, turn. Whatever that was. Logie could be a palace, a clan, a county – none of them had paid as much attention as they ought when Anna was being taught about her future country. Wemyss might be one of the most powerful men in Scotland, or a nobody, or one of the hundreds wavering in the hinterland between.

Knowledge was his coin. Turn, change partners. What did that mean? Merely that anyone in any court needed to know secrets in order to survive, or something darker? Men who bought and sold knowledge could surely only be spies – so who was Wemyss spying for? And who were his targets?

He knew about her sister. Leap, kick, land. But how much? That Ilsa should be more careful would be apparent to anyone who'd had more than two minutes' conversation with her. That Ilsa had connections to witchcraft might be the subject of tavern gossip – in which case, who else knew? Who were the associates Wemyss had mentioned – Scots, or Danes? For a Scotsman to know what Margareta prayed the Danish court didn't chilled her bone-deep.

The music skirled to a halt; the minstrels flexed fingers and rolled shoulders. Anna laughed, clapping her hands in girlish delight, while her ladies rubbed pinched toes, dissolving into giggles at their own miscues or their partners'. Margareta crossed to the sideboard where silver decanters held small beer and poured herself a cup, gulping with a clumsiness she hoped others saw as breathlessness rather than worry.

Wemyss was almost certainly a spy, and one who knew far more about her than she did of him. She ought to fear him.

'Places!' the dancing master trilled. 'Ladies are now gentlemen and vice versa!'

Margareta took her place opposite Vibeke, wondering if she could remember the gentleman's part.

These were the steps Wemyss would tread. He would bow like this, take a woman's hand like this.

And he had taken hers. Could that mean anything beyond mere intrigue? Had he wanted to dance with her, or only her secrets? Whatever the answer, whatever the danger, Margareta knew that if he asked her again, she would snatch at the opportunity.

But if he didn't?

Common sense told her it was better to be snubbed than endangered. Yet, for all that, every surge of her blood was crying out for Wemyss's hand to reach for hers, and let the danger come.

Wemyss had said not every Scot wanted King James to marry Anna. If any of the Scots at Anna's proxy marriage held that opinion, they certainly hid it well.

Carrying Anna's silver taffeta train as King Christian led his sister into the chapel gave Margareta an opportunity to do some spying of her own. The beauty of both the jewel-bedecked princess and her new gown, adorned with hundreds of roses made of seed pearls, were ideal distractions for anyone who might have glanced at Margareta.

The Earl Marischal awaited his master's bride, inscrutable as ever. Was this a responsibility he relished or resented? And the lords at his side, their robes no less resplendent for their sober hues – which among them had hoped to sabotage the marriage negotiations and now churned with rage at their failure? Could Anna rely on any of them to protect her?

And what of the Danes? Who was Ilsa working for? Did she know any of these Scots, or had someone already in Kronborg bought her service?

Whom could Margareta trust?

King Christian placed his sister's white hand in the Earl Marischal's callused one and stepped aside. As the minister began intoning the words of the ceremony, Margareta felt someone's gaze alight on her.

She knew whose it was before she looked up into those green eyes. And she also knew the answer to her question.

Trust me, he'd said. But she knew that the answer was *no one*.

Crimson and sapphire ruptured the blackened sky. If you looked away from the fireworks, the bobbing shadows of boats could be made out as men hurriedly rowed to keep the display on time without capsizing the stacked pallets carrying the fireworks.

In Kronborg's gardens, courtiers gasped obligingly. No one wanted Sophia to think the celebrations for her daughter were anything less than splendid, or any less so for the absence of the true groom. The fireworks certainly were impressive – they just couldn't distract Margareta.

Wemyss hadn't asked her to dance. She'd performed in a masque about Greek goddesses with Anna and her other ladies; she'd danced with Elline's paunch-bellied uncle, then a Scots lord with fingers so gnarled it was like being held by a crab, followed by one of King Christian's over-eager, coltish friends, who didn't realize how long any of his limbs were – and that was all. Five dances she'd sat out, pretending to enjoy discussing everyone's gowns and yanking her eyes away from the corners Wemyss moved between.

At least he hadn't danced with Elline or Vibeke either. She couldn't have borne their delighted crowing about their handsome partner and his strong arms. Instead, Wemyss had, like all the Scots lords, danced once with Anna, and then withdrawn to the edges of the hall, where he'd spoken with his countrymen, sipped wine, and once, she was certain, murmured something to a steward and, she was less certain, passed something to a page.

He was a spy. He had to be. But who was he spying on – and who for?

Despite the balmy midsummer evening, she shivered.

'You are cold, Mistress Vinstar.'

He'd arrived at her side silently, and she fought to still her startled limbs.

'The sea breeze is often chilly, no matter how hot the summer.'

'Or how hardy the Danes before it.' He arched an eyebrow at her. Was he teasing?

'Or the Scots,' she countered. 'Your cloak's thick enough for February.'

'I'd offer it to you, but I fear the queen would see my chivalry and immediately dispatch you indoors, which certainly isn't my aim.'

'Your aim?' Her tongue thickened; she stumbled away from the flirtatious tone Elline would have adopted. Here was an opening – and here she was, fearing to approach, convinced she wouldn't fit through.

'We never did finish our conversation.'

White sparks cascaded through darkness like glass shards. Shadows chased across Wemyss's face, too swift for Margareta to catch his expression.

'We never did,' she agreed, cursing her parroting of his words – yet struggling to add any of her own.

That arching eyebrow again. 'You must have questions.'

'Of course I do,' she hissed, unease and bewilderment riling her. 'You told me to be on my guard – you told me Anna and Ilsa are in danger – yet failed to tell me where the threat will come from!'

His darkening eyes crackled with reflected ruby and gold. 'Then I hope I won't fail you again.'

'So tell me – what exactly am I supposed to be afraid of?'

'So much …' He stared across the harbour at the silhouetted ships as if his eyes could bore through their hulls. 'Intrigues run deeper and faster than rivers, Mistress Vinstar. You see white water rippling, and it might be caused by hidden rocks, but it might just as easily be pike twisting in the darkness. Eddies which seem safe may prove tainted; currents might sweep you into peril or carry you into safe harbours. The more you know, the deeper you wade, and then you're surrounded by things you cannot see, yet must withstand. If I tell you any more than I already have, you will be a part of this.'

'Even though I don't understand what it is. Even though I cannot hope to unless you make me a part of it.'

'Yes.'

'Why do you offer this knowledge to me?' She leaned against the parapet's cold stone, trying to push her gaze into his. 'You haven't vouchsafed any of this to Anna herself, or her other ladies, I trust? Why me?'

'Because they're still innocent.'

'And I'm not?' She should have marched away in outrage. But she stayed, fascinated.

'None of the others have a sister who seeks out conspiracies.'

She froze. 'How do you know that? Even the queen—'

'If you imagine anyone could have kept your foster sister secret from Queen Sophia, perhaps you are an innocent after all. She knows. She has always known.'

How much? Conspiracies were dangerous – but witchcraft was deadly. 'But—'

'Why raise you alongside her own daughter? For the same reason she told me who your sister was. If a hand holds a blade, better it turn outwards than inwards.'

'You're working for Queen Sophia? You're her spy?' Her eyes narrowed. 'How? When did you meet her?' *And how long have you been watching Ilsa? Or me?*

'I came with Colonel Stewart's embassy last December and saw an opportunity to offer my services.' He smiled. 'I also saw a black-haired girl slipping out of the castle to meet a silver-haired girl in the snow.'

Margareta ransacked her memories. December – what had she and Ilsa talked of then? She'd brought Ilsa a pair of fleece-lined gloves, and Ilsa had been furious, and grateful, and even more resentful because of her gratitude. They hadn't said anything about their darkest family secret, though. Or had they? 'You watched us?'

He shrugged. 'You interested me.'

'Me – or Ilsa?' She fought the urge to ask what he'd thought of Ilsa. Whether he'd admired her. What man wouldn't admire the ethereally slender Ilsa, with her hair shimmering like a moonlit sea?

'Both. But you especially. When I saw you escape from the castle, I knew you'd been raised to be one of us. A spy.'

'You're wrong.' Margareta shook her head, stepping backwards. 'Anna likes me, that's why I'm in her service—'

'Do you think Anna likes anyone her mother doesn't wish her to like? Or even speaks to anyone who hasn't been placed in her vicinity? Sophia *chose* you, Margareta, to protect her daughter and, in due course, to become her spy. It was only ever a matter of time. Do you choose to accept the role?'

'You call it a choice! If what you say is true, I've never had any alternative!'

'You can choose to help me willingly. To protect Anna from those who wish her harm.'

'Or I'll be forced to do it anyway.'

'Better that Queen Sophia believes you willing. If she trusts you, how much easier than if she distrusts you?'

As well ask if she'd rather leap off a cliff or be pushed. She risked a glance along the parapet at the regal figures of the queen and her daughter. Only a fool would ever cross Sophia. Only a villain would do anything to hurt Anna.

She turned back to Wemyss. 'Very well. I enter into this willingly. Now tell me what I've embroiled myself in.'

He smiled, and the glow of the falling sparks stained his face like blood. An hour ago, what wouldn't she have given for a smile from this man? Now, it offered no comfort. 'The salvation of Scotland.'

Margareta waited in Helsingør Square. The evening shadows slunk over cobbles as rain pocked the ground, driving the canopies of abandoned stalls low; in the harbour, the wind had torn the water into ragged waves. Huddling deeper into the shelter of a leaning building, Margareta prayed the weather would calm before their sailing in a week's time.

A figure was crossing the square, straight-spined, with none of Margareta's furtive caution. Didn't Ilsa realize someone might be watching? When she reached Margareta's shelter, she pushed her hood back, shaking rainwater from her eyelashes. It was a gesture so like Johanna that for a moment Margareta almost thought her foster mother had come in Ilsa's stead. But she couldn't bear to think of Johanna, not anymore.

'This makes a change, Greta. I can't recall the last time you asked to meet with me. And such a fine night you've chosen!'

No point hiding how Ilsa's words grated: feigning amusement would only invoke the suspicion Margareta deserved.

You're doing this to help Ilsa too, she reminded herself. Protect her from whatever allegiances she's forged across the sea. You can't help her unless you know what she's up to.

'There aren't many opportunities to get away now,' Margareta said defensively. 'What with the proxy marriage, our travel preparations—'

'How irksome for you,' Ilsa drawled. 'Feasting and dancing every night.'

'It isn't all pleasure!'

'Today,' Ilsa said, holding up red and blistered hands, 'was laundry day. Please, do tell me about your suffering.'

'I didn't come here to argue.'

'Then why are you here?' Ilsa cocked her head in challenge.

'To tell you …' Margareta hesitated. This *was* a betrayal, however much she told herself it wasn't. But she had no choice. Many lives were at stake here, not just Ilsa's. 'I've changed my mind.'

Ilsa's face remained guarded, but Margareta could read the tug at her lip, the flicker of her eye: Ilsa was pleased. 'Why?'

'Because you deserve my help.' Ilsa never needed much convincing of her own worthiness. 'It isn't fair that I have so much and you so little. So I want to help you. But only as long as it keeps us both safe.'

The traditional note of caution: without it, Ilsa would never believe her.

Ilsa's expression loosened a touch. 'You mean you'll stop at the first sign of danger?'

'How can I know that unless I understand what sort of danger there'll be?'

'You won't know that,' Ilsa said. 'You can't. Not until you face it.'

'Yes,' Margareta said, starting to flounder. She couldn't fall back now. 'What I mean, Ilsa, is that I'll be brave for your sake. But I'll have to do some things differently from how you might, that's all.'

For a moment, she thought Ilsa would slap her. But then her milk-sister let out a laugh, scarcely warmer than the falling rain. 'Ah, my Greta mouse. You'll need to be twice as brave as you've ever been.'

'So what *do* you need? You mentioned a name. Gisela, was it?'

'Geillis,' Ilsa said, eyes narrowing. 'Her name's Geillis Duncan. She's apprenticed to Agnes Sampson.'

'Are they at the Scottish court?'

Ilsa snorted. 'Certainly not. Though half the folk there owe Agnes their health, or their family's. They're not far from Edinburgh – ten, twelve miles.'

'Twelve *miles*! There must be hundreds of folk within that distance of Edinburgh! How on earth am I supposed to find these women?'

'With as little exertion on your part as possible, I expect,' Ilsa retorted. 'You won't have to look for her. The Earl of Bothwell will arrange things.'

'Bothwell? Wasn't he the prisoner who went mad? Who kidnapped the old queen of Scotland and forced her into marriage?'

'If that's the version you want to believe. Anyway, that man died eleven years ago in Dragsholm. This is his nephew. He's going to help us.'

This made no sense to Margareta. 'How can a couple of Scottish midwives help an earl? How can you?'

'They have information,' Ilsa said calmly. 'As do I. And it is worth far more than pearls.'

She thought of Wemyss. *Knowledge is my coin of choice.* Was Ilsa's plan to use her wits to rise any different from Wemyss's?

'In return for what?'

Ilsa smiled. 'What do you think? For Scotland.'

'You mean he'd usurp King James? But Anna—'

'Do you think I would ask you to knowingly hurt Anna? Even though she cares more about her gowns than she ever will for you?' Ilsa smiled bitterly. 'No, Greta, this will help Anna fulfil her destiny too. You and Geillis will both be integral to that. And by choosing to help Anna, you can help me too. Your sister.'

But Margareta had already made her choice, and she tasted the bile of treachery.

'Be on your guard,' Ilsa said, pulling her hood up. 'Not, I imagine, that you need the warning.'

'Warning? Against what?'

A sudden sliver of moonlight cast an eerie blue light over Ilsa, as if she were a goddess come from the sea. 'There's a storm coming, Greta. Be sure you ride it out.'

6

Scotland

For days the talk had been of nothing but the dinner. Lamprey pies and stuffed capons, lemon possets and cinnamon jumbles, parsley sauce, almond sauce, apple, onion, and orange sauces – if there was an earthly sauce they hadn't made, Geillis fully expected Mistress Katherine would appear at the kitchen door, insisting they concoct one immediately. Her latest addition to the feast had sent Geillis and Jeanie traipsing along hedgerows, trying to find enough wild violets to garnish a salmon salad. Now the pantry was full of purple blooms in jugs of water, vinegar, and sugar and, frequently, an anxious Jeanie, checking that they weren't wilting. As far as Geillis was concerned, you only ate flowers when the nets came up empty and rats got in the barley; she couldn't imagine caring about a few petals when there was salmon to be had.

'Well, you're not a lady,' Jeanie retorted, 'so what would you know?'

'I know the importance of having a full belly.'

Jeanie surveyed the heaps of feathers and chicken carcasses on the table. 'If they're not full after this lot, they must have caverns for guts. Mind you, Master Patrick's is certainly vast enough.'

'Master Patrick?'

'Mistress's brother. As ruddy-faced as she's pale, and as flabby as she's skinny. If he eyes you at table, make sure you keep his wine topped up – he normally passes out after the syllabub's served, if not before.'

Geillis flexed her fingers; they ached from plucking feathers. 'I can't imagine Mistress Katherine having such a brother.'

Jeanie trussed a chicken's legs together. 'They say he eats so much because he's ashamed. He took his wife's name when they wed, and she wouldn't sign over her property to his family, the Moscrops, and now he overeats to make up for it.'

'That makes no sense.'

'Mistress Napier said it last time she visited.' Jeanie threw out the rich Edinburgh woman's name as if it made the story indisputable. 'Bigger he gets, the manlier he feels.'

Geillis didn't see anything manly about a bulging paunch.

'And he can't sire a son on her,' Jeanie went on. 'They've three girls and one boy in the graveyard. I hear she calls on Agnes Sampson every month, pleading for new remedies.'

'What's the wife's name?'

'Euphame MacCalzean.'

A friend – a customer of mine, Agnes had said. This woman was behind Geillis's employment with the Setons, and yet Geillis hadn't heard Agnes speak of her since. Stupid child, she scolded herself, sweeping the feathers into a tub for washing. Agnes wasn't her mother. She didn't have to tell Geillis everything. Especially since Geillis certainly didn't tell Agnes everything.

'They even say,' Jeanie whispered, 'she got Agnes to poison her father-in-law because he tried to bully her into signing over her property to Master Patrick.'

'Nonsense,' Geillis snapped, ignoring the unease sneaking down her neck. 'People always spread rumours about women with their own opinions.'

'I could believe it of her though,' Jeanie retorted. 'A tongue-lashing from her and you'll not sleep for a week.'

'Gossiping, are we?'

Jeanie almost dropped the half-trussed chicken in her haste to curtsey; Geillis bashed the tub against her hipbone as she shoved it onto the table before dropping into her own clumsy effort.

Mistress Katherine stood in the doorway, arms folded stiffly across a bodice already rigid with brocade. 'I had imagined the preparations for tomorrow night would keep you far too busy for such trivial matters. Am I wrong?'

Jeanie swallowed. 'No, Mistress.'

'You deny gossiping?'

'I—'

'Then you must have been denying the scale of your tasks.' Mistress Katherine's smile was belladonna-sweet. 'Let me remedy that.'

Jeanie opened her mouth to protest, then thought better of it.

Geillis said, 'How may we assist you, Mistress?'

Mistress Katherine surveyed Geillis's stained apron and reddened hands. 'Geillis, is it not?'

Geillis bobbed and said, 'Yes, Mistress,' knowing the woman was no more likely to forget any servant under her control than the Lord's Prayer.

'I hope you had vast reserves of good sense when you joined us, for spending time with this slattern must have robbed you of half your wits.'

'You must be the judge of that, Mistress.'

Mistress Katherine's lips thinned, as if disappointed. Had she come here spoiling for a fight? What kind of woman needed to vent her wrath on such lowly specimens as Jeanie and Geillis? But no anger came forth; instead she said, 'Nasturtiums.'

'Beg pardon, Mistress?'

'We must have nasturtiums to adorn our salads tomorrow. I have just learned the earl prefers them to violets, and we must all endeavour to please him in every possible way.'

'Of course,' Geillis said. 'We'll pick some this afternoon.'

Mistress Katherine rolled her eyes. 'Not this afternoon, girl. Now. When you receive an instruction pertaining to the Earl of Bothwell's pleasure, you do not follow it at your leisure. You obey at once.'

Bothwell. Geillis reached for the table to steady herself.

'Do you hear me, girl?'

'Yes, Mistress,' she heard herself say, but the words were far away, above the surface of a roiling sea. All she could think of were Agnes's words.

A more dangerous man will not be found in all Scotland. And he was coming here.

She wanted to consult Agnes – ask what on earth she should do, how she should be in a room with the man she'd been warned to avoid above all others. But there was no time: preparations for the dinner marched on, inexorable as an army.

How exactly did Agnes know Bothwell? Through her connection to Euphame MacCalzean? And what was that? Assisting a desperate woman in her quest for a living son, or something more?

Geillis's parents had always taught her that if a man was dangerous, you kept away from him. The drunk fisherman who'd swing an oar at you if you walked too close. The blacksmith who couldn't keep his hands to himself. Such men were found in every village. You learned to avoid them, taking longer walks home and perfecting the art of seeming benign but deaf. You didn't befriend their friends, if they had any. You didn't put orphaned girls in houses where they'd be forced into contact with such men.

Agnes must have known. She knew Euphame MacCalzean, she knew the Setons, and she clearly knew Bothwell. Impossible to know all three points of the triangle without realizing they were connected. And Agnes had deliberately placed Geillis in Bothwell's path – only to warn her. Why?

No time, no time. Her thoughts battered against her skull like carving knives. Salmon to fillet, capons to baste, asparagus to steam, cheese fritters to fry. All cooked in one vessel and served in another, and sand fetched to clean the cooking pots so they could be used for some other course. They had so much to do that they'd lashed one of the hounds to the turnspit wheel. He whined plaintively as he trotted, bewildered that his frantic paws weren't bringing the roasting pig any closer.

Finally Geillis's part in the cooking was done, and she was ordered to change her apron, tidy her hair beneath a cap, and ferry wine into the dining hall. Fumbling with her apron strings, Geillis caught a glimpse of Jeanie behind clouds of steam, face twisted with envy.

If only she knew how swiftly Geillis would have changed places with her.

Geillis might have been clean and neat, but as she waited at table she'd never felt so shabby.

Mistress Katherine was always elegant; now, in midnight-blue silk foaming with lace, she looked positively regal. At the opposite end of the table even David Seton looked imposing, despite his small stature, his black doublet slashed with steel-grey like the rivets in a suit of armour, surveying his table like a battleground. And in between the Setons, the combatants.

For all the wine purpling his beard and his raucously braying laugh, Patrick Moscrop, now MacCalzean, was a catapult of a man, hurling jests and judgements like grapeshot. 'James grows more foolish by the hour. Fawning over the Lindsay whelp as if his skin were covered in sugar. Unnatural, that's what it is.'

'He can kiss whomever he wishes,' Euphame MacCalzean retorted, the slashes of silver in her red hair gleaming like hidden blades. 'But such things should be private, whereas James makes them more prominent than any Act of Parliament.'

'Really?' Mistress Katherine challenged her. 'You do not care that our king is a sodomite?'

Euphame sipped her wine, revelling in the attention. 'I care not what a man does in private – I certainly wish no man to intrude on what *I* do in private. But I care very much about Scotland's sovereign behaving like a lovesick boy with one handsome man after another. He would make our country a laughing stock, and I despise the prospect of my daughters growing up to be ridiculed because an idiot sits on Scotland's throne.'

Geillis didn't dare look up. Meeting their eyes, alerting them to her presence – only a simpleton would do that. They might read her glance as impudence, as judgement. Worse, they might remember she wasn't a puppet who poured wine at the twitch of a string, but a girl who might repeat words to anyone with enough coin. Instead, she fixed her eyes on the vines writhing across the carpet at her feet.

They were talking of the king. Talking *rudely*. Where was the line between mere rudeness and actual treason? Or between conspirator and witness?

'What say you, Bothwell?' Seton asked, tilting the wine in his glass as if he couldn't both question Bothwell and look him in the eye. 'Is sodomy the worst of James's vices?'

Bothwell had been the quietest man there all evening, yet everyone had deferred to him. He'd been offered the choicest cuts, and no one had partaken of a dish he declined – such waste, Geillis thought, as if there wouldn't be enough already when they'd cooked sufficient for fifty. No one laughed at a jest before he did, or for long after he stopped. When an opinion was voiced, they all glanced to Bothwell. Even the powerful feared this man.

Now, Bothwell lifted his glass to his lips and drank deeply, in no rush to reply, knowing no one would dare steal into the conversation before he spoke. 'There's not a man at court whose soul isn't stained with sin. I could tell you tales of cardinals and choristers, chamberlains and chambermaids, men whose desires would make a harlot blush. None of us can pretend we are free from perversion, not even anointed monarchs.'

'Well,' Patrick began, before a sharp glare from his wife skewered him into silence.

'Is James more corrupt than other men?' Bothwell shrugged languidly. 'I daresay my sins are as dark as his. That's not what concerns me.'

'Nor me,' Euphame said with quiet glee.

'It is his folly,' Bothwell continued. 'His weakness. His mewling pleas for counsel on matters so simple a child could pluck a dozen solutions forth. I care not what manner of man a king is, except in one regard – his fitness to be king. There James fails abysmally.'

'Well said.' Seton nodded. Geillis imagined he'd have said as much if Bothwell had announced he'd seen kelpies flying over Prestonpans.

'So,' Euphame said, 'will you tell us more of your scheme, my lord?'

'Not in front of the servants,' Mistress Katherine muttered.

A smile coiled at the corner of Bothwell's mouth. 'Actually, it's your servant I wish to speak to. Alone.'

Geillis froze. Let him mean Jeanie, let him mean the steward, the gardener – anyone but her. She wanted nothing to do with Bothwell; she wanted Bothwell to behave as an earl should and pretend she didn't exist.

'Her?' Katherine spat out the word as if she'd found a bullet in her capon. 'Why her?'

'Now, wife,' Seton began blustering, 'you cannot hope to understand the complexities of my lord's stratagems. Men's minds work on larger scales than women's.'

'Not all women's,' Euphame snapped. 'Besides, I'm as much a part of this as you. I deserve to hear the reason for this girl's importance.'

Bothwell merely looked at her. Euphame bristled – but far from fearsome, she seemed shrunken. It was like seeing a strutting cat, having terrorized mice and sparrows, suddenly notice she'd strayed into the path of a wolf.

'I will speak to the girl alone. Seton can show you that Rhenish he hasn't ceased praising all evening.'

And just like that the master and mistress of the house, and their even more powerful kin, were dismissed, leaving Geillis Duncan, fisherman's daughter, alone with the Earl of Bothwell.

Footsteps died away. A bird called out somewhere in the night beyond the damson velvet curtains. The room seemed too large, the half-eaten fowls and congealing sauces grotesque.

'Geillis Duncan.'

No one had ever spoken her name with such guile, choosing it as if it were the card that might win the hand.

A more dangerous man will not be found in all Scotland. Was this what made him dangerous? Did he seduce people with honeyed words, bestowing attention on them until they turned their backs on the sun and faced him instead?

'When an earl speaks to you, it is polite to acknowledge him.'

Cornered, she lashed out. 'Even earls must ask questions if they wish to hear answers.'

Mistress Katherine would have whipped her for such insubordination. But Bothwell laughed. 'You'd be surprised how keen others can be to spill all their secrets without my proffering any questions at all.'

'Perhaps I have so few that I'm unwilling to give them away freely.'

'Perhaps you do not know the true value of what you have.'

Geillis's tone was brittle. 'I own two dresses, a mouth harp, a set of pipes, and a pair of pattens. Impossible to undervalue my possessions.'

Bothwell leaned back in his chair, watching her. 'You also own a mind. Eyes. Memories. And, I believe, a medicine bag.'

How did he know that? 'Yes.'

'In order to cut herbs, you must also own a knife.'

'Everyone owns a knife. How else would we eat?'

'So. You're a girl with thoughts and a blade. Few combinations are more intriguing.'

Other girls might have preened at such words from an earl. But Geillis didn't want Bothwell to be intrigued by her. Had Agnes, with her sharper thoughts and scalpels, been daunted or beguiled by his interest?

'Everyone owns a knife,' she repeated stubbornly. 'Why do I interest you?'

'Because you keep both your blades sharp.'

She'd avoided his gaze until now – but at these words she could no longer look away. Their eyes met and she knew Agnes had been right.

'Do you know what most servants do as they wait at table?'

Geillis shrugged, seeking refuge in truculence. 'Pour wine.'

'Your average servant,' Bothwell continued, 'does one of three things. The most simple-minded merely gawp, as if silken garb were more astonishing than the very word of God. Others, less dull-witted, listen with glazed eyes as they struggle to memorize gossip that will impress their companions. The brightest, meanwhile, bow and scrape, fawning over us in their eagerness to please, for they know even servants can rise if they win enough favour. But you did none of these things.'

'Perhaps because I haven't been a servant long.'

'I can tell. You weren't just inspecting Euphame's gown so you could coo over trimmings with other maids. You didn't watch Patrick so you could compile a tale about his drunken boorishness. You listened, and you thought very carefully about what you were listening to. So tell me, Geillis Duncan who has not been a servant long, who are you working for?'

She gaped. 'You think I'm a spy?'

'Why else would an intelligent girl skivvy for David Seton?'

'My parents are dead,' she retorted. 'He threw me out of our cottage. I've nowhere else to go.'

'So you bear a grudge against Seton? That hardly bolsters your defence.'

'I'm not a spy! I'm alone in this world – who would I be spying for?'

'Any of my enemies might have hired you to spy on me.'

'Then don't you think I'd own a pair of boots without any holes?' Geillis shot back.

'Maybe you appreciate the art of a good disguise. Or maybe' – he suddenly leaned forward – 'you're lying to me.'

'I haven't—'

'You told me you were alone. Yet I've seen you with a friend. Or did you imagine I'd overlooked you when I rode past?'

She stared. 'You saw me?'

'You were sharing a horse with Agnes Sampson. I would hardly overlook such a sight.'

'I don't see why that makes me special. I can't afford a horse of my own, so I shared Agnes's.'

Bothwell smiled ruefully. 'Agnes has never made friends easily. How could she, when she tells people their coughs will kill them, and has the power to poison with a single herb? She knows too much to be a comfortable friend for anyone – except those like her. And you, I believe, are very like her.'

Geillis swallowed. 'She's been … good to me.'

'Is that why you agreed to spy for her?'

Geillis gripped her apron to stop her hands trembling. 'No – I mean, I never did!'

But Agnes had told her as much. *After all, we're on the same side.* Yet Agnes had never asked Geillis for any information, hadn't demanded she share Seton's secrets. Had Agnes drawn knowledge out of her through kindness rather than interrogation? Had she been using Geillis all along?

'You're certain?' Bothwell pressed, gentle, cajoling. 'I'm sure you know how foolish it would be to lie to me.'

Too late to admit she was – even if she hadn't known it at the time. 'I am no spy.'

'How would you like to become one?'

She'd expected dismissal. Not an offer of employment.

'I don't understand. Who would I spy on – the Setons? I thought you were allies.'

'Even allies keep secrets from one another,' he said, a look in his eyes that made her wonder if he understood her relationship with Agnes. How one knew so much more than the other.

'But—'

'Geillis,' he sighed, and the false fondness in his voice made her skin crawl, 'you told me you were poor and friendless. Let's not pretend you don't need friends like me.'

'You're hardly offering me friendship, my lord.'

'I rarely do. I offer something you need far more.'

'Which is?'

'Protection.'

The fire had died down; remnants of logs shifted against the grate with a cough of sparks. There was no other sound.

Geillis's whisper jarred in the silence. 'Protection against what?'

'Whatever danger you may face,' he said simply. 'I am one of the highest men in Scotland. Some say I should be the highest. Few threats can touch me. Do you imagine anyone will offer you a better deal?'

Geillis thought fast. If few threats could touch him, the threats he could make must be far greater. It might well be unwise to accept – but it would be foolhardy to refuse.

'What must I do?'

He smiled at her grudging acceptance. 'A group of people hereabouts are carrying out a scheme at my behest. You will offer them your assistance and, when they accept, you will tell me everything.

How closely they follow my instructions. Who argues, who urges caution, who looks so frightened they might babble all to the next living thing they see. Everything.'

'But …' She had so many questions; she settled for the most practical. 'How will I find them?'

'You already have.'

Agnes.

'Won't she suspect? If I suddenly say I know she's part of your plan – such knowledge can only have come from you.'

'Oh, Agnes will deduce everything in moments.' There was a strange, mocking fondness in his voice that unnerved her.

'Then—'

'Perhaps I was mistaken regarding your intelligence.' He frowned at her. 'I want her to know I'm watching her.'

Was he threatening Agnes, or shielding her? Geillis couldn't tell.

'Am I supposed to tell her that?'

'What would a good spy do? Lie, Geillis. Learn to lie. You have no family, no riches. Your words are your only weapons, and you must learn to wield them if you wish to survive.'

Outside she could hear harnesses jangling, hooves stamping, impatient in the cold night. Laughter, a belch: Patrick MacCalzean being heaved onto his horse. He couldn't be packed off soon enough – him, his wife, and above all Bothwell.

Geillis stacked the salvageable pastries onto one plate. Most of the leftovers would do for pies and stews; they'd divide the rest between the servants' table and the pigs. Any other night, Geillis would have paused to gnaw a chicken leg to the bone or run a finger round the lemon posset bowls before ferrying the crockery back to Jeanie in the kitchen. Tonight, she'd be sick if she tried.

More harness-clinking, a needle-sharp reproof. Euphame MacCalzean, furious at her oafish husband. Small wonder they had no boys. If he ended every night like this, she'd never get with child again. Or perhaps Master Patrick feared the rumours were true and dared not touch his wife.

A third set of harness, that deep voice bidding farewell. He was gone.

Geillis let out a breath; slumping against a chair, she realized how long she'd been holding it. When she tried to breathe again she could barely haul in air: raking gasps that shredded with every tremor of her shoulders.

'Are you unwell, Geillis?'

She yanked herself straight, reached for another bowl to stack. 'Quite well, Master.'

Would it be worse to turn round or not? Keeping her back to him would be disrespectful – but so was looking him in the eye. Besides, he liked watching his servants from behind.

Seton's boots whispered against the carpet. 'A little tired, perhaps?'

'Not too tired, Master. I'll finish here and then be off to bed.'

'Yes,' he said, and she felt his breath, warm against her neck and reeking of meat. 'And will you sleep soundly, Geillis? Dreaming sweet dreams?'

He was trying to purr the way Euphame purred, to drawl the way Bothwell drawled – but his tongue slapping against his wine-stained lips and his barely swallowed belches ruined the effect.

'I never remember my dreams.'

'A shame,' he said. 'I should have liked to hear them.'

There was a sudden edge to his voice, turning ordinarily risible leers into something that couldn't be laughed at.

'My dreams would hardly interest a man like you,' Geillis said, aiming for flattery and instantly fearing it might seem encouragement.

'If they interest the Earl of Bothwell, I imagine they would entertain me greatly.'

Geillis sidestepped to clear another plate, striving to get as much space between them as possible. 'We didn't talk of dreams.'

'But you must have,' Seton said, and the edge was hardening. 'For he must have made you an offer, and an earl offering anything to a girl like you is the stuff that dreams are made of. Tell me, Geillis – what did he offer you? Coins? Gowns? A kiss?'

'No!' she burst out, stung into words. 'Nothing like that!'

'Many women would claw each other's eyes for a kiss from Bothwell. I'm surprised you could resist his wiles.'

'I'm not—' Geillis dropped a platter; fish bones scattered. 'He didn't.'

Seton laughed. 'Oh, Geillis, can't you see I'm teasing? I don't need to know what Bothwell's offered you. I simply need you to remember something.'

Suddenly her face was on the table, fish scales clammy against her cheek, honey sauce sticky beneath her left palm. Seton's hand was in her hair, driving her head down; her cap fell askew, covering one eye. His thighs pressed hard against hers; the table edge dug into her hips.

'That I am your master,' Seton rasped. 'I – not Bothwell – own you, Geillis.'

'Yes, sir,' she gasped, trying not to enrage him by struggling and yet twisting away from the cold fish.

'You need to learn this lesson,' Seton grated out, and she knew then it wasn't just anger thickening his voice and strengthening his arms, and she was even more certain it would be foolish to struggle.

His hand tightened around her hair, so tight he'd pull some from her scalp. His other hand fumbled somewhere behind her. At his breeches. And then he rucked up her skirts, her shamefully threadbare petticoat, and the fire must have gone out entirely because the air was cold enough to raise goose pimples on her thighs. She tensed, and then she thought resisting would make it hurt more, but not resisting might make Seton think she welcomed this. But there was no more time for thought because he shoved a knee between her legs, pushing them apart, and then he pushed himself, not inside her, but at her. Drunken fool, some distant part of her mind hissed as he groped blindly with his prodding manhood, then with rough, blunt fingers. For a moment she hoped he might fail, give up, and leave her alone – but that was when he found his way in, and she would have cried out, but her cry was muffled against meat and sauce and tablecloth.

Tansy, she thought as he thrust into her, every stroke making her cap flap feebly against her eye like a flag of surrender that no one noticed. Rue. Pennyroyal. Mugwort. She'd pick them every day until she knew she was safe, because if there was anything worse than this it would be bearing Seton's bairn. Over and over again: tansy, rue, pennyroyal, mugwort.

Then later: belladonna, mushrooms, yew berries. The right amount of anything, if you knew what you were doing. Enough to make a man sick. Not to kill him, because Geillis was no fool, but to make his life a misery, and to make sure he knew who'd ruined it.

When at last he slumped over her, groaning and panting, and whispered, 'Remember, Geillis, I am your master,' she thought: You're wrong. You haven't won, David Seton. You've only made it certain you will lose.

7

Denmark

This was the face of a spy. Margareta caught her own gaze in the mirror over Anna's head. They couldn't have looked more different. Anna, all silver-white and petal-pink, holding up a succession of earrings to see which best complemented her lapis-blue eyes. Behind her, Margareta's face was so guarded she seemed to be lurking even when merely arranging Anna's hair. One blithe, innocent, eager to meet her new husband. The other furtive, fearful, and eager for nothing.

Had Sophia seen her as a spy from the very beginning? When Gabriel Vinstar's coffin descended into the crypt, had she glanced at his child and thought *Such dark hair will be perfect for hiding in the shadows?*

Did all royal women look at children and see weapons? How long until Anna was forced to consider people in terms of usefulness or threat? As soon as they crowned her in Edinburgh?

'I think these,' Anna said, selecting a pair of pearl earrings set in silver filigree. 'They remind me of mermaids caught in fishing nets.'

Margareta smiled. 'When did you last see a mermaid?'

Anna laughed. 'When did you last look? I shall lean over the sides all the way to Scotland, searching for one.'

There was the difference between them. Anna looked for mermaids; Margareta would always be looking for the nets.

She didn't only have a face for espionage then; she had the heart for it too. Was this what she'd been all along?

* * *

They would sail tomorrow, and if Margareta feared leaving her home-land for Scotland, she feared leaving Ilsa far more. She couldn't pretend to have been close to her sister since she'd left home, but two miles' distance in Helsingør was infinitely different from the breadth of the North Sea. However much she cared for Anna, leaving Denmark meant leaving the only kin with whom Margareta shared memories. However painful those memories might be.

They met on the shore below the palace at dusk. The tide had crawled away, leaving lumpen detritus in its wake: fragments of lost boats, their bright flecks of paint abrupt against the salt-darkened wood.

Ilsa stood below the tidemark, green skirts whipping in the wind, salt spray glinting on her cheeks. Out of her element and yet no less imperious for that. Like a mermaid, Margareta thought, picking her way through the shallow pools that stippled the beach, demanding the tide return.

'Packed all your jewels in muslin, have you?'

'Let's not argue tonight,' Margareta pleaded as she reached her sister. 'Can't I have a peaceful memory of you?'

'Don't be daft. You'd only look back on it suspiciously.' It was as affectionate as Ilsa ever managed and Margareta gave her a half-smile in half-gratitude.

'Will you write?'

'When I can afford it. In a few months the captains will charge three times the price, claiming winter voyages are triply hazardous.'

'When you can,' Margareta pressed. 'Otherwise—'

'You'll scold me? I'd like to see that.'

'I'll worry.'

'You'll worry regardless. Some women embroider, some pray, some beat carpets ever harder, and my Greta worries.'

Margareta wrapped her arms tight around herself. 'Ilsa, I worry you'll end up like … like your friend Dorthea.'

Ilsa's eyes glinted, needle-bright. 'That won't happen. We have powerful allies. And unlike you, I'm not afraid to use them.'

Margareta flinched, the old excuses flailing silently as stranded fish. She'd never been able to convince Ilsa – or herself – that the irrevocably, unjustly different fates of their family were not her fault. 'But your enemies are also powerful.'

Ilsa smiled. 'No doubt. But we'll have struck them down long before they know who we are.'

Oh, Ilsa, Margareta thought. They already know.

What was she doing? How could she even consider spying on her own sister? Even if Ilsa's allies were as powerful as she claimed, her enemies included Queen Sophia and King James. Letting Ilsa stand against them without warning her would be the cruellest act Margareta had ever committed. And the thought of Johanna's face if she knew what Margareta had become ...

'Ilsa, you need to be careful.'

Ilsa laughed. 'You always say that.'

'Because you never are!'

'I'm still here, aren't I? I must have been careful enough.'

'But this time—'

'What? This time I'm asking you to be involved, is that it? Honestly, Greta, do you wish to back out now? I won't despise you for it, you know.'

Once, years ago, when Margareta and Ilsa had been carrying eggs back from the market, swinging the basket between them, a dog had chased a cat across their path; Ilsa darted one way and Margareta the other, and the inevitable had happened. Yolks stiffening on their aprons, they fled home to Johanna, where Margareta had wailed, 'Do you hate us now?' But Johanna had smiled. 'Of course not. I'm just disappointed we won't have baked eggs for supper.' She'd meant it kindly, but her words had almost been worse.

Ilsa couldn't know the extent of Margareta's betrayal. She deserved Ilsa's hatred – dear God, she did! But the prospect of disappointment in Ilsa's eyes was unbearable.

Margareta sighed. 'This time I won't be here, nagging you to keep safe.'

Ilsa laughed. 'As if I could forget! You're the good angel on my shoulder, Greta. Always reminding me to watch my step. Which must make me the imp on yours.'

Margareta managed a smile. 'I suppose it does.'

'I'll miss you, Greta.'

'I'll miss you.'

They hadn't embraced since they were children, all bony shoulders and long limbs that surprised them daily. But now they did, each bundling the other tight, Margareta's fine woollen cloak draping over Ilsa's worn homespun. As salt stung Margareta's eyes, she tried to pretend it was sea spray or the wind wrenching tears loose. Nothing whatsoever to do with her deceit.

None of Anna's ladies looked forward to private audiences with Queen Sophia. She only ever wished to speak alone with them for two reasons: to reprimand or to demand.

Outside Sophia's private apartments, Margareta steeled herself before nodding to the guards, who knocked then stood aside.

'Enter.'

Inside, Sophia was studying a chessboard intently. As Margareta approached, her footsteps silenced by rich Turkish carpets, Sophia extended a white hand and moved the black bishop. Then she reached for the raised ivory platform on which the board lay and spun it around. Now she was playing with white.

Sophia leaned back in her chair and eyed Margareta across her vast mahogany desk. 'Do you play chess, Margareta?'

'A little.' Chess wasn't popular in Anna's chambers: she rarely sat still long enough for a game.

'You should. Anyone who works for me should understand the game. If you cannot find an adequately skilled partner, then do as I do.'

'Are other players less skilled than you?'

Sophia smiled thinly. 'If they were more skilled, I would not wish them to know it. No, I play against myself because I like to know my own vulnerabilities. How my choices might appear to others, and how they might seek to turn them to their advantage, and thus my disadvantage. You need to develop this skill.'

This was how Sophia drew you in: promises to share her wisdom – yes, even with someone like you!

'But surely you know the next move each side intends?'

'Of course. Yet when I turn the board I can discern how transparent my intentions are. Besides, no skilled chess player thinks only a few moves ahead. There is always a deeper scheme at work. Can it be foiled in one or two moves by your opponent? If so, it is not a good scheme. Can it adapt in response to your opponent's actions? If it is to succeed, it must.'

This had never been about chess. Yet taking up the threads of Sophia's speech and weaving them was irresistible. Even if the pattern had been set by the queen.

'How can you play against yourself without bias? Don't you always want one side to win?'

Sophia raised an eyebrow. 'No, Margareta, I do not choose sides. Perhaps you meant if I thought one side represented my better self. But anyone's better self is the one that learns how to win – sometimes through defeat, and through resilience, determination, and ingenuity. Skills you must also learn.'

'Is this why I am here? For a chess lesson?'

'Not on this board,' Sophia said, frowning sharply. 'One should never abandon an unfinished game. No, I called you here for another reason entirely. You are to be betrothed.'

'Betrothed?'

It was the last thing she'd expected. Years of gossip with Anna, Elline, and Vibeke had taught Margareta that betrothals required power. Money, titles, status – all requiring either a living father or one who'd lived prudently. Betrothals had always seemed like Anna's gowns: cut from finer cloth than Margareta's, decorated with richer jewels – and something she could never hope to obtain.

'Indeed,' Sophia said, narrowing her eyes the way she always did when warning her daughters that, had she wished to breed parrots instead of princesses, she would not dwell in Helsingør.

'But – why me?' Who would want to marry the penniless daughter of a drunkard and the foster daughter of worse? Even if Sophia alone knew the full story of Margareta's childhood, surely the absence of a story would speak just as loudly to any prospective suitors.

'Because it is my will,' Sophia said simply. 'I require this marriage for my daughter's sake.'

Of course. A marriage not for Margareta but for Anna. Anna was all that mattered.

Margareta dipped her head obediently. 'May I ask whom you wish me to marry?'

'John Wemyss of Logie.'

A few days ago she would have leapt at the prospect. The idea of looking into his green eyes to speak her vows, of his lips touching hers, would have set her blood racing. But now?

He was a spy. She was a spy. Marriage was supposed to be a safe harbour, and instead she would be cast adrift on uncharted seas where storms threatened and rocks lurked.

'It's a fitting match,' Sophia said, her scrutiny returning to her game. 'He is high enough that Anna will not be shamed by one of her ladies marrying him, though not so high as to provoke questioning. Except, I imagine, from you.' She met Margareta's gaze with an expectation that seemed almost gentle and yet couldn't be.

Margareta swallowed. 'I am very grateful for your attention to my future happiness. But I must ask why.'

Sophia nodded. 'I would have been disappointed if you had not. A good mind never accepts any change in circumstance without thoroughly probing the whys and wherefores.' She leaned back, scrutinizing Margareta's reactions. 'Here in Denmark, no one would be surprised to see the two of you together. There are only so many Scots here, and only so many women who are going to live in Scotland – what could be more natural than for you to spend time together? Not too much, of course – there is friendly curiosity, and then there is indiscretion.'

Margareta remembered the night she'd danced with Wemyss, how she'd feigned a fall and he'd helped her aside. Then Sophia had been stern and disapproving. They hadn't been subtle enough to satisfy her.

'In Scotland, however,' Sophia continued, 'the two of you often together would inevitably raise suspicion. You are Anna's lady-in-waiting, he is one of King James's gentlemen. In the Scottish court, where there are so many more Scots, what reason could you have to seek out the company of one above all others? None that would not bring shame on Anna, and so I must give you a reason, for I need you to work together. What better disguise than a marriage? Nothing is so dull to gossips as a married couple, and if you and Wemyss speak quietly together in a corner, everyone will assume you are discussing a new steward or ordering linens for a baby.'

Wemyss's baby. Margareta blushed. This might be a marriage arranged under pretence, but once rings were exchanged, it would no longer be artifice. Would Margareta even know where the act ended and life began?

'I will announce the news at dinner tonight,' Sophia continued, 'and you shall be married once you arrive in Scotland – leaving a suitable gap, of course, after Anna and James's marriage has been celebrated.'

'Of course,' Margareta echoed.

'Because she comes first,' Sophia said, suddenly fierce. 'No matter what vows you give your husband, no matter how many children you bear, remember that Anna always comes first. On your chessboard it is not the king whose fall will lose you the game, but the queen, and you must protect her at all costs. And she will need protection in Scotland.'

So Margareta was to be Sophia's eyes and ears in Scotland. Not a wife first, nor a mother, but an informer.

'Do you swear to do as I command?'

A vow before Sophia taking precedence over a vow before God? What could be more fitting – and more damning?

Stepping outside was like emerging from underwater – finally air slipped into her lungs without a struggle, and she could walk without tangling weeds hauling her down. Margareta blinked as she crossed the gardens, as if that might make either the sunlight or Sophia's designs less blinding. She was to be married.

Girls were supposed to be delighted by the promise of marriage. Their lives were lived with no other goal. They were supposed to be grateful, eager, and unquestioning. Which made Margareta a wholly inadequate bride.

She rested her elbows on the garden wall, staring out at the distant white sails that wavered above the harbour. Tomorrow she would sail for Scotland with the man she was to marry and the woman she was to serve above all others. It would be a voyage of bitten tongues, for Margareta couldn't confide in anyone and even the slightest tremor of doubt across her face would be suspect.

This was to be her life. Always on the edge, guarding her thoughts like a vixen baring her teeth before the den where her pups slept.

'Lady Margareta.'

Couldn't she have even a moment alone? But she would never be wholly alone again – however lonely she might feel.

Margareta pulled a smile across her face and turned. 'Master Wemyss.'

Wemyss rested his elbows beside hers. Nodding at the gap between their hands, he said, 'I assume Queen Sophia's told you these are to be joined.'

'Once we're in Scotland.' She hated the trepidation in her voice – like a green girl nervous of her wedding night. If only that were the darkest of her fears.

'You sound less than enthused,' Wemyss observed mildly. 'I'd hoped the prospect wouldn't be too disappointing.'

'It isn't that,' Margareta said, staring at his hands, unable to look at his face. 'It isn't *you*.'

'What a relief,' he said, his dryness convincing Margareta he was laughing at her. 'But we both know there's very little of the personal in any marriage. At least we have an advantage over James and Anna – we've actually met one another.'

'How lucky we are,' Margareta retorted. She could match him for dryness if that was how he intended to conduct the business of their life.

'Well, aren't we?' Just like that, the sarcasm vanished. 'All marriages are allegiances formed on grounds of money and status, regardless of the age, wit, infirmity, or affability of either partner. We, however, are both young, in possession of our wits, apparently healthy, and not, I'd thought, entirely unlikeable. Moreover, our marriage isn't for money, which neither of us have in abundance, but for something far more valuable.'

'Status?'

'No.' His hand covered hers; she felt the heat of his palm easing into her skin. 'A hand.'

She looked up in surprise. 'What do you mean?'

He held her gaze. 'The shadows are dangerous places in which to dwell. Sometimes a hand to hold in the darkness – or pull you back into the light – these can be better defences than a dozen concealed daggers.'

'A dozen?' she said, trying for lightness in the face of his dauntingly tender sincerity. 'Is that the number you carry?'

He smiled. 'Always imagine anyone carries at least one more than you've found. Let that advice be my first way of keeping you safe.'

'Surely a knife of my own would be more effective.'

'Or knives.' The wryness was back. 'We'll have a whole voyage in which to practise. And fair weather for the sailing, by the looks of things.'

'Yes – God be praised.'

But even as they shared a smile, Margareta couldn't quell a twitch of fear.

A storm's coming. Could Ilsa have been wrong? Or was this merely the calm before the thunder struck?

8

Scotland

Geillis's fingers stung: the rue in her basket had left red welts on her knuckles that her knife now scraped with every cut, but she gritted her teeth. Better this pain, now, than the alternative. Besides, some of the mugwort she was gathering would go into a salve for her hands, healing her twice over. Easier to think of what she was doing as medicine, soothing a rash until it disappeared like a memory. Easier than thinking about what Seton had done to her.

She added the mugwort to her basket, alongside the rue and some pennyroyal. They were all supposed to keep things away – her mother had planted rue near raspberry canes to deter insects, and her father had kept crushed pennyroyal in his pockets to keep off midges in summer. And the mugwort, folk claimed, repelled evil spirits if you put it under your pillow. Geillis stared at the leaves, their odd, splayed shape – like gull feet, she'd thought as a child. What had come first – the discovery that these herbs could keep the consequences of brutal men's actions at bay, or the belief in their power to repulse? Did it matter? Geillis needed both.

She rocked back on her heels, tilting her head up. Out here on the clifftop path, the smells of the sea air and fresh herbs could smooth frown lines and make lungs swell. They slipped beneath your mobcap like a cool hand, stroking the strains of the day from your neck.

Her mother used to do that. First to Geillis's father when he came home, bones creaking from hauling nets, skin taut from squinting into the winds. Then, when Geillis sat beside her to darn by firelight, she would lift a hand away from her own tasks and her fingers would circle on Geillis's neck, rubbing her worries away. Had Geillis ever done the same for her mother? Had it ever occurred to her that becoming a woman wouldn't mean outgrowing worries, but becoming even more bound by them?

Geillis let her knife fall into her basket, dropping her head into her blistered hands. She'd scarcely paused to grieve since that day when her mother had bled to death in the rickety shepherd's hut. Instead, she'd flung herself into hard work – for the Setons, and with Agnes – refusing to let herself think of the life she'd lost. Her mother. The sisters who'd never drawn breath. And all the unborn babies before, all the possibilities that had been taken away from them.

Now, she wanted to be here, above the beach where her father's boat had washed up last winter. To remember a time when she'd had a home, had come through the door to smiles, not commands. If this had happened when her parents were still alive, perhaps she could have wept in her mother's arms. Perhaps she wouldn't have eyed the pulling grey of the tides with thoughts she barely dared name to herself.

Every village in Scotland could tell tales of girls who weighed their pockets down with stones and waded into the sea, rivers, lochs. Everyone presumed it was for the same reason, and women whispered with judgemental glee: *Should have been more careful*, while men watched silently because such things were women's business and nothing to do with them. But at the thought of Seton's wordless smirking, Geillis gritted her teeth. She would not be such a woman. Nor, thanks to her growing knowledge of herbs, would she be like her mother. To meet such an end for a man she loved, a baby she wanted, would be one thing, but to meet such an end for David Seton's pride? Never.

'Geillis?'

She forced herself to look up.

Agnes halted beside her, surveying the shore. 'I expected you to help with Janet Stratton's toothache.'

'Sorry.' Geillis spoke quietly, dully; no one could have mistaken her tone for genuine contrition.

'I suppose you have a good reason.'

'I had to pick some herbs.'

'I see.' Agnes peered into Geillis's basket, and Geillis flinched with angry shame: Agnes would grasp the situation immediately. 'You should wear gloves when gathering rue.'

'I don't own any gloves.'

'And I imagine you couldn't afford to wait to borrow any.' Agnes sighed and sat down beside Geillis. 'Who was it?'

She'd expected bluntness; that didn't stop Agnes's words striking Geillis like flat palms. 'I …'

'Best to say it,' Agnes advised. 'Then it becomes something you own, a tale you can control. If not, all the unsaid pain will eat away from within. Besides, better to speak of it before he does. Then he'll be the one defending himself. The second version of any story is the one people assume is the lie.'

'No one would believe me over him.'

'At least half the folk in any village might. The female half.'

'The half too frightened to speak up. The half who'd avoid me in the street, as if I were plague-ridden.'

Agnes gave her a sharp stare. 'Must sympathy be shouted from the rooftops for it to matter? Women might not make pronouncements in courts or from pulpits, but that doesn't make their pity worthless.'

'So I shouldn't remain silent, but other women can?' Geillis shook her head. 'Where's the sense in that?'

'You're not other women. I know you, Geillis Duncan. I know you yearn for a vengeance you think can never be yours. You chafe against a world that gives power to undeserving men and none to women who might truly merit it – who might even do something worthwhile with it. Silence for you would be a cage – but to speak could be the beginning of a great journey.'

Geillis returned Agnes's stare – equally sharp, but also bewildered. 'What are you talking about? You think I have an opportunity?'

'Was it Bothwell or Seton?'

There was no point asking how Agnes knew. It would have been more surprising if she hadn't.

'Seton.'

'Ah.'

'Does it make a difference?'

'Yes and no. Did he speak to you?'

'He said he wanted to prove he was my master.'

'Thus proving himself master of nothing. So David Seton's feeling weak. How interesting.'

'What does that make me? A mere worm.'

'If he thinks so, more fool him – and the wiser we are.'

Geillis hissed through her teeth. 'You sound glad! Did you put me in Seton's house with this in mind? Did you *want* this to happen?'

'I would never wish this on anyone. But what's done is done. No use crying over it. Instead, decide how you'll use it to your advantage.'

'My advantage! How on earth am I supposed to gain from this? I only wish to destroy David Seton, and that would just destroy me in turn!'

'If you were caught, aye.' Agnes's gaze was deliberately fixed on the mugwort leaves.

'What do you mean?'

Was that a small smile on Agnes's lips? 'There are better ways to ruin such men than with violence.'

Hunger rushed Geillis's words out. 'Tell me.'

'He wants to be like Bothwell. He thinks by taking part in Bothwell's schemes he'll become his equal. You could ensure that never happens.'

'What do you mean?'

'Bothwell asked you to help him, didn't he?'

'How did you know?'

Agnes shrugged. 'Why else would Seton feel such need to assert his mastery? Think, Geillis: Bothwell's demanded your assistance, so you must find a way for him to assist you.'

Geillis snorted. 'An earl help the likes of me?'

'Wouldn't be the first time he's helped a woman far below his station,' Agnes said quietly. Then her strident tone returned: 'Even if he doesn't know it. If you're telling him tales, you can choose how to tell them. Decide who to paint a hero, who a villain. You don't have to ruin Seton. You just have to make Bothwell want to do so.'

'Just manipulate the most dangerous man in Scotland?' Geillis shook her head incredulously. 'You make it sound so easy.'

'If you hoped for an easy life, you should have ensured you were born a man.' Agnes sniffed – and then, in a gesture that almost made Geillis fall off the rock in surprise, touched Geillis's hand. 'I never wanted any of this for you. Your parents, Seton, Bothwell ... But nor could I protect you from any of those things. I can only help you cope with them – if you're willing to trust me.'

Geillis stared at Agnes, her iron-shot hair, those blade-sharp cheekbones. Trust Agnes? Who'd placed her in Seton's house, in harm's way, who'd lied to her several times that Geillis knew about and God knew how many more besides. How could Geillis trust anyone, let alone Agnes?

Agnes sighed, as if reading Geillis's thoughts. 'I know it seems too much to ask.'

'Trust must be earned,' Geillis said bitterly.

'Then come with me to Inchkeith tonight.'

'Why?'

Agnes smiled grimly. 'If I know some of your secrets, it's only right you learn some of mine. Let me show you what Bothwell's planning.'

The oars plucked echoes from the sea as the boat moved towards Inchkeith island. Ahead, moonlight sliced stark angles into the rocky cliffs, as craggy as the abandoned garrison buildings high above.

Geillis hugged her knees against the sea wind, her shivers threatening to overwhelm her. Agnes had told her nothing about what they were coming here to do. Only that they were carrying out Bothwell's orders, and that was no reassurance at all.

None of her companions seemed to share her anxiety. Agnes rode in the prow, surveying the waves as if they were hers to command. At the oars, two men: John Fian, the Prestonpans schoolmaster, who always spoke to people as if they were ignorant boys, and the hulking Robert Grierson, whose boat it was. Her father had never spoken Grierson's name without grim envy; despite always being last to take to sea, Grierson inevitably returned with the largest catch and a roguish smile, his pockets filled with coin he didn't have to spend on wife or bairns. Between Geillis and Grierson sat Bessie Thomson, a girl Geillis had played with as a child, leaping off the sand dunes in a time before work became their lives. Geillis had always thought Bessie, with her buttery hair and round cream cheeks, as simple as the milk she spent her days with. Was Bessie here for her gullibility? Or had Geillis underestimated her erstwhile playmate? She remembered Agnes berating Robert Dixon for pawing at Bessie when she delivered curds – had Bessie's other customers abused her even more cruelly?

No one spoke. The only sounds were the plash of oars and the winds writhing up the firth. Perhaps the rowers were tired after the long journey from Prestonpans. Perhaps they all were. The sun had set hours ago, and everyone else in the parish would be long abed. Or perhaps they shared Geillis's fear after all. And if they were afraid, knowing what they were about to do, then Geillis, in ignorance, ought to be even more afraid.

They reached Inchkeith's shore. Fian and Grierson shipped the oars and clambered over the sides, hauling the boat onto the shingle, where the women disembarked.

'Tide's coming in,' Grierson said. 'Best secure her.'

Geillis frowned. The boat was above the tideline. It was the wrong time of year for spring or neap tides. Why the precaution?

As the men lashed the boat to a jutting rock, Agnes set off up a steep track, through scrub already brittle with autumn, though September was scarcely a week old. Bessie followed; the men fell in behind. Geillis had no choice but to do likewise. And as they ascended, she realized the others had all been here before. They'd prepared for something.

They emerged onto the clifftop overlooking the Firth of Forth as it wove inland. To the south, Geillis could see the flickering lights of Edinburgh; to the north, the dark hills lurking behind the Burntisland parish.

'There,' Agnes breathed, pointing out into the water.

What was she looking at? Pinpricks of lantern light aside, all Geillis could make out were different depths of blackness. But then the others nodded, and Geillis squinted, unwilling to be the only one who didn't see.

Something large was moving across the water. Stately, smooth, steady. A ship.

'Is it the right one?' Bessie asked.

'Of course,' Agnes said sharply.

'The *Margaret*,' Fian announced, as if lecturing small children. 'Sailing from Burntisland to Leith at King James's request. He wishes Jean Kennedy, sister-in-law to his adviser, Sir James Melville, to become Anna of Denmark's lady-in-waiting.'

'He can wish all he likes,' Grierson snorted. 'Let's get on with it.'

It? What was *it*?

With every ripple of waves, every breath of wind, Geillis's confusion was giving way to suspicion.

Why else would they have come here? Why else look for a ship?

They were going to sink Jean Kennedy's vessel.

But where were the lanterns for signalling, the oil, the tinder? Were they going to the old lighthouse on the hill behind them? It was practically derelict; there probably wasn't even a working lantern there anymore, let alone oil. They'd brought nothing with them. How would this be done?

'Agnes,' Geillis whispered, trying not to sound like a pleading child. 'What are we doing? Are there no lanterns?'

Agnes turned, moonlight striking her face like lightning. 'We have no need of lanterns, Geillis. Only faith.'

Trust me, she'd said. Was trust the same as blind faith? Whatever she was asking Geillis to believe in could have nothing to do with kirk.

'We must begin,' Fian said, intoning his words as solemnly as the creed.

Grierson started to whistle: a low, continuous note that seemed to drone too long for natural breathing. Fian clicked a pair of flints together in a steady rhythm, as if beating drums for a marching army. Agnes and Bessie crouched down, pulling trowels from their pockets and hacking at the earth – digging, Geillis realized, a trench in the shape of the firth itself. Agnes produced a skin and tipped water into the hollow.

Still Geillis had done nothing. She clung to that, as if none of it would matter if she could say she'd done nothing. But then Agnes caught her eye.

'Whistle,' she commanded. 'The more whistles, the stronger the wind.'

Geillis didn't want a strong wind. Or any wind at all – she wanted to be home, safely tucked up in bed.

But she had no home. And she hadn't been safe since her father drowned.

Geillis softened her lips and began to whistle.

Agnes dipped her forefinger in the water. Bessie did likewise. Slowly they circled their fingers, Agnes clockwise, Bessie anticlockwise, five times, then reversed. They too began whistling.

Now the air trembled with their notes, shivering, wavering. Far below, the water stirred. Tides, Geillis told herself, tides, that's all. It wasn't them. How could it be? God alone controlled the winds and waves, so this couldn't be happening.

Blackness seeped across the stars. The darkness thickened, as if a dozen clouds had just pressed closer, lowering like pillows towards unsuspecting sleepers. It began to rain. Gently at first, soft as whispers. Then harder, faster, a drumbeat chasing the whistling, until bullets of water ricocheted off the island's ruined buildings, turning the clifftop to marsh. Squinting through darkness and rain, Geillis saw the water around Agnes and Bessie's hands jerk, flail. Ripples spread, clashing with other ripples; more raindrops shattered them. Still they stirred. And now the water began to heave, surging against the sides of their hollow.

Then Agnes dropped a piece of wood into the trench.

It was tiny. It was nothing amidst the writhing water. Falling raindrops shoved one end underwater, sent spray flying over it. Within seconds it was drenched dark and spinning, twisting, tilting. Before long, it would sink.

The whistling grew shriller. Without thinking, Geillis changed her own pitch: higher, thinner. Winds charged up the firth, raking up black waves. Geillis's skirt whipped violently, rain driving it against her legs, wind tearing it away. Water spilled across her face, silvered ropes tangling before her eyes. Let me be blinded, she thought. She didn't want to see this. But neither could she look away.

Far below, the ship was struggling. Its sails arched like spines on the rack. Tiny silhouettes scuttled about the deck, hauling ropes, bellowing commands that couldn't drown out the screams. Rearing waves quenched the lanterns; the only light came cold and pale from the moon. But it was enough. Geillis saw what came next.

A stampede of waves, hurling themselves against the bow. The weight of them bore down on the vessel, flinging gouts of salt water across the deck, flicking men overboard as if taking chess pieces. Wood creaked and it sounded like a howl. Then a cracking, rending noise, and the mast split – but not in two. It collapsed into the sea, the tangling sails anchoring the ship. Now the shrieks grew louder and Geillis's whistle trembled like a sob. They knew. They all knew.

The ship tilted, the half-severed mast dragging it to port. Geillis saw figures throwing themselves overboard, taking their chances with the wild sea. Others clutched at the mast, as if something so broken could save them.

Then the ship struck the rocks.

Thunder roared in triumph. Every crash of the waves revealed black rocks punching holes in the stern. And with each wave, the ship sank lower.

Later, much later, the screams faded and Fian said, 'Enough.' They stopped whistling. Geillis opened her mouth, stretching her aching, salt-tight lips; if her throat hadn't been so dry, she would have let out a whimper. When had it stopped raining? Her skin was numb but almost dry, and she didn't understand how. She grabbed at the flask Grierson passed round, choking down the whisky as if its heat could wash away what she'd done.

Dawn was breaking. Ashen light seeped across the firth, nudging the clouds aside, exposing the wreckage below.

The rocks made a cradle for the ship, though no cradle had ever been so treacherous. The split mast lay trapped between dark stone pincers. Planks jutted like broken bones; fragments bobbed nearby. Bodies were tangled in ropes, faces bloated and grey; others floated, butting blindly against the rocks. How many more were lost in the sea? Geillis knew better than most how few bodies came back. But some did. Would they be dragging corpses up the Prestonpans sands in the weeks to come?

'It actually worked,' Bessie breathed, eyes wide.

Had it? Couldn't it have been a coincidence? They all knew how unpredictable and merciless the North Sea could be, and Scottish Septembers were never free of rain. Perhaps they'd had nothing to do with it.

'Of course it worked,' Fian said brusquely. 'We have faith, knowledge, and patience – our schemes are bound to succeed.'

Geillis closed her eyes, wishing his words could be blinked away. Behind her eyelids, swollen corpses turned in waves, slack faces staring up at calm skies.

'Right then,' Grierson said, rubbing his hands. 'You know the tradition. First to a wreck claims the spoils.'

'But …' Geillis swallowed. She hadn't meant to speak. 'Sun's barely up – if we arrive back laden with loot, won't folk wonder how we got here so soon?'

Grierson shook his head in disgust. 'This is what comes of involving women – worry and nagging.'

'Forget the trinkets,' Agnes said, her voice serene as the sea, her authority unquestionable. 'We may have succeeded tonight, but much remains to be done – and swiftly. Word must be sent. The Danes will sail any day now, and we must be ready.'

The Danes? What did a Danish fleet have to do with this Scottish ship?

Then Geillis understood.

They were going to kill the Danish princess.

9

The North Sea

Lightning flared. Everything seethed white: the narrow bunks, over-flowing buckets, the taut faces of Anna and her ladies. Then it was gone and darkness swarmed in. Margareta, gripping the edge of the bunk in one hand, the chest she perched on in the other, braced herself.

Sure enough, the waves hit. The whole ship dived down, down, and just when she was certain they would never rise again, the ship reared like a terrified horse. Then the settling, or what she'd come to think of as settling: the pitch and heave that had long ago extinguished their lanterns. Margareta didn't dare relight them.

Someone moved. That gasping lunge, the blind groping, the relief and desperation as they found the bucket: these were familiar sounds now. Then the stench of hot bile, crawling over the already-stale air. Was it Anna, Elline, or Vibeke? Elline, Margareta thought, as the vomiting gave way to whimpering. Vibeke usually groaned as if furious at herself, whereas Anna sighed almost apologetically, perhaps imagining Sophia's disappointment. And Margareta? She dived for the bucket herself, and when her belly was empty, gritted her teeth. She wasn't here to be an invalid. She was here to protect Anna.

But how could she protect Anna against a storm?

The journey had started so smoothly. They'd ridden down to the harbour in Anna's new silver coach drawn by six pure-white palfreys. The Danish and Scottish royal flags fluttered against a cornflower-blue sky, the three azure lions and the single scarlet lion rampant on their golden cloths. On the flagship's deck, the Earl Marischal had kissed

Anna's hands, saying what a fine day it was to start a voyage. They'd set sail with the folk of Helsingør cheering them off, and Margareta hadn't wanted to inspect the waving crowd in case she glimpsed Ilsa's silvery hair, glimmering like unseasonal frost. Instead, she'd glanced away, and her gaze had caught Wemyss's, and for a moment she'd thought there was nothing deceptive in his smile.

Fool to hope. Three days into the voyage and he'd talked to her of nothing but the Scottish nobility's convoluted intermarriages, testing her recollection. Then the storms had hit.

Margareta hadn't been outside the cabin since the first rains fell. 'A brief shower,' the captain assured Anna as the women trotted below decks, Anna worrying about watermarked silk. But peering out of the porthole later, Margareta had seen smoke-black clouds rolling towards them like siege towers, and she knew he'd lied.

The ship bucked again. There was a yelp and a thud: the Bible Vibeke clutched had tumbled from her grasp. Lightning flashed; in the sharp glare, Margareta saw Anna's face glistening with silent tears. Hesitantly, she touched her hand.

'All will be well. It's only a storm.'

'Only,' Vibeke breathed. 'An endless, hideous torture – but it's only a storm, so never mind! It's not as though it could—'

'Do you remember?' Margareta burst in, before Vibeke could utter the ominous words. 'When we were twelve, a storm struck while we were out hunting, and your brother wanted to hide under the trees?'

Another flash of lightning. Anna's cheeks were clammy, but she managed to curve her fingers around Margareta's. 'My mother told him that was a stupid place to hide.'

'*Kings cannot be ignorant*, she told him,' Margareta said, daringly trying to capture Sophia's imperious brusqueness. '*Especially when their ignorance endangers their subjects.*'

'I thought Christian would cry,' Elline croaked.

'But then you spoke to him,' Anna said to Margareta. 'You told him the horses were frightened, and we had to ride back as fast as possible so they could be tucked away safely in the stables. You said, *A good king always looks after anyone who's afraid.*'

'And he had to prove how good a king he was by galloping fast enough to break his neck,' Vibeke added.

Anna smiled at Margareta. 'You always know how to make us feel better.'

Even before Margareta knew the extent of Sophia's plans for her, she'd understood her duty was to cajole and coerce, smooth over any rows, ensure the royal children were happy, regardless of her own happiness.

But soon Anna gave a strangled moan and flung herself towards the bucket. As the princess vomited, Margareta stretched out a floundering hand and rubbed Anna's back gently, her palm rasping against sweat-damp silk.

'There now,' she murmured. 'There now.' Meaningless words that meant so much. Johanna had said them dozens of times to Margareta and Ilsa.

Anna sat back, still trembling. 'I can't help it,' she whispered, half-plaintive, half-sheepish.

'None of us can.'

'No – I mean, I can't stand the smell. Why has no one come to empty the buckets?'

During a storm, Margareta imagined there were hundreds of tasks the sailors deemed more important than disposing of ladies' vomit. 'I could take it outside if you wish.'

Just once, she thought, it would be nice if someone spoke up for her. If Elline or Vibeke protested 'Oh no, it's too dangerous!' or 'Surely a groom could be found?'. Instead there were only self-pitying groans from the bed and Anna smiling up at Margareta, saying, 'You're so kind. Thank you.'

Moments after the door closed behind her, Margareta regretted volunteering. The passageway was tight with shadows, and she needed to press her free palm against the wall to find her way. With every halting step the bucket banged her shins. Something slopped and she winced, dreading the state of her cloak.

The ship pitched to starboard and Margareta stumbled; the bucket whacked her kneecap and she gasped with pain. Something creaked ominously. Dear God, she wanted air. Blindly, she quested forward. There was a ladder here somewhere – surely it couldn't be far. How much room could there be below decks given Anna's cramped cabin supposedly represented the ship's finest state room?

There! Her hand found the steps. Grappling skirts in one hand and an ominously sloshing bucket in the other, Margareta half-crawled to the top, where she fumbled for the door handle.

Immediately the wind tore it out of her hand. The door whipped away so fast the force of its bang sent it flying back; only Margareta's up-flung hand prevented a broken nose.

Everything on deck was chaos. Rain fell in great spears, not just downwards but yawing in all directions. Dark figures dashed across decks slick with water, shouting commands, knotting ropes, hauling and winding and tightening. Some were scrambling up the rigging to sails that belled low with the weight of water. The men kept having to stop, wrap wrists in rope, and cling on for dear life as the wind yanked the rigging this way and that.

She should never have left the cabin. She'd thought she was helping Anna, but she'd only be a hindrance here.

But she couldn't just dump the bucket. They'd need it again before long.

Keeping her back against the wall, Margareta edged sideways, aiming for the port railings. Within moments, her skirts were sodden anchors, her cloak plastered to her legs. Fingers numbed white, she could barely hold the bucket, let alone grasp any handholds to pull herself closer. But it had to be done.

Then at last she was there, hauling the bucket up and tipping it over the side. Only when it was empty did she glance up.

The wave struck.

A great wall of salt water smashed into her with all the force of falling stone, sending her flying across the deck. She couldn't see. Everything was grey-green, pouring into her nose, mouth, ears. Only the crack of elbows and knees on wood told her she hadn't been hurled into the sea. Then a thump, a scrape, and a heavy grunt that wasn't hers, and she came to rest against something solid and warm.

'What do you think you're doing?' The voice was rough, deep, and unmistakeably Scottish.

Margareta blinked fast to clear her eyes. They were wedged against the starboard rail, Wemyss's arms tight around her shoulders, her back pressed against his chest. Amazingly, ridiculously, she still clutched the bucket in one hand. 'I had to—' A hacking cough overrode her words and, no longer able to care for dignity, she spat out a mouthful of salt water.

'The only thing you have to do in a storm is stay safe! Good God, Margareta, it's far too dangerous out here!'

She twisted her neck to glare up at him. 'If it's so dangerous, why are you outside?'

'You were nearly washed overboard! You nearly drowned!'

'You could have too!'

They stared at each other, furious, frightened. Something that was neither rage nor fear quickened their breath.

Another wave struck. The ship staggered; the tilt thrust them hard against the side and the lurch back to port would have sent them tumbling back across the deck if not for Wemyss's tight grip on the rail. Just before they plunged back down, Margareta glimpsed the sea over his shoulder, vast and roiling. But the sight when the ship came level was no less frightening.

'Dear God!'

Wemyss followed her gaze, past waves rising and falling like scythes. They'd left Helsingør with four other ships; two were struggling nearby. One tossed about like their own, its sails straining. But the other …

Its masts had split. Like a felled tree, the mainmast had toppled against the rear mast – and now that one fell. Even over the storm, Margareta heard screaming – and then wood shattering as the masts crushed the quarterdeck. Where the cabins were. Who had been in them? Had some courtiers been clinging to bunks on that vessel just as they were here?

'Can't we help them?' Margareta breathed, aghast.

'Not unless the storm abates.'

'But—'

Lightning flashed. The broken ship gleamed like bones – then all was plunged into shadows again.

'Far better to lose one ship than two,' Wemyss said.

Margareta wrenched her gaze away from the damage. 'How can you speak so callously?'

'Sometimes you have no choice but to watch people suffer.'

The words were cold as the waves – and yet his eyes told a different story. Why was he forcing himself to become so ruthless?

Wemyss scrambled to his feet.

'Come. We must get below!'

He pushed her forward and she wanted to object, but the storm was too loud. They ran across the deck, his arm tense around her waist, braced to catch her if she fell. The deck heaved beneath their feet, hurling them against the door. Margareta cried out as her palm struck wood; Wemyss grunted as his shoulders took the brunt of their fall. He groped for the handle, wrenched the door open, hustled Margareta through and stumbled after her. The door slammed behind them, then banged open again. Wemyss leapt forward to seize the handle.

'Bolts!'

Margareta fumbled at the wet catches. 'I can't – pull harder!'

'Don't you think I'm trying to?'

But he launched his weight backwards, dragging the door closer, and Margareta drove the bolts home. They slumped against the door. Outside, the winds howled, waves crashed, the ship moaned. Yet there was a stillness around them as they rested at the top of the steps, chests heaving, rainwater and salt water coursing down their faces.

Margareta had been afraid since the storm first struck. Now, as she looked up into Wemyss's eyes – the same dark green as the thundercloud edges – she felt a new fear ripple through her.

'I suppose I should thank you.'

'I suppose you should,' he agreed. 'Lucky I was there to stop you drowning.'

She frowned. 'Why *were* you there? You said it was too dangerous to be outside.'

He hesitated.

'You were watching me!' she realized.

'Apparently you need someone to keep an eye on you.'

'Is this why we're to marry? Not just to help us watch over Anna – but to watch one another too? I thought you said I should trust you!'

'You should!' His face now seemed too close, his eyes too green. A rain-silvered scar cut through one eyebrow; she wanted to brush the water away. 'If not me, who can you trust?'

'Did Queen Sophia tell you to spy on me?'

'Christ's wounds! There are other reasons for men to watch women! Besides, I'm perfectly capable of making my own decisions!'

'How can I believe you?'

'Was saving your life not enough? Let me prove it to you again.' Roughly, he pulled her close and kissed her.

For a moment, she couldn't move for shock, unable to think of anything but his lips on hers, the taste of salt, the chill of their skin making the warmth of his mouth even softer. And then her hands reached for him of their own volition, wanting him to kiss her forever while the storm raged outside.

Two days later, the battered fleet limped into Oslo harbour, the ship that had lost its masts trailing behind the others on ropes like a cowering hound. 'Repairs,' the captain had said and everyone else had thought *refuge*. Land that didn't pitch and sway. Winds that couldn't shove your bedchamber on its side.

The royal party barely spoke as they mounted their equally shaken horses. Anna was paler than sea spray. Elline gripped her belly, trying to hold it steady. Vibeke slumped against her horse's mane. Margareta, climbing the mounting block, stubbed her toes twice, unable to lift her feet high enough. Even Admiral Munck, the commander of their expedition, looked drained, his patrician forehead carved deep with weariness – or guilt? She'd only ever seen him looking thoughtful and austere with King Christian's other councillors. When was the last time he'd presided over voyages from a deck rather than prodding model ships across maps?

Exhausted, they fell in behind Munck and the governor of Oslo, journeying towards Akershus Fortress.

'We are glad to see you returned safely,' the governor was saying. 'I can't recall such terrible storms in years – perhaps even in my lifetime.'

'And scarce abated now,' Munck grunted, hunching into his cloak as rain beat down on his shoulders. 'The captain doubts our fleet will be fit to sail again for at least a fortnight.'

'Or until winter's passed if you leave it much longer,' the governor said lightly. 'Though I can't imagine any natural storm keeping you here that long.'

'If it was natural,' Munck said. 'Seemed more like witchcraft to me.'

Witchcraft.

Ahead of Margareta, the governor laughed and steered the conversation towards Oslo's amenities. But Margareta could never hear that word and feel mirth.

It was a storm, that was all. It couldn't be anything more.

Because if it had been something else, she would have to question what part Ilsa had played.

10

Scotland

Geillis had barely slept since that night on Inchkeith. The tiredness, and the dry ache of her eyes, she'd long been accustomed to; scouring fire-places and beating tapestries left her muscles burning. But she wasn't used to guilt. That was what kept her awake at night, staring at shadows, her bone-weary body crying out for sleep until the birds began to stir.

She didn't even know how guilty she ought to feel. The *Margaret*'s sinking might have had naught to do with their whistling. Lady Jean Kennedy and all the other drowned souls might not need to be on Geillis's conscience. But they were.

As for the second time …

They hadn't rowed out to Inchkeith, and Geillis had almost been relieved – if everything they were doing had no influence on the weather and a storm still struck, being stranded on that abandoned island was a terrifying prospect. Instead, they'd ridden east to North Berwick and climbed the Law. Facing out to sea, wrapped in Jeanie's cloak as well as hers, she'd known, as Agnes dug a hollow, that another group would be standing on the shores at Leith. Agnes had sent her west three days before to deliver a letter to a grim-faced woman, while Bessie had passed another message to someone further east. Elusive messages commanding the other groups to 'act' on a night chosen by 'our friend'. Groups outsiders would have called covens. And everyone knew what happened to covens.

Even while whistling, Geillis had prayed it wouldn't work. But what they were doing had nothing to do with God, and maybe that was why He hadn't answered her. For there had indeed been another storm.

It had begun out on the horizon. A dark spot, growing larger with every breath, like a flock of crows flying closer. The mass had swelled, pulsating with veins of lightning, its blackness bleeding into sky. She'd heard thunder crack, felt winds slap against her head and rain claw her cheeks, and the fisherman's daughter in her hissed that they should all flee from such weather, bolt the doors, and huddle together until it passed. But she couldn't run. She'd been more afraid to run and face Agnes's wrath than to stay with the others – if nothing else, they were other living beings and you clung to anything living in a storm.

But the storm hadn't come for them. It had turned, a great black beast uncoiling, and stalked eastwards. Fian and Agnes had exchanged smiles.

'Now we wait,' Fian said, eyelids low in infuriating smugness. 'Word of the sunken fleet will come soon enough.'

But Geillis didn't want word to ever come. She didn't want to know she was a murderer.

A peace of sorts could be found in the gardens. Leafy with September life, the vegetables were sprouting fast and Geillis could barely pick the raspberry canes clean before more ripened. She was glad – the simplicity of plucking and washing and cooking could dull a mind until it was as edgeless as washed-up pebbles. So while Jeanie swept hearths and made beds, Geillis knelt in soft earth and gathered cabbages, leeks, and carrots. She cut sage and thyme for cooking, lavender and rosemary for the rushes. All the while feeling, not thinking, aware of the satiny squeak of leaves against her palms, the herbs' scents stirring every time she moved her fingers. Never letting herself notice the holes in the earth where she'd pulled up cabbages, how similar one hollow could be to another.

Sage, she thought, imagining a dialogue with Agnes as she dropped velvety leaves into her basket. For wasp stings, or inflammation of the throat. 'And for cleaning your hands before a birth,' Agnes would point out mildly, an Agnes with arms too full of herbs to dig hollows, talking too much to whistle, impossible to reconcile with the wind-whipped woman on the Law, rain flashing on her flexed hands like broken glass. 'The scent calms, and no mother wants you handling their baby with fingers still covered in soil.' Most of this sage might be going straight into a chicken pie, but Geillis would keep some aside for her own stores.

Geillis rocked back on her heels, rolling her aching shoulders. Her basket was full; she'd give these to Jeanie, then come back out for the beans. Brushing earth from her apron, she stood up.

'Geillis! Jeanie!'

Geillis didn't recognize the shrieking voice at first: it was the last she'd have expected to be raised in panic. Mistress Katherine.

As Geillis hurried across the garden, Jeanie burst out of the kitchen door, hands red from chopping beef.

Mistress Katherine rounded the side of the house, cap askew, face red. They'd never seen her so dishevelled. 'You must go now! Ride as fast as you can!'

'Beg pardon, mistress?' Jeanie said blankly. 'Ride where?'

'Fetch Agnes Sampson at once! My daughter – Lucy's gravely ill!'

Jeanie stared, frozen with fear. Geillis thrust the basket at her, wiping her hands on her apron. 'What manner of illness?'

'Gravely ill!' Mistress Katherine repeated, eyes swimming with frightened tears. 'Are you deaf, girl? Fetch Agnes Sampson!'

But Geillis didn't want Agnes here. She didn't want to bring the memory of Inchkeith or Berwick Law here, into the peace of the garden. She didn't want Agnes to see Geillis move around and away from David Seton when it was Agnes who'd sent her within his reach.

'We don't need Agnes,' Geillis said firmly. 'I can help.'

She spoke in Agnes's voice, and she would use Agnes's knowledge, and she would prove that she no longer needed her.

Lucy's chamber was different from any other Geillis had visited. A featherbed, not a tick mattress; velvet curtains instead of oiled linen nailed to window frames; leather-panelled walls embossed with the Seton arms rather than bare wood. It was a chamber entirely for sleeping, not a curtained-off corner or a nest for dozing hounds by day. Nevertheless, it smelled like any other sickroom: stale sweat, rancid breath, dried vomit.

Mistress Katherine paused at the threshold. 'Are you sure we shouldn't send for Agnes Sampson?'

Geillis tried not to grit her teeth – the woman had a sick child after all. 'I know what I'm doing. Trust me.'

Mistress Katherine looked torn. 'I suppose you're here at least. Do everything you can.'

The unspoken *or else* hung in the air like an axe.

Geillis crossed to the bed where Lucy lay, her spindly body fragile in a linen nightgown. Geillis pushed the covers down to Lucy's waist, the better to see the rise and fall of her narrow chest; it fluttered like broken wings. Swiftly, gently, Geillis inspected her patient. Flushed, sticky face, dilated pupils. Lips dry. Flinching away from candlelight. Hot skin. Geillis sniffed the bowl Lucy had been sick into. Bile and some half-digested bread. Jeanie had baked bread that morning – they'd all eaten some so it couldn't be that. No suspect mushrooms, no spoiled meat.

What would Agnes do?

The thought sneaked up on her like a cutpurse, reaching out to steal her faith in her own abilities. Geillis shook herself impatiently. She didn't need Agnes's advice, real or imagined. She could do this herself. A fennel and ginger infusion for the vomiting. An angelica and camomile poultice for the fever. Rosemary tea as a restorative. Lucy's stomach would hurt after all that retching, so mint to soothe that, perhaps cloves for any pain elsewhere. She didn't need Agnes. She didn't need any of them.

'I'll need water heated,' Geillis said, and she no longer heard an echo of Agnes, but a voice all her own. Calm, confident. Somewhere between a mother and a minister, whose words you believed without question. The voice of a wise woman.

'Fine muslin,' she added, 'to make the poultices softer against her skin. New rushes laid down, lavender mixed in to calm her sleep.'

They obeyed her. Jeanie first, then Katherine, forgetting her rank in the face of her daughter's sickness. Left alone, Geillis splashed cold water from the brass ewer onto strips of linen and folded them against Lucy's forehead and chest. That would help while she prepared. She opened her medicine bag and drew out pestle, mortar, and the herbs carefully folded within labelled slips of paper, then began.

This was the work she loved. Plants between her fingers, their rising scents promising hope and health. The growing ache between her shoulder blades, the warmth of fingers close to cramping. Hard work, and worth it. Not like serving dishes that would barely be touched or scrubbing at thoughtlessly soiled cuffs. No, healing was the work she wanted to do all her life. And if this succeeded, if Lucy recovered ...

She didn't let herself dream. Instead, she applied herself to Lucy's care. All day she ground herbs for poultices, steeped them in boiling water, changed sweat-soaked sheets, emptied bile-filled pots into the privy ditch, sang soothing lullabies as Lucy whimpered herself into fitful dozes.

By nightfall Geillis was worn out and it didn't matter. Jeanie had brought a platter of food, which Geillis pecked at absently, tearing off a crust here, gnawing a heel of cheese there. Tossing a raspberry into her mouth, she removed a poultice from Lucy's forehead and placed the back of her hand against the child's skin.

It was markedly cooler. Was it just the poultice? Geillis tested Lucy's cheeks, neck, chest: all cooler.

'Is she better?'

She'd barely noticed Katherine's presence. Kneeling on the far side of the bed, hands clasped in desperate prayer, Katherine raised reddened eyes to Geillis.

'Have you healed her?'

'The fever's broken. She hasn't vomited since dusk and she's kept down rosemary tea.' Geillis hesitated – but in the sickroom she couldn't hesitate. She had to be the brave one, the one her patients could believe in. 'We must still pray. But I think we can be hopeful.'

Katherine's face crumpled with relief and she covered Lucy's hand with kisses. 'Thank you!'

'I was glad to help.'

'Why?'

Startled, Geillis cast a wary glance at her mistress. 'She was sick. She's a child and she needed help.'

'But you didn't have to be the one. We could have sent for Agnes Sampson, or a physician from Haddington, even Leith.'

'It would have been wrong to let her suffer while someone else was fetched. I was here and I could help.'

'So you didn't pause to think of the wrongs done to you?'

Geillis swallowed. 'Beg pardon, mistress?'

'Don't feign ignorance.' Katherine watched Geillis thoughtfully. 'I know we haven't always treated you well.'

'You've given me no cause for complaint, mistress.' Blurted out, her words sounded insincere.

'I doubt there's a servant alive who wouldn't complain of their mistress. Besides ...' Mistress Katherine's nostrils flared. 'My husband has certainly given you cause.'

Geillis flinched. She didn't want to see the pity in those stony grey eyes.

'You aren't the first,' Mistress Katherine said calmly. 'Though you've enough knowledge of herbs to avoid our last maid's fate.' She looked up; it was impossible not to meet her frank gaze. 'I know what my husband is, Geillis. But I also know what I would be without his good name.'

'So you turn a blind eye?' The words spilled out before she could choke them back.

'Not blind. I am always watching. Over the years I've observed that men never look at a woman and overestimate her capabilities. They see subservience, dowries, wombs. Sometimes they see us as whores, with deceit and avarice in our every movement. But they never consider that our minds might be wilier than theirs.'

Despite the banked fire, Geillis fought a shiver. 'What are you suggesting?'

Mistress Katherine didn't smile, but her lips twitched in something like satisfaction. 'You spoke with the Earl of Bothwell. You know my husband hopes to gain by his conspiracy.'

'If he gains, so do you.'

'Not necessarily.'

'I don't understand.'

Again, that twist of satisfaction on her lips. 'Perhaps my husband has ceased to be quite as useful as he believes. My suggestion is this: if you can find a way to hurt David Seton without harming me or my daughter, I would have no objection. I might even see a way to help you.'

Geillis had known Bothwell was dangerous. She'd known Seton could damage her. But now she wondered if there was anything so terrifying as a wronged wife, or a mother who'd feared she might lose a child. Katherine Seton was more dangerous than she could have imagined.

11

Geillis hadn't known a knock could be both furtive and panicked. But the one that came late one Monday night somehow was. Jeanie, deep in sleep beside her, merely muttered and rolled over to wedge her face against the kitchen cat's ginger flanks. Geillis grimaced: visitors after dark rarely brought good news.

Geillis padded across cold flagstones to the kitchen door. Quietly, she slid back the bolts and peered out.

'It's Agnes!'

Geillis took one look at Bessie's whey-pale cheeks and trembling lips and decided not to risk waking Jeanie. Slipping her shoes on, she led Bessie over to the shadow of the pear trees.

'What's happened?'

'She's been called a witch!'

Geillis's blood turned to ice. Had someone found out about Inchkeith? 'Has she been arrested?'

'She's to stand trial in Haddington. Tomorrow.'

Trial. The word was frightening enough – educated men all glaring at you, their judgements heavy with power. But a witchcraft trial would never be as simple as letting Agnes stand in a dock while people argued.

Geillis swallowed. 'You should go home, Bessie.'

'But shouldn't we help her?'

'How? They wouldn't listen to us.' Or perhaps they would – and that would be even worse. If they asked whether Agnes had ever tried to work spells, how could Geillis deny it? Geillis had a talent for silence, not lying, and courts never let you stay silent. 'Besides, if we try to defend her, what do you imagine they'll do next? We'd be clapped in irons too.'

'Maybe they'll let her go!'

'Don't be such a fool!' Geillis grabbed Bessie's shoulders. 'As soon as we open our mouths, they'll shout us down as witches too.' They ducked accused witches, pricked them, forced them to walk over red-hot coals. Anyone lying to save a witch couldn't expect any kinder treatment.

'But she's—'

'Innocent?' Geillis glanced behind her, checking they were still alone. 'None of us are innocent. Not anymore.'

'I wasn't going to say that,' Bessie snapped. 'I was going to say she's our *friend*.'

Was she? She remembered Bothwell saying Agnes didn't make friends easily – and small wonder, if the way she treated her friends was to send them into houses as spies, knowing their new masters were lecherous conspirators.

But how could Agnes have protected Geillis against Seton's lust or Bothwell's machinations? Kin to royalty, however distant, and the most powerful earl in Scotland – how could a midwife protect a servant from such men?

And how could a servant protect a midwife from accusations of witchcraft?

Geillis set her jaw. 'People accused of witchcraft no longer have any friends.'

The dark warmth of the corridors was stifling. The rushes *tsked* underfoot like disapproving gossips. Ahead of Geillis, the door to Seton's study loomed up like a clenched jaw. She'd been summoned to face the man who had raped her.

She'd seen him since, of course. The house wasn't so large, nor so well supplied with servants to make it avoidable. She'd poured his wine, her arm aching from trying to keep her skin as far away from his as possible. She'd passed him in corridors, wedging linen on her hip to keep something between them, as if cloth could armour a girl against her master.

The thought of being alone with him now made her skin crawl. Her thighs clenched defensively, uselessly. She couldn't evade him forever. Blinking back tears of shame, Geillis knocked on Seton's door.

'Enter.'

The fire was crackling. Seton, blue satin bulging like veins through a slashed white velvet doublet, sat at his desk.

He wasn't alone.

The other man was a stranger, his face taut as a bowstring, eyes arrowhead-sharp. But she knew the brindled horsehead crest on his livery: Bothwell's.

Seton took a swig of wine. By the state of his cuffs, it wasn't his first. 'This is the girl, Chirnside.'

He didn't even bother to name her. As if he hadn't stripped away enough of her dignity.

Chirnside looked Geillis up and down. 'Can you ride?'

The question threw her. 'I ... yes.'

Chirnside's eyes narrowed sceptically. But Bothwell had chosen Geillis. Was it fear of his master that prevented him from challenging her? 'Then we'll leave at once.'

'Where are we going?'

Both men frowned. It hadn't occurred to them that she might ask questions.

Chirnside's answer seemed to close around her like iron. 'Haddington.'

To defend Agnes, or to condemn her? It wasn't for Geillis to decide. Bothwell had already made up his mind.

They rode fast, the urgency of their pace echoing the severity of Chirnside's expression. Geillis was breathless trying to keep up, and couldn't gasp out a word, let alone a question.

When they reached Haddington, she expected to go straight to Agnes's trial, wherever that might be – the gaol, the kirk, the town hall. Or the river, for a ducking stool. Instead, they went to the tavern, and she knew immediately who would be waiting inside. Chirnside tied up their horses, dismissing the grooms with a cursory glare. Gripping Geillis's elbow, he steered her through the bustling taproom, past barmaids carrying bowls of stew that made Geillis want to retch, and upstairs to the top floor.

Chirnside had barely knocked before the voice came.

'Enter.'

Chirnside pushed her in ahead of him. It was not a room where anyone would imagine an earl to be – plain, almost bare, apart from a table and a few chairs. It was the room where they were least likely to be overheard.

'Swift work, Chirnside,' Bothwell said, with a sardonic note of surprise. When the earl's attention switched to her, Geillis schooled herself not to flinch. 'You've heard about Agnes.'

She nodded, wondering if she'd ever be able to tell him anything he didn't already know.

'And you didn't come at once to save your friend.'

'You told me Agnes didn't make friends easily.' Where had that daring come from? More from terror than bravery.

'Touché.' He didn't smile. 'Well, you must be a friend to her today.'

What sort of friendship was commanded by an earl? 'How may I be of service, my lord?'

'I need you to keep Agnes alive. Preferably out of gaol too.' Bothwell's dark eyes were unreadable; Geillis wondered why Agnes's survival, Agnes's freedom, meant so much to him. The earl gave a hollow chuckle, as if he'd read her thoughts. 'The longer she's imprisoned, the more likely she'll talk.'

Geillis wanted to insist Agnes would never talk. But what did she know about how gaols loosened tongues, or minds? 'How can I do that?'

'Expose this trial as a farce. Tell them Agnes has never dealt in witchcraft. She's a healer surrounded by ignorant fools unfit to lick her boots.' Anger and something else flashed across his face before cold command returned. 'You have knowledge of herbs – you can explain everything away.'

'Even the ship at Inchkeith?'

'You mean the surprisingly inclement weather?' Bothwell's voice dropped, low and threatening. 'I think you'll find that was God's doing. Perhaps He disapproved of that vessel's reason for sailing. Anyway, I believe you and Agnes were attending the schoolmaster John Fian that night. What was his affliction again?'

Geillis hesitated. 'Chest pains. We gave him parsley boiled in wine and infusions of mint.'

Bothwell snorted. 'Next time you lie, don't knot your fingers in your apron. But the charges no longer relate to that night.'

'No longer?'

'Indeed. They relate to a Sunday in summer and a sick man and his sicker son. Who is now a dead son. Hence, I imagine, the charges.'

'Robert Dixon?' Geillis remembered that filthy, untended cottage, the feverish child. When had he died? On a night when Geillis and Agnes were out raising storms? Storms that would have brought winds to rattle tiny chests, chills to make fleshless limbs shiver uncontrollably. Had Dixon tried to get help – and had she and Agnes been nowhere to be found?

'The storms cannot be mentioned,' Bothwell said quietly. 'I cannot be mentioned. Fail me, and I will withdraw my protection from you both – and for women like you, only my protection can save you from the flames.'

Geillis's head pounded; she wanted to grab something to stop herself swaying. Scraping your own mind raw with fears was one thing; hearing them spoken aloud, especially by Bothwell, the kind of man who might pass such a sentence, was far worse.

'But I cannot foresee such problems arising,' Bothwell went on, a dangerous purr under his words. 'After all, you're sensible enough to appreciate the value of keeping quiet.'

Geillis swallowed. 'I'll do my best, my lord.'

'Your best?' He sneered. 'I've no interest in that. Either do my bidding, or you will prove the instrument of your own undoing.'

The kirk where Agnes's trial took place was cold. Geillis had never noticed what iciness old stones could bleed, as if centuries of sea-frets and winter frosts were slowly worming out of the cracks. Perhaps it was the relative emptiness: no Sunday crowds jostled in the pews today. Instead, the minister sat in a row of other black-robed men Geillis didn't recognize: one grim-faced powerful man looked much like another.

She knew one face though: the sickly grey slab of Robert Dixon's. His jaw was set in the same scowl as before. She might have pitied him – but not today. Not when he was accusing Agnes – who remained locked in the tolbooth, forbidden even to be present, let alone defend herself. It was all up to Geillis.

'That woman killed my boy,' he grated out, voice raw from grief – or guilt because he'd never bothered to fix his roof.

'Use her name, Master Dixon,' a black-clad man sighed, tapping quill against inkpot. 'For the sake of the court records, please be specific.'

Dixon's scowl veered into an affront he didn't dare voice. 'Agnes Sampson. Everyone knows she's a witch.'

'We must have particulars,' the scribe pointed out. 'Tell us how you reached your conclusions.'

'Because she did it,' Dixon insisted. 'She gave him herbs and potions – devil's brews, no doubt – and he died.'

'Do you recall what manner of herbs or potions?'

'Course not.' Dixon looked horrified at the thought. 'I wouldn't know anything about them.'

'So you let your son imbibe substances you didn't recognize?'

This was wrong. Trapped in a pew by Chirnside's wiry frame, Geillis felt certain this wasn't how trials normally proceeded. That the trial was indoors and quiet, not at the riverside with a mob braying for the ducking stool, was strange enough. But for the prosecution to be sceptical, even faintly impatient – surely this wasn't normal?

Dixon frowned. 'Well, yes. The lad were sick! I were desperate! Any father would've done the same!'

'Any … father … would have … consulted … witches,' the scribe said, pausing as his quill caught up with his words. His, not Dixon's. It didn't matter what anyone said. All that would ever be remembered, or used to decide a verdict, was what that man chose to record.

'Did Mistress Sampson not tell you what she was giving the child?'

Dixon hesitated, clearly tempted to lie. 'What I remember her saying, plain as day, is that my boy would die! She foretold the future and that's witchcraft, no denying that's witchcraft.'

'Accusations of prophecy,' the scribe observed, writing something probably entirely different. 'That is a serious charge, Master Dixon.'

'More serious than causing my boy's death?'

The scribe glanced up. 'Have you anything further to add, Master Dixon?'

Dixon hesitated, bewildered by the direction the trial was taking. 'I … that is—'

'Very well.' The scribe straightened his papers and turned to the man beside him. 'Sheriff, I believe you said we had another witness?'

The sheriff nodded. 'One Geillis Duncan.'

'A woman? Has she provided a deposition?'

'There's been no time. Ordinarily, I would be reluctant to permit a woman to testify in person. But … there are circumstances. As you are aware.'

Beside Geillis, Chirnside shifted slightly, the merest tilt of the head. Enough to let the men know he was watching – and someone else watched through his eyes.

'Call her forth,' the scribe said.

The sheriff jerked his head at Geillis. She yearned to ignore such a peremptory summons, but she obeyed. Chirnside had already stepped out of the pew, taking a position that would block her flight if she decided to bolt.

As Geillis approached the front of the kirk, Dixon glared at her with resentful blankness. He didn't recognize her. One of the women who'd tried to save him and his son, and he didn't recognize her. Of course, if he had, she might well have been denounced along with Agnes.

'Geillis Duncan,' the scribe said. 'What is your connection to this case?'

Geillis wet her lips. This was fine. They hadn't mentioned Inchkeith, or storms, only a sick man and a child who'd deserved a better father. In the law's eyes, she had nothing to feel guilty about – and neither did Agnes.

'Here!' Dixon suddenly burst out. 'She were at my cottage – she should be locked up with the other one, not allowed to defend her.'

Eyes shifted. Did the black-clad men agree? Geillis's wrists itched at the threat of irons.

But the scribe merely tutted. 'Master Dixon, hold your tongue or you'll be found in contempt of court. Mistress Duncan, did you assist Agnes Sampson on the occasion in question?'

'Yes.'

'Tell us, in your own words, what you found there.'

Her own words. As if he would record them if they didn't please him. She no more owned her words than the air required to utter them.

'We went to Master Dixon's house after kirk and found both father and son were sick.'

'So they hadn't attended a service that day?'

Neither had Agnes, for that matter. 'No – but the child was too sick to sit up unaided, let alone leave the house.'

'Very charitable of you, Mistress Duncan.'

She shifted, awkward at the suggestion of kindness. 'I helped the child eat and made poultices for his chest. Agnes – I mean, Mistress Sampson – administered to Master Dixon.'

'What did she administer?'

'Pennyroyal for his cough and mint to ease his chest. Simple, godly receipts, passed down for years.'

The scribe grunted. 'What of this other accusation, that of prophesying?'

Geillis threw Dixon a contemptuous glare. 'She did say he might die – but only because his father was too lazy to do anything but drink while his poorly thatched roof filled the cottage with smoke and corrupted that poor child's lungs. That wasn't a prophecy, sirs, that was common sense. Any man who can't see that has none himself or seeks to conceal his own guilt.'

'Thank you, Mistress Duncan,' the scribe sighed, 'but if you could confine yourself to answering the questions rather than indulging in speculation.'

'Beg pardon, sir.'

'In your opinion, was the child's sickness entirely natural?'

'He was underfed, in a badly kept home. I was sad to hear of his death, but I wasn't surprised.'

The scribe made a note. 'To the best of your knowledge, has Agnes Sampson ever dealt in witchcraft?'

Her throat tightened. She couldn't remember how to breathe normally – how deep, how fast. *Do not think of Inchkeith.*

'Well, Mistress Duncan?'

She'd hesitated. Was a pause as damning as an affirmation? Would they believe her lie now? Admit to Inchkeith and she'd have to admit her own part in it. Besides, silence was one thing, but to be the voice that condemned Agnes?

'Never,' she said. 'I've never seen Agnes do anything that could be called witchcraft.'

The scribe nodded, leaning back in his chair. Coins rattled at his hip, echoing around the nave. 'Gentlemen, we've heard enough. I suggest releasing the prisoner without charges.'

Outside the kirk, Chirnside steered Geillis towards the lych gate, his hand in the crook of her elbow; they might have been taken for a courting couple.

'You spoke well,' he told her, without warmth. 'Our mutual friend will be satisfied.'

Friendship with Bothwell. Geillis wanted, madly, to laugh. 'I was glad to be of service.'

'You aren't done yet.'

Geillis swung to face him; his hand held her manacle-tight. 'But – the trial's finished.'

'The trial, yes. You, however, must establish exactly how much Mistress Sampson said before it took place. Whether she protested. Whether those protests mentioned anyone by name.'

'She wouldn't!'

'When the gaol's bolts slam home, there's no telling what a person may say.' Chirnside's mouth was stone-firm. 'You will wait for her. Offer her a lift back on your horse.'

'My horse?' He couldn't mean the serene white mare she'd ridden here: it was worth more than she'd ever earn.

His lips moved slightly; she didn't mistake it for a smile. 'The Earl of Bothwell rewards those who serve him well.'

He left her in a quiet square emptying of the last market stalls, waiting for Agnes.

Geillis sank down, leaning back against the Mercat Cross. She had a horse. All it had taken was a lie in court. How much would she have been offered to sink even lower, to become Judas? For if Bothwell could bribe juries to set his minions free, he could just as easily bribe them to reach a different verdict. It would be his whim, or part of a scheme grander than they could imagine, and they would never know until it was too late.

'I hear you healed Seton's daughter.'

The last time she'd heard Agnes's voice, there'd been winds seething around the Law and black clouds stalking across the firth. Neck crawling with cold, Geillis almost darted away – but the thoughts of Chirnside, of Bothwell, were even more chilling and so she forced herself to face Agnes as the grey-haired woman crossed the square.

Had Dixon's accusations been believed, a pyre would have been built here, and a baying crowd gathered, wild with bloodlust and with relief it wasn't them.

If Agnes shared Geillis's imaginings, she hid it well. She walked as she always walked: straight back, straight shoulders, insisting on taking up space in the world. The only sign she'd spent the night in gaol was a smudge of dust on her shoulder. As she reached Geillis, Agnes tilted her head expectantly. 'Did you use coriander seeds for the fever?'

Geillis shifted, hating how childish she so often felt in Agnes's presence. 'I didn't have any. Angelica and camomile worked well.'

'Hmm. White horehound for the vomiting?'

'I hadn't any of that either.' Geillis suppressed a snarl. 'I used fennel and ginger, and Lucy managed to walk in the garden today, so evidently my remedies succeeded.'

'I never imagined they wouldn't. After all, I taught you.' Agnes eyed her shrewdly. 'I hardly expected to find you here. After our last meeting.'

'I was asked to speak in your defence.'

'Who asked?'

'I'd have thought you'd be grateful!' Geillis snapped.

'I would be,' Agnes said, softly, 'if I believed you'd offered freely. But something tells me you had to be dragged here.'

'Lucky the jury couldn't see through me as easily as you claim to,' Geillis retorted. 'Or they'd have seen I lied to save you.'

Agnes grew very still. 'Lied?'

'Yes, lied!' Geillis shot to her feet, hands on hips. 'They asked if I'd ever seen you dabble in witchcraft and I denied it, I denied it to save you!'

'Then where was the lie?'

Geillis stared. 'But ... on Inchkeith. On Berwick Law. You led us in raising storms.'

'You saw me dip a finger in water,' Agnes said lightly. 'Think, Geillis, of all the occasions you've put your hands in water – relief on a summer's day, washing your face, scrubbing linen. What has any of that to do with witchcraft?'

'What about the whistling?'

'Whistling!' Agnes laughed. 'Who doesn't whistle at least once a day? I never sweep my floors without a melody to speed my broom.'

Geillis glared. 'Don't treat me like a fool, Agnes. We raised storms. We sought to stop the Danish princess ever reaching Scotland, to prevent the king's marriage.'

'That cannot be true,' Agnes sighed. 'If it were, a good honest girl like yourself would surely have told the jury. She wouldn't have perjured herself in court.'

'Are you threatening me? After all I did for you?'

'No, no.' Agnes laughed again. 'I'm *teaching* you, Geillis. Just as I taught you how to turn a breeched baby.' She took Geillis's hands. 'There's skill in these hands. Some you've taught yourself, and some I've taught you. But all of it is God-given and naught to do with the devil.'

Geillis tried to yank free; Agnes's grip held her fast. 'Do you think I'm an idiot?'

'I'd hoped not,' Agnes said, brow creasing in concern. 'I'd thought you far wiser than most girls your age. You're no Bessie Thomson – or are you?' Taking Geillis's scowl as answer, Agnes continued. 'Girls like Bessie see selkies in every wave. She might see something wholly innocent and work herself into a frenzy imagining it witchery – but not you, Geillis.'

Beneath her gentleness was unfathomable strength. To listen was like swimming in calm waters until you found you were far out to sea and a black gulf lay beneath you, ready to haul you under.

'A girl like you,' Agnes said, 'would see through superstition and fear to the heart of the matter. She would see the reasons behind Inchkeith and Berwick Law, and she would understand that it was not witchcraft, but *statecraft*.'

'Statecraft!' She'd never even heard the word.

'Exactly.' Agnes smiled. 'You've met the earl. Isn't it clear now?'

A twist of shame from that part of her eager to please Agnes. Geillis muttered, 'No.'

'It isn't witchcraft that matters,' Agnes said, as if it were clear as a summer tide. 'It's fear. Bothwell wants Scotland afraid. He wants King James afraid – and nothing makes people so frightened as whispers of witchcraft. That's why he needs us.'

'To behave like witches? But what if people believe it? Dixon already denounced you!'

'Now, Geillis, don't tell me you're afraid! We must spread terror, not succumb ourselves!'

'They burn witches, Agnes!'

'They won't burn us. We have Bothwell's protection. All we have to do is what he wants.' Agnes's voice was seductively menacing. 'A wave of fear will sweep through Scotland, faster and deadlier than any plague. Others will fall victim to it, but not us. We don't need to be afraid, for once the wave has washed away, we will be left in a land where Bothwell reigns and we, his helpers, will finally gain what we deserve.'

12

The world had come to Leith to watch the royal party depart for Oslo. King James was leaving his kingdom for the first time to bring his bride home. Enterprising hawkers thrust trays of pies under noses – some of which, Geillis thought, might even contain the meat they promised. Surprisingly popular too were the girls offering posies of wildflowers 'to give to an earl' – as if grown men had any interest in wilting daisies, especially men who owned the fields they'd grown in. Geillis remembered her own hapless attempt to sell flowers the day her mother died. If only she'd been successful, she might never have taken the position with Seton, and then she might never …

Foolish. No one could sell flowers all year, let alone for a lifetime.

As they elbowed past ribbon sellers and whelk stalls, Bessie nudged Geillis. 'Look how many ships! He must be taking the whole court with him!'

The fleet looked more like a forest, the masts of a dozen vessels swaying in the harbour, their leaves of scarlet, gold, and azure rustling on a gentle breeze. Wagons packed the docks as baggage was ferried on board, while grooms persuaded horses up gangplanks.

'Not all the court,' Geillis pointed out. 'Someone must stay to govern.'

'But there are hundreds going!'

Bessie couldn't count past her fingers accurately, but her awed guess couldn't be far wrong. The courtiers were a magnificent sight as they boarded. Damask purred against taffeta; sarcenet whispered beside furs; everything was adorned with brocade trims, spills of lace, elaborate embroidery. They were like stained-glass figures come to life.

'And we're meant to frighten these people,' she muttered.

At the front of the crowd, those of higher status watched from carriages or horseback, elevated above the masses. Euphame MacCalzean and her husband, she dripping with jewels, he in a turquoise velvet hat adorned with enormous feathers. Seton, nodding obsequiously at passing earls, Mistress Katherine tensing every time her husband went unnoticed. And beside the flagship's gangplank, the black-clad figure of Bothwell, sable-edged cloak flung rakishly back from one shoulder, one hand at his hip, a position so relaxed you might have overlooked the embossed hilt a hair's breadth from his fingers. As Bothwell bowed to the man approaching, Geillis realized the king had arrived.

Sunlight splintered against metal at King James's throat: beneath frothing lace and crimson velvet he wore a steel gorget. She remembered Euphame MacCalzean deriding the king's obsession with assassins, though was it as ridiculous as Euphame thought? There were conspiracies against James. They were all part of one.

'Not exactly majestic, is he?' Bessie said, her scorn somewhat undermined by the fact that she was chewing the ends of her hair.

Geillis might never have seen a king before, but even she could tell James didn't look or behave like the ruler of Scotland. His shoulders were more padding than muscle, his slightly bulging eyes gave him a startled appearance, and his straggling beard, clearly grown to cover a weak chin, was begging for a comb. As Geillis watched, the king's hand drifted to his codpiece for an unashamed, vigorous scratch. No wonder people conspired against him. But did a man deserve to be menaced, even killed, just because he wasn't handsome?

'Look at them both,' Bessie said. 'Doesn't Bothwell look much better? No wonder Fian says he's being left in charge. Along with the Duke of Lennox that is – but Lennox is a boy of fifteen and Bothwell's a man.'

'Why would King James do that?' Geillis watched the king reach the flagship's deck, wondering how much of his bulk was ermine and how much was armour. 'He imprisoned Bothwell for treason not six months ago and he must know Bothwell's ambitions. Why give him so much power?'

Bessie shrugged. 'Does it matter?'

'It just …' Geillis couldn't explain her reservations. Leaving Bothwell in command of Scotland while James sailed for Denmark in late October – he'd be trapped there over the winter. This decision seemed so reckless, so stupid – and yet, at that dinner, hadn't Euphame MacCalzean accused James of exactly that? Perhaps he hoped to flatter Bothwell into friendship and peace. 'It doesn't seem the sensible choice.'

'Isn't that why we're supporting Bothwell? Because James can't make sensible choices?' Bessie grinned, and Geillis almost envied her: when had she last taken pleasure in mocking someone? 'Like sailing in late October – Agnes says it's a very dangerous prospect.'

Geillis's belly clenched. 'Does she indeed?'

Bessie nodded. 'She said we're to join her for a moonlight excursion to pick herbs. Or that's what we'll tell everyone. She meant—'

'I know what she meant.' Geillis shook her head in warning: Bessie was speaking foolishly loudly. 'Danish princesses are one thing. But Scotland's anointed king? We can't target him.'

Bessie elbowed her, as if they were jesting. 'We're not targeting anything. All we'll do is dip our hands in water and whistle.'

She was reciting Agnes's words, but apparently without any awareness of what lay beneath them: Bessie's smile was frighteningly broad.

'You're not serious!' Geillis hissed. 'Even you can't be so—'

Bessie cut her off before Geillis could insult her. 'She's expecting us. Tomorrow night, on the Law.'

Geillis stared at the flagship, its sails swelling proudly on the breeze. If she did as Agnes and Bothwell instructed, would those sails be torn by gales, drenched, submerged? Perhaps there would always have been a storm tomorrow night. Perhaps it would be witch-whistled – or perhaps their whistling would be no more powerful than a shepherd calling his dogs.

Or it would kill a king.

Let Agnes expect her all she liked. Geillis couldn't do it.

*   *   *

She'd burnt the bread. Geillis swiped the ruined loaves into her apron, yelping as her fingertips caught the oven edge. She tipped them onto the table for inspection. Black patches the size of her hand on all three; cutting the crusts couldn't salvage them. She suppressed a groan. She'd passed a sleepless night listening to rain spattering the glass, incessant as a baby's cry, worming its noise into Geillis's skull and racking her with guilt and fear. Who had been swept away by the storm – and who among the living would seek revenge?

Jeanie, coming in from the garden with pails of water, tutted. 'Barely fit for the pigs, they.'

Geillis shoved the loaves aside and began mixing more flour and water.

'Best get them proving before you give the pigs their treat.'

'Yes,' Geillis said tightly, pummelling her dough as if it were Jeanie's face. Jeanie, who had snored all night, her chin shiny with drool. Who'd never burned a loaf in her life, never spilt milk or dropped eggs or cast spells on an island at midnight.

She thrust her knuckles deep into the dough, spun it, slapped it down. Too sticky, too wet, it was almost as unwieldy as her thoughts. Geillis scattered more flour on the surface, coughed as a cloud caught in her mouth. She couldn't ruin two batches in one day. Bread wasn't that difficult. Knead, turn, dust, knead, turn. Enough.

Geillis tossed her burnt loaves into the slop bucket and hurried out to the garden, knowing Jeanie would mock her temper later and fighting the urge to fling the slops in her face.

In the storm's aftermath, the air was raw and refreshed. Although the sheer weight of rain had bent the herbs double in their patch, they gleamed vivid with greenness. Geillis picked her way through sodden grass, past the stables to the yard where the pigs happily rooted through mud. She tipped the bucket into the trough, the greediest sow's snout already questing past her knee.

Something was stuck at the bottom of the bucket. Groaning, Geillis banged the bucket against the trough, hoping to loosen whatever mulch it was.

A hand closed on her shoulder. She spun; the bucket lifted in feeble defence.

It was Chirnside, Bothwell's man. Dear God, what now?

'I'm busy,' she flung at him, aiming for defiance and falling into a stammer. 'Can't someone else rescue whoever it is this time?'

'Hardly,' Chirnside said, his grip boring beneath her collarbone. 'The one who needs saving is you.'

'What?' Her knees felt loose as water; her legs thudded against the sow's flanks. 'Has someone denounced me?'

'They didn't need to. You've disappointed my master.'

'But I haven't done anything!'

'That, you foolish girl, is precisely the problem.'

Geillis reached out to clutch imploringly at his sleeve, the dropped bucket clattering against her kneecap. 'I don't understand.'

'You weren't recruited to stand idly by!' Chirnside leaned close, eyes flaring.

'Is this about last night? How—' But of course Bothwell knew. Word would travel fast to the most powerful man in Scotland; he would have countless informers.

'You did nothing.'

'But—' Geillis flailed for words. How could she tell Chirnside she feared to commit treason when in the same breath she'd be accusing his master of the same crime? She was a servant. She couldn't fling accusations at Scotland's regent.

'You were supposed to observe for my master,' Chirnside continued, ignoring her feeble interruption. 'What could you observe last night? Mould on the ceiling? How many mice the cat caught?'

'Nothing,' Geillis muttered grudgingly.

'Nothing. What use is that to my master?'

'None.'

'Speak up, girl!'

'I said none!'

Satisfied at having goaded her, Chirnside released his grip; her shoulder throbbed but she didn't dare show more weakness by touching it. 'Precisely. How do you imagine my master deals with useless servants?'

Geillis stiffened. How violent could Bothwell be? How cruel could Chirnside be on his behalf? Imagining Bothwell would protect her from Seton now seemed utterly foolish: he was a far greater threat.

'I don't know.'

Chirnside's voice was cold. 'He eliminates them. Sometimes in broad daylight with a sword. Sometimes he employs a judge and jury. Or he might come to you himself, after dark, when you think it safe to sleep. Bare hands could be all it takes. Or perhaps he'll use the objects around you. That fire you left smouldering. Your own pillow. Even your father's mouth harp.'

How could he know about that harp? She'd barely played it since her father's death, only taking it out when she thought herself unobserved. When she thought herself safe.

'When next you play it, imagine the wood crammed against your teeth until your lips bleed. Imagine splinters piercing your tongue, nailing it to your gums. Imagine fragments cracking into your mouth and sinking down your throat, into your gut, stabbing all the way down, so that you die choking on your own blood and the only music you'll ever hear again is the gargling as you attempt to scream.' Chirnside gave her a falsely pitying look. 'Anger him, Geillis Duncan, and best make sure you lock the door at night. It won't save you, but it might prolong your life by a few moments. Give you time to cry mercy. Time to hope God cares enough to listen.'

'I'm sorry!' The words hurtled out, a child's frightened plea.

Chirnside laughed scornfully. 'If you believe yourself sorry now, you haven't been listening.'

'No – I swear I was!' She was gabbling, near witless with fear. 'What can I do? What does he want me to do?'

His eyes tracked her up and down – not in Seton's lecherous way, but with complete disdain for her body, for all she could ever be. 'You will do his bidding. Take part in every activity Agnes Sampson and his other associates suggest. Listen to everything discussed by David Seton and his wife and whoever visits the house. Report back to my master. Follow these commands without question.'

'Yes,' she whispered.

'Yes what?'

'I will obey. Without question.'

'Glad to hear it,' he said, with a sudden, jarring note of geniality. 'In one week's time you will meet John Fian and Agnes Sampson, among others, at Prestonpans at midnight.'

'What will I do there?'

'So eager to please! My master will be delighted. There, Geillis Duncan, you will take to the sea.'

'On All Hallows' Eve?'

'Precisely.'

They wouldn't return to shore until November. And sailing in November … The tide had spat her father's boat up on the beach the following dawn, and she'd scrambled over driftwood and jetsam with sudden hope. But then she'd seen that gaping wound in the hull, and heard her mother scream, and she'd known their world was broken.

'Is something wrong?' His false kindness was far more frightening than any blade.

Geillis ducked her head. 'No. Of course not.'

Hooves clattered. Seton and Mistress Katherine rode into the yard, finely dressed. They must have been visiting someone important – the kind of visit Geillis ought to have known about if she were to have any chance of satisfying Bothwell.

'Can we help you, sir? Or is your business here merely to distract my servant?' Mistress Katherine peered down at Chirnside as if he were a common churl seducing kitchen maids.

'If you think the Earl of Bothwell's business mere distraction, then yes.'

Mistress Katherine's fingers tightened on the reins. Beside her, Seton grunted. 'You should bring the earl's business to me, not this girl.'

'The earl didn't mention you when he gave me today's commission.'

Seton bridled. 'This is my property, sir! Address me with respect, or I'll have you thrown out!'

Chirnside glanced at the rooting pigs, and back to Seton, as if he deemed the animals more dignified than their owner. 'Then, with all due respect, the earl requires your servant's service a week hence. She'll be gone a full day. My lord trusts this will be convenient.'

Seton looked ready to explode. Mistress Katherine said, 'The earl must know we value Geillis's service. He wouldn't request her presence unless it were a pressing matter. Geillis knows her duty and doubtless will ensure her responsibilities here are fulfilled before she leaves.'

She was reminding Geillis of their exchange by Lucy's sickbed. That, if there was a means to hurt Seton through Bothwell's schemes, she would help. But Geillis could no longer see a way to use any of this for her own gain. Every path she saw was shadowed with menace, and Bothwell's towering figure loomed behind them all.

The sea gaped dark around their boat. This far out the scents of gorse and samphire were gone; even the saltpans couldn't penetrate this gulf. There would be no island at the end of this voyage, no green life, nothing to cling to except black water. Clouds had blinded the moon; the only light came from Fian's torch, its flames spilling copper snakes across the waves. The winds were quiet, as if the air hardly dared breathe. But winds could change. In a few hours the month would shift, and none knew better than Geillis that you couldn't trust a November sea.

Were any other boats out tonight? Most would be long abed or watching fires from under blankets; All Hallows' Eve was no time to tempt evil spirits.

Agnes watched the horizon as if picking their destination out of the abyss, while Grierson hauled on the oars with brutal vigour. No one spoke. While the others' silence was for secrecy, Geillis's came from griping fear and a grief she'd never voiced.

Her father shouldn't have left them. The sail had needed darning, the hull caulking. Stormy seas never yielded large catches. There were so many reasons he should have stayed. Not least of all Geillis, Bridget, and the babies growing in her belly.

But perhaps that was the reason Allan had gone. It wrenched Geillis even to suspect it, but had some part of her father not wished to return? After all, what were their lives? Back-breaking toil, and for what? The dream of enough firewood, a pig to butcher, a day when no part of the cottage needed repairing. No matter how hard he worked it would never be sufficient to feed his wife so she could suckle the babes long enough that they might live. With another child on the way, had her father understood he simply couldn't dig another grave shorter than his shinbone, couldn't take another cold, stiff bundle away from a wife whose milk and tears hadn't yet dried, so that when he had to decide whether to battle a passage between beckoning rocks or simply let go, he had chosen the peace of darkness?

As Geillis peered over the side, she thought how easy it might be to slip into the dark water and fall away from the world, down, down, until invisible sand embraced her and seaweed held her in silken arms. Below the sea were no servants, no masters. No witchery. Only salt and sand, washing your bones white.

'There,' Fian breathed.

His words snapped her out of her bleak reverie. Geillis followed his torchlight. Ahead was a different shadow: more solid. She could pick out masts, dropped sails, a bowsprit. A ship, with no lights, in the mouth of the firth at midnight: a ship that didn't want to be seen.

As they drew alongside, Fian let out a series of whistles. An answering cluster of notes came back, and Geillis jumped as a rope ladder was suddenly unrolled by someone up on deck; she'd almost believed Fian could conjure up ladders as well as storms.

As Grierson secured the boat to the ladder, Fian's eyes alighted on Geillis. 'You first.'

No chivalry, this, she thought, reluctantly setting her hands to the rungs. As she began ascending, she wondered what would happen if she slipped. Her skirts might tangle around her feet, her hands too cold to grip the ropes.

But then the ladder jerked. Agnes was following her, and up was the only way she could go. Gritting her teeth, Geillis climbed.

At the top she swung herself over the side, her feet meeting solid wood gratefully. Straightening up, Geillis turned to see what manner of ship she'd clambered aboard, her eyes aching from squinting through darkness.

No fishing vessel: there were no nets. Nor a merchant's ship: she rode too high in the water to be carrying much cargo. A passenger ship? Or one commissioned for a single purpose: the Earl of Bothwell's plans.

There was no crew in sight. But the deck wasn't empty. A woman stood outside the cabins, her pale hair sheened silver, as if she were a selkie emerged from the sea. Except there was no moon and no reason for this woman to gleam so. Nor, Geillis thought, for that smile on her face.

'Geillis Duncan,' she said in strangely inflected Scots, and although she'd never heard the accent before, Geillis thought: *Danish.* 'I've been expecting you.'

Geillis gaped. 'H-how?'

'Choose whichever explanation you prefer.' Amusement rippled through her voice.

Bothwell must have told her, Geillis thought stubbornly. Though why would he trouble himself? To frighten her? Or perhaps the woman had a list of names and this was just a lucky guess – she might just as easily have said Agnes or Bessie.

'You didn't want to come aboard first,' the woman observed, sending another shiver through Geillis. 'Perhaps I shall choose an explanation for that.'

Was she threatening Geillis? But then why the mirth in her voice?

The woman's eyes drifted past Geillis to the railings, where the others were arriving on deck. As Fian joined them, torchlight cascaded over her, revealing a homespun cloak no thicker than Geillis's own. If her confidence didn't spring from money or status, then where? And how did she know Scots when Geillis couldn't have guessed a word of Danish? Geillis shrank away from an explanation, wondering instead whether the woman would greet them all by name. But she merely nodded approvingly as Grierson's thud completed their group. 'We will go within.'

Going anywhere with this woman was at once the last thing Geillis wanted – and irresistible.

13

Inside the cabin candles flickered, casting a bronze glow across a table set with a jug and several cups resting on a spread of intricate charts etched in green, blue, and black ink. A captain's charts – used here as a tablecloth. They weren't here to discuss trade routes. At the far end of the table stood another fair-haired woman, older than the first, who without raising her head in greeting, began pouring them each some wine.

'Welcome,' the younger woman said, gesturing for them to sit. 'My name is Ilsa, and this is Erna. We bring news from across the sea.'

'You sailed here?' Geillis blurted out, almost missing her chair in shock. 'But – the storms.'

Ilsa's smile glittered. 'Ah, yes. Terrible indeed. And yet both wind and tide favoured our voyage.'

'Unfortunately,' Erna said, her Scots more halting than Ilsa's, 'they didn't show as much ill favour to the Scottish fleet as we'd hoped.'

Had they whistled up winds too? Had other Danes? The chill that had settled on Geillis weeks ago seeped deeper at the thought of yet more covens gathered on clifftops, conspiring to thwart King James and Princess Anna's voyages from both sides of the North Sea. Did the royal couple know how many people despised the thought of their union?

Agnes said, 'Then they've reached land?'

Ilsa nodded. 'Your king's ships were blown off course, but not enough to prevent their landing on the Norwegian coast two days ago.'

'Enough to send him three weeks north of Anna.' Erna spoke contemptuously. 'Unless the snows strike hard, he'll reach her in Oslo before November's out.'

'Then we've failed,' Grierson said, disgusted.

'Not at all,' Ilsa countered. 'This was but one stage in our lord's plan.'

She said *our lord* as if she were in church; the near-blasphemy made Geillis shudder. If they were worshipping Bothwell, what did that make them?

'Now,' Ilsa said, 'we simply move on to the next stage.'

'Enlighten us, do,' Fian pressed, sounding disgruntled by his ignorance, especially compared to such a slight young woman.

Ilsa rested her forearms on the table as if delivering a sermon. 'It may be too late to prevent James meeting his wife. But not to convince him this marriage is cursed. Already rumours chase through Denmark, suggesting God doesn't wish Anna to be queen of Scotland.'

'Helped along, I daresay,' Agnes remarked caustically.

'Perhaps a little,' Erna said with relish.

'We can assist them further,' Ilsa said. 'While both are in Denmark, we can contrive all manner of ill omens.'

Erna said, 'If enough black cats are bundled into Akershus Fortress, at least one must cross James's path. Perhaps even as he walks alongside his bride.'

'Cockerels can be made to crow in the afternoon,' Ilsa added. 'Any gown Anna wishes to wear might be unaccountably soiled; the fish they dine on could be black and putrid when they slice into it.'

'Tricks,' Fian pronounced. 'Mischievous tricks.'

Ilsa smiled. 'Isn't everything we've done a trick of sorts? It's what others believe that matters. Even the most rational folk will waver when faced with so many ill omens.'

'What of us?' Agnes asked. 'Short of rounding up cats, what would Bothwell have us do?'

Anything he wanted, thought Geillis. *Only my protection can save you from the flames.* He'd already commanded them to sink ships; Geillis knew they'd be doing something far more sinister than aggravating a cockerel.

'For now, you are limited.' Ilsa's condescension would have earned Geillis a slap – yet Agnes merely arched an eyebrow. 'Without James here, it will be harder for you to frighten him, and few messages will reach him over winter. But just because it isn't the season to pick roses doesn't mean we shouldn't sow their seeds. You will prepare the land for the arrival of a queen no one wants and the return of a king God's turned his back on.'

Geillis had never heard anyone describe the princess so contemptuously. Bothwell had saved such a tone for the king, dismissing Anna as if kicking a stray cat out of his path. Where did Ilsa's venom come from?

'You wish us to prattle gossip?' Fian queried.

'To cultivate rumours,' Ilsa said dryly. 'Your object is to make Scotland afraid. Make people fear the king's return and the princess's arrival – make them see it as barely a breath away from the end of days.'

Geillis imagined the rumours growing, tangling. Nothing could spread faster than fear.

Agnes shook her head. 'It won't last. However many tales we tell of ravens dropping bones at the hooves of James's horse, it will all come to nothing once Anna's belly swells.'

'That's where you come in.'

But the Danish woman wasn't talking to Agnes. Her eyes bored into Geillis's.

'Me?'

'You,' Ilsa said calmly. 'You must ensure Anna doesn't conceive – and if she does, you will make sure the child dies before it can be born.'

Geillis choked on her wine. Before she could splutter out any words, Agnes broke in.

'Why Geillis? I've more experience of midwifery than anyone in East Lothian – I've served the rich ladies of Edinburgh for years.'

'Rich ladies and royalty are far more different than the former like to think,' Ilsa said, with startling spite.

'All the more reason to choose me!' Agnes snapped. 'Why on earth is this task being trusted to my apprentice?'

Geillis would have bridled at the insult – but not only did she agree with Agnes, she didn't want this task. She didn't even want to name it.

'Are you questioning our lord's decisions?' Ilsa purred.

Bothwell had chosen her himself? Geillis stared, horrified at the thought of Bothwell discussing her at all, let alone with this woman. Let alone as a potential murderer.

'Don't question my loyalty, child!' Agnes hissed. 'I knew the earl when you still had milk teeth!'

'Then you'll help him,' Ilsa said matter-of-factly. 'No need for us to quarrel. He wishes you to do as I've said.'

'And he's conveying his wishes through you now?' Agnes shook her head in furious affront. 'Forgive my scepticism.'

'You are forgiven,' Ilsa said lightly, ignoring Agnes's sarcasm – and the deliberate insult angered, or stunned, Agnes into silence.

Before Agnes could compose herself, Geillis found her voice. 'The queen will have royal physicians at her beck and call – why would she seek my services? Or even know my name?'

'She'll be told it,' Ilsa said. 'One of Anna's closest confidantes is my sister.'

'Your sister?' Fian looked askance at Ilsa's homespun gown. 'Forgive me, madam. I hadn't perceived we were in the presence of a member of the Danish court.'

Ilsa threw back her head and crowed. Then, glee vanishing like a smothered flame, she replied, 'Fear not. You haven't been impudent – at least not in that regard. She's my milk-sister. Margareta Vinstar. My mother nursed her when her own died, and now she waits on the princess.'

While you … Geillis wanted to hear more but Ilsa continued, explaining future plans, so composed she might have been giving directions to market.

'When the Danes eventually land in Scotland, my sister will seek you out, Geillis. You'll advise her, and she'll advise Anna.'

Geillis fiddled with her cup, unconvinced. 'Won't they realize I'm giving false advice?'

Ilsa curled her lip. 'Girls of the Danish court know nothing of the world, still less of womanly matters like conceiving and carrying children. You could tell my sister and her friends to wear cobwebs beneath their clothes and eat only apples for a week and they'd know no better.'

Agnes spoke again, rage honed into coldness. 'You appear to be confusing innocence with stupidity. That would be a grave mistake.'

'Then make your lies as clever as possible,' Ilsa retorted. 'We both know of herbs that in one measure can aid conception and in another make any hope of a child bleed away. Believe what you wish about Anna and my sister's understanding – but trust me: we're far wiser.'

Did Ilsa hate her sister or love her? Geillis couldn't tell.

'Are we agreed?' Ilsa asked, and it was no question.

Agnes held Ilsa's gaze. At last, she said, 'We are agreed.'

Neither of them waited for Geillis's agreement. As if they were the chess players and she a piece of wood flicked from white to black.

'Excellent,' Ilsa said, pouring more wine. 'Then let us toast. To our lord's schemes – and our own advancement.'

Geillis awoke to stabbing pains in her shoulders and a certainty that she'd only just dozed off. The cabin had three bunks, one each for Ilsa, Erna, and Agnes, relegating Bessie and Geillis to the floor.

The others were still asleep, and small wonder: the drinking had continued well past midnight. Geillis had hunched in a corner, desperate to be alone but not daring to ask about beds, knowing she'd sound like a child. Only when Bessie fell asleep, knocking over the jug, had Agnes declared enough was enough. But even if she'd had a feather mattress and furs, Geillis doubted she'd have had much rest. Not after Ilsa had revealed Bothwell's command.

Was Bothwell testing her loyalty? Or was this a punishment for her failure to go to the Law? Agnes was right – there was no sense to choosing Geillis for this task, because no mother would choose the apprentice over the midwife who'd delivered hundreds of babies safely. So why was Bothwell sending Geillis to kill the queen's unborn baby? Unless it was Agnes's loyalty, Agnes's obedience he was testing – but why?

Above all, whatever Bothwell's reasons, how could Geillis bring herself to do something so vile?

Geillis pushed herself up, massaging her neck. Her mouth was fuzzy with sleep and the aftertaste of dread. She needed water.

Stifling a groan, she rose and stretched, scraping her knuckles on a bunk as she pushed the cabin door open.

A mist had come up overnight, holding onto the ship like a smothering hand. She could barely make out the railings, let alone the other end of the ship.

And there was something else she couldn't see.

Where was the crew? Even with the ship at anchor, shouldn't someone be on watch, keeping the lanterns lit so no other vessels ran into them in the fog?

Quiet closed in on her. No thump of bare feet on wood, no calls from the rigging. Only the slap of unseen waves against the hull, only the slowly creaking masts.

Something was wrong.

Her footsteps cracked like gunshots. She fought the urge to tiptoe as she made her way to the hatch leading below decks. As she heaved it open, the hinges yawned, needing oil. It was dark: no lanterns below either. Perhaps that was a normal precaution, Geillis told herself, stepping into the darkness – a fire in such cramped quarters would be disastrous.

She could see the first few stairs, but only shadows beyond. Geillis descended, feet fumbling for the next step. At the bottom, waiting for her eyes to adjust, a familiar smell reached her nose. Stale, acrid: the sweat of sick men.

She had to help them, no matter what Agnes thought. There must be a medicine chest somewhere – perhaps in the captain's cabin? Best to find her patients before she sought any cures. Less fearful now, Geillis moved forward, imbued with the confidence of duty.

Her foot hit something soft, yielding. And because the smell was worse, because she heard no noise, Geillis knew what she would find before she knelt down.

He was dead. She couldn't see his face, but he was beardless and skinny – no more than a boy. From the stench, he'd either vomited or excreted himself to death. Gagging, she pressed a hand to her mouth, forcing herself to think.

There was still a crew to be found and helped; this wasn't a ghost ship from her father's fireside stories. There was nothing to fear from sickness, only remedies to be found and administered.

Moving further into the ship's belly, her questing fingers met a door handle, and Geillis pushed it open.

The smell crashed over her like a breaking wave. *Breathe through your mouth. Don't show your patients your distaste – if they think you find them disgusting, how will they ever trust you to heal them?* It chafed Geillis to admit it, but Agnes's lessons straightened her spine.

Her adjusting eyes made out dozens of hanging white shapes. She almost screamed – but they were only hammocks, lumpen and pale as larvae.

The first sailor she reached was dead too, his mouth crusted with the vomit he'd choked on. So was the second, his hammock damp and stiffening with everything he'd voided. Geillis was on the verge of despair when she heard a groan. Immediately, she rushed towards the sound. The man making it reached out a sweaty, trembling hand.

'I'm here now,' Geillis said gently, sponging vomit away from his mouth with his thin blanket and touching his forehead. Burning up. If only she could see whether his eyes were discoloured. Or the colour of his vomit – that might help deduce what had struck them all down. Rotten meat, perhaps. Or something in their water supply – maybe a dead gull?

'Don't help them.' It was a command.

Geillis turned. If the Danish accent hadn't given Ilsa away, that silvery hair shimmered even in the gloom.

Geillis squared her shoulders. 'They're sick. They need help.'

'You won't help them,' Ilsa said calmly.

'Why not?' She couldn't keep the fury from her voice.

'Because it's too late,' Ilsa told her. 'They all sealed their fates when they chose to sail on this ship.'

'What do you mean?'

'None of them will leave this ship alive.'

There was something odd in her voice – something almost satisfied.

Geillis hesitated. 'How did they get so sick?'

Ilsa smiled. 'I think you know.'

Horror crawled over Geillis's skin like maggots. 'You did this to them?'

'Well … Erna administered the poison.'

'How convenient for you,' Geillis spat, now hiding her fear behind anger.

'For *us*,' Ilsa corrected her. 'It would have been disastrous if these men had lived to speak of what – who – they'd seen here. I considered cutting their tongues out, but Erna and I could hardly manage so many. Besides, some may even have their letters, so it wouldn't have guaranteed our safety.'

'You could have paid them,' Geillis hissed. 'Bothwell has coin enough!'

'Dead men need no wages – and this way Bothwell will keep his coins to reward us better when the time comes.'

Geillis shook her head in disbelief. 'So you killed these men hoping for *money*?'

'I did it for our security,' Ilsa said coldly. 'This was the only way to ensure silence. We shall take axes to the hull before we leave this vessel. After all, a ship's name and charts reveal where they sailed from, and where to. Then questions will be asked.'

'But you can't just make a ship vanish and hope no one questions it! Someone will be waiting for this ship – dozens will be waiting for the crew to come home!'

'This is common sense,' Ilsa chided. 'We wish fear to spread – what could be more frightening than a ghost ship? A vessel glimpsed through mists, its lanterns luring men onto hidden reefs. Should any jetsam wash up on Scottish shores, that will prove an excellent opportunity to spread such tales. Should one of the bodies wash up, even better.'

'But some are no more than boys!'

'And you and I aren't much more than girls.'

Was that a threat? Geillis wasn't sure she wanted to know.

'Don't we deserve protection?' Ilsa pressed. 'Boys' voices are louder than girls'. Men's voices louder than women's. Better if there are fewer voices to be weighed against ours.' Ilsa was close now, her skin pearly against the darkness. 'I've done this to help us all, Geillis. Aren't you grateful?'

'I never asked for this,' Geillis whispered. 'I never wanted anyone to die for me.'

Ilsa's smile was wistful. 'So often the only choice is whether someone else dies – or you.'

'That's not a choice.'

'Perhaps you'd prefer death?'

'I didn't mean—'

'See?' Ilsa touched her cheek. 'You've made your choice. Too late to turn back now.' Her cold fingers stroked Geillis's jawline; there was nothing tender in the gesture. 'Bothwell was right about you.'

Was she referring to Bothwell's reasons for choosing Geillis as a weapon? 'What do you mean?'

Ilsa's thumbnail caught her chin, gentle but unforgettably sharp. 'You remind me of my sister. Both of you imagine your fears and scruples make you kind. But in truth it is helping me – and your friends – that will redeem you, not this irksome dithering.'

Geillis swallowed. 'There's nothing wrong with caution.'

Ilsa laughed. 'It's boldness we need. Not cowardice. Can you be bold, Geillis Duncan?'

Geillis lifted her jaw defiantly. 'Why did your sister have scruples? If she doubted you, why should I trust you?'

'Margareta believes safety lies in silence,' Ilsa said coolly. 'She was wrong before, and she's wrong now. Perhaps you can persuade her into courage.' She chucked Geillis under the chin. 'Remember, a silent enemy is a victory won. But your own silence? Never be the one to strangle your own voice, Geillis Duncan.'

From anyone else the words might have been encouraging. But all Geillis could think about was how moments ago Ilsa's fingers had been creeping closer to her throat.

14

Far better, Margareta thought, to be journeying to meet another, than waiting for the travellers' arrival. A few weeks ago, she would never have imagined entertaining such thoughts.

They'd tried to sail for Scotland again in October, after a month lingering in Akershus while the fleet was repaired. Fair winds would have seen them land after three, perhaps even two days. Instead, they'd spent four tossed about on furious seas, battered by roaring gales, and Margareta, peering out of the porthole, had been certain she could still see Oslo's lanterns flickering behind them. Once again they'd been forced back to shore, and ever since they had been dreading the inevitable third attempt to cross the North Sea.

But that was before they began waiting.

When they'd received news of James's arrival in Norway nearly three weeks ago Anna had read the letter and declared, 'Excellent tidings. King James writes that since we could not find a way to cross the North Sea, he will come to us.'

As cheering courtiers had raised toasts, Margareta hoped no one else had noticed Anna's voice waver on *we could not*. Had James simply written a fact – or made an accusation?

'How romantic!' Elline had said. 'Crossing stormy seas to bring his bride home!'

Even Vibeke had looked impressed. 'It's very touching.'

But Wemyss's face had hardened. 'This is most out of character for James.'

'What – romance? Perhaps any new bridegroom—'

'No. Sentiment, melodrama – James is no stranger to those.'

'Then what's so unusual?'

He'd met her eyes, his jaw set. 'His bravery.'

Since then, Anna had barely sat still. Every time a page knocked at her chambers, she shot out of her seat like a falcon loosed from her jesses, hurriedly smoothing hair, skirts, face. As the page revealed his errand – a dropped glove, a tray of lemon possets, local minstrels hoping for royal favour – Margareta saw Anna sigh as she remembered to breathe again. But how much of that sigh was secret relief?

She hadn't shared Wemyss's disclosure with Anna. How would it help to tell her James wasn't renowned for bravery when here he was, having crossed the North Sea, battling through snow-smothered forests and half-frozen fjords and jagged mountain ranges – whereas Anna had twice failed to sail to Scotland?

Other things troubled Margareta. Wemyss had told her of James's reign, how the regents who'd vied for supremacy in his infancy had all been assassinated or executed – and of his mother's legacy. 'All his life,' Wemyss had said, 'James has been told his mother was a whore, a French traitor, a witch who murdered his father and connived to steal James's crown.'

'Her own crown?'

'Not in James's eyes. He doesn't think women should rule anything, least of all a country. "It's called a kingdom for a reason," he'll say, and insist his mother was only ever holding the throne until he, its rightful occupant, was born. Of course, he'd never say this to the English queen, for he hopes to inherit Elizabeth's kingdom before long.'

Just as unsettling were the favourites. Wemyss had shaken his head when Margareta asked who these men were. 'Since I left Scotland, James's fancy may well have moved on to another. But you can guarantee they'll have handsome faces, be granted more power than their lineage warrants, and either have worryingly astute minds behind their long lashes or be entirely swayed by relatives wiser than themselves.'

'But if they change so often, what do they matter?' Margareta had pointed out. 'All kings have favourites – even young Christian gets infatuated with heroes who ride faster than him.'

'They wouldn't matter,' Wemyss said darkly, 'if James weren't so susceptible to gossip. But he believes the worst of everyone – except these favourites.'

Margareta had conveyed this to Sophia, wondering how much the queen already suspected. But to tell Anna that Scotland hated women who sought power, or that James distrusted everyone … to say such things while looking into Anna's summer-blue eyes would have been like drowning kittens before a child. So Margareta kept her worries to herself. Better that she struggled to sleep, better that purple shadows lurked beneath her eyes than Anna's. It wasn't Margareta who had to win the approval of a king.

There was so little to distract them. At least travellers beheld new sights – mountains rearing skywards, ice creeping over fjords like giants' breath. All they had in Akershus were the same walls, the same gardens. However beautiful frost and snowfall made those gardens, they could only stay outside until their toes went numb and their cheeks red in the stinging winds. Even Anna's imagination was running dry when it came to evening entertainments. She'd summoned troupes of acrobats, fire-eaters, sword-jugglers; they'd learned every Scottish dance the men could remember and taught the men all the Danish ones they knew. Despite the ladies' increased fluency in Scots and English, they'd found few books written in either that the Earl Marischal deemed suitable for Scotland's future queen.

Another girl, trapped in a castle with her handsome betrothed, might have relished the opportunity for clandestine trysts, for kisses beside frozen fountains – but not Margareta. Being so close to Wemyss reminded her how enforced their closeness was: by winter and by Queen Sophia. Even if something surged in her belly when their eyes met, even if she relived that kiss in the storm every night, even if he sometimes spoke as if she meant more to him than a useful accomplice, she couldn't forget he hadn't chosen her for herself, and she'd been given no choice at all. Would she ever be able to love this man honestly – and would he ever truly love her?

They were sewing when the knock came, embellishing clothes with decorations that boredom rather than fashion dictated. Anna jolted upright, dropping the gloves she'd been working on; instinctively, Margareta knelt to tidy up after Anna. Glancing up, she saw Anna's jawline, rigid as midwinter ice, barely moving as she commanded, 'Enter.'

The Earl Marischal always bowed deeply, but this bow was reverent even by his standards. 'I bring urgent tidings, Your Highness.'

Anna's imperious demeanour was all Sophia; the fast pulse in her throat was all Anna. 'Please deliver them.'

'It gives me great joy to tell you that King James is but half a day's ride from Akershus.'

'Half a day?' Anna echoed, dazed. 'Why …' Her eyes dropped, searching the dove-embroidered silk of her gown, the silver satin of her slippers, as if they might offer advice. Lifting her head, she said, 'Why then, a great feast must be prepared. How many in his party?'

'Three hundred courtiers, Your Highness.'

'Three hundred!' Anna blanched. Margareta wondered if her own party's paltry five dozen would now appear insulting. 'But where are they all to sleep? What will we feed them?'

'If I might be so bold,' Keith said carefully, 'perhaps a more intimate supper would be better tonight. His Grace will be weary after his journey. And you might both prefer to meet for the first time in a less … crowded situation.'

Anna blinked rapidly, thinking. Great celebrations were what Anna knew. How else to impress anyone, let alone a king, without offering up your finest garb, twenty courses, fireworks, and dancing until dawn? 'An intimate supper? That sounds …'

'Romantic,' Margareta breathed up at her. 'Thus eminently suitable.'

'Eminently suitable,' Anna said, her voice now smooth as satin. 'Lady Margareta, inform my steward. I trust you to ensure our guests are welcomed in the comfort and splendour they deserve.'

Margareta rose. 'Of course, Your Highness.'

Where would Anna's steward be? Totting up accounts, terrorizing cooks or interrogating seamstresses? Margareta aimed for the chamber the steward had appropriated for a study, hoping for a swift errand.

'Margareta!'

Only one man could address her thus. He'd emerged from a side corridor, his cloak speckled with sleet.

'Wemyss,' she said, not sure whether she was pleased to see him. 'I'm looking for Anna's steward.'

'He went to the kitchens. Why?'

'Because King James will arrive within the day!' Margareta let her words out in a brittle sigh. 'Anna wants me to make arrangements for three hundred courtiers! There aren't enough beds for them, let alone any servants they might bring, and we'll all starve before the month's out because it will take weeks to round up supplies to feed a king's court and—'

'Calm down,' Wemyss said, extending his hands as if approaching a rearing horse. She wanted to hit him.

'Didn't you listen to a word I said?'

'To each one,' he assured her. 'I've been listening for weeks.'

'To me?'

'Naturally – but also to the chatter in Oslo.'

His tone made her pause. 'Is that where you've been?'

He nodded. 'No royal party could stir a step through Danish territory without every witness chattering about it. We've known they'd arrive around now since they landed. There's nothing to worry about. The highest nobles will stay here, while Oslo's aldermen are delighted to welcome such elevated guests. Merchants have been bringing in food and wine for weeks. All's in hand.'

'You knew?' Margareta stared. 'You've known – you and however many other Scots – for weeks, and you never thought to tell me? To tell *Anna*?'

'We thought it best.'

'*We?*'

'The Earl Marischal, for one—'

'Who are you to decide? Anna will be your queen! She should be the first to receive news, not the last!'

'Would it have helped?' Wemyss folded his arms. 'Tell me honestly, if Anna had known the hour of James's arrival, how would she have behaved?'

Margareta tightened her jaw defensively. 'That's not the point.'

'Would you rather she'd been apprised of every hindrance James encountered, every snowfall driving them indoors, every thrown shoe and buckled wheel? Or would Anna have misinterpreted such events as omens?'

Margareta scowled, unwilling to concede aloud that he was right. Anna was already frayed with anxiety, twitching at the sight of magpies, recoiling at mentions of ships and storms. If she'd learned of anything obstructing James's passage, her mind would instantly have leapt to the rumours of witchcraft that had dogged them since September. Her panic would only have worsened over time.

'My task,' Wemyss said patiently, 'is to protect Anna. Sometimes that means keeping things from her.'

'What about my task?' Margareta retorted, infuriated by his genial tone. 'How can I protect Anna if I don't know what I'm protecting her from?'

'Am I supposed to know everything you're not aware of?' Wemyss shot back. 'If I told you every detail of my knowledge, you'd accuse me of condescension!'

'So I should be flattered that you're hiding the truth? Why thank you, kind sir!'

'Flattered that I assumed you might be capable of finding things out for yourself? That you were suited to the task Sophia gave you? Given the alternatives, Margareta, I think you might prefer the way I chose!'

'You arrogant, patronizing *idiot*!' Margareta hissed. 'Do you think any woman would be pleased to discover her future husband's been lying to her?'

'I didn't *lie*—'

'Hiding information amounts to the same thing! For the love of God, Wemyss!' Margareta flung up her hands in exasperation. 'What sort of a marriage will this be if we cannot trust one another?'

His smile was bitter. 'Very like James and Anna's, I imagine.'

'Is that what you want?'

'What I want – or what you want – has never mattered.'

'But ...' Had he not hoped? That they might value their marriage for what it meant to them, not merely how it served royalty? That they might even, one day ...

The words died on her lips and silence stretched between them.

'I must go. Anna will want to know what her steward said.'

He nodded curtly. 'Perhaps I'll see you at dinner.'

'Perhaps.'

Where did they go, all the unsaid words? Hurrying away, Margareta imagined a vast graveyard, its stones carved with unsent letters, feelings bitten back, promises never made, all beaten into fragments by the wind and vanishing along with the years.

Anna dressed for meeting her husband as if her ivory silk and warmed pearls were battle armour. Margareta wondered if James would be more impressed if Anna actually wore armour, see her as a kindred spirit, given his own habits. Or would he view Anna as an opponent? Wemyss said James disliked the notion of a woman seeking power; did that include the power to save her own life?

Margareta pushed irritably at a stray lock of hair. The more she thought of Wemyss, the more she thought of all the things they'd said and all they ought to have said.

The chamber hummed with suppressed nerves. Elline fretted at a loose thread on her bodice, for once unable to chatter away. Anna scratched a nail against her ornate chair's armrests.

'Should I be seated?' she whispered to Margareta. 'Won't it seem rude, my greeting him like a supplicant?'

'He can't expect you to stand all evening,' Margareta said reasonably. 'As long as you rise to greet him, he'll find nothing to criticize tonight.'

'Tonight,' Anna repeated, and Margareta instantly regretted the word. 'But what of all the nights to come for the rest of our lives? I don't know how to be ...'

A wife? Neither did Margareta.

Footsteps approached. Too many to count – though surely fewer than three hundred. Keith had said James wouldn't wish for more than a dozen. Anna's panic seeped into Margareta like smoke from a burning, all choking and wrong.

The doors opened. Should they have arranged a herald? Keith had implied the less pomp the better – but would it appear insulting?

Keith bowed. 'Your Highness, allow me to present His Grace King James the Sixth of Scotland.'

Anna rose and said in Scots, 'Welcome to Akershus, Your Grace.'

The man beside Keith stepped forward, and Margareta had to suppress the thought that he couldn't be the king. He appeared broad at first, but then she noticed his arms hung closer to his body than the shoulders. He was richly, albeit soberly dressed, but even the most skilled tailor in Christendom couldn't have made those legs look anything other than bowed. The calves of his stockings were so padded his knees seemed oddly shrunken. All this Margareta might have overlooked, were it not for his face.

An unoiled beard straggled over a weak chin, drawing attention to moist, pink lips, licked too often: out of nerves or lasciviousness? These too she could have ignored, for kings only had to be handsome in stories, although queens always had to be beautiful. It was James's eyes that were most disappointing. They were dark, like the water of a seldom-used well, but far from steady. She'd seen flies remain stiller above rotten meat. When Vibeke coughed, he started as if a gunshot had gone off.

At last he spoke. 'We are pleased our journey is ended. We hope its arduousness will prove worthwhile.'

On another man's tongue, those words might have been a flirtatious jest, even romantic. Margareta couldn't pinpoint the precise moment where James's tone slipped. But it fell as a thinly veiled accusation.

Anna winced. 'That is also our dearest hope.'

'Well then,' James said. 'May we expect some of your Danish hospitality this evening?' He licked his lips, and the query suddenly seemed lecherous.

A blush began to stain Anna's chest. 'If it please you, we shall dine here in my chamber. Your Earl Marischal told me you would enjoy that.'

James snorted. 'Keith doesn't decree what I do or don't enjoy. That is my prerogative.'

He was trying to be witty, teasing, independent – and missing the mark. If it hadn't so clearly distressed Anna, Margareta would almost have pitied the Scottish king.

Anna straightened her spine. 'Of course. But as your wife, I hope I may increase your enjoyment of Danish food and music tonight.'

James glanced around his courtiers, catching the eyes most likely to wink. 'As my wife, I hope you'll increase my enjoyment of many things.'

And because he was king, they smirked obligingly – and because Anna was their future queen, they refrained from laughing aloud. But it was enough to stain Anna's cheeks crimson as she held out a hand to James, indicating the seat beside hers. Before joining her, James gestured to the Scots, who moved to the seats nearest the royal pair, leaving the Danes to sit furthest away.

Was this how things were done in Scotland? It was as though they'd decided any Danish ranks must give way to Scottish ones. Moreover, they showed no interest in mingling with the Danes, but had merely transplanted their cliques and cabals from Edinburgh to Oslo, without the slightest intention of accommodating Anna's companions in their court.

'A toast,' James said, 'to our arrival in Oslo. Since my bride was unable to come to me, I have come to her. Let us drink to intrepid voyages and dauntless men.'

Margareta watched Anna's face as they all drank. The blushes had gone. Next to the ruby darkness of the wine, her skin had a shroud's pallor.

* * *

She remembered thinking the proxy marriage strange – the clumsy symbolism of crossed ankles, vows spoken to the wrong person. But was there anything less strange about James and Anna's actual marriage?

Most of the Danish nobility barely knew their spouses before their wedding day. Some might have been childhood playfellows whose parents envisaged uniting their lands through matrimony; the majority would have seen their partner at court, if not actually exchanged words, while a lucky few might even have been attracted to each other. Love matches were for folk tales – and most of those ended tragically. Still, for a couple to know one another as little as Anna and James was rare indeed.

'Four days,' Wemyss said the evening before the royal wedding. 'You and I have had months – how privileged I am, to know you so intimately.'

Bitterness cut through his wry tone: clearly he hadn't forgotten their last quarrel either. Yet, for appearances, for convenience, for the knowledge that they must do Sophia's will, they were playing cards together. Around them, tables rattled with dice and coins, while the minstrels strummed alternately Danish and Scottish tunes, a well-meant but jarring medley. Margareta eyed her cards sourly: not a single pair or sequence.

'If you know me so well, what's my favourite colour?'

'Why?' He picked up a card and discarded the four of clubs. 'Will guessing correctly determine whether you'll smile on our wedding day?'

She mimicked his taut lightness. 'So you admit it would be a guess?'

'A deduction based on observation. For instance, I deduce that the card you've just selected is of little value to you.'

It was: the five of spades, and her only other spade was a ten, rendering a sequence impossible. Even so, Margareta tucked the five into her fanned cards, and discarded the four of diamonds, arching an eyebrow at Wemyss. 'Tell me then. What deductions would you make about my favourite colour?'

Wemyss eyed her thoughtfully. 'You often wear black and dark blue. A less astute man might select one of those – but I doubt you ever have much choice in the colour of your gowns, and I imagine Anna prefers her ladies to contrast with her silvers and whites. Do you envy the delicate hues of her skirts? No – I think something bolder.'

'To match your presumptuousness.'

'If anything matches between us, we're lucky – many couples aren't so fortunate.'

'I'll count my blessings then.'

Why couldn't it always be like this? The easy pleasure of batting words back and forth – and yet they were only easy because they meant so little.

'Let me see,' Wemyss mused, setting his cards face down and tapping his fingers together. 'You've always lived by the sea – yet you don't love it, for you know how dangerous it can be. So not blue or green. I've never seen you admire gold and silver ornaments. Surely not purple, in a kingdom turned away from Rome. Am I correct thus far?'

'You haven't dismissed my favourite yet.'

'Of course, this presupposes that your favourite is a constant.' He tilted his head. 'Are you loyal, Margareta?'

'Always,' she said quietly. 'Even if my loyalty feels like a betrayal.'

'So you're drawn to a certain hue, but you think you shouldn't be. Fascinating.'

'You're mocking me.'

'Always,' he told her. 'And yet never. I laugh that you might join in, not to make you feel small.'

'Perhaps you ought to be wittier then.'

He winced. 'Clearly you don't take my approach.'

'If the approach takes hours, why would I wish to? Have you an answer yet?'

'Sometimes, Margareta, the journey can be as pleasurable as reaching your destination.' He met her eyes and she blushed. Was this gentle hint at their future what James had hoped to deliver? But there was none of James's leering in Wemyss, no seeking of other men's approval. His words were for her alone.

'And yet we must reach it eventually.'

'True.' A softness in his eyes – was he thinking of their wedding night too? But then his eyes narrowed, relishing the puzzle. 'So, a colour you think you shouldn't love – and knowing you, your reasons aren't like anyone else's. Not red then – that's too obvious: reminders of blood and so forth. Brown's similarly too easy to dismiss as the colour of mud, even if it's also spaniels' ears, mountain slopes, and hawk feathers.'

'Is that your favourite?'

He laughed. 'You've beaten me to the guess.'

'Not so much a guess as eliminating everything it isn't.'

'The logical approach. Or just long-winded. But I think I've guessed.'

'Do you indeed?'

He leaned closer. 'The colour of the sun – of spring after a long winter. Warmth and hope, primroses and daffodils, a hearth to come home to. Your favourite colour, Margareta Vinstar, is yellow. Am I correct?'

'Yes.'

'But why do you also dislike it? Could it be because yellow is often the colour of cowardice?'

Margareta held his gaze. 'It could.'

'But it isn't.'

'No.'

'And you aren't ready to tell me why?'

He knew Ilsa was a conspirator. But he didn't know that Margareta's family hid an even darker secret. Or at least she prayed he didn't. Only Sophia knew the truth, and she couldn't tell him. 'I might never be.'

'Then you don't have to.' He brushed his knuckles against hers. 'Shall we play on?'

Margareta managed a smile. 'Let's.'

As he picked up a card, she wondered if James would let Anna keep secrets with so little resistance. Somehow, she doubted it.

Even in Helsingør, the wedding celebrations couldn't have been more splendid. A full month of festivities was planned: wolf hunts, skating on frozen lakes, masques, fireworks, dances, jousts, and a banquet every night.

'If we eat like this for a month, Anna will look pregnant even if she's not,' Elline muttered as they watched roast swan follow roast boar follow roast venison into the great hall.

'We all will,' Margareta pointed out. 'Far worse for us unmarried ladies.'

'All the better that gossip concentrates on Anna then.' Elline eyed a marchpane palace as if planning to devour the four-foot-high sculpture singlehandedly.

Margareta knew Elline didn't speak out of cruelty, only the pleasure-loving carelessness most girls spent their days in – and which Margareta had never known.

But even Margareta, who could worry about snow on a summer's day, had to admit everything had gone far better than expected. The vows had been declared without so much as a cleared throat. Someone had trimmed James's beard and matched his doublet to the wine, so his habit of waving his goblet while speaking wouldn't spoil his clothes – at least, not from a distance. Anna looked as beautiful as ever. Not a radiant bride, perhaps, but a gleaming one, the pearls at her throat and the gemstones in her bodice twinkling as if she were a constellation of stars deigning to walk among mere mortals. Yes, she thought, sipping her wine, despite everything it had all gone rather well.

Elline and Vibeke giggled as they scampered along the corridor to Anna's bedchamber, even the normally staid Vibeke overwhelmed by the situation. Their mistress was married. They'd known each other as virgin girls; now one of their number was a woman. How else to cope with this change than to laugh and elbow each other's ribs?

'She might be with child already!' Elline whispered as they reached the door. 'Just think!'

'It's not that fast,' Vibeke objected.

Elline sniffed. 'Only takes once.'

'Hush,' Margareta hissed. 'They'll hear you.'

'Only what everyone else will be saying,' Elline mumbled – but she subsided as Margareta knocked.

The door was opened – and not by a guard. Ermine robes over his nightshirt, his bare legs pale as clams, his beard straggly again, as if it had grown overnight, James himself met Margareta's stare.

'Have you brought breakfast?'

'Ah – no, Your Grace.' Margareta dropped into a belated courtesy. 'Sorry.'

James snorted. 'Suppose I'll have to find some myself. Out of the way, girl.'

She hadn't risen from her curtsey and had to scuttle crabwise to avoid his bulky furs as he strode past. Elline slid to the floor, helpless with laughter. While Vibeke tried to drag her upright, Margareta slipped inside.

Anna was sitting up in bed, her hair satin-smooth. Surely James hadn't brushed it for her? No – Anna was holding the comb herself, pressing its teeth against her wrist, so hard the flesh was turning white.

'Anna, what—' Margareta stopped. 'Vibeke, order some food.' She bumped the door shut with her hip as if by accident and hurried over to the bed. 'What are you doing?'

'Have you got a knife?'

Horror-struck, Margareta stared. 'Why?'

'There must be blood on the sheets.'

Every hair on Margareta's body rose. 'You mean he didn't—'

'He tried.' Red bloomed on Anna's cheeks. 'He heaved and thrust, but … it didn't work.'

'Oh, Anna.' Margareta fumbled for her belt knife. 'It's not your fault.'

'No?' Anna took the knife and lifted the covers, reaching for the hem of her nightgown.

'No – don't.' Margareta snatched the knife. 'You mustn't.'

'It has to be done.'

'Yes – but not by you.' Margareta pushed her sleeve back and pressed the blade to her wrist, not caring about the sharp sting. Blood welled and she smeared it against the sheets. 'That much?'

Anna shrugged. 'How should I know? I'm a virgin still.'

'It isn't your fault,' Margareta repeated.

'I think it must be.' Anna dropped her eyes. 'While he was trying, he said a name.'

Behind Margareta, Vibeke and Elline stumbled in. Hastily, she sheathed the knife and rolled down her sleeve. In little more than a whisper, Margareta asked, 'Whose?'

Tears welled in Anna's eyes. 'Alexander.'

Margareta squeezed Anna's hand.

As they set about dressing Anna and stripping the sheets to display to the court, that name echoed in Margareta's ears.

Alexander.

The King of Scotland had spoken a man's name on his wedding night and failed to bed his wife. No one would ever blame James, of course. It was never the man's fault. If this ever got out, Anna would be blamed. Margareta had to help her.

If only she knew how.

PART II

Our fears do make us traitors.
'Macbeth'

15

Icicles hung from trees, shining like inverted candles. Every so often, a blast of wind dislodged snow from the higher branches, showering white on the frozen ground. Any movement in these woods seemed eerie; falling snowflakes became hidden *hulders*, luring men off safe paths, drawing their victims deeper into the forest. Even a court's progress seemed hushed – the beat of sacking-wrapped hooves against packed snow, the jangling sleigh harnesses: the Danish winter muffled each sound. To know yourself so small was humbling, and Margareta wondered how the Scottish king would respond to being humbled. All she could see of the royal couple were the backs of their heads above their ermine-lined sleigh: Anna straight-backed, her velvet cloak the colour of frost, James lounging away from her against the side, his head resting on a gloved hand as though bored. They'd had to leave Akershus because the fortress couldn't support so many Scots for long. Perhaps James was wishing he'd risked a January sailing rather than the prospect of a sojourn in Helsingør. Or perhaps he was bored with Anna.

'Spiced wine?' Elline nudged Margareta, one hand poking out of their nest of furs, proffering a wineskin.

'Thank you.' Margareta extracted her own hand and instantly felt the cold bite through her gloves. The wine had been hot that morning, and even though Elline had been hugging it under blankets ever since, it was barely tepid now. Still, the cinnamon and nutmeg tasted like fireside evenings and Margareta could almost pretend she felt warmed. Passing the wineskin back to Elline, she returned to watching Anna and James. Was it her imagination, or had he leaned even further away from his wife?

His wife. If he could call her that without flushing. Almost two months since their wedding night and the only blood ever staining Anna's sheets came with the full moon. The Scottish ladies assigned to Anna had inspected the sheets with cold disapproval – then glanced at Anna, their judgement stiffening into blame. As for the man James had invoked, Alexander Lindsay, his face was inscrutable whenever he looked at Anna – which he did almost as often as he forced himself to look away from James. Now, Margareta saw the fair-haired Scot, riding behind the royal sleigh, turn his head back to the white-veiled trees, and she wondered whether it was respect for the Danish royal family or pained jealousy that made him twist away. Or if he were hiding his delight at Anna's unconsummated marriage and what it suggested about James's feelings for him.

No one had spoken of it – not openly, although the sidelong glances were as damning as a judge passing sentence. The court had danced and feasted and laughed through December, seemingly united in celebration. But Margareta knew where the conversations that truly mattered occurred: in corridors, or in the gardens after dark, the figures moving between statues as carefully as stalking foxes. A spy who couldn't find a way to overhear those discussions would be worthless.

But there were two sorts of person who sought such secluded spaces: conspirators, and lovers.

Sophia had been right. Betrothing Margareta to Wemyss provided them with the perfect excuse to sneak away together. To an outside eye, their meetings in Akershus's gardens looked like romantic liaisons. They'd walked together past mulberry trees strung with ice, and instead of vowing eternal loyalty or comparing the depths of their love to oceans, they'd spoken of Anna and James.

'Should we tell Sophia?' Margareta had asked as they passed rose-bushes with white-tipped thorns. 'Though how to phrase such a letter …'

'A letter that may be read by others.' Wemyss nodded grimly. 'There's enough damaging speculation about the marriage already. If it were known their union remains unconsummated ...' He let the unsaid words hang, drifting coldly with the air he breathed.

'But—' Margareta clenched her fists in frustration. 'She thinks it's her fault. That she's offended him – that she's hideous to him—'

'Perhaps she is!' Wemyss winced at his own harshness. 'I mean – through no fault of her own, or James's, for that matter. But she cannot be what attracts him.'

Margareta narrowed her eyes. 'Don't we both know attraction in marriage is a fortunate accident, not a necessity?'

He didn't bite at a retort. Instead, he said, 'Look, this isn't the first time a man's had to marry a woman he doesn't love. Or the first time a man's preferred men to women. Even kings – they say Edward the Second of England had no love for women, yet he sired four children. Perhaps it will just ... take time.'

'Waiting isn't a solution!'

Wemyss sighed. 'No one can offer solutions for other people's marriages. They must find one themselves.'

But watching Anna and James now, five days and two hundred miles away from that conversation, Margareta doubted they could.

Suddenly there was a commotion up ahead: shouts rising, horses whinnying. Then two swift horn blasts, the signal to stop. Never an easy task on snow – the sleigh runners skidded, while the drivers fought to keep the horses moving just enough so their withers wouldn't be clipped, but not so much they barged into the sleigh in front.

'What's happening?' Elline asked, twitching bolt upright. 'Is it bandits?'

'Don't be ridiculous,' Vibeke groaned. 'You'd need an army to overwhelm this train, not a gang of hungry peasants.'

As they bickered, Anna glanced back and Margareta recognized the summons in her eyes. Extricating herself from the furs, Margareta clambered down onto the snow. Away from the hot bricks and heat of Elline's body, the cold coiled around her, and she hastened for warmth as much as obedience.

'Your Grace?' No intimacy here, not with James so close, drumming his fingers impatiently.

'Can you discover why we've stopped?' Anna asked. 'And how long for? If there's time, I should like some refreshment, and I'm sure many would like to stretch their legs.'

James snorted. 'Women! Always seeking comfort when any sensible traveller knows the only true comforts will be found at journey's end. Patience and fortitude, that's what you need.'

Anna's jaw tensed, but as she turned to her husband it softened. 'You are very wise. But might it not be helpful to know the length of our delay? Sitting still in a Danish January can be deadly.'

'Deadly dull,' James agreed – and there it was again. Something – his tone, his countenance, the lack of warmth in his eyes – twisted his attempts at jocularity, rendering them callous. Who was he trying to imitate? For it wasn't so much wanton cruelty on James's part as bad acting. The gestures were rehearsed, the lines learned – but he'd been woefully miscast.

'Margareta,' Anna said, ignoring her husband's last remark, 'see if Admiral Munck can tell you more.'

Margareta curtseyed and set off, limbs tense with cold and trepidation. Where the sleighs had run, the snow was slick and treacherous, and she tried to keep her footing by advancing along the very edge of the track, where rails and hooves had flung the softest powder. Her footsteps crackled, their echoes shivering in the bitter air.

Margareta halted, suddenly alert. Were those just her footsteps echoing? She squinted at the trees. Snow swirled in the shadows between black trunks. Was it just the weather? Or was something – someone – moving through the forest?

It couldn't have been, she told herself, hurrying away. But for a moment she'd been certain she'd seen Ilsa's silvery hair flick behind the pines and heard her laugh spiralling on cold wind. Yet how – and why – would Ilsa be in this forest, at this time?

At the front of the train, men were barking at one another, vying for supremacy in solving their dilemma. Two trees had fallen, blocking their passage.

'Unharness the horses,' the Earl Marischal insisted. 'They can pull them aside.'

'They aren't plough horses,' another Scot objected. 'Strap them to trees this size and they'll refuse to move.'

'Nonsense!' someone else snapped just as Wemyss said, 'Or worse, they'll try to bolt. We'd have frightened horses or crippled ones – and we'd still be stuck in the middle of a forest.'

Margareta felt a strange warmth at his words; it took her a moment to recognize it as pride. Her betrothed had made the most logical observation so far. Her irritating, untrustworthy betrothed.

'Or,' Admiral Munck said, cutting through them all with a voice used to command at sea, 'we could take axes to the trees. No risk to the horses, and we can gift the wood to the next village.'

Wemyss nodded. 'It wouldn't hurt to impress the local folk with King James's munificence.'

Margareta wondered whether James's acting might prove convincing in that scene – the merry monarch bestowing bounty on ruddy-cheeked paupers. Somehow she doubted it.

'Axes it is,' Keith declared, immediately rattling out orders as if it had been his idea all along.

Wemyss caught sight of Margareta and joined her. 'What are you doing here?'

'Admiring your work,' she said dryly. 'How many men it takes to solve a problem.'

He laughed. 'Then you'll find much to admire in Scotland.'

'Anna wants to know how long we'll be delayed. Whether it's worth getting out of the sleighs.'

Wemyss glanced at the trees. 'They'll not be moved swiftly. Admiral Munck, what would your estimate be?'

Munck joined them. 'These are large pines, and our axes are more used to splitting kindling. An hour at least.'

'Thank you,' Margareta said. 'I'll let Queen Anna know.'

'Of course,' Munck continued, 'the real question is why they fell at all.'

Wemyss looked sharply at him. 'The weight of snow, I imagine. Or strong winds.'

Munck shook his head. 'We haven't passed a single fallen tree today. Yet here are two healthy trees toppled across the road King James and Queen Anna wish to travel. Strange, no?'

'You think they were felled deliberately?' Wemyss frowned. 'But the roots are up. No axe was taken to these. Perhaps too many beasts dug winter dens beneath their roots.'

'Or perhaps they fell for the same reason our ships were twice driven back by the worst storms I've seen in my career.'

Margareta stared. 'You cannot mean—'

Munck nodded grimly. 'Witchcraft. And mark my words, witchcraft will not go unpunished.'

Ilsa. Margareta felt the cold within her, as if she'd swallowed snow.

Witchcraft is in your blood, Greta. You cannot deny it.

She knew what witch-hunts led to. Flames and baying crowds, the smell of burnt flesh lingering not for hours, or days, but forever.

An arm was around her waist. She hadn't realized she'd swayed, or that she couldn't stand without help. Wemyss was speaking.

'It's been a fatiguing journey for the women, Admiral. I'll escort Mistress Vinstar back to her sleigh.'

Snow crunched under her boots. Whiteness all around, stinging her eyes. And then shadows brought softness, and she was sitting on a tree stump and being told, 'Wait there.'

As if she could move. As if she hadn't drawn enough attention to herself already. She pressed her fists against her thighs and tried to draw in steady breath after steady breath, wondering if the blood pounding in her ears would ever quiet.

'Here.' Wemyss was back, pressing a steaming flask into her hand. She could barely hold it. As though she were a child, he lifted it to her lips. Not wine, or ale – something warm and smoky that made her eyes water and her nose sting, then spread through her belly like a sigh of relief.

'Impressive,' Wemyss said. 'Most people splutter and cough when given whisky. Perhaps you'll fit in well in Scotland.'

Margareta blinked, trying to focus. 'I must see Anna—'

'I've seen her. Everything's fine. We're waiting here while the trees are chopped. There's stew warming, and some of my dafter countrymen are even having a snowball fight.'

He'd taken care of everything. He was taking care of her. It ought to have been easy to love him.

But he wouldn't love her if he knew the truth.

'Now.' Wemyss sat beside her. Their hips pressed together through furs and wool; the heat of it set the blood hammering in her ears again. 'Why did Munck's words unsettle you so? You're no delicate fainting flower.'

She couldn't speak. Instead, she fumbled for the whisky flask again.

'Surely,' Wemyss said quietly, 'you don't believe there's a coven of witches working to destroy James and Anna's marriage.'

I know there is. But he believed Ilsa no different from other conspirators. Or so she thought. Hoped.

'Surely, Margareta, you don't believe in witchcraft.'

This was how they caught you. 'The Bible tells us there are witches.'

'Yes, along with talking snakes and enchanted fruit.'

She whipped her head up. 'That's heresy!'

Wemyss shrugged. 'Many new thinkers find the lines between heresy and common sense rather blurred. Galileo. Giordano Bruno. Doctor Dee.'

'But – you cannot disbelieve the word of God!'

'The word of God, no. The word of man? I disbelieve that every day, especially when men claim forces of evil lie behind events with rational explanations.'

'Easy for you to say,' Margareta retorted. 'You're a man. You serve the king. No one would ever accuse you of witchcraft.'

He tilted his head quizzically. 'You serve our queen, and yet you seem afraid. Why?'

She could tell him about the real reason Ilsa hated her. About what she'd failed to do to help her. But how could you unlearn years of silence?

Margareta twisted her fingers together. 'It's different for women. As soon as someone mentions witchcraft, the world becomes a mob.

You might not believe in it, but you're one man, and anyone standing against a mob will be trampled.'

'Do you think Anna would let that happen to *you*? Do you think *I* would let that happen?' Wemyss laid his hands on hers. 'One of my wedding vows will be to protect you. And they won't be empty words.'

She wanted to let her lips meet his and the simple warmth of a kiss become the world. But she couldn't.

'And maybe,' Wemyss said, steel beneath his soft voice, 'one day you'll honour me with the same favour.'

'Me, protect you?'

'Why not? But, I meant with words that aren't empty. With openness. About why you're really afraid.'

Easier, though, to snap out a brittle riposte: 'You know why we're betrothed. You must know that's impossible.' She thrust the flask at him and rushed away across the snow.

16

Rumours seeped through Scotland like burns slithering beneath moorland, slowly turning firm ground into traps. A calf was born with two heads in Fife. Three girls went into the sea in Galloway and never emerged – but three seals had watched their village ever since, black heads gleaming beneath the moon. A child in Leith was taken by the faeries and in his place they left a malformed, drooling thing who could only cackle and groan. Up in Aberdeen, snow fell for ten days, burying a cottage entirely, and when the snow cleared, the cottage had vanished; in the empty space were footprints with cloven hooves.

'Devil's work,' women hissed as they broke the ice on the wells. 'The devil's taking hold of Scotland.'

'Do you think it's because the king left us?' another would ask, lowering her bucket past frost-rimed stones. 'All this has worsened since he went across the sea.'

'A sign,' others muttered. 'God didn't wish him to go.'

'Or perhaps,' one would suggest, 'God doesn't wish him to come back.'

Some flinched then, turning for home. But others moved closer, hungry for gossip.

'Has God ever loved the Stuarts? Look how many met bloody ends. This king's own mother lost her head; every King James before him had a gruesome death.'

'Cursed,' they agreed in low voices. 'No doubt about it.'

'If I were Danish, I wouldn't want my princess marrying into such a tainted family.'

'That's unpatriotic.'

'Being against the Stuarts doesn't mean being against Scotland.'

'After all,' someone would eventually say, 'we got rid of his mother, didn't we? Why not James too?'

As a child, Geillis had looked forward to market day in Leith with such eagerness she'd skipped along the coast road, imagining all the different coloured ribbons for sale, the glossy-maned horses that snorted happily if you brought them an apple, the smells of fresh-baked pastries and whelks straight from the harbour. But now? She couldn't remember the last time she'd skipped, or even wanted to. And the prospect of the day before her was tarnished beyond repair.

The weather didn't help. Snow, so deep pattens were useless, trodden to slush the colour of congealed porridge. On her own, Geillis could have muttered rude words at patches of ice, snarled as snow leapt over the top of her boots. But in Mistress Katherine and Lucy's company, she could hardly swear. Moreover, every time they encountered deep snow, it was Geillis who dismounted, nearly fell over, and then floundered along, leading the horses, while Lucy blithely swung her heels, and Mistress Katherine held her head as straight as if she were balancing towers of coins atop her hood.

But far worse was what Geillis had to do when they reached Leith. Not the errands, though waiting for Mistress Katherine to choose lace and Lucy to be measured by a seamstress weren't particularly exhilarating ways to spend a day. No, it was the rumours Geillis was expected to plant.

She hated doing it – and this, she knew, made her terrible at it. When Geillis muttered about misshapen animals and missing children, far from sounding ominous, it was stilted and resentful, and surely everyone listening could tell.

But what choice did she have? She touched her cheek where Chirnside and Ilsa's fingers had gripped. They might not have left bruises, but they'd left something worse.

How could she possibly murder the queen's unborn child? And why had such a task seemed less like a sin to Agnes and more like a prize? She'd thought Agnes privy to Bothwell's schemes, but if that were the case, why had Agnes and Ilsa argued on the now-sunken ship? Or if Agnes had known Bothwell's plans all along, why had she recruited Geillis, if not as a potential murderer? Her thoughts clung to her, far colder than the snow numbing her skin.

By the time she, Mistress Katherine, and Lucy reached Leith, the pale sun had pushed through the clouds and the sea shunted against the harbour walls, slow waves crosshatched with light, like glass on the point of shattering. Geillis heard hawkers selling baked codlings, oysters, hot chestnuts; her stomach growled, remembering the stale bread she'd shovelled down that morning. The Setons had broken their fast, of course, with lark pasties she'd kept warm on the oven bricks all night, wrapped in sacking so they wouldn't burn. Geillis had kept waking up in a panic, certain the cloth would catch alight.

'Seamstress first,' Mistress Katherine announced as they rode into the yard of the inn where they always left their horses – where the grooms didn't insist on accidentally fondling Mistress Katherine's hips as she dismounted. 'Geillis, see to your errands, then meet us by the seamstress's door.'

So I can carry the parcels. 'Yes, mistress.'

'Before the noon bells strike.'

'Yes, mistress.'

The crowds parted immediately for mother and daughter, as if at the scent of expensive wool. Geillis watched them go, not envious of them as such, but of anyone who wasn't her. Anyone who didn't have to work for Bothwell.

Of course, she thought, making her way to the ironmonger for a new cleaver, the Setons were in league with Bothwell, and they certainly weren't his equals. But they'd have had far more choice in joining him than she had.

She wrapped the cleaver in the sacking brought for the purpose, knowing Leith tradesmen charged extra for wrapping. Then she collected Seton's boots from the cobbler, and Mistress Katherine's freshly starched ruffs from the laundress, before bargaining with spice merchants for mace and pepper. Oil for horse harness next, and a promise from the farrier to come out to shoe all Seton's horses, and then to the butcher to order a side of venison.

Errands done, Geillis glanced about the market. Where to place herself? Far away from the street preacher beneath the Mercat Cross – anyone listening to his Bible verses would shun superstitious gossip, within his hearing at least. The queue for the bakery was sure to be full of gossip. What she really wanted was to sit down, but the slush of the marketplace rendered that a foolish hope. Besides, Geillis had never been the sort of woman to whom gossips flocked.

Perhaps she could just tell Agnes she'd sown some stories? She'd come up with some on the way – cockerels crowing the Lord's Prayer backwards, sick children coughing up moths. If she could invent rumours, surely she could invent tales about planting those rumours. And none of them would involve a ship full of dead men sinking into the black firth, axe holes gaping in its hull like ruined eyes.

Almost decided, Geillis wandered towards the seamstress's shop, vaguely hoping her early arrival might impress Mistress Katherine. She was almost there when jeering erupted behind her. Geillis jerked round, on guard.

But they weren't mocking her. No one was even looking at her.

Three men had emerged from the tolbooth in chains, flanked by savage-faced guards. The prisoners' hair was blood-matted, their jaws mottled purple.

'Traitors!'

'Beasts!'

'Burn them!'

Geillis flinched. Turning away, she caught a woman's eye. 'What's happened? Who are those men?'

'You heard – they're traitors.' The woman crossed her arms, as if such brusqueness would firmly establish her own loyalty.

'But what are they accused of?'

'Found guilty of,' the woman corrected her. 'Sinking a royal ship, that's what.'

Had another ship sunk on the way to Denmark? Surely Agnes would have heard? Geillis fought to keep her voice steady. 'When was this?'

'Didn't you hear? Back in September. These men sank a ship sailing from Burntisland. Drowned Lady Jean Kennedy what used to wait on the king's mother.'

The *Margaret*. Geillis saw the black waves thrusting it under, the broken mast dragging it down. And all the while the whistling.

'How ... how did they sink it?'

'Lured it onto rocks, then plundered the wreckage. Got caught trying to sell jewels – as if men like them come by ruby necklaces honestly!'

Geillis's throat was dry. 'Then it wasn't witchcraft?'

The woman looked suspicious. 'Why would it be?'

'No reason.' She tried to shrug, but her heavy packages meant she could only shift awkwardly.

'What have you heard?'

This was what she was here for. 'It's just ... with all the other stories, I wondered, that's all. Talk of missing children, malformed beasts – and now this.'

The woman frowned. 'They were uncommon storms, I'll grant you.'

'And just happening to strike when King James's bride was trying to cross the sea? Twice?'

'Could be coincidence.' The woman sounded sceptical.

'Maybe,' Geillis said, forcing even more doubt into her voice. 'But it seems too convenient, wouldn't you say?'

'True.' The woman grabbed her neighbour's elbow. 'Here, Mairi! Lass here heard it wasn't just lanterns those men used – it was witchcraft!'

'No!' Her neighbour's eyes widened gleefully. 'And everyone's milk in Haddington was sour today, to say nothing of the fish they're selling on the docks – all tentacles. Wouldn't surprise me if that was unnatural too.'

'I heard of a witch over in Fife who cursed the wife of the man she wanted to marry. Strong as spring one day, dead without a mark on her the next.'

They were off, gossiping so loudly everyone nearby heard – and then more rumours sprang up. Like weeds, you couldn't cut one back to get rid of them all. The only way to end them was burning.

Geillis felt sick. Only words, she tried to tell herself. But words were thoughts and plans, memories and promises. They raked up the past and foretold the future. Nothing was so dangerous – and Geillis was encouraging them. She turned away, not wanting to watch the crowd spitting on the men, and caught a glimpse of fox furs – and their wearer.

'Mistress MacCalzean!'

Euphame MacCalzean turned. 'Do I know you?'

Her steely glare ought to have made a girl of Geillis's station quail. But she'd seen things far more frightening than haughty ladies. 'I'm Geillis Duncan. I work for the Setons.'

Euphame peered down her nose at Geillis. 'You're the one Francis spoke to.'

Francis? With a start, Geillis realized she meant Bothwell. 'Yes, mistress.'

'What do you want, girl? I've better things to do than stand in the street talking to servants, however interesting earls think them.'

Geillis stepped closer. 'Those men who've been arrested. Did they have anything to do with … with what was done? I know there were other groups, not just Agnes's. Were they part of this?'

Euphame's face twisted – with scorn or discomfort? 'I don't know what you're talking about, child. But if they truly had any part in Francis's plans, do you think we would have allowed them to be arrested?'

'You mean they're innocent? Won't Bothwell say something?'

'Don't be such a fool!' Euphame shook her head grimly. 'Their innocence is the very reason he won't. And neither will anyone else.' She swept away, her fox-edged cloak whipping behind her like a flame.

Conspiracies were one thing. Trying to save your own neck another. But letting innocent men take the blame? One more sin Geillis was too frightened to stop herself committing.

17

Denmark

They shouldn't have come back to Helsingør.

Royal brides didn't return home. Anna's departure in September, heralded by fireworks and feasts, should have been the last time she beheld her homeland for years, perhaps even forever. Royal brides who came home without consummating their marriage would face a swift annulment and a lifetime in veiled seclusion. Was James planning to cast Anna and their cursed marriage aside?

None of them were wanted in Helsingør – but you couldn't have guessed from the welcome they received. Pageants and cheering crowds lined the streets. Girls tossed dried rose petals before James and Anna's sleigh and Margareta wondered how many others in the crowd had been paid: no roses grew in January. When they reached the castle, minstrels hailed them and bears danced either side of the procession, capering with the blind fear of creatures who knew that not feigning joy meant punishment.

Queen Sophia stood beside her son at Kronborg's entrance. Margareta was too far away to read Sophia's expression, but she knew what would be there. Regal welcome, and an icy determination to conceal the fury beneath.

She would be even more furious when Margareta revealed the truth.

'You are certain?'

'Yes, Your Grace.'

Sophia placed one finger on her desk as if impaling the problem. 'Two months married and still not consummated. Who else knows?'

Margareta swallowed. 'None that I'm aware of. I cut my wrist to stain Anna's sheets so we might conceal it, and I do not believe she's confided in anyone else.'

Sophia's gaze flicked to Wemyss.

'It's hardly the sort of thing a man shares. Especially given what your daughter told Margareta. The name.'

'Ah yes, the name.' Sophia frowned. 'Who is Alexander?'

Wemyss rocked on his heels. 'It's a common Scottish name.'

'No doubt you have a candidate in mind.'

'Alexander Lindsay. Fourth son of the Earl of Crawford.'

'A nobody?'

A man who always carried nuts and seeds for horses. Margareta had seen the king's lover soothe several mares when a barrel had crashed off a sleigh. If Alexander Lindsay hadn't been – deliberately or otherwise – undermining Anna's chance of happiness, Margareta might have warmed to the gentle Scot.

'Not anymore,' Wemyss said. 'King James appointed him Vice Chamberlain and Lindsay lent the king ten thousand gold coins towards this expedition. In return, James will raise him to the peerage.'

'The sort of favour granted to royal mistresses.' Sophia waved a hand dismissively. 'All kings take lovers. Lindsay will produce no bastards, at least.' Sophia turned to Margareta. 'What counsel have you given Anna?'

'I …' Margareta hesitated. 'I told her to be patient. King James might come to care for her.'

'He doesn't need to care for her to get a son on her.' Sophia eyed Margareta thoughtfully. 'But what other advice could an unwed girl have given? One virgin counselling another – as well ask you to teach her how to joust.'

Margareta winced at the disappointment in Sophia's tone. 'I'm sorry, Your Grace.'

'Then make amends.' Sophia sighed. 'Another irksome consequence of those storms. If not for them, you'd have been in Scotland and safely wed months ago. Now, we have only a few weeks before Lent delays any weddings for a further two months – and I've had quite enough of delays. You must marry at once.'

'Your Grace?' Margareta knew she was blushing.

'Thursday will do very well.' Sophia glanced at Margareta's pink cheeks. 'Oh, come now. You've been betrothed long enough no one will suspect there's a reason for haste.' She turned to Wemyss. 'She'll need guidance. To be taught how to please a man. I trust you are up to the task.'

Wemyss rocked on his heels again. 'I shall do my best, Your Grace.'

He was trying not to laugh. How dare he find their predicament, *her* predicament, amusing?

'Good.' Sophia arched an eyebrow. 'Well? You have a wedding to prepare for. Off you go.'

The wedding was small. Little wonder, given that preparations were underway for celebrating James and Anna's marriage for the third time, as if more feasts and dances might compensate for the union's hidden frailties. There were no such lavish entertainments for Margareta and Wemyss's wedding, and she couldn't help wondering what there might have been had her family been here. But then she imagined Johanna and Ilsa in their homespun dresses, one quiet, one furious with discomfort, and acknowledged the idea of Ilsa dancing at her wedding was absurd.

It took place in the chapel in Kronborg with a handful of guests – Elline and Vibeke, a few Scottish lords. The bride wore an old green damask gown with hastily added ivory brocade trimmings and a lace ruff lent by Anna.

'I can't come,' she'd said, eyes limpid with apologies. 'Mama says I must accompany James on a tour of Helsingør. But wear this, as a token of my regard for you.'

It was oddly appropriate; if Anna couldn't be there, part of her wardrobe would. Most brides would have been secretly glad: royalty at your wedding rendered it impossible for even the most beautiful bride to be centre of attention. But as Margareta walked down the aisle on the arm of Sophia's chamberlain, with whom she'd spoken twice, she wished someone else was there to draw everyone's eyes. Not her. Not too-tall Margareta Vinstar, daughter of a drunkard. And the way Wemyss was looking at her, too tender, too soft – wasn't it yet another lie?

Their vows rang in the near-empty chapel, echoing solemnly on the marble. When the minister pronounced them man and wife and Wemyss leaned forward to kiss Margareta, she couldn't help remembering their first kiss, that clash of tempers and bodies in a storm, and she didn't know whether this brief, gentle brush of lips was a relief or a disappointment. Surely you shouldn't hope for anger in your husband's kiss – and yet hadn't all Anna's ladies dreamed of passion in marriage? Was she doomed to be as disappointed as Anna in that regard?

Afterwards, a small supper in rooms she assumed were Wemyss's, for Margareta could think of no other reason why they would have come to a small inn overlooking the harbour. Certainly not for the overcooked venison, so dry any conversation faltered as they chewed. From downstairs a bawdy song drifted up and Elline caught Margareta's eye with a mischievous smile. The verses grew lewder, the chorus more raucous. A nervous laugh trembled silently at the corner of Vibeke's mouth. The Scotsmen nudged one another and winked. Calmly, Wemyss reached for his ale. Margareta wanted to slide beneath the table.

'Well,' Wemyss said eventually, 'my thanks to you all for joining us. But even dear friends must bid farewell on such a night.'

'The earlier the better!' one of the Scots laughed.

Vibeke's giggle escaped, piercingly shrill. Elline snorted and both blushed. Margareta suddenly realized she'd spent every night for the past eleven years sleeping beside either these two or Anna, and as they left along with the Scots, it seemed her old life was walking out too.

The door closed, and she was alone with her husband.

Her *husband*. The word tasted strange, like the first time she'd tasted hippocras: rich, heady, and she knew she was meant to like it.

She didn't know where to look. Wemyss stood in the centre of the room; behind him was the door to the other chamber, and behind that door ...

'Margareta, will you join me?' He held out a hand.

'Of course,' she said. 'I vowed to obey you, didn't I?'

He smiled, seeing the trepidation beneath her offhand defence. 'I'm not ordering. I'm asking.'

She doubted it would have occurred to most men to ask. That was one of the reasons why she lifted her hand and took his. Her other reasons? Duty – as a wife, but also to Anna and Sophia. And the greatest reason, the one that made her belly tense and flutter at once: desire.

In the next chamber, a sturdy table held wine and a bowl of hazelnuts; a sheepskin rug lay before a crackling fire. And in the centre was the bed. Their bed. Her stomach clenched; her borrowed ruff trembled with every breath.

Margareta swallowed and turned to face him, her eyes latching on to the black velvet trimming his doublet. 'Well then. I suppose we'd best get on with it.'

His chest heaved with suppressed laughter. 'I suppose we'd better.'

'How should I ... proceed? Perhaps you could explain first so I know what I'm doing, then I can advise Anna later.'

'Margareta.' She heard his wince. 'Please. The rest of our lives will be given in service to royalty. Let tonight be for pleasing one another.' He ran his forefinger along her cheek and down her neck as he spoke.

'But—'

'Later. Tomorrow.' His fingers traced the neckline of her bodice. 'Or never.'

'I must—'

He kissed her, and there was no duty or obedience in his kiss. It was tender at first, then deep and lingering, and her body arched towards his. She wanted his lips on hers, his body on hers – and had she cried out? She couldn't tell – couldn't have silenced herself if she'd tried. He was unlacing her gown, peeling her clothes away, caressing each emerging inch of skin. She yearned for every stitch to be gone, to be naked in his arms – and to linger over this pleasure too: his lips at her collarbone, her breasts. She fumbled at his clothes, the unfamiliar fastenings, her fingers touching his skin tentatively, wonderingly, as if tasting him.

'Margareta,' he whispered, and it was almost a groan. She knew what he was asking, and her kiss was her answer. He lifted her and she wrapped her legs around his waist as he carried her to the bed. She sank into the furs beneath his weight and remembered Vibeke had always wondered about this – the practicalities of breathing and arranging limbs and not squashing or being squashed. But his weight wasn't oppressive; she wanted to pull him closer, as if they weren't close enough already.

'Tell me if I hurt you,' he breathed, and his hand parted her legs, stroking her, and then it did hurt, but she didn't care. Some part of her wondered how she could be doing this with a man she couldn't trust, and another part murmured *But you do trust him. He will not harm you. He will take care of you.*

All the rest was consumed with desire for him. There was no point trying to think, so she gave herself up to this moment, this man, this marriage, and if the floorboards in the bedchamber were like those next door, the sounds Margareta and John Wemyss made would have drowned out any bawdy songs and likely inspired the writing of several more.

Could there be anything more delicious than this? Margareta stretched, arching her back and pressing closer to John. He grunted approvingly, pulling her even more snugly against him.

'Do that again, and I won't be held responsible for my actions.'

'Good.' She ran a hand down his chest. 'Then perhaps you won't hold me accountable for mine.' She draped one leg across his, arching an eyebrow in playful promise. What made her so daring? She'd never been mischievous. Sarcasm and caustic observation were her forms of wit, yet here she was, teasing a naked man, entirely without embarrassment.

'I intend to hold you entirely accountable,' he retorted, pulling her onto him; as he kissed her, she felt him hardening against her belly and pressed herself close in gleeful provocation.

'Why, Mistress Wemyss,' he murmured, 'you have a wealth of undiscovered talents.'

'I like you calling me Mistress Wemyss.'

'You have a lifetime of it to look forward to. And I—' he caressed her thighs '—have a lifetime of *this* to look forward to.'

'You enjoyed it then?'

'Can't you tell?'

She pushed herself up to see his face. 'So could I suggest this to Anna?'

'What?'

'Me, on top of you. Is that something all men like?'

'Christ's wounds, Margareta!' He propped himself up on his elbows. 'Is this really the best time to discuss that?'

'We have to discuss it at some point.'

'Bloody hellfire.' He slumped back against the pillows. 'Look, I know we told Sophia we would, but … her plan is utter nonsense. I'm not James. I don't share his tastes in wine or horses, never mind our proclivities in the bedchamber. What excites me is unlikely to excite James.'

'There must be some things all men like.'

He grimaced. 'Margareta, I don't want you to care about what other men enjoy. If you want to know what I'd enjoy, I'll happily enlighten you. But discussing James's bedchamber habits is not what I want to do in the midst of creating our own.'

'But if we don't help Anna, James will cast her aside!'

'What? What makes you say that?'

'His kinsman did it.'

Slowly, John sat up. Margareta, dislodged, followed suit. Feeling newly exposed, she tugged the blankets up to cover herself.

'How long has this worried you?'

She shrugged. 'Since Anna first told me, and we had to pretend she'd bled on the sheets.'

'But you did pretend. And as far as I know, no one's questioned it.'

'Not yet – but in six months, a year? If there's no sign of an heir, people will question it. And Anna will be blamed, just like Anne of Cleves fifty years ago. The English king got rid of her, and no man in Christendom would touch her afterwards.'

'That was different.'

'How? A king had an unconsummated marriage annulled – why not this one?'

'Many reasons!' John moved as if to take her hand in reassurance, but changed his mind, thrusting his arm behind his head. 'Look, James is no King Henry. He needs Anna. Think about it. By the time Henry divorced Anne of Cleves, he'd ruled for over thirty years. He already had a son and heir, he'd had three wives, God knows how many mistresses. Yes, he was desperate for another son, but he didn't need to prove himself as James must.'

'Prove himself?'

'As a king, and a man. James has no acknowledged bastards crawling round Scotland. His liking for men is an open secret. No one names it aloud and everyone pretends they haven't noticed, but I doubt the court will be quite so tolerant if they discover he hasn't lain with his wife – or cannot. Scotland needs an heir, and if James cannot provide one, many might think themselves a better prospect. Some men already fancy themselves heir.'

'So setting aside Anna would make him look weak?'

'Exactly. And he looks weak enough already. King Henry took his throne at eighteen, a Spanish princess for a queen. They called him the most handsome man in Christendom. He towered over his court. He was ruthless – he and his father destroyed every claimant to their throne. No one in the land could touch him, let alone match him. But James?' John shook his head. 'His mother's crown was given to him when he was a baby. No one believes he can rule Scotland alone. People doubt him from afar. Then they see him up close ...'

'And he doesn't look like a king.' No wonder Margareta had thought he looked like a bad actor: James knew the role didn't suit him.

'Exactly. James won't dare set Anna aside. He needs the marriage to work as much as she does.'

'Then Anna's safe?'

'No.' His eyes were dark with grim sadness. 'She cannot be. All those hoping to take Scotland's crown for their own are already seeking ways to hurt James further. Anna will be an easy target. Foreign, young – and unable to fulfil her duties as a queen.'

It was worse than Margareta had thought. She'd imagined the risk lay with the king's disinterest in Anna. Now it seemed James wasn't a threat to Anna, but her protector. And that was a terrifying prospect.

18

Geillis wished she'd never mentioned witchcraft in the marketplace. Never seen those men. The memory wouldn't leave her head. Seated in kirk, half-listening to the sermon, she saw their battered faces in place of the minister's. Jointing a chicken, she'd slice into its flesh and wonder what instruments had bloodied theirs. Even in the garden, the rustling herbs and whispering winds would transform into her stupid, clumsy words: *Then it wasn't witchcraft?*

No good claiming the words were harmless. Nor could she pretend someone else would have said it before long: *she* had said it. Now three men were dead on Castle Hill, and no one remembered that they'd officially hanged for sinking the ship. Only that the men had been witches – and everyone knew male witches always acted alongside female witches.

'They're saying someone must have taught them the art,' Geillis told Agnes as they returned from assisting a farmer's wife in childbed – a slow labour; both women were leaden with weariness. 'Some wise women.'

'Or a relative,' Agnes said grimly. 'One of the men was Bessie's distant cousin.'

'You mean …' Geillis almost dropped the reins in horror. 'They *were* involved?'

'No.' Agnes harrumphed in the way that meant she was worried – and furious that she had to worry. 'They were just imprudent young men trying to sell washed-up wreckage. But there's a connection.'

'But Mistress MacCalzean said there wasn't,' Geillis objected. 'She said Bothwell wouldn't have allowed it.'

Agnes snorted. 'We're to consider ourselves lucky if rich folk remember our names, let alone notice who our cousins are. They probably think we all sprang up fully formed, ready to serve their purposes.'

'And yet you trust Bothwell to reward you?' Geillis shook her head in frustration. 'He doesn't care about us. Never did.'

'That isn't true. Once—' Agnes stopped. 'I trust him to honour his promises – and to remember that keeping us safe might also keep him safe.'

'You wouldn't dare say that to him!' Geillis shot a glance at the older woman. 'You can't threaten someone like Bothwell!'

'You don't have to make threats as long as the other person knows you carry blades.'

A lifetime ago, Geillis had protested to Bothwell that everyone had blades – even children had belt knives. Bothwell had deemed her weapons useful. Agnes believed her own capable of true menace. But Geillis knew there was a world of difference between knives used for dicing onions, and steel swords. And that was without considering the hand that gripped the blade – how much strength in their arms, and whether they had the slightest idea of how to wield it.

Seton's satisfaction rose off him like a stench. Geillis never wanted to be close to him, but when pouring his wine at dinner it took all her willpower not to recoil.

'Lucy learned a new madrigal today,' Mistress Katherine said, toying with a sliver of hake. 'She wishes to play it for you. I told her perhaps tomorrow before supper.'

Seton snorted. 'As long as it's short. I may need to go to Edinburgh this week.'

'Edinburgh?' Mistress Katherine stopped short of adding *You?* – but her surprised tone was insult enough.

'Aye, Edinburgh.' Seton narrowed his eyes. 'It's likely the Privy Council will call on me.'

'For what purpose?'

Seton smiled. 'To give evidence in a trial.'

Mistress Katherine grappled between curiosity and a reluctance to pander to him by asking questions. 'Whose?'

'The Laird of Auchinleck,' Seton said, taking a swig of wine. 'He's been consulting witches.'

'What has that to do with you?'

Seton smiled again. 'I denounced him.'

The colour drained from his wife's cheeks. 'What on earth possessed you?'

Seton's face darkened. 'I despise the man. Pompous, self-righteous, far too quick to insult me. Well, he'll get his comeuppance.'

'Then you have no evidence?'

Seton shrugged. 'What's evidence got to do with it? Man deserves punishment, and with the whole country wild with chatter of witchcraft, it's a good way to attack him.'

'But …' A vein pulsed in Mistress Katherine's forehead. Geillis had never seen her so close to losing control. 'Auchinleck's an associate of Bothwell. He may be involved in the scheme – he could know too much!'

'Nonsense,' Seton retorted. 'He doesn't know nearly as much as he claims. Besides, I've paid that Fian fellow to run an errand in Ayrshire. He'll have been seen on Auchinleck's estate.'

John Fian. Who'd whistled up winds and scuttled the corpse ship.

'And in your company!' Mistress Katherine exclaimed. 'Fian's part of this! If he's called to testify, what else will he reveal?'

'Nothing,' Seton said testily, 'because I paid him very well.'

'We haven't enough coin to pay a man to resist Privy Council questioning!' Mistress Katherine shot to her feet. 'You've not only made a foolish, dangerous error, you've wasted money – money I brought to this marriage!'

'And which belongs to me!' Seton snapped. 'As do you, and everything in this house!'

Mistress Katherine's lip curled in disgust and she stormed from the room.

Geillis listened to her steps fade away, wishing with each one that she'd return.

'More wine, girl! I shouldn't have to ask!' Seton banged his cup on the table furiously. Geillis hurried forward. His hand shot out to seize her wrist. 'Put the jug down.'

She set it on the table carefully and stepped back.

'Don't move.' He eyed her up and down. 'You're an obedient girl, aren't you, Geillis?'

There was only one answer. 'Yes, sir.'

'Take off your dress.'

She felt her stomach drop. She'd dreaded this. And now it was here.

'Do as you're told, Geillis. You know what could happen to a disobedient servant.'

'Yes, sir.' Her voice was thin, high, not her own. This wasn't happening to her, but to someone else, some other girl with a voice Geillis didn't recognize. Slowly, she lifted her hands to untie the laces of her dress.

'That's it.' He leaned back in his chair, his breath growing shallower. 'Keep going.'

Unable to bear looking at him, she fixed her eyes above his head, on the leather panels she'd oiled that morning, and pushed her dress off her shoulders to the floor.

'Now don't be untidy, Geillis. Pick it up and place it on ... that stool, over there.' He pointed to one by the fireplace. A low one. Geillis, horribly aware of how thin her shift was, so worn in patches you could almost see through it, bent to obey. Behind her, Seton's breath quickened and she knew what she would see before she turned round. He'd untied his breeches and slipped a hand inside.

'The shift too, I think.'

She wanted to cry. She'd seen him humiliated by Mistress Katherine, and he had to show her who held power in the house. Perhaps show himself too.

That gave her a glimmer of courage. He wasn't doing this because he was strong, but because he was weak. Steeling herself, Geillis pulled her shift over her head.

She'd never been naked before a man. She'd never wanted to be. Nor did she want to see any part of Seton's body exposed, and she kept her eyes high so she couldn't see his hand moving, or his eyes tracking over her body like a hound trailing through mud.

'Skinny thing, aren't you?' He groaned, and she wondered if it was disappointment or arousal. 'You must be cold, Geillis. Come here so you can warm up.'

Away from the fire? She wanted to spit at his stupidity. Agnes would have. Ilsa too. But Geillis obeyed.

'Good girl.'

She felt his eyes on her like a stain. His every command stained her; every time she obeyed him stained her. And afterwards, he'd be able to say he hadn't touched her – it had been Geillis tempting him.

'Climb astride me, Geillis.'

Even now, as she lowered herself into his lap and he fumbled himself inside her, he would still say it was her fault, since if he'd forced her, she'd be on her back, struggling, crying out. Instead, she was silent.

'You are mine, Geillis. All mine.' He grabbed her waist, so hard she knew he'd leave bruises. 'I am your master. Say it!'

'You are my master,' she echoed, and the syllables meant no more than Latin. They weren't her words. It wasn't her body he thrust into, only some shell of a girl saying, 'You are my master, and I am yours to control.'

The next morning, the tide tossed up fragments of sunken boats. Rain bent the mugwort stems back like fingers, and gulls battled against brutal gusts, shrieking futile protests.

There were always winds. Waves rose and fell every day. How could you tell which ones were natural and which had been summoned – if such a thing were even possible? How could a woman know if she was a witch? Not the warning hissed to any girl with an interest in herbs, not the rumours spread by vindictive neighbours – but a woman with the power to change her fate.

All week she was desperate to ask. When she next saw Agnes, there was no waiting until after they'd seen their patient.

'Agnes,' Geillis whispered as they followed the coast path to Prestonpans. 'I need to know. What you did at Inchkeith, at Berwick Law – was it real?'

Agnes appeared more interested than irritated. 'Haven't we had this talk before? Why are you so keen to tread over old ground?'

'Because …' Geillis hesitated. 'Because I need it to be real.'

'I see.' Agnes stared ahead, as if fascinated by the winter-shrivelled heather. 'Far be it from me to instruct people what to believe. I'm no minister. My word isn't law when it comes to laying down what's God's miracles, and what's devil-sent delusions.'

'Agnes, please.'

'But I will say this.' Agnes stopped suddenly, turning to face Geillis. 'Faith matters. Not just to open St Peter's gates, but here on earth. When I give someone a remedy, is it my herbs or their trust that most helps their recovery? They have to believe I can help them, and if I can bolster that belief by telling them the herbs were picked under a gibbous moon, or by murmuring a little cantrip over a poultice, I'll do it. Is my power real? Real enough that every woman from Berwick Law to Leith asks for me when their babies are coming. Real enough to frighten half Scotland. Real enough to catch the Earl of Bothwell's attention. So, Geillis. Do *you* believe I can help you?'

Fear warred with desperation. Years of listening to ministers preaching hellfire and brimstone, death to any tempted by the devil, grappled with the memory of Seton's flesh breaking into hers, invading where he had no right to go. He would do it again. Again and again and again. Unless she stopped him.

'Yes,' Geillis whispered, and the wind whipped harsh echoes from her words. 'I believe you can.'

Agnes smiled. 'Then what is it? Healing, foretelling, charming?'

Geillis's jaw clenched. 'Purging.'

19

Denmark

After weeks of celebrations, the quiet of Roskilde Cathedral was welcome. Here, the steady, solemn hymns could be trusted not to break into galliards; instead of performing in masques every other night, Margareta could relax beneath the vaulted stone, unwatched. No more sides of still-bloody venison, no more hogs turning on spits, their juices hissing on the coals. Finally the simple white flesh of cod and the reliable softness of bread. Lent had never been such a relief.

'I can barely remember a time when I wasn't celebrating Anna's wedding,' Elline sighed as they drifted in the royal party's wake. 'I've danced through ten pairs of slippers – I'll be dancing barefoot if this carries on much longer.'

'I never thought I could be sick of fireworks,' Margareta said. 'But wouldn't it be nice to spend snowy nights indoors, rather than shivering in the gardens?'

'I suppose it will all be worth it,' Vibeke mused. 'Once there are a few princes in the nursery, what will cold fingers and sore feet matter?'

Margareta looked away. If anyone at court could read her face, it would be Vibeke, who paid far more attention to others than Elline. But if Vibeke spoke with unruffled confidence about future royal babies, she couldn't possibly suspect the truth – so surely neither could anyone else. Even the arrival of Anna's courses that morning didn't seem to have concerned Vibeke, though according to Anna it had made James's departure from her bed even more hurried.

They still hadn't consummated their marriage. Nor could Margareta see any way of helping them. Anna had asked her what John most seemed to enjoy in bed, and when Margareta, blushing furiously, had mentioned that he liked fondling and kissing her breasts, Anna had frowned.

'Through your nightgown?'

'No – he takes it off.'

'And his own?'

'Yes.'

'So you're both naked together?' Anna had knitted her brows. 'Might James prefer it that way?'

Margareta had shrugged helplessly. 'Maybe you'd both prefer it. You'd be … closer.'

But the next morning, Anna had come to her in distress. 'He wouldn't let me undress him! When I tried to remove my nightgown, he demanded where I'd learned such whore's tricks.'

'Did you …' Margareta hesitated. If James thought Anna a whore for attempting to lie naked with her own husband, she wasn't sure she wanted to ask. 'Did you try anything else?'

'I tried … sort of pushing myself against him. So he'd accidentally end up touching my breasts. But he just rolled over and pretended to fall asleep.'

'Perhaps it will be better in Scotland?'

Anna had looked up, blue eyes wavering behind tears. 'How?'

But Margareta had been unable to answer.

Now, watching Sophia and Christian lead James on a tour of the cathedral, Margareta remained at a loss; judging from Anna's imploring glances at the carved Christ on the rood screen, so was she.

How long before others started asking questions? In six months, the world would know Anna hadn't conceived on her wedding night. But gossip would spread before then – and the longer it spread without the rumour of conception to soften it, the crueller it would be.

As they moved past the chapter house, someone moved in the shadows. Margareta knew at once who it was.

'Ah!' she breathed, pretending to stumble. 'I've wrenched my ankle – these new boots!'

'The pains of a married woman's new wardrobe,' Vibeke said dryly. 'Shall I stay with you?'

'No – Anna might want you. I'll just rest a while.' She hobbled to the nearest pew.

As the royal party's footsteps died away, the figure emerged to sit behind Margareta. Ilsa rested her clasped hands on the back of the pew.

'I hear you're married. My invitation must have been lost.'

Margareta winced. 'Hardly anyone was there. It was a small occasion – we couldn't afford anything else.'

'No? What are those boots made of – potato peelings?'

Margareta stopped rubbing her ankle and slipped her feet beneath her skirts.

'What's your husband like?' Ilsa turned, peering after the royal party.

'He's tall,' Margareta said haltingly, reluctant to discuss John with Ilsa. 'And kind.'

'Tall and kind,' Ilsa repeated in a mocking sing-song. 'What a fortunate wife you are. Would I like him?'

'I doubt it. You argue with everyone.'

'How do you know I don't save all my arguments for you, dearest sister?'

'Because you haven't changed.'

Ilsa laughed. 'Nor have you. Married woman you may be, but you're as cantankerous as ever. Maybe John Wemyss isn't such a wonderful husband after all.'

'Never mind him,' Margareta snapped. 'What do you want?'

'Would you believe me if I said to see you?'

'Of course not.'

'I thought as much. Well, it seemed a good opportunity to tell you how our schemes are progressing.'

'Our? Don't speak as if I'm a part of this.'

'Who says I did?' Ilsa's face tightened. 'I am part of things outside our bond, Greta. Don't you dare begrudge me that.'

'I didn't mean …'

Ilsa sniffed haughtily. 'I merely came to tell you that your task has been made easier.'

'What?'

'I met with Geillis Duncan and her associates. They know who you are – who you are to me. They'll be seeking you out.'

Margareta gritted her teeth. 'You mean you didn't trust me to find them myself?'

'Honestly, Greta?'

Margareta bit her lip. 'How did you find them? Did they come to Denmark – through those storms?'

'I went to them.'

'You've been to Scotland again?'

'Not exactly,' Ilsa said evasively. 'We never set foot on shore.'

'We? Who is *we*?'

'My friend,' Ilsa said, her voice needling. 'Erna Koldings.'

'I've heard that name. Isn't she a cunning woman?'

'She's like me,' Ilsa said flatly. 'Whatever you want to call us. Midwives, cunning women, wise women. Witches.'

'Ilsa, for heaven's sake be careful!' Margareta peered round. The royal party might have disappeared into a chapel, but voices echoed all too easily in a cathedral.

'Always caution with you!'

'I'm serious. Admiral Munck claims the storms that delayed us were caused by witches.'

'He would – better that than his own incompetence.'

'It doesn't matter why he's saying it!' Margareta hissed. 'He's a powerful man, and even more powerful men will listen to him! You have to be on your guard. Especially if—'

'If what?'

Margareta hesitated. 'There's a possibility he's right.'

'Do you think there is?'

Margareta didn't meet Ilsa's eyes. 'If I thought that, I'd have to believe you tried to drown me.'

'Now why would I do that?'

Spite. Jealousy. Or worst of all, blame and revenge for what happened after Margareta left home all those years ago. Margareta swallowed her reasons; they tasted like bile.

'You see!' Ilsa crowed. 'All nonsense. Did you think me some sort of *draugar*, creating darkness in daylight and sinking ships on a cruel whim?'

Margareta stared at her sister, unable to quash the thought that Ilsa prowling the shore as an undead shapeshifter wasn't hard to imagine at all. 'Ilsa, did you try to drown me?'

'Oh, don't be ridiculous. You didn't drown.'

'You weren't there, Ilsa! You have no idea how terrifying that crossing was!'

'Terrifying?' Ilsa echoed. 'You've been afraid all your life, Greta.'

Margareta paused. 'I never thought to be afraid of you.'

'Nor should you be,' Ilsa said silkily. 'Not as long as you do as I've asked and meet with Geillis.'

'Ilsa, this is too dangerous!'

'Midwives are the opposite of dangerous, Margareta. Especially Geillis. Offensive as you may find being compared to a commoner, she reminded me of you. A thoughtful, lonely, awkward thing.'

Margareta winced. 'Ilsa—'

'But clever. She might even be able to help you.' Ilsa leaned forward. 'With matters concerning your precious Anna and her husband.'

'How do you know about that?'

But when Margareta twisted round, there was only the echoing quiet of the cathedral. Ilsa was gone. Conniving words, delivered in a voice twisted with envy: would they be the last she'd ever hear from her sister?

20

A year ago, Geillis would never have left her house at night. The prospect of her mother's scolding would have daunted her as much as the shadows. But her mother was long buried, and Geillis had learned there were far more frightening things in the world than darkness. To overcome your fears, you had to become something that frightened others.

Moonlight slid between the bare branches of Ormiston woods. Barely any light reached as far as the disused well. A hush had fallen over the clearing – no distant calls of hunting owls, no whisper of bats' wings. Only the women's footsteps. One by one, they took up places around the well: Bessie west, Geillis east, and Agnes north. Beneath their hoods, their faces were dark masks.

'Are we ready?' Agnes asked, and two faceless women answered, 'Aye.'

'It isn't enough,' Agnes had told Geillis, 'for you alone to believe this. Seton must believe it too. And for us to be safe, he must believe it comes from a higher power, not us.'

What better way to make Seton believe than having Bessie spread whispers faster than the pox? Geillis didn't smile – she could scarcely remember the last time she did and meant it – but her face hardened with satisfaction.

Agnes reached for the pail. 'Whatever we bring out of this well will be the destruction of David Seton.'

Bessie went first. As she poured, she let out a nervous giggle – then cut it short at one look from Agnes. In the hush, the plash of the pail meeting the water, the creaking pulleys echoed like gunshots. Bessie hauled the pail out and turned to Agnes, who was spreading a large muslin square out on the ground. Bessie tilted the pail and poured.

What had Geillis expected? Some malformed creature, snarling and spitting blood? It was almost a relief to see dark water disappear through the cloth, leaving scraps of moss and several pine cones behind, then a pebble with a hole in its centre.

Geillis's turn. She lowered the pail and paused before hauling it up, letting the water settle. When she began pulling, she knew immediately there was something inside. She could hear it scratching, scraping. Christ in heaven, was something alive in there after all? As it swayed into view, she almost didn't dare reach for it. But this had been her idea. If Bessie could do it, so could Geillis. She took the pail and poured.

It wasn't a creature. But nor was it anything she'd expected to find down a well. Broken glass lay on the cloth, some green and blue, some clear, enough for a stained glass window. How had so much glass found its way to the bottom of Ormiston well?

'Geillis.'

She was still gripping the pail. Agnes held out her hands, waiting.

What would Agnes bring up? Doubtless nothing as mundane as pine cones. As Agnes lowered the pail, Geillis suddenly wondered: could Agnes have put the glass in there?

Whatever your trouble, do you believe I can help you?

She believed in Agnes. Did that mean she believed Agnes capable of conjuring? She dared not think of the answer – not in a forest after dark, not when the final pail was emerging and Agnes was tilting it.

Agnes met Geillis's eyes. For a moment, neither moved. As though Agnes was waiting – for a signal, even for permission. Slowly, Geillis nodded, and even more slowly, Agnes poured.

When all the water had drained away into the earth, what remained on the cloth was grey and brittle; some gleamed smooth, some jutted sharply, and some was tangled in what might once have been cloth.

Bones. Not bird bones, or fox, but unmistakeably the bones of a small child.

'We have it,' Agnes said softly. 'The destruction of David Seton.'

They left the kirk on the first Sunday in Lent as they always did, according to their stations. Seton gave his arm to Mistress Katherine, who touched her fingertips to his sleeve as if it was soiled. At their heels came Lucy, chattering happily about how they'd see lambs in the fields before long. Then the servants, led by the steward, Geillis and Jeanie falling in at the rear.

As they walked along the lane, Jeanie wittered about a recipe she'd heard recently. Geillis struggled to listen. She was watching for Agnes. Agnes always met her after kirk; everyone knew they visited the sick on Sundays.

'The sauce hardly used any spices, and any sauce for lampreys is meant to cover up their taste, so—'

'What's that?'

Mistress Katherine's words rang out with such force everyone halted, peering at what she'd seen.

It was laid out across the path, a circle too smooth to be found in nature. A ring of moss and pinecones, surrounding a ring of broken glass and, at its centre, the child's bones.

'Was that there this morning?' Jeanie whispered. 'Have we already passed over it?'

'I've seen these before,' a groom muttered. 'My mother says whoever passes them first will sicken before the week's out.'

'A curse,' Jeanie breathed.

Geillis said nothing. Even as Mistress Katherine turned, her eyes seeking Geillis's, she remained silent.

So did Seton. She couldn't see his face, but she saw his shoulders were rigid.

Hoofbeats drew near. Jeanie clutched Geillis's arm.

Agnes emerged into the lane, mounted on Blossom. 'Why Master Seton,' she said calmly, 'you look as if you've seen a ghost.'

'You!' Seton burst out. 'This is your doing!'

'Mine?' Agnes glanced down at the collection of objects. 'But my home lies to the east. What business would I have had on this path?'

'This business!' Seton hissed. 'You know what this is – how it came to be here!'

Agnes smiled. 'All I know, Master Seton, is that your sins will find you out. And you can be sure our noble friend has already discovered them.'

He must believe it comes not from us, but from a higher power.

What was Seton thinking? That Bothwell had decided to punish him, frighten him into believing himself cursed? Or was he wondering, as his head twitched left and right, whether they could take another path home? But that would make him look afraid, and weak – and nothing riled Seton more than being made to seem a fool.

Then he turned. Face blotched purple, his eyes bulged madly as they landed on Geillis. She returned his gaze calmly. *Let him think it was me. Let him understand I am not his victim. I have Bothwell's protection – and my own.*

Eventually Seton spoke, his voice taut with rage. 'This is a cruel jest meant to frighten us. But have we not just come from kirk? Are we not bathed in God's graces? We have nothing to fear from malicious japes and backwards superstitions. Let us continue home.'

Mistress Katherine stared at the arm he offered her, even less willing to touch it than before. 'David—'

'Lucy isn't afraid,' Seton snapped, grabbing his daughter's hand and pulling her alongside him. 'Look – she has more courage than any grown woman here!'

Lucy's lip wobbled – and then she looked up at her father with a hopefulness that made Geillis's heart twist.

'I'm not afraid,' she said clearly, and stepped forward.

'No!' Mistress Katherine shot out a hand to pull her daughter back.

But it was too late. All they could do was watch as a nine-year-old girl, golden curls bobbing, was first to step past the broken glass and bone.

21

Scotland

Geillis watched Lucy's chest rise and fall, every judder tightening Geillis's own. *Let it not be the last.*

Was it worse than before? Impossible to tell. Her memories of Lucy's last illness were blurred with sweat and steam from the endless preparation of tisanes and infusions. Moreover, the abiding memory was of the moment when Lucy had sat up and smiled, and Mistress Katherine's face had opened with relief like a new rose.

But Mistress Katherine was no longer that woman. Her cap had long since been tossed aside and her neatly pinned hair had slipped awry. Every so often she rubbed her jaw angrily, as if she might scour away the ache from clenching and Lucy's illness all at once. But most painful to see were the deepening hollows around her eyes.

I did that, Geillis thought. She, who ought to bring hope to the sick and their loved ones, not take it away.

Outside the sickroom, Lent was almost over. Days were stretching, nights shrinking. Not that they could tell. Geillis had wanted to keep the shutters open, let in some air, but Lucy whimpered in distress whenever daylight touched her eyelids, and so Geillis had closed them again. They had endured a month of darkness.

How could an illness last so long without changing? She'd tried every remedy she knew – poultices, lozenges, tisanes; camomile, feverfew, white horehound, probably every herb that grew in Scotland – and nothing had changed. Lucy still lay there, shivering yet burning with fever, waking only to vomit and sometimes not even then.

There was an explanation. But if true, it damned Geillis forever. *Witchcraft.*

Why had Lucy stepped forward before Seton? That pitiful eagerness to impress her father had drawn his punishment down on the child. Geillis wouldn't have tried like this to save Seton.

Would she have tried at all? Or exchanged this herb for that, doubled a dosage and watched in satisfaction as Seton breathed his agonizing last? Part of her wished she could be so ruthless – and part of her knew she was too much of a coward.

'My husband should have been the one to suffer.'

Geillis jumped. That Mistress Katherine had spoken at all was surprising; that her words were so close to Geillis's thoughts was unnerving.

'All this.' Mistress Katherine gestured at the chamber as if to swat it all away. 'If not for him, Lucy wouldn't lie ... afflicted. His arrogance, his foolhardy blundering – he's led us to this! You heard the Sampson woman. *Be sure your sins will find you out.* And Bothwell's already discovered them. Don't you see? This is Bothwell's vengeance. Agnes Sampson's his chosen weapon.'

How long before Mistress Katherine blamed Geillis too, as Agnes's apprentice? Geillis ventured, 'Bothwell's vengeance? For what offence?'

'For thinking he can be anything like Bothwell!' Mistress Katherine pressed the heels of her hands against her eyes in furious exhaustion. 'My husband thought he could wield power like Bothwell, with his idiot accusations. That trouble with Auchinleck – any fool could see that might lead back to Bothwell, and to us. So Bothwell sought to punish David for his stupidity – and yet it's Lucy who suffers! While David drinks wine and leers at servant girls!'

Geillis wondered who else Seton had abused. Had those girls merely borne it stoically, knowing this was the way of the world? Nothing to be done about it. Certainly not careless attempts at revenge that missed their target.

'The worst part,' Mistress Katherine continued, 'is how little I can do. Look at us. Sitting here, trying remedy after remedy, when no earthly cure can restore my Lucy. I can never hurt Bothwell or David as they are hurting me. As they are hurting her.'

Geillis wet her lips. 'We could try—'

'We've tried everything. Save running both men through with spears, and Lord knows I truly wish to. But that could only make things worse.' Mistress Katherine looked at Geillis. 'I once told you I would help you hurt my husband. But I cannot.'

'You don't have to think of helping me,' Geillis protested. 'Not now.' *Not after what I've done.*

'I do think of it. As I think about helping Lucy, and myself. All are impossible.' She ran a hand over her untidy hair. 'Whatever damage is done to a man, his women feel the pain. If my husband loses coin, status, respect, my household is pinched. However low he falls, I fall lower. As does our daughter. And all who rely on us for a roof and bread and safety. The last person to suffer is the man who caused the suffering.' She met Geillis's eyes. 'Hurting David would only hurt the three of us in this room.'

Geillis wanted to keen with remorse at the truth of her words.

'And that is also why,' Mistress Katherine continued, her voice suddenly poised, 'it will not be Bothwell who suffers for what he has done to Lucy.'

'No. It will be Agnes Sampson.'

Geillis whipped round at Seton's voice. He stood in the doorway, a week's worth of beard darkening his grim face. How long had he been there? How much had he heard?

'She did this to Lucy,' Seton said calmly. 'Everyone knows what she is.'

Geillis hardly dared ask. 'You believe Lucy's bewitched?'

Mistress Katherine shrugged helplessly. 'What else should we believe? Once I might have merely laughed at a pile of bones in the road. I would have scorned ignorant folk who think any drowned person has been taken by selkies. But now? You've tried every cure you know and Lucy's not healed. If it's not witchcraft that ravages her, what can it be?'

God, Geillis wanted to say. The same God who takes unborn babies so that their sister must bury them beneath tiny mounds of earth, who lets women die in childbed and the sons of drunkards waste away. Sickness had no rhyme or reason: the innocent were laid low as often as the corrupt. But how would blaming God comfort anyone? Better blame the devil – and since none could touch him, then blame his agents. Easier to blame witches than accept the truth. Except, for once, blaming witches was the truth. And it wasn't only Agnes who was responsible.

'Agnes Sampson hurt my child,' Seton said quietly. 'She must pay.'

Belief matters, Agnes had said. The Setons believed their daughter had been bewitched and that Bothwell and Agnes were to blame. Geillis could only tremble in her coward's silence, bereft of words to damn herself or defend Agnes.

They buried Lucy the day before Good Friday. Flowers bloomed in the kirkyard, a few late snowdrops giving way to daffodils, the trees soft with pink blossoms. Next to that gentle colour, the freshly dug grave seemed rough as an open wound. People wept. Not Lucy's father, who moved as if he were underwater and in two minds about whether to accept drowning. But her mother wept more than enough for both, all dignity forgotten in a tumult of grief. Other mourners shed tears too, if not so wretchedly. Even the servants cried.

Geillis couldn't. All those sleepless nights at Lucy's bedside had dried her eyes. Besides, if she'd wept, her tears would have been from guilt and fear as much as sorrow, and it would have sullied Lucy's funeral to shed such tears. Instead, she watched with fatigue-reddened eyes as clods of earth fell on that small coffin and knew she had no right to pray for forgiveness.

A week later, the summons came.

Geillis hadn't seen Chirnside since King James departed Scotland six months ago, leaving Bothwell as regent. From Chirnside's velvet sleeves and freshly starched ruff, she could tell those months had been profitable. Her own clothes were patched and darned, and she'd never owned a ruff. But if Lucy Seton's death was what it took to earn a reward, she didn't want one. As for what Bothwell had commanded her to do, she couldn't bear to think about it.

He hadn't summoned her to a tavern this time, but to Seton Palace: the estate where Lord Seton often played host to royal hunting parties.

The palace was the largest building she'd ever seen, with its four storeys and gleaming windows. How could anyone need so many rooms? What were they all for? Did nobles add chambers to their homes merely to impress others?

Chirnside saw Geillis's lips part and snorted as they rode into the busy stable yard. 'If you think this grand, you should see the earl's home at Crichton. He could change bedchambers twice a night and it would still take him a week to get through them all.' He swung down from his horse. 'Make haste. The earl's never pleased to be kept waiting. Since he's already displeased, irritating him further might be unwise.'

Geillis dismounted with a swiftness that shamed her, hurrying after Chirnside as he led her inside.

It wasn't the front entrance. She knew these weren't the grandest parts of the palace. And yet she'd never seen such splendour. While David Seton's corridors were merely a way of getting from one room to another, the corridors of Seton Palace were for flaunting wealth. The carved oak panels shone with polished crests. Portraits hung in golden frames; busts on elaborate pedestals flanked each door. Marble-topped tables basked in alcoves, not for writing or jointing chickens, but merely to showcase the blue and gold light pouring through stained glass windows. This house glowed with centuries of power. Geillis felt hideously out of her depth.

Chirnside stopped in front of a pair of doors carved with grapevines. Geillis wondered at the sight – no door she'd ever seen was thick enough to be whittled away for the sake of pretty patterns; even the kirk door could be blown open by a strong gust. It all came back to power: proving how much you had – or being reminded how little you possessed.

'He's waiting.' Chirnside's eyes glinted cruelly. He knocked three times, then twice more.

'Enter.'

Chirnside ushered her into a chamber more opulent than she could have imagined. Everything was soft: the rich tapestries, the bright carpets, the glow from a hearth as wide as Geillis was tall. Everything, except the man seated before the fire. Geillis remembered the last time she'd been alone with Bothwell. How she'd been made to pay afterwards.

'Geillis Duncan,' Bothwell said, gemstones glinting on his slowly tapping fingers; beneath his touch, a leashed mastiff with hooded eyes growled deeply. 'I hear you've been taking my name in vain.'

Geillis tried to imagine how Agnes would have weathered the earl's interrogation – without flinching, surely, for there were cliffs that would wear down faster than Agnes. 'Not … not in vain, my lord. In pursuit of spreading fear through Scotland – as you commanded.'

'David Seton is not Scotland.'

'But won't Scotland hear of his misfortunes? And—'

'Misfortunes!' Bothwell laughed coldly. 'Unfortunate indeed, for a sickly child to fall sick again and fail to recover. But this had nothing to do with fortune.'

'Won't everyone believe it did? That he's suffering because he dared to cross you …'

'I've no objection to Seton suffering.' Bothwell poured himself a glass of brandy from a crystal decanter. Geillis's throat felt dry at the sight; there was no chance she'd be offered any. If she so much as touched the vacant chair opposite Bothwell, the mastiff would prob-ably lunge at her. 'He overreached himself – a folly you'd do well not to replicate. But this is not the way I would have chosen.'

Nor I, Geillis thought. But what choice do you think I had left?

'I make no secret of my distaste for James Stuart,' Bothwell continued. 'But I'm not such a fool as to attack him directly – not yet. There are other ways to destroy a man.'

'How would you have destroyed Seton?' She hated the hunger in her own voice.

Bothwell smiled. 'I'd have let him destroy himself. Long before I tossed cursed detritus in his path, I'd have driven him to the edge of death with fear. He would have fled from shadows, shrieked at birdsong. To destroy a man, you destroy his mind.'

'So you'll drive James mad?'

'Precisely. A weapon that leaves no traces. There'll be no bloodstains on my clothes. But James's wounds will be no less fatal. He will be terrified, and a terrified king's no king at all.'

'Fear's a slow poison.' And while Seton was being poisoned, how many times would he attack her again?

'I'm a patient man.' Bothwell smiled again, fondling the mastiff's ears. 'I've been planning this for years. Long before his mother lost her head. I will not have my plans ruined because a gaggle of women choose reckless methods of revenge. Children will have to die – but not the offspring of petty fools.'

He meant James's future heirs – the babies Ilsa had told Geillis she must prevent being born. Geillis felt sick.

'Remember,' Bothwell said, his eyes burning so fiercely Geillis felt her flesh searing, 'you do not act for yourselves. You are mine, and you will do as I command.'

Almost the exact words Seton had used when he raped her. Geillis felt as deeply bruised by Bothwell staking his ownership of her life as Seton taking her body.

Bothwell sipped his brandy. 'James will return to Scotland any day now – though I don't expect his voyage to be easy.'

'Of course not,' Geillis said quietly, trying to dull the edge of bitterness in her voice.

'He will arrive in spring,' Bothwell observed. 'A time for planting what you will harvest in future. You will not seek your own petty vengeances. You will sow fear. Rumours and whispers, tales of danger and devilry. And when the time comes, you will reap the rewards.' He swirled his drink and Geillis thought of Agnes's fingers in the water atop Inchkeith; whatever spells Bothwell was working were far more sinister. 'I have another task for you, Geillis. One that Agnes cannot perform.'

'Why?' Her voice hunched low, a cowering dormouse of a question – let him decide she wasn't capable of this task. 'What can I do? She's braver, wiser—'

'And older.' Bothwell's smile gleamed like exposed bone. 'I usually prefer experience … but for this, I need a girl, not a woman.'

She stared in horror. He couldn't possibly mean to do what Seton had done to her. But there was nothing Bothwell wouldn't do.

He laughed scornfully. 'It's not your body I need, Geillis, but your wits. You will befriend Ilsa's sister, Margareta – and use this friendship to gain access to James's wife.'

The lady-in-waiting? 'But – surely Agnes should be the one. She's far more experienced with herbs.'

'After her teaching, no doubt your knowledge of herbs will suffice. Besides, I told you, Agnes doesn't make friends easily. This is why I need you – the Danish girl is far more likely to befriend a girl her own age.'

'Bessie,' Geillis blurted, offering up her childhood friend like a sacrificial lamb. 'People like Bessie—'

'I said I needed wits. Specifically, a midwife's wits. And nothing suits my purpose better than one who is a lonely, frightened orphan.'

On another's lips, those words might have sounded sympathetic. But on Bothwell's, each one sounded like a blade held over her bared neck.

'You and she are the same,' Bothwell continued. 'Why do you think I chose you to help me?'

Suddenly she remembered Ilsa's words on the corpse ship: *Bothwell was right about you.* Had he planned this all along? Had he been marshalling both Geillis and this Margareta lady like chess pieces, one black pawn and one white, at once opposites and identical? His unnatural foreknowledge, his cold calculation terrified Geillis.

'Befriend her,' Bothwell said. 'Help her – or convince her you bring aid. Even salvation. Make her trust you implicitly.'

'And then betray her?'

'Precisely.' He smiled again, and this time she felt the exposed bones were her own, and he could break them with a word. 'When the time is right, you will destroy her and the queen she serves. And then … the promised reward.'

She was bargaining with a devil; any reward would only come in exchange for her soul, already blackened with Lucy's death. The mastiff growled again; she smelt its hot breath as its jaws widened in readiness, waiting for Bothwell's command. She couldn't say no. Only now did she realize that Bothwell had always held her on a leash.

22

Scotland
May 1590

At last, they had arrived.

It hadn't been an easy voyage. September's abortive sailing had been far worse, but eight months' passage had dulled its edges. The memories of this journey, however, were nauseatingly fresh. Storms had assaulted the fleet again. Thrashing waves had tilted the vessels this way and that, hurling cannonballs of salt water across the decks. Once, Margareta had opened the hatch to see a sailor bowled over by a wave and dashed against the railing; bone had cracked and his shriek was shriller than wind.

It had been a long time before she'd dared step outside again.

But now they were on dry land. When she fixed her gaze on the horizon, no railings veered up towards it before bucking away – Leith's streets stayed blessedly still. She tried to tell her belly this, but the churning wouldn't stop; it was as though seawater had taken over her innards.

Ahead, James and Anna were stepping into Anna's silver carriage; for the courtiers, horses awaited close by. Hesitantly, Margareta approached a grey mare.

'Scottish horses don't bite.' John appeared at her side. 'No more than Danish ones, anyway. What's the matter?'

Margareta grimaced. 'I can't decide which would be more painful – jolting over these cobbles in a carriage or riding an unfamiliar horse with an unpadded saddle.'

'Definitely the carriage. Everyone will be gawping at the occupants and gossip will inflate each wince into a scowl. By the time James and Anna reach their destination, all of Leith will think their king hates either them or his new bride.'

'Don't jest about it.'

'I wasn't jesting.' His eyes were dark with warning. 'This doesn't feel like a town welcoming her king.'

John was right. As the royal party moved through Leith, it became increasingly pronounced. There should have been crowds cheering, children running forward to touch the horses' gleaming caparisons. Leith ought to have been wreathed in flowers, garlands dangling from inn signs and windowsills. Pageants should have greeted them in every square, comparing Anna to goddesses, biblical heroines, revered saints. Instead, what spectators there were kept their arms folded and their stares blunt. Paint peeled from walls; timbers were warped with damp; cobbles half-submerged in a morass of rotten vegetables and horse droppings. Unlike Helsingør's bright red roofs, Leith's grey houses were slated, and their drabness seemed yet another insult.

'Is Scotland always like this?' Elline's shocked whisper echoed Margareta's own anxieties.

Was this simply Scotland before summer transformed her? Dark nights and short days could break many spirits – but they hadn't looked like this in Helsingør or Oslo. Had the harvests been poor?

Or was this grim dissatisfaction a symptom of a greater sickness? A sign of how hostile Scotland felt towards her king – and now towards Anna too?

With all the ill will on the streets, Margareta had begun to doubt whether they would even eat that evening, let alone be given beds for the night – and their reception at Holyrood Palace was far from reassuring. The palace's situation didn't help; where Kronborg stood on a jutting foreland, backed by the sea, its curtain wall bolstered with strong bastions, Holyrood huddled in the midst of the city, surrounded by twisting, sloping streets on one side and hulking hills on the others, any of which could have concealed assailants until it was too late.

In the courtyard they were greeted by Privy Councillors, each wearing badges of office on their black velvet cloaks. As the men bowed to James and Anna, Vibeke elbowed Margareta.

'So this is what a court without a queen looks like. How long since his mother was pushed off her throne? Twenty-three years?' Vibeke pursed her lips disdainfully. 'A woman would have organized a better welcome. One that made us *feel* welcome, not like a horde of rats disgorged from the ship.'

'That cannot be the only reason,' Margareta said quietly. Even though they spoke in Danish, she had no desire for the other Danes to overhear. 'Queen Sophia's not the only reason hospitality's always offered in Kronborg.'

'You think Christian concerns himself with banquet menus and sleeping arrangements?' Vibeke sniffed. 'I tell you, Scotland's crying out for a queen.'

Could she be right? Had Scotland forgotten what a queen could do, in the tainted wake of their last, a woman who'd caused scandal and civil war? Or did they enjoy not having a powerful woman in their land?

At Holyrood's entrance, a tall, dark-haired man handed over a set of keys and the Great Seal to James. This had to be the regent. Handsome, confident, welcoming: he was everything James wasn't. And yet there was something about his beguiling appearance that unsettled Margareta, like the bait on a wolf pit: you wouldn't know the ferns and flowers concealed sharpened spikes until you'd already fallen into the trap.

'Bothwell,' James greeted him, and once more Margareta noted what a terrible actor he was. James's loathing couldn't have been plainer. 'I hope the country hasn't descended into anarchy under your rule.'

'Not entirely,' Bothwell said, with the easy grace of one wholly comfortable with their power. 'But no one's drawn up battle lines, so I deem my regency a success.'

Behind James, Chancellor Maitland's eyes narrowed. At Bothwell's left hand, a beardless youth laughed, overly eager to please the man who'd been pretending to be king for seven months. John had said the young Duke of Lennox had been intended to limit Bothwell's influence; evidently that had failed.

'We are glad to hear it,' James said. 'Having brought a wife into Scotland, I hope for peace throughout my realm.'

Bothwell laughed again. 'In my experience, marriage rarely leads to a harmonious home, particularly when the nursery starts to fill.'

He was smiling, jovial; his words could have been ribald teasing. But there was something barbed in Bothwell's eyes.

He couldn't know. How could anyone know, especially a man who'd never set eyes on Anna before?

'You won't have heard,' Bothwell continued. 'Whilst you were away, my wife bore a daughter. Our third healthy child, a little sister for my boys to protect.'

For a moment, James didn't speak. When he did, he sounded as if he were being strangled. 'Three heirs, Bothwell. You're a fortunate man.'

'The beginnings of a dynasty,' Bothwell said cheerfully. 'Do accept my sincere good wishes for your marriage, sire. I cannot tell you how I anticipate the advent of a prince in the royal nursery.'

His smile didn't reach his eyes. Neither did James's. It might have been spring in Scotland, but there was no warmth to be found in Holyrood.

Where their welcome into Scotland had been indifferent, Anna's coronation was lavish. Mythological tableaux lined the streets; minstrels played on every corner; dried rose petals were scattered underfoot as Anna and her train of nymphs proceeded through Edinburgh before entering Holyrood Abbey. Inside, the entire court bowed down as her silver taffeta gown was parted for her shoulders to be anointed with holy oil, and when the crown matrimonial was placed on Anna's fair hair, the applause could have been heard out at sea.

'No expense spared,' John said grimly that night. 'Even though there's little coin to be had. And no ritual left out, even Catholic superstitions.'

'The anointing.' Margareta had been surprised by that too. 'Why was that included?'

'Because James was anointed. Like his mother, like Elizabeth of England, like every monarch on these shores hoping to keep both throne and head. James is determined to make a point.'

Margareta nodded. 'He wants to enforce the legitimacy of his marriage. Which means he knows there are doubters. And he fears them.'

John met her anxious gaze. 'He's doing everything he can to establish Anna as the rightful queen of Scotland. Except the only thing that would succeed.'

In the midst of Edinburgh's bustle, Holyrood's deer park seemed like another world. Crags shouldered out of the ground, basalt ridges twisting through glens and hollows; gorse tangled at the shores of blue lochans. Riding up the great mound of Arthur's Seat, Margareta could see the castle on its black outcrop and the metallic glimmer of Nor Loch below, not so much a palace as a fortress. John had told her Edinburgh had been built atop dormant volcanoes; she couldn't think of anything more apt for a court simmering with secret conflicts.

Below, she saw James and his gentlemen galloping after the hounds. Not for them the appreciation of a view – and nor did Margareta believe that was why Anna had wished to ride up here. The Scotswomen assigned to Anna's household milled about at the foot of the hill, clearly longing to ride after the hunters, not loiter while their mistress gazed upon a city they'd seen a thousand times before.

'He was angry last night.' Anna spoke softly, fearing the winds might cast her words down to the Scotswomen.

'With you?'

Anna shrugged. 'At me, with me. I think I just happened to be there – bearing witness to his failure.'

Margareta winced at the allusion. 'Does he let you comfort him when he … fails? Just holding each other might help.'

Anna shook her head. 'If I reach for him, even just to brush his hand, he accuses me of being a whore. He wants me to lie still, in darkness, in my nightgown, while he fumbles and puffs and swears. If I ask him what's wrong, he just barks at me to stop fussing like an old woman.'

Margareta didn't know what to say. The problem wasn't Anna, but that Anna was a woman. In any other marriage this would have been sad, and yet would have been endured, for God didn't bless all marriage beds equally. But in the union of the king and queen of Scotland, it was disastrous – and dangerous.

'Ordinarily,' Anna said, 'he just rolls off me and stares at the ceiling. He prays, or drinks all the wine in the chamber, then calls for more. But last night …'

'What did he do?'

Anna closed her eyes; perhaps it was the skirling winds raking at them. 'He drove his fists against the bed. He stormed back and forth, pouring wine and drinking half, then hurling it onto the fire. I thought he'd injure himself, or me.'

'Why was he so angry? He cannot be surprised anymore – was it simply months' worth of frustration?'

Anna shook her head. 'Bothwell. You know what they say of him?'

'He stands to be James's heir.'

'Not just his heir. His replacement. And why not? His countess has given him three children, whereas I … Why wouldn't Scotland wish to replace us?'

'Because it would be treason,' Margareta said forcefully. 'It would lead to civil war. Bothwell might want that, but the rest of Scotland? Chancellor Maitland, the Duke of Lennox, the other earls? They won't stand for it.'

'Perhaps not now,' Anna conceded. 'But in six months? A year … five years? If Bothwell's countess produces three or four more babies in that time and I none, what will Scotland choose then?' She turned to Margareta. 'There must be something we can do. You have to help me.'

Horns sounded in triumph. Below them, the hunting party was returning, a bloody deer carcass trussed and dangling across a horse's back. At the head of the party, James rode alongside Alexander Lindsay, the newly created Baron Spynie, both men gore-spattered and laughing. As Margareta and Anna watched, James leaned out of his saddle to wrap an arm about Lindsay's waist and kiss his cheek, so close to Lindsay's mouth their lips brushed together. Lindsay tilted his head as if to return the kiss – but then caught himself. Had he glimpsed his lover's wife, or one of James's enemies?

'You see,' Anna murmured, her sigh brittle with longing. 'He isn't always incapable of love. Only with me.'

When she returned to the chamber she shared with John, a note lay atop the bed. Assuming it was for him, she sat down to exchange riding boots for slippers – then saw her own name on the parchment. Fingers taut with trepidation, she opened it.

Your sister wishes you to form a new acquaintance. Come to Barbara Napier's house on Cowgate after dark two nights from now. Come alone.

It wasn't signed. It was the kind of note that couldn't be signed.

Margareta looked around the chamber. Nothing seemed disturbed, nothing missing. But someone had been here. Someone who knew Ilsa – who knew what she was to Margareta. In the chamber that ought to have been her refuge, her skin crawled with fear.

She hadn't the faintest idea who Barbara Napier was. She might have learned the Scottish tongue, but she didn't know nearly enough Scotswomen, and as Margareta moved through the Edinburgh streets, wrapped in her blackest cloak, she realized what a hindrance this was.

John would have known. And she could have asked, and yet, where Ilsa was involved, Margareta didn't want to involve John. Whatever labyrinth she was about to enter, she had to negotiate its twists and traps alone.

Cowgate was a well-to-do street. Its cobbles had been recently swept; the upper storeys of the houses didn't tilt forward, pinching the night sky into a black vein, but rose serenely up. Strains of music emerged from one house: lutes, viols – far smoother than the chants barging out of Canongate taverns.

Which was Barbara Napier's? The note hadn't said, and she didn't dare ask. A lone cloaked woman with a Danish accent abroad at night would certainly arouse suspicion.

'Lady Margareta?'

A shadow detached itself from a nearby wall and suddenly a girl stood before her.

'Who asks for her?'

The shutters behind the girl cast arrows of firelight across a pale face. Red hair was thrust back beneath a brown worsted hood, and hazel eyes held Margareta's before jerking away. A girl who wanted to see but not be seen, and to be bold but feared she would never be bold enough. Margareta would have known those feelings anywhere: she saw them daily in the mirror.

'Geillis Duncan,' the girl said, and Margareta felt a jolt of recognition. So this was the girl who'd reminded Ilsa of Margareta. *A thoughtful, lonely, awkward thing.* Despite Ilsa's description, she'd half-expected someone like Ilsa – fey, wild, fiercely determined to be noticed. But there was nothing strange or intimidating about Geillis. As she lifted a self-conscious hand to tuck hair behind her ears, Margareta saw her fingers were stained green, probably from herb-gathering, and she found the thought oddly comforting.

Geillis glanced behind Margareta into the shadows. 'How do I know you're Lady Margareta?'

'The same way I know you're Geillis Duncan – we must take it on trust. Or – tell me something about Ilsa.'

Geillis bit her lip. 'I admire her … willpower. Although …'

Margareta almost laughed, nerves and understanding making her lightheaded. 'She frightens me too sometimes.' She glanced up at the house. 'I take it this is Mistress Napier's home, then?'

A shadow passed over Geillis's face. 'Yes, my lady. They're waiting for you upstairs.'

They? As she followed Geillis inside and up a flight of oak stairs, Margareta wondered how many people she was expected to meet.

Five doors led off the landing; Geillis pointed her to the one straight ahead. At the back of the house, Margareta noted. Further from any would-be eavesdroppers.

Inside, tapestries covered two walls, depicting Diana ordering Actaeon's destruction and Circe transforming Odysseus's men into swine. Velvet curtains and carved oaken panels covered another wall; the fourth was dominated by a fireplace, above which hung a portrait of one of the women seated before it. She was older than her picture – Margareta glimpsed grey hairs beneath a pearl-ornamented headdress, and the lines between her brows had deepened. But she was still attractive, in the way that good food and comfortable living could keep you. She had to be Mistress Napier, but what of her companion? She was also finely dressed, though her taut shoulders and tighter lips suggested she was far from satisfied with her life.

'Lady Margareta,' Mistress Napier said, spreading her hands in ostentatious welcome. 'Thank you for coming. Allow me to introduce our party. I am Barbara Napier. This is Euphame MacCalzean, and—'

'And I'm Agnes Sampson.'

Margareta wheeled round in shock. Behind her stood a tall woman, so imposing that, if not for her grey hair, Margareta would almost have thought Diana had stepped out of her tapestry. She hadn't heard the door open, or any footsteps – how had this woman arrived so silently? And who else might burst in on them?

Barbara cleared her throat. 'Agnes. I wasn't expecting you—'

'So early?' Agnes's smile mirrored the goddess again; she might have been watching hounds strip flesh from bone. 'I felt the occasion called for a swift ride. Though I find myself in need of refreshment.' Her eyes lighted on Geillis. 'Wine, I think.'

'Let me ring for—'

'I've dismissed them.' Agnes cut Barbara off again. 'Wouldn't want anyone bursting in on us now, would we?'

Barbara was speechless. Euphame was either suppressing laughter or rage. Into the silence, Geillis mumbled, 'I'll see if there are any honey cakes too.'

As the girl scuttled away, Margareta half-wished to flee with her – but she couldn't help being fascinated by this new arrival. At Barbara's limp gesture, Agnes swept to sit beside her. Sinking into her own chair, Margareta suddenly noticed Agnes's clothing; it was only slightly less worn and faded than Geillis's. Yet where Geillis had been given a servant's task, this woman sat imperiously with the two in damask and velvet as if she were not only their equal, but their superior. Who was she – and why had the others tried to keep her away?

Before Agnes could seize command of the conversation again, Margareta spoke. 'Why did you ask me here?'

Barbara patted at her skirts, as if asking the rich weave to remind her that this was her home, and she'd summoned Margareta. 'Why, your sister wished it. You are so far from home – surely it must be comforting to meet people associated with dear Ilsa!'

Ilsa, Margareta knew, would despise this woman with her wafting hands and feeble, sycophantic lies. Had Barbara ever met her? Geillis's assessment of Ilsa had rung far truer.

'My sister's acquaintances and mine rarely move in the same spheres.'

'But how sad! Let us remedy that now. Euphame and I would be only too delighted to help you know and love Scotland as we do.'

'In return for what?'

Barbara flinched at her bluntness. 'We wish to serve our queen—'

'And what else?'

Euphame MacCalzean leaned forward. 'You may take serving the queen for granted – but women like us cannot. Queen Anna's support would be a prize beyond jewels.'

Women like us. If they knew Ilsa, surely they knew Margareta had always stood on the outside of the court looking in. But Ilsa had never understood that this was a curse as much as a gift, and suddenly Margareta had the strange sensation of kinship with these women.

'Why do you need Queen Anna's support?'

'For justice,' Euphame said. 'My husband's family seek to wrest my property from me – but with royal favour, I could claim what is rightfully mine.'

'To clear my name,' Barbara said. 'I served the Countess of Angus until I lost her favour – no fault of my own, I assure you. I would prove myself more than worthy of serving a queen.'

'We have been wronged,' Euphame said. 'And we seek not vengeance so much as to rise above petty spite and be recognized for our true selves.'

Were they telling the truth? Margareta wanted to believe them – another reason to be on her guard.

'I shall inform Queen Anna of your offer. But she already has many ladies helping her improve her knowledge of the Scottish court.'

'The court is not Scotland.' It was Agnes who spoke. The others twitched – Barbara Napier swallowed hastily and Euphame MacCalzean's eyes jerked. Were they afraid of Agnes? Why would they fear a woman of her standing?

Margareta couldn't help gazing at Agnes with wary fascination. 'Why do you say that, Mistress Sampson?'

Agnes smiled. 'Because it's the truth. I imagine other countries like dismissing our kingdom as a little wilderness tucked away in the corner of maps, all mountains and mists. A country filled with people as miserable as the weather, led by men who wouldn't know warmth if you set them on fire. But that isn't my Scotland.'

'Yours? Do you fancy yourself her ruler?'

Agnes laughed. 'I fancy many wouldn't think me drastically worse than her current monarch. Perhaps you might be among them.'

Margareta bristled. 'I've served Queen Anna since we were children. She will always have my loyalty.'

'Ah yes, poor Anna,' Agnes said. 'Tied to a man whose affections lie elsewhere.'

'Euphame and I are more than aware,' Barbara simpered knowingly, as if Agnes hadn't spoken. 'It can't be easy for a beautiful queen like Anna, being married to a king who prefers men.'

'Especially a certain vice chamberlain with a talent for riding horses,' Euphame drawled, her emphases laden with innuendoes. In an uncomfortably accurate impersonation of James's reedy voice, she cooed, *'Alexander! Alexander!'*

She'd told Sophia no one else knew. How had the gossip wormed its way into Edinburgh's streets? 'How did you know that?'

'Oh, the king's favourites are common knowledge among circles such as ours.' Barbara toyed with her necklace, smirking.

'Yes,' said Margareta, choosing to ignore the pomposity of Barbara's tone, 'but how did you know he called Lindsay's name on his wedding night? That he couldn't—'

Margareta bit her lip, as all three Scotswomen stared at her. She shouldn't have said that. The gleam in their eyes made that abundantly clear. They'd already known about Alexander, but not about the wedding night, or that James's love went so deep.

'Are you suggesting,' Agnes said slowly, 'that the king's marriage was never consummated?'

'I can help Anna.'

Geillis spoke quietly from the doorway – yet in the stunned silence, everyone turned at the sound of her voice.

'How?' Margareta whispered. 'James can barely stand to touch her.'

Geillis was carrying a silver tray laden with a jug and glasses. As she approached the table by the fireplace, it rattled audibly – she was shaking. 'I …' Her voice was barely audible above the tinkling of glass. 'Perhaps—'

'I'll prepare you potions,' Agnes cut in stridently, 'that will inflame him so much he'll be unable to help fulfilling his kingly duties.'

'But …' Margareta hesitated. 'He'll be furious if he knows what they are.'

'Then it's up to you to keep them secret,' said Agnes. 'You must ensure he drinks whatever I provide. Can you do that?'

Margareta turned to Geillis, who was now looking at the floor, nervously pouring wine, then looked back at Agnes. There was something about her that made her yearn to deserve her trust.

Margareta nodded. 'I'll make sure he takes your potions.'

'As for Anna,' Agnes continued, 'I can give you remedies to aid conception and, should a child take root in her belly, help him stay rooted. Geillis will bring them to you.' She flapped her hand, rejecting the wine that Geillis was holding out to her. The curt gesture sent hurt darting across Geillis's face, chased swiftly by what Margareta suspected was an anxiety to please Agnes, and Margareta recognized the changing emotion; whenever Anna gave her a brusque command, it stung, and all the more because Anna wouldn't have noticed her own abruptness. 'It will take a day or two to gather herbs and such-like,' Agnes went on, oblivious. 'Meet Geillis in three days.'

'Where?'

'Why not in Holyrood itself? Give her your token and they'll have to let her in.'

She made it sound so simple. And yet … This couldn't be all that Ilsa had wanted. Her sister couldn't have known about James's predicament. What was Margareta missing?

Geillis was watching her beneath lowered lashes: deference concealing intelligence. Was there another reason this girl wanted admitting into Holyrood? What could a midwife's assistant hope to accomplish in the palace?

They were playing a dangerous game. But to turn away from the board now would mean never knowing what her opponent's strategy had been. Sophia would never have walked away.

'Very well.' Margareta set down her untouched wine. 'Here's my token.' She slid a ring off her finger – one of the few her father hadn't drunk or gambled away – and Geillis reached out shyly to take it. With that, Margareta stood to leave, batting aside Barbara's wheedling protestations that she sit awhile longer. She'd had quite enough of these strange women already.

'Oh, and Lady Margareta?'

She was halfway across the room when she paused, disconcerted by the amiable tone that had crept into Agnes's voice.

'How far gone are you?'

For a moment, Margareta didn't understand – was Agnes referring to the distance to the door? But that question, to a woman, could only ever mean one thing.

She'd thought it seasickness. The waves had tested everyone's bellies. After reaching Holyrood, she'd assumed the Scottish food disagreed with her. But how long since her last courses? Six weeks? Seven?

Margareta breathed out and turned back to Agnes. 'How can you tell?'

Agnes smiled. 'There isn't a woman in Scotland who knows more about children than I do – getting, carrying, or birthing them.'

'You have children of your own?'

Something flickered across Agnes's face, as if a lance had thrust a visor back, exposing raw flesh. 'Aye. But it's other women's babes I know most about. I reckon you'll be letting out your fine gowns before Michaelmas and spending Advent in your confinement.'

'You know that too? How?'

'Trade secrets.' Agnes raised her eyebrows mockingly. 'There are signs for those who know how to look.'

'It's a special time,' Euphame said, her sharpness suddenly softening. 'When life begins to grow – like carrying the sweetest secret inside you. Treasure it, Lady Margareta. I hope for your sake your child thrives.'

Margareta nodded, half-dazed. Her hands drifted to her belly; could there be a little life growing in there?

'You must have my lace caps,' Barbara trilled. 'I would be honoured to gift them – my own handiwork, of course—'

'Lace caps can wait,' Agnes said. 'My herbs come first. Expect Geillis in three days.'

As she turned to leave, Margareta glimpsed Geillis. Still silent, she was staring at the ring she clutched. She might have been fascinated – or she might have been avoiding everyone else's eyes.

Outside, the night air furled around Margareta like a black veil; she fought the urge to brush it away, as if she could clear eyes and thoughts with one palm stroke.

What had she done? The thought nagged at her that John would be shocked and Sophia disappointed – but why? She'd met with women who could help Anna. Yes, she'd given them private information, but they'd given her hope. This was part of spying: you had to give in order to receive. And guilt was just another integral part.

'Lady Margareta!'

For a terrifying moment she thought someone had followed her from Holyrood – but surely meeting respectable Edinburgh wives and a local midwife was nothing shameful?

But it wasn't anyone from court; it was Geillis, hurrying across the cobbles.

'What is it?'

The girl wasn't remotely out of breath; her wiry frame proved she was used to hard work. Yet something made her hesitate. 'I wanted … to suggest you eat plenty of red meat, to help your child grow strong. And start brewing ginger tea when you feel nauseous, with a little honey if it helps. I can bring you some ginger when I bring you the herbs for the king and queen. You needn't pay me any more for it.'

A servant girl with nothing, worrying about the comfort of the queen's lady-in-waiting? The irony made Margareta laugh aloud; it echoed like a raven's caw in the empty street. 'Why should you care to offer me your services unpaid?'

'Because …' Geillis searched the shadows, as if for answers. 'I enjoy helping women and their bairns to grow healthy. And having children, or not having them, has hurt all of us. Even those two – they're too proud to let their hurt show. But Euphame's lost every son she ever bore, her girls are sickly, and her husband's family are set on robbing her of her property, even though Master Patrick's brains are thicker than bogs. As for Barbara, she was thrown out by the Countess of Angus after the earl … made advances. The earl blamed her – easier that way.' Bitterness twisted Geillis's face. 'And the consequences nearly killed Barbara. Only Agnes could save her, but not the baby.'

Was that why Barbara and Euphame wanted to help her – and Anna? But there was something else Geillis wasn't saying. Invasive as it felt, Margareta asked, 'What about you?'

Geillis hesitated. 'My mother lost child after child. I had to bury all my siblings under a tree.'

There was such loneliness in Geillis's voice, a pain that gaped around ghosts no one else knew had existed, much less remembered. The same pain Margareta felt when she remembered her childhood home.

'Then I'm grateful.' Margareta shivered, suddenly desperate to be away and indoors. 'Perhaps before noon, three days hence?'

Geillis looked as if she wanted to say something else. But she merely nodded. 'I'll see you then.'

As Margareta hurried back to Holyrood, she pressed a hand to her belly and the new fears and hopes coiling within.

23

Lady Margareta's ring gleamed in the firelight. Stirring the tisane with one hand, Geillis examined the jewel: a ruby the size of her thumbnail.

She'd never seen anything so costly. This could have fed a family for years, built Agnes's cottage at least five times over. Even such a ring as this. The band was scratched, as if one of its owners had carelessly scraped it against stone. Perhaps all the gentry were so heedless of their riches; they'd have dozens of other trinkets. Whereas Geillis could never dream of owning anything so fine.

Unless Bothwell was true to his word. If he did reward them as he'd promised, would Geillis one day have a golden ring of her own, with gemstones that glowed like stars? Hardly likely, given that she'd failed to complete a sentence when trying to deceive Lady Margareta.

'Daydreaming?'

Agnes's wry word-prod called Geillis back to her cottage. To the knowledge that the fingers holding the ring were stained green from herb-gathering, that her hands had calluses rough as shingle. Not like Lady Margareta's hands, which might have been sculpted out of finest white beeswax, their nails perfect half-moons, unchipped, unsoiled, unscarred.

Just once, Geillis thought, I'd like to be the woman others envy.

'If that steeps overlong, it won't be half as efficacious.'

Geillis stirred the tisane. 'I thought a while longer.'

'Did you think that before you started mooning over that ring, or after?' Agnes left off chopping tansy and peered into the pot. 'Almost done, I reckon. Don't drift off again.'

'I won't.' Geillis tucked the ring into her apron pocket and stirred pointedly. 'Agnes ...' Geillis hesitated. 'Why are we giving this to King James? I thought we'd give them herbs to make things worse, not better.'

'Exactly.'

'But—'

'I could hardly say that to Margareta. You saw the adoring look on her face when she spoke of the queen. We'd never persuade her to give Anna anything harmful.'

'Then how—'

'She won't know what she's really giving Anna – or what she's taking herself.' Agnes gave Geillis a condescending glare. 'Honestly, Geillis, I thought Margareta the innocent fool, not you – not having an inkling about her own pregnancy and revealing that nugget about Alexander Lindsay. She's helped us without knowing already, and she'll continue to do so. Margareta will give Anna medicine for her husband, and for herself, and none of them will know what they're taking.'

'But this tisane,' Geillis objected. 'Won't it ... work?'

Agnes smiled. 'James will take genuine remedies. After all, the male side of things is a little harder to falsify, and from what we've heard, he needs all the help he can get. But Anna won't be taking parsley seeds, or valerian, or meadowsweet. Margareta will, so none can say my remedies don't work, only that she was a fool to muddle them. Instead, Anna will be taking mugwort, wormwood, and tansy. Should she conceive at all, her children will wither and die in her womb – and so will James's hopes of an heir.'

'How can you say such things about a baby?' Geillis didn't dare add, *And while smiling.* 'We're supposed to help babies live – to help their mothers live. What Bothwell's commanded goes against everything you've taught me! I don't understand why you want to be the one who does it!'

Agnes divided the tansy among small twists of paper. 'To help you, of course. Whatever Bothwell's decided, I can tell you haven't the heart or stomach to kill James's children. Especially after that sorry business with Lucy Seton. Now I've prepared the herbs for you, all you need to do is deliver them.'

Like a carrier pigeon, Geillis thought, and she would have been angered if she hadn't been so desperate for any way to absolve herself. 'But what if Bothwell finds out?'

'From whom?' Agnes wiped her knife clean. 'Certainly neither of us. As for Euphame and Barbara, do you think they care? They didn't address a single word to you – I imagine they've already forgotten your name. So you can let me take this burden.'

'Then ...' Geillis hesitated, wary of prodding Agnes much more. 'When you started teaching me about herbs, this wasn't your plan all along? You didn't intend to make me ...'

A murderer.

Agnes didn't answer at first, busying herself with sheathing her knife, blowing shreds of tansy off the table. Eventually, she said, 'No. That was never my intention.' She stood abruptly. 'Blossom needs fresh straw.'

Left alone, Geillis stared at the twists of paper. Even delivering them was cruel enough. If she went to meet Margareta, if she killed the queen's baby, she would never forgive herself.

But if she failed, Bothwell would never forgive her.

What choice did she have? Feeling sick, Geillis reached for the herbs.

Geillis was convinced they wouldn't let her in. The guards would take one look at the ring, then at her homespun dress, and laugh. 'As if a lady would give you her jewellery,' they'd scoff. 'You stole this. It's the tolbooth for you, girl.' And she'd be marched away and flung into a dark cell.

At Holyrood's gates, she approached the youngest guard, his chin pocked with cuts from inept shaving. Geillis drew the ring out from her apron, hoisted her basket and her head higher.

'I'm come to see Lady Margareta Wemyss.'

The guard swallowed nervously, glancing from ring to Geillis to the guard on the opposite side of the gate. She'd never thought men could feel as anxious and out of place as she did. 'Here – McHugh, is this Lady Margareta's token?'

A guard, grizzled from decades buffeted by wind and rain, peered over. 'Damned if I know. Which one's Lady Margareta? Can't tell these Danish wenches apart.'

'Who's the fair one who's always giggling?'

'Something like Ellen? What about the small one who looks like she's eaten lemons?'

'She's the black-haired one,' Geillis said, hoping her sigh was imperiously impatient – an Agnes sigh.

'I see,' McHugh said, trying to reassert his authority. 'And what business have you with Lady Margaret?'

'Lady Margareta,' Geillis corrected him witheringly, 'and it's women's business.'

The younger guard went scarlet. McHugh pushed the gate open hurriedly. 'Queen's ladies usually walk in the garden at this hour. Be on your way.'

Geillis slipped through.

Here she was. Geillis Duncan, fisherman's daughter, meeting the queen's lady-in-waiting in a royal palace. She wanted to laugh – but laughing in a palace seemed almost sacrilegious, and she didn't dare. It took all her courage to continue towards where she guessed the gardens might be. Sure enough, as she rounded the corner of the palace, the vista softened and colours bloomed before her. Not one herb in sight. The most useful plant in Holyrood's garden was the lavender edging the paths. No doubt they had a royal herb garden elsewhere, or traders queuing eagerly at the gates.

The queen and her ladies were walking between the lavender rows. Ambling without a destination. Was this what they did all day?

Geillis watched as Queen Anna wandered nearer. Her gown was stiff with seed pearls, its train smudged green from the damp grass; Geillis pitied the laundress who'd have to fish in her tub for scrubbed-off jewels later. The queen was young – younger than Geillis, with the silken skin of someone who always had a carriage awaiting her summons.

Geillis had tried to drown this woman.

It was one thing targeting an imagined woman, but seeing this girl-queen in the flesh, Geillis realized how delicate she was, how innocent. And here Geillis was, about to hand over potions that would murder Anna's unborn children.

Lady Margareta was walking with Anna, a raven beside a snowdrop. Catching Geillis's eye, she indicated a rose bower in the corner nearest Geillis. Stooping, Margareta murmured something in Anna's ear; the queen nodded before continuing her meaningless circuit. Her ladies glanced briefly at Margareta as she peeled away from their group. As they disappeared among flowers, Margareta reached the bower and ducked beneath an arch of thorns and petals. Not a hiding place if anyone truly sought you, but enough to fool casual glances.

'Well?' Margareta was abrupt, agitation fraying her patience. 'Have you the items we spoke of?'

Geillis nodded. 'Those wrapped in white cloth are for the king, brown for the queen, and green for you.'

'How often should they take theirs? Daily? Or only when—' Margareta broke off, blushing.

'Only when,' Geillis said. 'For him, that is. Once the queen conceives, she should take a dose every morning. For the first three months.'

'Three? But I thought it was too late for me to take the same herbs as Anna, and I'm less than three months gone.'

She was sharp, this Danish woman.

'The dosage must be built up over time,' Geillis invented. 'Otherwise it could prove dangerous.'

'So Anna might be at risk?'

Margareta was perilously close to prodding the truth out of Geillis, and she fought the urge to confess everything.

'This medicine will strengthen Anna's womb so she can better protect a child. But there are no guarantees when it comes to carrying babies. All I can offer you is a stronger chance.'

Margareta's frown deepened as Geillis spoke – and yet she nodded thoughtfully. Holding out a gloved hand for the basket, she said, 'I wish I understood more about herbs.'

'It's useful,' Geillis agreed, wondering if she could ask for the basket back: it was sturdy wicker, and she was loath to sacrifice it.

'My mother was a midwife,' Margareta said suddenly. She twisted the cloth wrapping the medicines. 'My foster mother, that is. I've thought of her often since discovering I'm with child. I wish she were here to advise me.'

'She's in Denmark?'

Margareta plucked again at the green cloth before replying. 'We lost touch when I joined Anna's court.'

A painful rift, if Geillis were any judge. But she dared not probe too closely. 'Isn't Ilsa skilled in midwifery? Couldn't you write to her?'

Margareta frowned yet again. 'Ilsa and I aren't as close as we once were either.'

'But if you want advice ...'

'She's across the sea. It would take weeks to get a reply, and by then I might not need her advice anymore, or I might have a thousand other questions. Besides, Ilsa hardly invites confidences.'

Geillis pictured the fey woman on the ship, her chilly laughter. 'I can see that.'

'You've met Ilsa – you'll know how ... single-minded she can be. Ilsa can never hide that. Nor would she wish to.'

'If more people were open about who they are, the world might be a better place,' Geillis said. Herself included – she avoided looking at the basket on Margareta's arm.

Margareta smiled bitterly. 'I doubt that. What's beneath the surface is often uglier than we could imagine. Unsaid words, secrets we cannot share. Exposing these things would mean exposing our very selves. Few are brave enough to do that.'

'Then you think Ilsa's brave?'

'On my kinder days. I think her reckless most of the time. Whereas she thinks I'm more cautious than a mother hen.' Margareta looked Geillis in the eye. 'Which are you? Brave to the point of carelessness – or does your own shadow make you start?'

Geillis hesitated. 'Neither. I wish I could be brave, but common sense tells me caution's wiser.'

Margareta nodded. 'And yet, for a woman to aspire to wisdom ... some would say that's the most foolish notion of all.'

'More foolish not to.'

Margareta smiled ruefully. 'That's what Ilsa would say.' She tucked the basket into the crook of her arm and frowned again. 'Be careful, Geillis. To be like my sister is a dangerous way to live.' Then she spun on her heel and walked away towards the palace.

Geillis stood alone among the roses, the ring weighing heavy on her empty hand.

All the women she'd envied – Agnes, Ilsa, Margareta – had reason to be afraid. But only Margareta was. Why? And if wealthy women were afraid, then someone like Geillis ought to be terrified.

The coastal path back to Tranent was quiet. Most people went to Edinburgh and Leith at sunrise and came back by sundown; Geillis, trudging along under the midday sun, had only her thoughts for company.

Ilsa had said Margareta and Queen Anna were as sheltered as roses. Yet although Margareta knew little about herbs and childbirth, she knew enough about life to be suspicious. As for the queen, was there steel beneath her silk? If Ilsa had underestimated both, did that mean she'd also underestimated King James? Had Bothwell?

What did Geillis know of James? From her own eyes, almost nothing. From gossip, that he was unwise, incapable of siring an heir. He was the last of a cursed line. Yet he was still alive. She remembered Bothwell sneering that people had been trying to kill James since before he was even born, as if this proved James's weakness. But couldn't it also show that James had a knack for survival – that he was far stronger than they'd given him credit for?

Hoofbeats startled her out of her tangling thoughts. Instinctively, she darted onto the verge. Most riders assumed you'd prefer to move than be trampled, and rarely slowed down.

But this rider did.

Bothwell. He was alone, and her heart sank – no leisurely hawking expedition, this. An earl alone on the Tranent road could only mean secrets, and danger for those he sought. He looked her up and down. 'What happened to the horse I gave you?'

She shrugged, ashamed. 'Seton rides her now.'

'Of course he does,' Bothwell snorted. 'Never was a man so convinced of his own grandeur on so little evidence.'

Had she imagined Bothwell might command Seton to leave her horse alone? There'd been promises of rewards, but never that they would keep them.

Bothwell eyed her irritably. 'Returning empty-handed from Edinburgh, I see. Unusual.'

He was right. She ought to have bought ribbons or horse harness, something to pretend her errand was for the Seton household. 'Perhaps I was selling, not buying.'

'Even Seton's not so witless as to let a girl carry his coin about the countryside without someone to guard her against unscrupulous bandits.'

Geillis rubbed Margareta's ring inside her pocket; it hadn't occurred to her that someone might try to take it from her. 'You're the only person I've seen on my journey, my lord.'

He laughed. 'And I'm the most unscrupulous of all. How did you like Holyrood?'

She couldn't help her lips parting in shock, and that made him laugh again.

'Come now, Geillis. It's my business to know your business. Our bargain was that you'd tell me everything you know – but you aren't a particularly diligent correspondent, are you?'

He was disappointed. Her safety depended on not disappointing him – on him never finding out about her secret agreement with Agnes. But he couldn't possibly know, unless Agnes told him. 'I'm sorry, my lord.'

'Then atone. Come – ride behind me.'

Unable to refuse, Geillis took his hand and he swung her up behind him. His back was broad and strong, muscles gained from sword drills, not honest hard work. The waist she reluctantly held was trim; beneath soft leather and velvet, she could feel concealed hilts. Until then, she'd been painfully aware of her own worn clothes, the sweat beneath her armpits. Now she was only aware of how breakable her skin was.

Bothwell clicked to his horse and they rode on. 'Tell me about the Danish women.'

Geillis swallowed. 'They're worried. There's no chance of Queen Anna conceiving.'

'So James cannot perform the act? Can't say I'm surprised.'

'Even if he does, we've given the queen tonics that will destroy a child. She'll miscarry within weeks.'

'Good. Will she suspect?'

'I don't think so. She and her ladies know so little of these things. They'll think they've done everything they should have ...'

'Yet still God forsakes the Stuarts.'

'And the queen will think that even more because ...' Even speaking of Margareta to Bothwell seemed a betrayal: one step closer to the deed he'd commanded. 'Lady Margareta is with child.'

'Ah yes. I must commiserate with John.'

'You know her husband?' She'd assumed the Scottish court was neatly divided into James's faction and Bothwell's, with no one crossing the line.

'John Wemyss is a useful man to know. His wife's pregnancy is even more useful – her growing belly will remind everyone of the flatness of Anna's. And it provides you with the opening I desired. Make sure the Wemyss child thrives. Take her more potions, make yourself indispensable.'

'But I'm not a court midwife! I'm not even the one Tranent folk ask for – it's Agnes they want!'

'Lady Margareta must want you. She must trust you. Remember my instructions.'

There was no arguing with him. 'Yes, my lord.'

'Good girl.'

Like patting a dog's head. He'd kick her just as carelessly.

They were approaching the turn for the Setons' house. Geillis shifted in the saddle. 'I can walk from here, my lord. I don't want to take you away from your business.'

Bothwell snorted. 'My business is with the Setons. David's been foolhardy again.'

By the time Geillis had splashed her face with water, donned a clean apron and ferried wine into Seton's study, they were all seated. Bothwell was in the most comfortable chair while the Setons twitched anxiously.

'Thank you, Geillis,' Mistress Katherine said. 'No need to wait.'

Witnessing Seton's humbling only led to one thing; gladly, Geillis dropped into a curtsey and turned to leave.

'Best Geillis remains.'

'We can pour the wine ourselves,' Mistress Katherine protested. 'Geillis has other tasks.'

Bothwell curled his lip. 'Indeed. Therefore, she remains.'

So much for Mistress Katherine's attempt to protect Geillis from the inevitable. Bothwell wanted to humiliate Seton, and her eyes would be the mirror in which he saw himself shamed. All she could do was pour wine and retreat to a corner.

'I thought,' Bothwell said slowly, 'I'd made my opinion of your gossiping perfectly plain.'

Seton ground his teeth. 'You did, my lord.'

'Yet here you are. Spreading rumours. Dangerous rumours that have landed one of my most valued assets in the Haddington tolbooth again.'

'She deserved it!' Seton spat. 'After everything she's done!'

Geillis froze. Did they mean Agnes? But she'd seen Agnes only yesterday, mixing herbs. She could barely have returned home before being arrested.

'She did nothing,' Bothwell countered. 'A sickly child sickened and died. That's all.'

'You know that's not true!' Mistress Katherine hissed. 'Agnes Sampson killed our daughter with witchcraft. Now she'll die for it!'

'But your daughter wasn't the target.'

Mistress Katherine jerked, confused. 'That's irrelevant. She's guilty, and the guilty must be condemned.'

'Then your husband should suffer. After all, his cowardice led to your daughter's affliction. If your daughter's death is anyone's fault, it's his.'

'You dare sit there,' Seton growled, 'in my house, drinking my wine, blaming me for Lucy's death? Watch your step, Bothwell.'

The knife was at his throat before he'd finished speaking. Seton's wine fell from his hand, spilling across the rushes.

'One more word,' Bothwell whispered, 'and the mere motion of your own throat will be enough. Do not imagine I will hesitate. Unlike Agnes, you are of very little value to me. Your death would trouble me no further than a sullied cuff. Do you understand?'

Seton tried to nod; blood beaded on his throat and his eyes bulged wide.

'Mistress, answer for your husband and yourself – as you usually do.'

Mistress Katherine's knuckles were white around the arms of her chair. 'We understand, my lord.'

'Glad to hear it.' Bothwell wiped his blade on Seton's doublet and sauntered back to his chair. 'Retract your accusations. Tell the sheriff of Haddington you spoke out of grief. Declare Agnes an upstanding member of your community, you'd be lost without her. And you'll compensate Agnes for the inconvenience you've put her to.'

Seton's hand fluttered towards his throat. 'Yes, my lord.'

'We meant no offence, my lord,' Mistress Katherine said, fighting for composure. 'We thought it would help. You wanted Scotland to be afraid of witchcraft.'

'Agnes Sampson locked up isn't an object of fear,' Bothwell snapped. 'Scotch these rumours. Deny everything. Or you'll be the ones in Haddington tolbooth, and no one will seek to free you.'

'Yes, my lord,' Seton mumbled.

'Well?' Bothwell arched an eyebrow. 'What are you waiting for? Go. Now.'

As they filed out meekly, Seton cast a look of disgust at Geillis. He would make her pay later.

Bothwell held out his cup. She hurried to refill it.

'Go back to Lady Margareta,' he said, sipping the wine. 'The moment she suspects, I need to know. And consider, Geillis, whose hands prepared those herbs.' He looked up at her, and she saw icy ruthlessness in his eyes. 'This household has already betrayed me enough. Should you ever be tempted to follow suit, just remember which of us has attempted to kill royalty.'

He didn't know she'd already disobeyed him. But that only made the danger worse. She could only say what they all said to him. 'Yes, my lord.'

24

A child. Before the year's end, she'd have a child.

At first she hadn't believed it, and Margareta told herself this was why she hadn't told John. After all, why should she believe a stranger, however authoritative her pronouncements? But as the weeks wore on and her courses didn't come, Margareta had to admit Agnes had spoken truthfully.

Sitting up in bed while John drowsed in the early morning sunlight, Margareta eyed their chamber. Where was she supposed to put a baby? Or a nursemaid? And what would the child wear? She hadn't spent time with children since being a child; Anna's younger siblings had all been dispatched to nurseries, even separate palaces, only re-entering court life once their table manners and conversation were deemed sophisticated enough not to embarrass their royal kin.

Would Margareta be expected to send her child away? To find a wet nurse in Edinburgh as Gabriel Vinstar had found Johanna in Helsingør?

'What are you frowning for?'

John rolled over, flinging an arm across her legs. His hand lay against her belly, and she wondered how close his fingers were to his child, how small it would be against his palm.

'Margareta?'

Now was the time. He knew her body better than anyone; he'd notice soon enough. But to say it aloud would mean it was real.

It would make their marriage real. Not a facade to allow them to spy more easily for Sophia, but a real union. A family.

'Something serious?' John gently enfolded her hand in his. 'Weightier than your usual need for fresh bread and honey in the mornings?'

Best to say it quickly, like yanking a splinter out of skin. 'I'm with child.'

He stared.

'I wasn't sure at first,' she blustered, 'and then I was. I mean, I am. Perhaps December.'

'A child,' he whispered. 'Our child. I didn't expect …' His hand cupped her belly, warm strength against her softness. 'Well.'

'You're displeased.'

'No!' He sat up and kissed her. 'I'm pleased. Delighted, overjoyed. Although I had hoped to have you to myself a while longer. So we could get to know one another better.'

Margareta scowled. 'Just because there's a baby growing inside me doesn't mean I'll be incapable of speaking for the next six months.'

John laughed. 'Nor of reprimanding me. I'm sorry.' He kissed her again. As he drew back, it was his turn to frown. 'You are pleased, aren't you? Having a baby – my baby – that doesn't displease you?'

'No! But …'

'Is it the birth? The finest midwives and physicians in the land will be squabbling for a chance to attend anyone at court. I'll make sure you have the best care.'

'It's Anna.' Margareta held his gaze. 'This will hurt her deeply. Discovering I've achieved what she cannot, what her husband prevents her from even having a chance to achieve, what her future and Scotland's depend on … I can't bear the thought.'

John was quiet a moment. 'Or …'

'Or what?'

'Perhaps this will be the spark needed to ignite James's passion. He was furious when he heard about Bothwell's third child. Perhaps seeing other men siring children will remind him how crucial it is that he follow suit. Before …'

He didn't finish. They both knew how dangerous the consequences could be.

Anna stared at her fingers, slowly turning her rings so that sunlight broke into shards against the gemstones. 'A child.'

Margareta nodded. 'In December, all being well.'

Anna gave a small smile. 'Do you remember the folk tales we heard as children? Now I think on it, they were filled with childless queens. Desperate women who struck terrible bargains with faeries, or stole the children of milkmaids and foresters, then raised them as princes. Perhaps we should find a goose girl who doesn't want her baby and offer her as much of Scotland's gold as Chancellor Maitland won't notice missing. What say you?'

'Oh, Anna.' Margareta took her hand. 'If I could change places with you—'

'I don't mean it!' Anna tried to laugh. 'Fear not, Margareta, I'm not asking you to exchange your baby for a few trinkets. I just meant ... there are so many childless women in stories. And they are always alone.'

'They might feel alone,' Margareta said gently. 'But they aren't.'

Anna touched Margareta's hand. 'I thought you understood better than anyone. No loneliness is so harrowing as that in a great crowd.'

Before Margareta could respond, the doors burst open and Elline came panting in.

'News from Denmark!'

Anna rose. 'Tell me.'

'They've burnt them! Burnt them all!'

Cold slid through Margareta's body.

'Start again,' Anna said, impossibly calm. 'Slowly and logically.'

'Admiral Munck ordered an investigation,' Elline said. 'Into the storms. He insisted it couldn't have been lack of skill that forced the fleet back twice. And now they've found the culprits.'

'Who? Did they sabotage our ships?'

Elline shook her head, gleefully grim. 'Witchcraft! They found six women in Helsingør and made them confess. They've all been burned at the stake and you're safe!'

Anna sighed. 'Thank God.'

'What were their names?' Margareta heard her own voice as if from underwater. 'Elline, what were the witches' names?'

'Oh, I can't remember them all!' Elline tossed her head carelessly. 'There was an Erna, an Astrid, and maybe an Ilsa was the ringleader, but who cares about dead witches' names? They've been caught and punished, that's all that matters.'

Ilsa. My Ilsa.

There was a roaring in her ears like the baying of a mob, and smoke-black darkness closed in. She was choking. She heard someone call her name, and then she knew no more.

The pyre was built last night, and now the faggots are dark with damp. Not so wet they don't catch fire – enough kindling has been added to ensure the crowd's satisfaction – but wet enough to smoke. Pale fingers creep over the woman's ankles, clinging to her skin, bare beneath a cell-stained shift. Smoke coils around her, writhing slowly up her body.

Then the coughing begins. Quiet at first, as if she's determined to be polite. But barely minutes later she strains against the ropes, and lets out a hacking, rib-trembling splutter. Then another. Another. Worse each time, more violent, more painful, and still the flames haven't touched her. Her skin turns grey, her eyes streaming pale veins through the soot. The fire toys with her feet like cats torturing broken sparrows, pawing, swiping; flames blister her legs scarlet.

Margareta, heavily cloaked in the shadows, prays for an ending. Gunpowder hidden in the pyre, a sympathetic guard levelling a crossbow at the woman's heart. She even hopes the accusations were true after all, that the woman will transform herself into a gull or a will-o'-the-wisp and soar away into the whitened skies. Instead, fire tears through her skin, turning white to red, red to black, and even through the gouts of smoke Margareta sees the yellow gleam of bone. The woman tries to scream, but smoke has scraped her throat raw and what emerges is a horrible keen somewhere between a croak and a moan, more animal than human.

'Help her,' Margareta breathes, the words wresting themselves free. But the crowd bay, 'Murderess! Whore! Witch!', hurling all three words at

random, for if the woman is guilty of one sin, she must be guilty of the others too.

The woman's lips part, gasping for life even when life is pain beyond imagining. It's almost a relief when her eyes close, her head lolls. But the guards continue to let her burn. Even the bodies of hanged criminals are released to their kin for burial; beheaded traitors are given a grave. But not witches. Witches burn until only shards of bone remain, and these will be buried at crossroads so the devil might take them. As the wind scatters ashes like white petals, Margareta acknowledges, shame curdling in her belly, that she will never dare ask which crossroads. She will never kneel there to ask for forgiveness.

And then she sees in the crowd someone whose eyes are red with tears as well as smoke, her jaw clenched in accusatory rage. Someone who will never forgive Margareta.

Ilsa.

'Margareta?'

She flinched away from the daylight pricking her eyelids, pale as Ilsa's hair. They would have shaved her head before dragging her to the stake, hacking bright hanks away to sell to wigmakers who would lie about its provenance. It wouldn't have been done carefully; Ilsa's scalp would have been crusted with blood, and her eyes would have seemed as vast as oceans.

'Margareta.' John placed another pillow behind her shoulders. 'Drink this.'

She smelled beef and thyme: broth. Her first sip was tentative, her second greedy, and before long the bowl was drained and John set it aside. Only then did she look at him properly. His doublet was tossed over a chair, his rolled-up shirtsleeves rumpled. His beard was scruffy, bristles askew, as if he'd dropped his chin into his hands too often.

'How long have I been asleep?'

'Four days.' He gripped her hand in both of his. 'The physician gave you a sleeping draught. He thought rest would do more good than anything else – possibly the first intelligent thing he's ever said.'

'What of—' She hardly dared ask. 'What about my child?'

'Well. Thank God. For a time they thought you might lose the baby. But you and the child are as stubborn as each other, and you've clung on obstinately.'

Margareta wanted to cry with relief. 'Perhaps they take after you in that regard as well.'

'Then we'll produce the most pig-headed infant in history.' He smiled, unable to manage laughter yet. 'Margareta ... I told Anna you'd felt unwell all day before you collapsed. I don't think anyone else made the connection with the news from Denmark.'

Margareta hesitated. 'About the witches ...'

'About Ilsa.'

He had waited long enough. Not only his vigil at her bedside, but all the weeks and months before, waiting for her to trust him, not knowing if she ever would.

Margareta placed her free hand atop his. 'You know Ilsa was my milk-sister.'

'Yes. Sophia told me you'd been fostered as an infant.'

'What else did you know of her?'

'Only that she and Erna Koldings were in touch with Scotland. With Bothwell.'

'She hoped to be rewarded,' Margareta said bitterly. 'She was always jealous of my court life. Gowns, palaces, feasts. She wanted more for herself. Ministers might declare that's no excuse for turning to witch-craft, but what would they know about empty bellies? All Ilsa wanted was to make things better. And Bothwell preyed on that.'

'You speak of her tenderly.' John tilted his head enquiringly. 'Yet, if the rumours are true – if they were guilty of the crime they died for – then she and her coven tried to kill us. You.'

Margareta shook her head bitterly. 'Ilsa knew how to use herbs to heal. She sold potions to lovesick girls, helped women birth their babies. As for dancing with the devil or calling the elements to do her bidding, I never saw any of that. She died because Admiral Munck wanted someone punished, because the court was frightened by a storm, as if we were no better than children. My sister was no saint, but she shouldn't have died like that! No one should ever die like that!'

Her voice had risen to a wild cry. John stared at her with dawning recognition.

'Ilsa wasn't the first person you've loved who died at the stake, was she?' He caressed her hand. 'Who was the first?'

She'd never spoken of this to anyone. But if she couldn't trust her husband, there was no hope.

'My mother.'

'Your foster mother?'

'The only mother I ever knew – mine died giving birth to me.' Margareta glanced down at her belly: time for that fear later. 'Johanna. She was so kind, so generous. People would come for her on midwinter nights, and she'd wade halfway across town through snow to help them. She brought more babies into Helsingør than any other midwife.'

'What happened?'

'Even the best midwife cannot save everyone.' Margareta gritted her teeth at the memory. 'There was a merchant. Rich, with several ships and all the influence they brought. His wife was scarcely more than a child. Ilsa told me her hips were slim as saplings – hardly ready for one baby, let alone twins. Her belly was three times as wide as she was. It was hopeless.'

'She died?'

Margareta nodded. 'My mother did everything she could. But the labour went on for three days, and by the third the merchant's wife had bled to death. So my mother tried to save the twins the only way she could – by cutting them out of the girl's womb. But when she drew them out, their bodies were grey and lifeless. Before she could try rubbing their bodies or breathing into their mouths, the merchant walked in.'

'Did he misread what he saw?'

'It must have looked like a butcher's yard.' Margareta didn't let herself shy away from the tale. 'My mother, arms and chest scarlet. His wife cut open, his babies stillborn. In kinder moments, I tell myself grief made him act as he did. But in truth … some men cannot bear for any part of their world to lie beyond their control. I think that was why he lashed out.'

'He attacked her?'

'He dragged her from the house by the hair and hauled her through the streets, bellowing that she was a witch who'd slaughtered his wife and sacrificed his children to the devil.'

'And people believed him?'

'Perhaps not all. But defending a witch guarantees they'll find another. If anyone remembered how my mother brought their babies into the world or saved them from dying in childbed, they kept silent. She was locked in a cell.'

'Did she even get a trial?'

'Such as it was. If she had a single mark on her – a mole, a scar – then she was a witch. If she'd ever spoken to a cat or dog, she was a witch. If a rich man said so, she was a witch. She never stood a chance.' Margareta blinked sharply. 'The court had been away hunting. By the time we returned, her pyre had been built.'

'You were too late to save her.'

'She couldn't have been saved.' Margareta shook her head furiously. 'Ilsa never accepted that – she thought I could have persuaded Sophia to stop the burning. 'Ask your rich kinswoman to save your poor one,' Ilsa spat at me. But I was fifteen and frightened … and what woman ever stopped a burning? Once you're called a witch, that's all you'll ever be. Queens can be ruined by such slander, you know that. The only power a woman has lies in her reputation being unblemished, and speaking out in support of a witch would tarnish anyone's irrevocably.'

John still held her hands, her one anchor to the present day. 'Did you have a chance to say goodbye?'

It was one of her greatest regrets. 'We were too late. But I went to watch.'

'You watched your mother burn?'

'I owed her that. She deserved to have people in the crowd who wept for her.'

If they ever put me on a pyre, I'd want you to bear witness. So I'd know not everyone despised me. Margareta's throat rasped at the memories of

Johanna's death and Ilsa's words; her lips dried. As if he knew, John poured small ale for them both.

'You couldn't have saved Ilsa. Nor could Sophia have intervened on your behalf – not without revealing your connection, and thus endangering you. And Anna. As you said, queens can be ruined by slander.'

Margareta nodded. 'I know. In my head, I know. But ...'

'I understand.'

She took a gulp of ale. 'Now you know who my mother was – what happened to her, to my sister – do you ... regret marrying me?'

He kissed her hand. 'You are not them.'

'I'm tainted by association. Ilsa said witchcraft was in my blood.'

'Then it's in our king's too, and the queens of England and France. All their mothers were accused of witchcraft. If we all had to suffer for the rumours spread about our parents, there'd be a queue to the scaffold from Edinburgh to Inverness. Besides, your mother was no more a witch than Queen Mary or Anne Boleyn, and probably even Catherine de' Medici. Witchcraft was just an excuse to persecute them further.'

'That doesn't make me safe,' Margareta insisted. 'If what women really die for is angering powerful men, none of us are safe.'

John pulled her into a rough embrace. Pressing his cheek against her hair, he whispered fiercely, 'You're as safe as I can make you – you and our child.'

At last she trusted him to try and protect her. But he was only one man. What could one person do against a world crying out *witchcraft*?

25

'They burned them,' Geillis repeated dumbly. 'Ilsa and Erna – burned for witches?'

Agnes swept hellebore roots into her mortar. 'Along with half a dozen others. No doubt the Danes are feeling very pleased with themselves.'

Geillis could well imagine. Would the mob have heard Ilsa's screams over their own yells? For even a girl that aloof would have shrieked when her flesh began to char.

No wonder Lady Margareta was said to be ill. Geillis had tried to see her again. But the guards had told her she was too sick for visitors. Geillis had been torn between sympathy for the Danish lady, and pity for herself at once again disappointing Bothwell. She'd known that was selfish: the woman lay mourning her sister. But altruism was a luxury Geillis couldn't afford. 'What will happen to us?'

Agnes paused her grinding. 'To us?'

'Now the Danish women have been executed. Hadn't we best stop before they arrest us too?'

'Oh, Geillis.' Agnes began trimming more leaves. 'That's exactly what they'll expect.'

'Because it's *sensible*!' Geillis leaned across the table, knocking the piled herbs askew. 'Women have *died*, Agnes! Two were burned in Aberdeen last week, three in Edinburgh last month. You've been arrested twice. Isn't it time we stopped?'

Agnes pointed her knife at Geillis. 'You're a coward.'

'Even the bravest soldiers know when to retreat! We might as well be staring down the barrels of a thousand cannon. It's too dangerous to continue!'

'That's precisely why we must.'

'Are you mad?'

'Not at all.' Agnes began chopping carefully. 'Think about it. All the Danish and Scottish nobles will be congratulating themselves, convinced they've frightened us into submission.'

'Well, they've frightened me!'

Agnes gave her a scornful look. 'It's they who should be frightened. When we increase our efforts, they'll discover we aren't afraid of them. To powerful men, there's nothing so incomprehensible – or so terrifying.'

'Increase our efforts?' Geillis gripped the table edge. 'We already tried to raise storms to kill the king and his bride – what more could we possibly do?'

Agnes's lips thinned. 'They aren't dead yet.'

She didn't want to kill anyone. Least of all an unborn child. Geillis tugged at her cuff, clenching her fist tight over the tiny pocket she'd sewn for Margareta's ring, feeling the setting gnaw her palm. She knew what it was to lose children. Whenever she'd passed the small mounds beneath the tree at home, she'd remembered the bundles. The only time she'd embraced her siblings was to press them close to her body so Bridget didn't have to see her take them away. Since then, Geillis had held the hands of weeping women while she explained what to do about the milk that would come anyway. And of course there had been Lucy. Yet she'd been ordered to bring herbs to Holyrood that would break the Danish queen's heart.

And Bothwell would ensure she took the blame for it.

Geillis found Margareta sitting outside the abbey, her back against the sun-warmed stones, staring across the parkland – eastwards. Towards Denmark. As she approached, Geillis realized the Danish woman was watching her. She hadn't stirred, but her eyes had hooked onto Geillis's movements.

'You came a long way in this heat. Please, sit down – rest your feet. Have a lemon cake, I've already eaten four.'

When was the last time anyone had cared about Geillis's comfort? Geillis almost smiled as she sat and took a cake; it melted against her tongue and she could have sighed with pleasure. 'I'm used to long journeys. Besides, what of your feet – any swelling?'

Margareta shook her head heavily; Geillis suspected the summer heat wasn't the only thing weighing on her.

'And your hands?' Geillis reached out tentatively. Gloved in lawn to protect that white skin, the knuckles were still clear, the flesh not puffy. 'What about morning sickness – has it abated?'

Margareta grimaced. 'This morning I scalded myself while making Anna nettle tea, and when I cried out, when I saw that tiny patch of pink flesh, I thought I should be sick. But that had nothing to do with the baby.'

'I know,' Geillis said quietly. 'I leaned too far into the oven this morning and felt utterly feeble for coughing.'

Margareta's face suddenly sharpened. 'Who knows about your connection to Ilsa?'

Geillis thought of the sunken ship, the poisoned sailors. 'No one who doesn't share that connection. Other midwives, that is.'

Margareta nodded, not completely reassured. 'Hardly anyone knows she was my sister. It feels like a betrayal, but we must pretend her name means nothing to us. Otherwise ...'

'You've done nothing wrong,' Geillis said, wishing she could say the same of herself. 'Why should you be afraid?'

Margareta shook her head. 'If people knew ... Being kin to a witch or friends with a witch is enough to damn us. Should the wrong words be spoken, we could burn.'

'But they haven't been spoken.' Geillis reached for Margareta's hands again, unsure whether she was soothing herself as much as the noble-woman, or why she so desperately wanted to assuage Margareta's fears. Because Margareta was a patient, or because Geillis was lying to her? 'If my silence can keep you safe, it will.'

Margareta squeezed Geillis's hands in gratitude. 'In which case I would owe you far more than a lemon cake.'

Their entwined hands rested above Margareta's belly. Geillis's chest tightened at the reminder of what she was doing and wondered if her promised silence would save either of them – or drag them further into danger.

In the moonlight the yellow clusters of tansy seemed to rise from the ditches like many-eyed ghosts, watching her every move. Geillis averted her gaze as she and Bessie hurried past, unable to avoid remembering that first time she'd harvested here, after Seton had assaulted her. And now she harvested to murder the queen's child. That first time she'd been desperate, grieving. Now she was selfish, callous, and treacherous. When she'd first handed over the little pouch of herbs to Margareta, she'd seen desperation turn to gratitude in the lady's eyes, and her deception had stung inside her belly like nettles. You were supposed to be able to trust midwives. To trust the herbs they gave you. Not swallow your own loss as if it were honey.

This tansy would kill a baby. Could even kill the queen if the miscarriage went badly. And how long before Margareta was accused of that murder?

Bothwell had commanded her to befriend Margareta. But he'd expected Margareta to like Geillis, not the other way around. She knew it was ridiculous to imagine friendship with a court lady, that only her own pitiful loneliness was tempting her to latch on to such small kindnesses. What did one cake cost a lady who'd just devoured four? Besides, what kind of friendship entailed poison? No true friend brought death in scented flowers.

It was Lammas Eve. She ought to have been helping with the harvest, carrying golden sheaves through golden fields, eager for the feast they were earning. Races would be held on the beaches and artisans would sell their finest wares, and Geillis might have had enough coin for a new cloak pin. Instead, she was once again outside at midnight, climbing the Fiery Hills overlooking the saltpans, dreading what she'd be forced to do at the top.

At her side Bessie shivered, and Geillis glanced at her in surprise. Bessie's face was drawn and pale in the moonlight; it was the first time she'd seen her afraid.

'Courage, Bessie,' Geillis whispered, hoping it would make her brave too. 'In a few hours we'll be tucked up in our beds again.'

'You don't know that,' Bessie hissed. 'The devil stalks the land on Lammas Eve and drags people down to hell by their bootlaces!'

'Best tie yours tightly then,' Geillis said, as stoutly as she could muster.

Ahead, jagged orange cut through the darkness on the hillcrest. Cloaked figures moved around a fire, malformed with shadows. Behind them, trees stood sentinel, their branches hissing in the scouring winds off the sea.

'Why so many?' Bessie whispered.

Geillis didn't know. She'd expected their usual group – Agnes, Fian, Grierson. But more than two dozen figures moved on the hilltop. Could they all be trusted?

As Geillis and Bessie reached the fire, Agnes called, 'Welcome to the Fiery Hills, my girls.'

More warrior than woman, she stood over the fire, her face like carved bronze, eyes glittering with determination. Around her the other figures were sitting down, pulling dark cloaks tight, hoods low, but all looking to Agnes.

Bessie muttered a nervous greeting as they joined the circle. Someone passed Geillis a steaming cup; she didn't want to call attention to herself by refusing, so she took a gulp. Bitterness raked her throat, sharp, sour, then suddenly sweet. She gagged, almost spitting it out. What on earth was it? She sniffed the cup, would have sniffed again if Bessie hadn't snatched it. Had she smelled salvia? Belladonna? Did she feel strange, or just think she ought to feel strange? Carefully, Geillis sat down, letting her hood hide her face like everyone else.

Only Agnes kept her hood down. She remained standing, surveying them all.

'Most people wouldn't dare venture here. Not this night, when they fear the old tales of what walks abroad in the darkness – and not this place.' Agnes smiled. 'In bygone days, they called it the Faerie Hills. On nights like this you can hear the distant drums and pipes of the faery dancers, calling to you, drawing you deep into their songs. But once you enter their dance, you will never leave. Even if your feet

bleed, even if your very bones are exposed, you will never stop dancing.'
She looked at them as if she could see through their lowered hoods,
through their skin to the stuttering hearts beneath. 'You are all part
of our dance now. You cannot break away.'

Whispers rustled, fearful, urgently hushed. No one dared speak.

'Joining us,' Agnes continued, 'is the one who will lead our dance.'
She extended a hand towards the trees.

At first, Geillis was certain there was nothing there. Then a shadow
became darker than a shadow, and the sea mist writhed about it like
snakes.

'The devil!' Bessie gasped.

Every time Geillis blinked the shadow changed shape, and flames
rose up to meet it, red and blue crackling as if it were truly the devil
incarnate, walking through the fire.

It was the belladonna. Of course, the belladonna – or whatever it
was – had addled their vision. And Bessie's girlish superstition was
nonsense.

'Greetings,' the shadow said. She knew that voice. He was worse
than the devil. 'We are here with a sole purpose – the destruction of
James Stuart.'

'God has forsaken him,' someone whispered – Fian?

'And the devil too,' another man hissed – Grierson? 'Let him die then.'

Let him die – and not us. That was their wish, their cruel, selfish,
human wish. Not everyone could survive. Why should James Stuart
have that privilege? The hisses bred, vicious and biting. *Let him die.*
Let him die.

'Tonight,' Agnes said, 'we make a working that will bring down
James Stuart.'

Neither of them called him king. Easier, perhaps, to deny treason
if he were just a man. Easier to kill a man named James than murder
the king.

The shadow stepped into their circle, and yet somehow seemed to
hover above it. 'Each of you will play a part in this. Serve me well
and you will be rewarded. Fail me ... and hellfire and brimstone will
be as snowflakes compared to my wrath.'

They said he'd ripped a man to pieces for insulting him. They said he'd made a pact with the devil, so cunning that now the devil was in his debt. They said he drank blood, bathed in blood, spilt blood as often as others breathed. If even half the rumours about Bothwell were true, hell truly would be nothing compared to his retribution. Geillis could already feel the flames scorching her skin. How many would rather burn to death than risk Bothwell's vengeance?

Agnes drew a package out of her cloak. Unwrapping the linen folds, she said, 'Each of us will name it. Then I will speak the final invocation.'

Through the flames, Geillis made out something small and pale in Agnes's hands. For a moment she thought it was a baby rabbit, and she was almost relieved when Agnes said, 'I name this manikin *Jacobus Rex*.' And then Geillis knew relief had been madness.

How could Agnes explain this away? Whistling on a cliff, mixing potions – all so calmly dismissed Geillis had almost believed in Agnes's innocence, and her own. But this?

'I name you *Jacobus Rex*.'

'*Jacobus Rex*.'

'*Jacobus Rex*.'

It was moving around the circle, too fast. Geillis heard Fian's solemn preaching, Grierson's satisfied anger. Dozens more, all taking the object, saying the words, their obedience either blind or vindictive. The name became a hiss seething through the night.

Bessie whispered, '*Jacobus Rex*,' and passed the thing to Geillis.

It was warm to the touch; she almost dropped it in revulsion. *Just wax. Softened by too many hands.* White, expensive wax, carved into the shape of a crowned man. It would have made a week's worth of candles for Geillis's parents.

But they had no need of light now.

'I name you *Jacobus Rex*.'

Geillis thrust the manikin to her right, wanting it gone – the slackening wax, the clammy warmth, the knowledge of what they were doing.

Jacobus Rex, Jacobus Rex.

Then it was back in Agnes's hands and her smile was cold. Opening a vial, she said, 'Let the body of Jacobus Rex sear with pain. Let his skin blister and his flesh rot. Let him suffer as he has allowed his people to suffer.' The vial tilted. Liquid hissed and Geillis caught the scent of toad venom.

'And now,' Agnes said, 'let him burn.'

She tossed the manikin into the fire. Sparks spat blue. Then flames crawled over the waxen king, feeding on his sunken white flesh.

He burned as Ilsa had burned. But there were no screams, no baying mob. Only the raking wind and the cold laughter of the man who would be king.

26

The court spoke of nothing but witchcraft. In Edinburgh two more women had been executed for cursing a young laird who'd spurned them. Anyone pointing out that the sweating sickness usually visited cities in summer was browbeaten into silence with endless stories of hexed men, of women wielding potions.

'After all,' Elline pointed out at dinner, 'if someone miraculously recovers from an illness, no one hesitates to say it's God's will. Why shouldn't a death be the devil's work?'

The sauce on Margareta's venison was congealing; dark, misshapen lumps clung to the meat. She wanted to push it away, but unless King James rejected a dish it was not for his court to make up their own minds. Though he wasn't enjoying dinner either; he spent more time prodding meat with his knifepoint than eating, and even his ever-present cup of wine remained untouched.

'But how can anyone prove witchcraft killed that laird?' Vibeke pressed. 'It's not as if witches leave daggers in their victims' backs.'

'All it takes is someone else's words,' Margareta said quietly. 'Someone whose voice is louder than the witch's.'

Elline tossed her head. 'If we can't prove their guilt beyond doubt, they can't prove their own innocence either.'

She seemed so certain she spoke of justice. So oblivious that her arguments could apply to any of them. Once one witch burned, the flames crept closer to everyone. Even queens' ladies – even queens themselves.

'That's ridiculous,' Vibeke protested. 'You're just being stubborn—'

'The king,' Elline whispered, staring at the dais. 'Look to the king.'

James had half-risen, but then doubled over as if someone had thrust a blade into his guts. But he wears armour, Margareta thought, and only Anna is near enough to stab him. Yet James swayed, his jaw clenched against pain. Then a spasm rocked his body, and he was violently sick.

The hall erupted. Men rushed forward; Anna, reaching for her husband, was all but elbowed aside by Maitland and Bothwell. Above the furore, as the king was carried from the hall, Margareta heard Elline hiss, 'Witchcraft! He's been cursed!'

'There could be a hundred explanations,' John pointed out as they lingered in an alcove near James's bedchamber. 'Meat spoils easily in summer, and I certainly didn't enjoy last night's venison. Disease spreads fast in a crowded city – dozens have probably fallen sick in the shambles too. Or he drank from a stream while hunting, and a dead sheep lay around the bend.'

'But there's only one explanation anyone wishes to hear.'

'Aye. And you can guarantee James will be listening.'

'Listening and feverish.' Margareta shook her head. 'A dangerous combination.'

John watched the door leading to James's rooms. A physician carrying a bowl of blood emerged. 'Perhaps that's what someone wants.'

'What do you mean?'

'James was already frightened. Now he's sick. Few people are more fearful than the sick, especially if they're convinced their sickness isn't natural.'

'Plenty are willing to convince him.'

'If James wasn't already persuaded witches are trying to murder him, he will be by the time he leaves that bed.' He didn't say *if*. Even discussing the possibility of a king's death was treason. 'So. We have several explanations. Firstly, the king's illness is natural, but someone's encouraging rumours to the contrary, perhaps to make the king even more frightened. Secondly, someone's made the king ill through earthly means – rotten food, even poison – and wants to exploit the situation, again spreading fear. Or …'

Margareta braced herself. 'Thirdly?'

John's jaw was rigid. 'The king's illness *is* unnatural.'

'Witches are trying to kill him? You don't truly—'

'I don't know what to believe. But one of those explanations must be true.' He met her eyes. 'Your mother was accused partly because of her knowledge of herbs. Who knows more about poison than cunning women?'

She hid her alarm at the thought of Geillis's herbs. But James had been taking them for months already without consequence – this sickness couldn't have anything to do with Margareta.

'And perhaps,' John continued, 'it helps if others believe the devil guides their hands.'

'That way leads to the flames! No woman would be so reckless!'

John shook his head. 'Not all women fear the same things. You fear the flames – wisely. But others are more afraid of men who beat them, who could evict them from their homes – who wouldn't dare do such things to a witch.'

'You think some Scotswomen *want* to be known as witches?'

'I think they might want what everyone else in Scotland wants.' His eyes were grim. 'Power.'

A court with an invalid king was no place of peace, but neither were the Leith docks. Margareta had hoped the sea air and the bustle of people whose lives continued regardless of James's sickness might be a distraction. But the scent of oysters and whelks, the chiding of waves against harbour walls, the sun-silvered ripples: all reminded her of another dockside and the sister she'd so often met there, and it wasn't the child turning in her belly that made her nauseous, but the thought of tainted smoke rising over Helsingør's red roofs.

She'd arranged to meet Geillis here at noon, but the Scottish girl was late. Margareta could only assume Geillis's employers had kept her; she heard Ilsa's mocking reproof: *Geillis's tasks will be ever so slightly harder than fastening pearl necklaces.* Grimacing, Margareta turned away from the sea, as if Ilsa's whisper had emanated from the surging foam.

'Lady Margareta!' There was Geillis, leading a white mare. 'Forgive me – my horse threw a shoe and—'

'Your horse?' Margareta eyed the mare's lines admiringly. 'She's beautiful – I hadn't thought …' She trailed off, hearing Ilsa's scorn again: *Too good for the likes of us, you mean?*

Geillis flushed. 'She's my master's horse, of course. I only meant I rode her here.' She rummaged in her cloak. 'I've brought you more valerian and meadowsweet. I wondered … does the queen need more herbs yet? It's just that tansy doesn't grow past September and I'll need to gather enough to dry over winter.'

Margareta shook her head. 'There's been no … opportunity. And now that the king's ill, who knows when or …' She stopped before the treasonous *if* could tumble out.

Geillis hesitated. 'Is he very ill?'

'His physicians are worried.'

Geillis wound her horse's reins around her fingers; the tips whitened. 'Are they conferring in corners and pasting on smiles? When Agnes and I realize a patient can't be saved, our smiles betray us. They're too broad. Too kind. Because we can't help remembering they're the last she'll ever see.'

'They don't smile. Isn't that worse?'

Geillis shrugged. 'Perhaps physicians have a different way of being kind to the dying than midwives.'

'I know which I'd prefer.' Margareta shivered at the thought. She imagined James, a fearful man even in health. How terrified must he be in the stale cage of the sickroom, with only those cold, measured men to help him? 'Geillis … when the time comes, will you be my midwife? Not Agnes. Just you.'

Geillis stared. 'Just me? In Holyrood Palace? Where the king and queen might …' She looked suddenly horrified, twisting her hands as if all too aware of their calluses. 'I couldn't – you should ask Agnes, she's far more experienced—'

'No.' Margareta shook her head. 'In my darkest hour, if it is to be dark, I know I'd want your kindness and no one else's. I know I could trust you to take care of me.' She reached for Geillis's hand, trying to convey how little its roughness mattered to her, how much Geillis's support did matter. 'Please. Say I can count on you.'

Geillis hesitated. Then her fingers closed around Margareta's. 'Of course you can.'

Despite the physicians' warnings, James recovered – and perhaps, John suggested, this was what the conspirators had wanted. A dead king was a void that could only be filled by the fallout of a civil war. But a frightened king was an opportunity. He would be compared to braver men and found wanting. Then he would be no more of an obstacle than draped lace, easily torn and crushed beneath their boot heels.

In Holyrood Abbey, they offered up prayers of thanksgiving for the king's recovery. Margareta wondered whose were genuine. After all, if James had died, who would have gained? He had no son. Queen Elizabeth was his closest relative, but she was an old woman who would never bear a child. Scotland and England might have been briefly united, but then hungry claimants would have snapped at both thrones.

The vast Gothic window turned golden light pale, greying the courtiers' faces. There was Chancellor Maitland, solemnity carved around his mouth, eyes alert even when cast down. He was indisputably powerful but lacked royal blood. A quick mind wasn't enough to take a throne – but it could make you the power behind one if its occupant were malleable enough. Such as Ludovic Stewart, the sixteen-year-old Duke of Lennox, whose pretty face resembled that of his late father, James's one-time favourite. The boy's head was respectfully bowed, but where Maitland remained watchful, Lennox didn't seem interested in anything beyond his ruffled sleeves. He'd been left jointly in charge of Scotland while James came to Denmark, true, but only as a figurehead. If he were James's heir, he might wear the crown, but he wouldn't guide the crown's decisions.

What of the other regent? Bothwell knelt beside Lennox, all swarthy strength beside the boy's delicacy. He was warrior enough, powerful enough – but was he popular enough? From what she'd learned of Scottish clans, Margareta doubted anyone could claim universal respect, let alone love – but was Bothwell any less favoured than other men? Would he care? She knew he was conspiring against James; John said he'd been imprisoned for rebellions before: twice trying to separate James from a favourite, once demanding James invade England to avenge his mother's execution – never physical assaults on the king himself, but sedition calculated to emphasize James's weakness. He certainly wouldn't shy away from naming himself James's heir – and who would stand against him?

Suddenly Bothwell's gaze reared up and gripped Margareta's. Dark, calm, shrewd. He'd caught her watching and wanted her to know.

Margareta wrenched her eyes away. Before her now was Anna, her ruff a web of frost about her neck.

How would Anna have acted if James had died? A widow in a strange land. After a season proved there was no heir in her belly, the Scots would lose interest in her. Could she marry again, to a man who might give her a child, who might care for her? Or would she be so tainted by rumours – the cursed wife, the barren girl – that no other prince would ever touch her? Did Anna need James – or need him gone?

The thought left her cold. Anna wasn't like that.

But Anna was Sophia's daughter. And Sophia knew that sometimes you had to make sacrifices in order to win.

No wonder James had spent his life in fear. Less than six months at the Scottish court and Margareta saw shadows everywhere, and even the pure seemed corrupted.

'Perhaps I should organize a celebration,' Anna said as they left the abbey. 'Nothing too strenuous, of course. Some masques, some music. We've had so little pleasure of late.'

'An excellent idea,' Elline put in. 'We'd love to dance again.'

'You'd have to choose the masque's allegories carefully,' Margareta said. 'No King Arthur – if a great warrior's wounded, won't that suggest someone attacked him?'

Anna glanced at her sharply. 'Something about seasons renewing would suffice.'

All their lives Margareta had offered prudence when Anna was flighty. Was queenship changing her? Or had this sensible, considered woman been there all along – and would she still need Margareta?

Margareta was gnawing her lip as one of James's grooms approached.

'Your Grace, I bring a message from the king.'

'He is well?'

'Improving, Your Grace. He wishes to take supper with you.'

Anna frowned. 'In private?' James never asked to see her alone, other than on their fruitless nights together.

'A small supper, Your Grace. He also asks that Lady Margareta and Master Wemyss attend, as his carefully chosen guests.'

Carefully chosen words: the boy's concentration as he delivered the rehearsed phrase gave that away. What did James want? He'd never spoken to Margareta directly, only tossing generic instructions at whichever of Anna's ladies happened to be present. Had his sickness rendered him suddenly gregarious?

It had to be something more sinister.

No one spoke as the food was served. Taking their cue from James, they sipped wine as the servants laid out simple fare: roasted capons, manchet loaves, chicken pie. Margareta fervently hoped James wouldn't drink at his usual pace tonight: nerves and her baby's odd bubbling movements made wine roil in her stomach. She caught a wary look from John as a dish of buttered parsnips was laid down between them. Was his concern for her health, or for the reason behind this strange summons?

Opposite Margareta, Anna was humming softly – a sure sign of anxiety. The only person who remained calm was the one for whom it was least characteristic, the one who'd just recovered from either sickness, or poisoning, or a witch's curse.

James gestured curtly at the servants. 'Leave us.' He watched them go with irritation. 'See how reluctantly they depart? Nothing is so infantilizing as wearing a crown. People assume I cannot cut my own meat without a coterie of assistants, as if I were still a beardless boy.'

'Perhaps they just want to help,' Anna offered.

James addressed John. 'Do all Danish women have the same naive faith in the altruism of others?'

John smiled. 'No doubt Margareta can tell you that herself, Your Grace. Perhaps women are generally less exposed to the world's harshness, thus less inclined to cynicism.'

James looked at Margareta with his eyes only, turning neither head nor body, as if she wasn't worth his full attention. 'Do you find that true, Lady Margareta?'

Margareta summoned up a smile. 'I think women are exposed to different parts of the world – perhaps no less harsh. But I've always been inclined to cynicism.'

'Do you believe my servants can be trusted?' The question came scything out of the air. James leaned closer. 'As a cynic, surely you look for suspicious behaviour. So tell me – what have you seen?'

Margareta wanted to read John's face for clues about how to answer. But looking away from the king now was unthinkable. 'I haven't been at Holyrood long enough to judge.'

'Nonsense. We all judge within moments of meeting another person.'

'Then to judge soundly, sire. Are you asking about intelligent decisions or merely prejudice?'

She could have bitten her tongue in two. You couldn't speak to men so tartly, let alone kings.

But James merely raised his cup to John. 'You were right. A fiery temper and a sharp mind. Not qualities all men would desire in a wife.'

Anna flinched. Margareta was too disconcerted to consider Anna's feelings further. Did James and John often discuss matters alone – and was she herself a frequent topic of conversation?

John, wholly unflustered, raised his cup in response. 'Not all men, sire, but certainly this one.'

'Ha!' James slapped the table and laughed. 'You say that in her presence, Wemyss, but what about when your cheeks are out of range of her fingernails?'

John smiled. 'Even then.'

'See this?' James swung his attention to Anna. 'Your lady-in-waiting has married a most loyal man.'

Anna's eyes flickered between them. Don't do that, Margareta wanted to urge her. Keep your eyes steady, or nothing you say will seem sincere.

'We are both fortunate in our husbands,' Anna said, her composure ringing hollow.

James watched her for a moment, then turned away. 'Eat. All of you – eat, drink, be merry. Merrier than I've been,' he grumbled, tearing off a hunk of bread. 'Nothing sucks the cheer out of a chamber faster than physicians.'

'But we are grateful to them,' Anna reminded him, 'for restoring you to health.'

James grunted. 'Not everyone desired my restoration.'

No one responded. Which was worse – silence or speaking?

James speared a morsel of chicken on his knifepoint. 'You know it's true. Wemyss, you know it better than most.'

What did he mean by that? The pie tasted like sawdust in Margareta's mouth.

'After all,' James continued, 'you seem to know many things better than most. You've always been a good man for observing and reporting.'

John cut a slice of bread. 'I am only glad of such talents insofar as they serve Scotland.'

'Then be glad of an opportunity.' James tossed wine down his throat. 'I want you to investigate a matter for me.'

'Which matter, sire?'

'Does it matter?' James snorted, amused by his own wordplay. 'Is my wish not your command?'

'Naturally,' John assured him. 'But I can hardly investigate without further knowledge.'

'You've all heard the rumours.' James picked at breadcrumbs. 'I've been plagued by them for over a year. Witchcraft.'

No one spoke. Margareta risked a glance at Anna. Although her face was turned dutifully towards her husband, her eyes darted anxiously. Who could hear that word without fear? Especially when the rumours also named Anna as the witches' intended victim.

'This year alone,' James continued, 'a dozen witches have been executed in Scotland. And the whispers would have me believe those dozen are but an oozing sore, warning of a vast canker beneath.'

'And do you?' John asked quietly.

James stared past them, at the darkness beyond the table. 'All my life people have wanted me dead. Some believe this has rendered me a craven wretch, who cannot blink without thinking an assassin's creeping close. And they're right. I am afraid. What man wouldn't be? My father, my grandfather, my great-grandfather were murdered. My inheritance is steeped in blood; my blood is that of victims, not victors.' He leaned forward, dark eyes blazing. 'But this doesn't make me a coward. It makes me more determined to purge Scotland of traitors. When you know others would happily shed your blood, you do not shy away from bloodshed. You thirst for it.'

John cleared his throat. 'Sire, it's possible all this talk of witchcraft is just that – talk. Bluster and vengeful gossip, no more.'

'There are too many rumours.' James shook his head. 'One sick man doesn't mean the plague's come to Edinburgh, but a dozen cases, a hot, fly-ridden summer and talk of more people feverish, riddled with purple sores? If you still chose to believe there was no plague, you'd be a fool. Scotland is infested with witchery and I will see her cleansed, even if I have to set a fire from here to the Tweed.'

'You wish me to turn witch hunter?'

'I do.' James smiled. 'And you will begin your hunt close to home.'

Margareta froze. Surely he couldn't know about her connection to Ilsa?

But James was looking only at John. 'You've always been a useful man,' James said softly. 'Useful to many, I believe.'

John's smile was too calm. 'Such is the minor laird's lot. Either we make ourselves useful, or the world tramples us.'

'Have you ever made yourself useful to the Earl of Bothwell?'

John paused. And Margareta suddenly recalled words uttered during a dance in Kronborg: *she met with some … associates of my associates.* She'd only thought about Ilsa at the time. But now, she stared at her husband, uncertainty smouldering. Had he introduced Bothwell to Ilsa?

'The earl has sometimes asked me questions a mere laird couldn't refuse to answer. But if you're asking about loyalty—'

'Do I need to?'

This was a different James. Not the terrible actor struggling to fit himself into someone else's role, the clumsy youth attempting crude jests, or the fool manipulated by councillors. They weren't onstage now. And it suddenly occurred to Margareta that it would require a very good actor indeed to play the part of a bad one.

'In the circumstances, of course you must ask.' John wet his lips. Margareta had never seen him nervous before. Was he guilty – or desperate to prove his innocence? 'You said so yourself – several Stuart rulers met violent ends, caused by Scottish traitors. If the King of Scotland didn't question everyone's loyalty, would he remain king long?'

Stop, Margareta wanted to scream. You go too far – you're talking treason now!

'But there's a vast difference,' John went on, 'between a boy telling an earl something in exchange for a new horse or a seat at the table – and a man who in his heart believes that earl might make a good king. I was that boy once. But I am not that man. I am a true subject, and I serve you ahead of any other man.'

But not ahead of any woman? Of Sophia? Or your wife?

James watched John thoughtfully. 'You speak well, John Wemyss. I'd like to believe you speak true. Of course, if you don't, I have your wife and unborn child close by to remind you of the rewards of serving your king well.'

So that was why Margareta had been invited: to threaten John. She was James's hostage.

'I have an excellent memory, sire. I rarely need reminding of important details.'

'Then you shall serve me well,' James said calmly. 'You will not forget anything overheard during your investigations. Nor will you forget the value of subtlety.'

'You do not wish anyone to know you're investigating?'

'Not yet.' James's red-stained mouth curved with the taste of future satisfaction. 'Let them incriminate themselves even further. Why build a pyre for the witch when you can watch her lay the wood herself?'

'Very wise, sire.'

James's face hardened. 'So many think my fears have robbed me of my reason. But they are wrong. My fears might grow every day – but that only makes me more determined to defy them.'

Abruptly he thrust his chair back and held out an arm to Anna. 'Come, wife. I'm minded to defy my enemies still further tonight.'

Margareta barely slept. Nor did John. They both tossed and turned in the darkness, but always one spine drew a barricade down the centre of the bed. Sometimes a hand crept towards a shoulder, so close they could feel the warmth from the other's skin. Sometimes lips parted and a sound emerged that might have been the beginnings of the other's name – or merely the murmurings of a dream. Every time, they turned away and silence fell. The trust between them was as fragile as new ice, the darkness beneath too close and cold to ignore.

Bleary-eyed with sleeplessness, in the morning Margareta went to Anna's chambers, only to find Elline emerging.

'She's not there. Her bed hasn't been slept in.'

Margareta blinked. 'Then – she must have spent the night with the king.'

'Should we go there?'

'I'll go.' Margareta seized Anna's robe, already turning. 'I'll escort her back – you lay out today's gown.'

When she reached James's chambers, she'd barely addressed the guards before the door flew open and James, fully dressed, sauntered out.

'Good morning, Lady Margareta,' he said. 'A fine morning to go hunting, wouldn't you say? I rather hope Wemyss will agree.'

'He'll be delighted, Your Grace.'

With a bark of laughter, he was gone. She didn't want to know what so amused him.

Inside, Anna was sitting up in the vast bed, her hair spilling around her shoulders. As Margareta approached, Anna pushed back the covers and smiled.

There, blossoming on the white sheets, was the unmistakeable crimson of blood.

27

Autumn had always been Geillis's favourite season. Sunlight peeled the morning mist back like a chestnut shell, revealing the glistening world beneath. She would walk along the hedgerows until her basket creaked with the weight of blackberries, elderberries, rosehips, and hazelnuts. It would be cool enough to need a shawl but not so cold she'd ever shiver; cool enough that she didn't envy the fishermen already bobbing out on the waves, but warm enough that she wasn't filled with envy for those still abed. On such mornings it was almost impossible to be afraid. When berries purpled her fingers, how could she think of toad venom dripping on manikins? The world seemed clean and pure again, and Geillis could pretend she was too. Pretend she'd never cursed the king – or wondered, when the curse failed, whether that had been Agnes and Bothwell's intention all along: not to murder the king, but to frighten him.

She'd filled her basket; the little sacks separating the berries and nuts bulged. A steady walk home then, to protect her hoard: let that be the excuse. The prospect immediately awaiting her was hardly daunting: kneading dough, chopping onions – rhythmic tasks that would lull her into thoughtlessness. It was what would follow in the evening that made her reluctant to return – and what might drag her out into the night.

Lost in her thoughts, Geillis barely registered the kirk as she passed, and almost collided with someone emerging through the lych gate.

'Mistress!'

'Geillis!'

They both stepped aside, backwards, an awkward dance. Eventually, they managed to arrange themselves so they walked beside one another.

'You're abroad early, Geillis.'

'Best start on the day's chores before the day starts without you, mistress.'

'That sounds like an inherited saying.' Mistress Katherine made a thoughtful noise. 'Your mother's?'

'Yes.'

'You lost your mother last Easter, did you not? Just before you came to us.'

'Yes, mistress.'

'Once, I thought the worst thing in the world was to lose one's mother. Now I know that isn't true.'

Geillis clenched the basket tighter. How dared Mistress Katherine dismiss her grief? But then Geillis remembered her own role in Lucy's passing and knew she had no right to rage.

'Is that why you're abroad early, mistress? You've been to ... see Lucy?'

'As well say I am abroad late. I do not sleep much these days.'

Mistress Katherine's exhaustion was clear. Every line in her face was etched deeper, as if the artist drawing her had leaned too heavily on his charcoal.

'I could brew some camomile tea. It might help you rest.'

Mistress Katherine shot her a surprised look. 'How could I rest, knowing my little girl's alone in the kirkyard? She never liked it there, not after dark. The yews cast such strange shadows – have you seen them?'

'Yes,' Geillis said hesitantly, not wanting to encourage her.

'Like wild horses rearing,' Mistress Katherine mused, pulling at weeds as they walked, heedless whether she plucked cow parsley or nettles. 'Lucy was fond of horses, but I think that makes the yews more terrible. Far worse when something you love betrays you, don't you agree?'

What did she want Geillis to say? 'Yes, mistress.'

'That Sampson woman, for instance.' Mistress Katherine absently scratched her stung fingers. 'She helped bring Lucy into the world. I trusted her. And then she ripped my girl away.'

Geillis swallowed. 'Mistress—'

'Do you know, I thought you were her today?'

'Beg pardon?'

'When you appeared at the lych gate. You have her way of moving now. As if you're taking a place in the world, no matter who might already be there. Once, I could have admired that. Perhaps I might have tried to emulate her too.'

Geillis wanted to deny it. But she searched for plants in places Agnes had pointed out, chopped herbs and spoke to the sick in Agnes's manner. She'd been striving to be like Agnes for over a year; it was too late to reverse the changes.

'But now,' Mistress Katherine continued, 'I do not think anyone should aspire to imitate that woman. Far better to be content with your own station in life.'

Easy to say for a woman who'd never washed her own linen, Geillis thought bitterly.

They'd reached the house. Geillis heard the chickens clucking eagerly as Jeanie fed them; the stables already rang with horseshoes being struck. Before they could step through the gates, Mistress Katherine seized her arm.

'Do not seek to be like Agnes Sampson, Geillis. Do not even seek to be near her.'

Was she trying to protect Geillis? From what? Guilt and fear cramped in her belly. 'Mistress—'

'Believe me, Geillis. No one wise will want to be associated with that woman.'

'The Earl of Bothwell does.'

Mistress Katherine stared, astonished by Geillis's boldness. 'You'd be making a grave mistake to assume power and wisdom go hand in hand.'

Grief changed people in different ways, Geillis had learnt. Some lashed out, some withdrew – and yet there was always the same sensation at the heart of it: a gaping absence, like a wine jug that would never be filled again. She'd seen it in Mistress Katherine, and now, at the stalls in the Grassmarket, she saw it in Margareta: a listlessness as she picked up and discarded ribbons and lace, a distractedness when she spoke, as if the words she truly wanted to say could never be spoken to the person she needed to hear them.

'I've been craving rødgrød,' Margareta said, holding violet ribbons in one hand and scarlet in the other.

'Rødgrød?'

'Stewed berries,' Margareta said vaguely. 'Redcurrants, bilberries … my mother used to add raspberries too. They serve it with vanilla cream in Kronborg, but she just made it with milk, and that's the kind I really want.'

'Some women start eating coal,' Geillis said dryly, 'so no reason why you shouldn't have this.'

Margareta smiled bitterly. 'Ah, but there is. It reminds me of Ilsa.'

Geillis couldn't help a nervous glance over her shoulder. Yes, there was safety in a crowd, where dozens of rich ladies wandered the stalls with their maids, and hardly anyone in Scotland knew Ilsa's name. Nevertheless, those two syllables made her think of a cold laugh on a cold sea – and a raging fire. 'Why?'

'She used to eat it so fast her mouth was smeared crimson,' Margareta said. 'Then she'd bare her teeth and snarl that she was a *draugar*, about to eat me up and curse me with ill luck for all my days, and I'd scream and hide in our mother's skirts.' She selected the scarlet ribbon and handed it to the stallholder. 'Sometimes I wonder if she truly did curse me. Or if any such curse landed on her instead.'

Whenever Geillis bought ribbon, it was two handspans tucked into her pocket; now she stared as the stallholder wrapped yards and yards of Margareta's chosen colour in muslin. 'You mustn't …'

'I know.' Margareta took her package and they moved away through the crowds. 'Most people would think all the ill luck fell on Ilsa, and I'm a self-pitying fool. But then I think about the storms. And I wonder whether my milk-sister really tried to kill me. After all, they say those we hold dearest can also hurt us the most.'

But the Helsingør coven hadn't been the only ones sending storms out into the night. Or giving poisonous herbs to unsuspecting women, winning their trust all the while. Geillis swallowed, wishing her secrets tasted less like blood and bile. 'Sometimes what people take to be curses is just life. Just normal cruelty.'

Like Lucy Seton. *A sickly child sickened and died. That's all.* But Bothwell's dismissal was cruelty too – and Geillis knew he was wrong.

'Normal cruelty,' Margareta repeated. 'Maybe that's how everyone sees a burning – until it happens to someone they love.'

Or until you feared you might be the one to burn. How could you ever atone for sins so terrible you deserved an eternity in hell?

She was serving at table when the steward slithered in, his face taut with reluctance.

'Well?' Seton demanded, skewering duck on his knife. 'There'd best be a decent reason for this interruption – can't you see we're eating?'

He was, Geillis thought, noting the abandoned morsels on Mistress Katherine's plate.

'I beg your pardon, sir,' the steward said, 'but there's an urgent message.'

'Deliver it then,' Seton snapped, beckoning Geillis to refill his cup.

'It's for Geillis, sir.'

'Her?' Seton glanced at Geillis with angry revulsion. 'Who would bring a message for her?'

The steward hesitated.

'Out with it, man!'

'It's Agnes Sampson.'

'What?' Seton sat bolt upright. 'Here?'

'Yes, sir.'

Seton pointed his knife at the steward, a gesture that might have been threatening if not for the meat waggling on the end. 'Did I not give orders that the Sampson woman must not be admitted?'

'You did, sir.'

'Then send her off – with the hounds on her heels!'

'She says it's urgent. She insists on seeing Geillis.'

Seton's jaw jutted. 'Geillis is my servant. She sees only those I wish her to see, when convenient to me.'

The steward braced himself. 'She said you'd say that, sir. And to point out—'

'That sick people and babies have no interest in your convenience.'

Agnes stood in the doorway, hands on hips. *Taking up a space in the world*, Geillis thought, *no matter who's already there.*

'You dare enter this house?' Mistress Katherine hissed. 'After what you've done?'

Agnes gave her a forthright stare. 'Must other children die because yours did? Your husband might bear such a senseless grudge, but you're not so foolish.'

'Get out!' Seton snarled, half-rising. 'Leave now, or you'll be chased off my land!'

'I'm no deer to be hunted.'

Seton bared his teeth. 'You think yourself invulnerable because Bothwell currently finds you useful. But what would you know of men like him?'

'Every woman learns about powerful men,' Agnes retorted. 'That's how they change from girls to women.'

Seton sneered. 'If you think he'll always protect you, then you're the fool. And when he's done with you, I won't be.'

Agnes sighed wearily. 'If all drunken idiots fulfilled their vows of vengeance, half of Scotland would perish. Enough, David Seton. I need Geillis's assistance, and I won't leave without her.'

'You'll leave when—'

'Who's the patient?' Geillis asked.

It was as if they'd forgotten she was there. Agnes recovered her briefly lost composure first. 'Breech birth in Prestonpans. The mother's only twelve and the father's the blacksmith – even if the babe wasn't breech, she'd struggle to deliver his child, or any child, with her hips.'

'But the blacksmith's wife—'

'Exactly.' Agnes nodded. 'This girl's frightened and alone. Her father's useless with drink and fury, and the sister who fetched me is barely nine. You see?' She flung this at the Setons. 'There are other children in Scotland, other parents.'

Neither spoke. Geillis set down the wine jug and stepped towards Agnes.

'Geillis!'

She turned at Seton's bark.

His eyes were coal-black with fury. 'If you go with her now, you'll regret it.'

She shook her head. 'I'll regret it even more if I don't.'

And Agnes and Geillis were gone, out into the night to help a child bear a child, while the men who ought to have kept girls safe glugged wine and curled their fists in brutish threats.

28

Margareta watched John, not as the awkward and infatuated girl who'd watched him in Kronborg, but as a woman who knew her husband couldn't be trusted.

He was a spy. He'd always been a spy, but now, after the dinner with James, there was no forgetting it. Perhaps it behoved a spy to be able to stroll among Bothwell and his friends, laughing, jesting, occasionally murmuring into an ear. If John couldn't gallop after stags with the earl's men, bellowing encouragement and bloodlust, he wouldn't have been the man James and Sophia needed him to be. But what kind of husband did that make him?

Margareta didn't want to be a nagging wife, growing more shrewish daily, as if the bulge forcing her to let out her gowns wasn't a baby but a festering canker of resentment. Yet before she could stop herself, barbs shot from her lips.

'You're playing cards with Bothwell again?'

John dug through his clothes chest for a doublet, his previous one in a wine-stained heap across a chair. 'A few hands, yes.'

'I thought you were coming to bed.' Margareta was already there, propped up against pillows yet still feeling the weight of the seven-month lump in her belly.

'Afterwards. I'll try not to wake you.'

'If you drink as much as last night, I doubt you'll manage that.'

'I wasn't drunk,' John objected, pulling on a fresh doublet.

'I could smell it on you.'

He laughed. 'Spilling wine on my clothes doesn't mean I've drunk too much – logically it means the opposite.'

'What about the singing and stumbling and snoring?' she retorted. 'All caused by eating marchpane, I suppose?'

'They're just part of me.' He planted a kiss on her nose. 'I might be late.'

'Might?'

'Bothwell always draws games out – trying to make his opponents nervous. Or drunk.'

'And poverty-stricken. Our child will be born a beggar at this rate.'

'Only if I lose.' He grinned. 'Why do you think I've changed my doublet?'

She stared. 'You're not going to cheat?'

'If necessary.'

'And you have a special doublet for cheating?'

'Several – otherwise someone might notice I win in green and lose in blue.' He adjusted his sleeves. 'A few extra pockets here and there, that's all.'

'But if you were caught—'

'Of all the things I do, cheating at cards is among the least dangerous.'

She shook her head. 'If you're discovered to be dishonest in one respect, they'll realize you're untrustworthy in others.'

He reached for her hand; her fingers hung limp in his. 'There won't be a single trustworthy man at Bothwell's table. That's why they're at his table. I may not be good enough at cards that I can reliably win without resorting to cheating. But in the greater game, I do know what I'm doing.'

'Bothwell isn't a simpleton to be easily gulled. What if he discerns what you're up to?'

'Then I'm a dead man.'

'How can you say those words so carelessly?'

'Because I've been saying them for years.' John sat down on the bed. 'When I came to court, I knew I couldn't rely on wealth or family connections to make my way. Nor was I willing to advance by seducing rich women, or men for that matter. Like I told you, my wits were my only coin. I dealt in information and observation, and I knew my targets wouldn't be best pleased to discover what I was up to. So I gave them a share.'

'You were a double agent?'

'Double? Try triple – or quadruple.' He grimaced at the complexity. 'My role is to convince everyone that I seek to help them above all others.'

'Including me.'

His eyes met hers. 'You still doubt me.'

'You've just told me you deceive everyone – why should I believe I'm any exception?'

'Because you're my wife!' He seized her shoulders and kissed her. 'You have to trust me, and I have to trust you, because otherwise we'll drown in this sea of lies. When the door to this chamber closes each night, all deception is left outside. This marriage, our love – they're the only honest things in my life, and I intend to keep them thus. Do you believe me?'

She didn't know. Then the baby turned, and as the ripples moved through her, she knew she had to. Because true faith meant believing without any proof. She had to believe in John for their child's sake, and for theirs. She needed something honest to cling to.

'On one condition.'

'What's that?'

'Never wear that doublet to play cards with me.'

Margareta was dressing Anna's hair when the queen observed, 'That gown looks familiar.'

Margareta glanced down at the pale blue silk. 'It used to be yours.' Most of Anna's old gowns were passed to Elline and Vibeke; only those with the longest trains could be adjusted to accommodate Margareta's height – and now her belly.

'It's very pretty,' Anna said. 'I might have to ask for it back one day soon.'

Their eyes met in the glass. Anna's danced with mischievous delight, and Margareta couldn't help smiling; it had been so long since she'd seen Anna happy.

'Are you sure?'

'It's only been six weeks,' Anna conceded. 'But my last courses were at least two weeks before ... that night. And James was so – so *determined* I cannot help believing it must have produced a child.'

'Oh, Anna!' She wanted to hug her; perhaps two years ago, they might have embraced. But Anna was a queen now, and carrying a prince. 'I'm so pleased for you.'

'So am I.' Anna clasped her hands over her belly. 'And you'll have to find me more of those herbs. What was the midwife's name again?'

Margareta paused, suddenly remembering Geillis's fear at the thought of attending her inside Holyrood Palace. How would she feel about attending the queen? Besides, it was Agnes who had prepared the herbs for Anna and James, Agnes who'd taken Geillis as her apprentice, and Anna would want the more experienced midwife. And some part of her also wanted to keep Geillis to herself, as she'd once kept Ilsa to herself: a bond Anna didn't need to lay claim to.

'Agnes Sampson.'

'Agnes Sampson,' Anna repeated, smiling. 'She's served us well. We shall have to show our gratitude somehow.'

29

She'd never met Margareta inside the palace; when the sun was shining, Geillis hadn't cared. But now, with clouds hiding the summit of Arthur's Seat and rainwater worming through her boot soles, she wondered what the chambers were like. The smell of roasting pork that wafted from the kitchens made her stomach growl. Somehow, she doubted they were smoke-filled like Robert Dixon's, or shared with two pigs like the cottage where poor Kitty McNeill had to tie her new baby to her chest with a shawl to keep him safe from the greedy sows.

'Have you walked all this way?' Margareta asked as Geillis reached her. Moisture gleamed like crystals on her fur-lined cloak; the rain had driven most courtiers indoors, leaving the gardens all but deserted. 'You're soaked.'

Geillis glanced down at her own worn woollen cloak. Although she was certainly cold and damp, soaked wasn't the word she'd use. 'I'm fine. But you – are you still comfortable walking?'

Margareta swatted the air impatiently. 'I might be outpaced by snails, but I'd go mad if I didn't walk every day. Please don't tell me I shouldn't.'

'Far from it – walk as much as you can.' Geillis hesitated, loath to bring the conversation to its inevitable focus; her basket suddenly pulled like a millstone. 'I've … I've brought the herbs.'

'Thank you.' Margareta reached for the pouches; their hands brushed, soft kidskin against knuckles sore from picking rue. 'Geillis – don't you have any gloves?'

Geillis almost laughed. 'I've never owned gloves.'

'Then have these.' Margareta pulled hers off and thrust them at Geillis.

'I can't—'

'Go on. I have others. And this too.' She handed Geillis a coin purse. 'Why not hide some from Agnes?'

Geillis shifted awkwardly at the reminder that she was being paid for services. If Margareta knew ... 'Thank you.' She slid the gloves on; supple and warm, it felt like moving someone else's hands. No one could buy whelks or pick crab apples in these gloves. 'They're too rich.'

'And you're too cold, even if you say you're used to it.' Margareta smiled tightly. 'I know what people look like when they're pretending to be strong.'

'So do I.' Geillis narrowed her eyes. 'Are you worried?'

Margareta tried to laugh. 'I'm rarely not.'

'Is it the baby? Or ... the birth?'

Margareta swallowed. 'My mother ... my birth mother, that is, died in childbirth. The closer my time comes, the worse I fear it, and the more I grasp how useless my fears are.'

'Are you much like your mother?'

'I don't know.' Margareta shrugged, eyes glistening. 'I never knew her, and no one here remembers her.'

How many people remembered Bridget? Agnes had seen her wracked with labour pains, but what of the real woman, the one who'd lived before and beyond the birthing chamber and had hoped to raise her children, not just deliver them? Geillis hesitated, then wrapped Margareta's hands, bare and white, in her own, their calluses hidden in softness. 'What happened to our parents doesn't have to determine our lives. There are no promises where childbed's concerned. Yes, it can be frightening. But being afraid and carrying on – that's what proves all mothers brave.'

Margareta squeezed her hand. 'Not just mothers, I think. Thank you, Geillis.'

Geillis looked away from her gratitude. If Margareta knew all they'd done, she would know what Geillis truly deserved.

* * *

A sea fret had crept in while she and Agnes had been attending a birth, and an insistent drizzle fell, damp seeping into Geillis's cloak from all directions. On days like this, Geillis's father had tossed a coin before putting to sea, saying, 'A gold coin makes the mists lift.' Except they hadn't been gold coins, but wooden buttons or battered nail-heads. 'Play your pipes, Geillis,' her mother had suggested. 'Charm the mists away.' Did fishermen and their wives still say such things? Did they dare, with all the people burned for witchcraft this year? Or were they like Geillis: steeped in so deeply they couldn't climb out again? As if witchcraft were a clinging fog, turning her colder every moment.

As she entered the Setons' courtyard, a shadow loomed out of the mist and she almost gasped in fright: Chirnside was waiting.

'A message,' Chirnside said, without preamble. 'There'll be a gathering at North Berwick kirk on All Hallows' Eve.'

'The kirk?' Geillis frowned. 'Are we praying for something?'

'In a way.' His smile was chilling. 'You told Bothwell the Danish queen is with child. After the gathering, she won't be for much longer.'

How many more times would Geillis have to see this? Men deciding to plant their seed in women's bodies, men deciding to end women's pregnancies, all for men's gain. Bothwell had commanded Agnes's herbs would poison Queen Anna's baby, driving home the message that God had forsaken the royal marriage. Geillis had drunk rue, wormwood, and tansy, desperate to ensure Seton hadn't got her with child. Were none of them to have a choice about whose children to bear, or when?

'Remember,' Chirnside said softly, 'you're in no position to refuse this invitation.'

Geillis closed her eyes in resignation.

The dead walked abroad on All Hallows' Eve. People spoke in low voices and hung yew branches above their doors before locking them and huddling around fires no one dared let go out. They spoke as if the dead were the ones to fear.

Riding towards the dark peak of Berwick Law, Geillis thought of her own dead. Her parents. Lucy. She'd run towards their spirits, not away. To berate her father, embrace her mother – and beg Lucy's forgiveness. Some feared the dead's revenge; Geillis feared the anger of the living, and if she hadn't feared Bothwell's most of all, she'd have been locked safe indoors tonight.

Beneath the Law, the kirk clung to a promontory that jutted out into the sea like an accusatory finger. Fires blazed in the kirkyard: one great pyre, flames leaping as high as pikes, braziers wedged against the stone walls. Against the flames, Geillis saw figures. Dozens – well over a hundred. She'd rarely seen so many people in one place. Even in Edinburgh, the flow of people never stayed still, and narrow streets pinched crowds into small pockets of buyers and sellers. But this assembly was vast. Did so many despise the king? How many plotters had Bothwell intimidated into joining his schemes? Was this the scale of his power and hatred?

'Geillis!' Bessie appeared from nowhere. 'Have you brought your harp?'

Geillis patted the pack across her shoulders. 'Harp and pipes. But I don't see—'

'Hurry!' Bessie half-dragged Geillis into the kirkyard.

This isn't like hell, Geillis told herself as she stumbled past grave-stones. It cannot be like hell. And yet there were flames, so wrong against the kirk tower and ranks of the dead lying all around. Somewhere a drum was beating, faster than a heart, and Geillis felt her own pulse striving to meet it. They passed a goat turning on a spit; her stomach clenched at the smell. Bodies everywhere, laughing too loudly, their faces looming up at Geillis, leering savagely.

'Sit here.' Bessie thrust her onto a blanket near the pyre. 'He wants you to play the harp until it's time.'

'Time for what?'

Bessie shook her head impatiently. 'You'll see. Just stay there!'

Then she was gone, leaving Geillis alone with the heat almost scalding her cheeks. Surreptitiously, as if someone were watching, she shuffled as far back on the blanket as she could, then pulled her mouth harp from her pack.

She hadn't played for years, but it had been impossible to refuse to bring it. Her father had once produced animal noises on it – sheep, ducks, cows – but it had been a long time since he'd been in the mood for such frivolity. Usually the instrument's noise was so plaintive, so insidious you almost hated it – but just as you itched to break it in two, the sound was suddenly part of you. It was the hair on your neck, the skin over your spine, the place where eardrums met skull. As Geillis set the harp to her lips, she knew its music was entirely fitting for this gathering.

At first, her lips and fingers were awkward, notes jarring. Like trying to walk after sleeping on frozen ground. Then her body remembered, and the music came.

They just swayed to her melody at first: men and women absent-mindedly shifting as they spoke and drank. Swaying became stepping; stepping became turning; turning became twirling became leaping. Bodies gyrated, sinuous as eels. John Fian wielded a burning branch in each hand, flames illuminating a wild jeer, boots flying faster than drumsticks, for once looking as imposing as he believed himself to be. People dared each other to dance with him, leaping closer and closer, shrieking as sparks snapped at flesh. Was that Bessie, dancing with an otherworldly elegance? The Bessie who'd stumbled down sand dunes with Geillis couldn't possibly move so smoothly, so seductively.

Two figures cut through the crowd like steel through flesh, making their way to a platform near Geillis. Agnes, hood tossed back, unashamed, and Bothwell, who knew how terrifying the darkness could be, leaving his cloak to cast misshapen shadows across his face. Behind them, the kirk tower strained away towards a sky that was all blackness.

The drums stopped. Immediately, Geillis set down her harp. Everyone turned towards the platform, unable to resist Bothwell's sinister draw.

'Friends,' Agnes said, her voice carrying over the sea winds. 'He has called us, and we have come. Our master wishes to address us.'

'My people.' Bothwell lifted his arms, a gruesome mockery of a crucifix. 'Tonight is the night others fear most, and rightly, for we are fearsome indeed! What can you not achieve under my instruction? This night, we will make such a working that all of Scotland will quail before you!'

Cheers leapt up: raucous, unfettered.

'We aim to destroy James Stuart,' Bothwell continued. 'Tonight we will make him suffer worse than ever before. The Danish girl is with child. But not for long.'

If any dared express sympathy, they were drowned out by glee and spite.

'Her child will be lost in blood!' Bothwell cried. 'James will know his marriage is cursed. He cannot give Scotland an heir, and Scotland will not give him her loyalty. We will not serve James Stuart!'

'Aye!'

'Down with the Stuarts!'

Bothwell's voice rang out over the roars. 'Whom do you serve?'

As one, they breathed, 'You,' and the scything winds and crashing sea echoed the word.

'Until death,' Bothwell hissed. 'But tonight, we celebrate the destruction of James Stuart and his wife. Throw them on the fire!'

Agnes unwrapped two wax figures and offered them to Bothwell. He took one in each hand and brandished them.

'These people are not fit to rule – only to burn!'

He hurled them high. For a moment the wax was bone-stark against the night sky. And then the flames devoured them.

Silence stretched. Then shattered.

Roars clashed with screams; laughter surged through shrieks. The drums beat again, faster now. Bodies slammed against bodies, stamping feet churning the earth. Geillis scrambled back as two people spun across her blanket, whisking her ankles away just in time. She tried to push herself up, but a dancing boot crashed down onto her knuckles and she cried out. Twisting onto hands and knees, she crawled, clutching her father's harp to her chest. Someone stumbled against her and Geillis grabbed their cloak, hauling herself upright. She dived for the wall, for its promise of stillness.

'Here! Take this!' Someone thrust a cup into her hand and whirled away. Her throat was rough from the smoke; without thinking, Geillis lifted it to her lips. But then she caught its scent. Salvia, henbane, belladonna. The same concoction passed around on the Fiery Hills, and no wonder many swore they'd seen the devil that night. Slowly, Geillis poured the contents into the earth.

Someone was watching her.

A man stood a little further along the wall, his back to a brazier. A position that would hide his face in shadow if he looked out at the gathering – but his face was turned towards her. He was young, with a courtier's beard, neat and presumably fashionable, and a fine velvet doublet. There were plenty of wealthy folk here, not least Bothwell himself. But this man was still, composed. He hadn't drunk the belladonna concoction either.

He moved towards her. She almost fled – she didn't want another rich man ordering her around. But in the midst of this chaos, she needed to stand beside someone calm.

'You don't dance,' she observed as he approached.

'Only when I know the steps,' he answered. 'This jig has no plan I can fathom. Why aren't you dancing?'

'I prefer waking up unbruised.'

'Very wise. I suspect there'll be sprained ankles and blackened eyes before dawn – not to mention aching heads.'

'Why are you here, if not to join in?'

'I could ask the same of you.'

'I was commanded.'

'I see.' His gaze flickered across the dancers. 'In a manner of speaking, so was I.'

'Then in another manner, you weren't,' she pointed out. 'You chose to come.'

'I wanted to see what drew so many here.'

She shook her head. 'You weren't merely passing by. Your clothes betray you – I know you're from court. Which means you must be in league with—' She broke off. Did she dare name him?

'It would certainly seem that way.' His grim tone made her suspect it wasn't that simple.

Geillis thrust out a hand. 'Geillis Duncan.'

He had no choice but to take her hand and answer. 'John Wemyss.'

Perhaps the John was false; it was common enough. But the second name? 'Is your wife Danish?'

His eyes flashed; he might as well have bared his teeth, he looked so savage. 'What do you know of her?'

'I – gave her herbs,' Geillis said, his suppressed rage forcing the stammer. 'To help with her child – your child.'

He rocked on his heels, still guarded, still angry. 'Then I must thank you – the child grows strong. Are you a midwife?'

'I'm learning. Agnes Sampson's the midwife.'

'Strange.' His gaze pierced her. 'You concern yourselves with bringing lives into the world – yet you willingly aid the destruction of the queen's child.'

She snorted. 'Do I look as if I'm here willingly?'

'No one dragged you in chains,' he pointed out. 'Therefore you've chosen your life over that of an unborn baby.'

Geillis lifted her chin. 'And if that baby lived to become king, do you think he'd care about my life? Or make it any safer?'

'Has Bothwell said you matter more to him than to the king?'

She stared at him, suddenly cold. Who was this man, really? What did he want? 'He knows my name. That's more than I imagine James Stuart ever will.'

'What's Bothwell promised you?'

She hesitated. What *had* Bothwell promised? Nothing. Vague talk of power and riches, dangled out of reach like bright threads before kittens. 'That we'll be rewarded.'

'Empty promises,' Wemyss said, as if reading her mind. 'Is that how you justify yourself?'

'Who are you to judge?' she snapped. 'You're here, aren't you? I didn't hear you speak out when the queen's baby was mentioned. You're as guilty as any of us.'

'Perhaps,' he said coldly – but his coldness wasn't for her. 'Perhaps I'm as great a sinner as any here.'

'Maybe you should pray for forgiveness,' she retorted. 'We're in a kirkyard, after all.'

'There's nothing holy about this place anymore.' He looked her in the eye. 'If I wished to repent, I'd go to a kirk in Edinburgh. St Giles', perhaps, on the Canongate.'

She knew what he was asking – but not why. What did he want her to confess? And what would Bothwell do if he found out?

'I don't know that kirk,' she managed. 'I'm sorry.'

'If you change your mind … Thursdays after dark are often the quietest time.' He turned to leave.

'Master Wemyss?'

He looked back at her, gentle patience in his face.

'I—' She hesitated. 'I hope your wife's childbed goes well.'

His smile was both pleased and disappointed. 'Thank you, Geillis.'

He turned, and disappeared among dancers and darkness.

30

Anna's pregnancy hadn't yet been announced; it was too early to be certain. Nevertheless, the court's mood was altered.

Nothing dramatic, Margareta conceded. But whenever James rode back from a hunt, red with exhilaration and gore, he kissed Anna's cheeks as well as Alexander Lindsay's. In the great hall, Anna no longer sat at the royal table like a remote star – cold, silver, and alone – but chattered to ambassadors and lords. She and James even laughed together now, not in the discordant way of before, one beginning, the other's echo jarring, afraid they were somehow targeted by the jest. The changes were there if you knew to look for them – and Margareta wasn't the only one looking.

Bothwell hadn't met her gaze again since that time in the abbey. Why should he? Surely to him she was just the wife of a friend, and wives interfered with gaming and drinking. She wasn't the prettiest of Anna's ladies; her face didn't capture eyes like Elline's. A fortnight away from entering confinement, Margareta felt more ungainly than ever. Some men ceased to see pregnant women at all; some looked faintly repulsed, others irritably bewildered at a process they neither fully understood nor controlled. If Bothwell ever looked Margareta's way, his eyes skimmed past onto someone more interesting, more powerful. Which made it easier to observe him without being observed.

He'd been furious at first. As if Anna's pregnancy were a personal insult. But then his face had settled back into its customary certainty: that everything would work out according to his wishes. And that was frightening to behold.

* * *

On All Saints' Day, Margareta woke to find John sprawled across the bed, fully clothed, face buried beneath pillows. His boots were abandoned near the door, spattered with still-soft mud. She was tempted to wake him, but a mild pang of compassion and a less mild compulsion to use the chamber pot persuaded her otherwise. She levered herself out of bed, stifling the grunts that accompanied rising now, and squatted over the pot. Then she poked her head out of the door and ordered the page to bring some food. Unable to bear the prospect of a stomacher or even the loosest of her let-out gowns, she wrapped herself in a robe and set about untangling her hair. By the time she'd tamed its knots, the page had returned, his tray piled high with still-warm bread rolls, golden pats of butter, and two bowls of beef pottage. Margareta carried it over to the bed and settled herself against the pillows.

At the smells of meat and thyme, John stirred. 'Breakfast already?'

'It's daylight,' Margareta pointed out. 'If you don't want yours, I'll happily eat both portions.'

'You'll have to wrestle me for it.' He hauled himself up. 'I'm famished.'

'I'm not surprised – how late did you come to bed?'

'God knows,' he sighed, dipping generously buttered bread in his pottage. 'A blasted cockerel crowed as I reached the stables, though it was far too dark to be dawn.'

If only she could stay in this simplicity: breakfast with her husband, a warm bed, peace before their baby was born. But this was not their real world. 'Where did you go?'

His eyes told her he shared her wish. 'I followed Bothwell. To the kirkyard at North Berwick, and what looked like a vast convention of witches.'

'In a *kirkyard*?'

John nodded. 'More than a hundred people. Dancing and drinking Christ knows what – most were reeling after a few cups. They seemed convinced Bothwell was the devil come amongst them to lead them to greatness – though none knew exactly what that greatness would involve.'

'Did he know you were there?'

'I took pains to remain unseen. By Bothwell, anyway.'

'What do you mean?'

'I had to be seen by someone. I hoped to persuade one of Bothwell's acolytes to turn informer.'

'And did you?'

'Perhaps.' John swallowed a mouthful of small beer. 'I made her an offer – we'll see if she accepts.'

'Who was she?'

'Geillis.' He met her eyes. 'You know her, I believe.'

Startled, Margareta nodded. 'Yes – she gave me herbs to help the baby grow.'

'Did she seem happy about it?'

'What?'

John looked thoughtful. 'Geillis struck me as one of the unhappiest women I've ever seen. She didn't want to be there. Bothwell has a hold over her – maybe not just Bothwell. Whatever she's doing, she does it unwillingly, which makes her a perfect mark for a double agent. But I wondered …'

'What has this to do with her giving me herbs? She's a midwife.'

'How did you meet her?'

'At Barbara Napier's house.'

'Archibald Douglas's wife? She's kin to the Earl of Angus; she served him before he died. Rumour was he'd raped her then dismissed her, and she avenged herself by poisoning him.'

And poisoners used herbs. But people died for many other reasons – and many wronged women didn't murder their attackers. Was Barbara one of them? Or had Margareta made a horrible mistake?

'There was an older midwife too,' she said, trying to justify herself. 'Agnes Sampson.'

John's face whitened. 'Agnes Sampson?'

'They said she's the best midwife in Scotland.'

John lowered his head into his hands. 'Christ's wounds, Margareta. Agnes is working with Bothwell.'

'What has that to do with my baby?'

'Dear God!' He shook his head despairingly. 'Are you suddenly convinced the world is full of kindly folk who want to help? You've never been this naive – surely you must see through these women? They know who you are! They knew who you were long before you even knew their names!'

'But I'm nobody!'

'You're Anna's closest friend!' John thrust the bowls aside and seized her hands. 'You're their connection to the woman they seek to harm. Did they mention Anna?'

'Yes,' Margareta whispered, a horrible, gaping abyss opening inside her. 'They ... they wanted me to recommend Agnes to her. I thought they just wanted royal patronage, influence at court—'

'You fool,' he whispered with furious tenderness. 'They don't want to help Anna. They want her child dead.'

He was still talking, something about fires and wax figures, but she wasn't listening. That artless query at Leith docks about Anna needing more tansy – Geillis's concern hadn't been innocent or helpful at all. It had been murderous.

'The herbs,' Margareta choked out. 'The herbs!'

'What? The ones they gave you? Christ, Margareta, have they done something to our child?'

'Not ours,' she managed. 'They gave me herbs to help James do his part. And some for when Anna conceived.'

'The same as yours?'

Mutely, she shook her head.

'Has Anna taken any of them yet?'

She could barely utter the traitorous word. 'Yes.'

His grip tightened on her wrists. 'You must stop her. Now, Margareta, before it's too late.'

She couldn't run. Her belly was too heavy, and the last thing they wanted was Bothwell seeing her fly panic-stricken to Anna. Nevertheless, Margareta hurried as fast as she dared.

How many doses could Anna have taken? It had been weeks since Margareta had started giving her Geillis's herbs – if Anna drank an infusion every day, that made over twenty. What was too many – fifty? One? It had to be a large number – Agnes and Geillis weren't stupid. Treacherous, murderous witches, but not stupid – they'd know that if one dosage caused a miscarriage, everyone would blame them. But gradually poisoning an unborn baby would make it far harder to pinpoint the poisoner. Perhaps it wasn't too late. Perhaps Anna's child would still live.

And Margareta wouldn't have killed him.

How could she have been so stupid? She knew Geillis and Agnes had worked with Ilsa, and what Ilsa had died for. But she'd been so determined to believe Ilsa was falsely accused, not corrupt or malevolent or violent. She'd wanted to believe Geillis was like her – and Agnes like Johanna. Wise women. *Good* women. Women who could never harm another's baby, because how could anyone be so cruel? Especially those who knew how desperately a mother-to-be needed to trust those around her.

Except Ilsa hadn't promised never to hurt Anna. She'd promised to help Anna fulfil her destiny – and she'd used Geillis as her weapon.

Margareta had been blind – and now Anna might suffer for it.

She burst into Anna's chambers. And stopped.

They were empty. No – abandoned. Embroidery frames lay on the rushes, loose silks trailing, thread baskets overturned. A harp stood silent; sheet music fluttered on a stand. It was as if some spell had spirited Anna's ladies away.

Except they hadn't gone far. From behind the door leading to Anna's bedchamber, Margareta heard Vibeke's voice raised.

'Get a physician! Quick!'

The door crashed open and Elline hurried out, barely glancing at Margareta.

Horror seeped through her. She looked down at her belly. How could she take this in now?

But she served Anna. Now that Margareta had betrayed her, it was even more important to serve her. Steeling herself, Margareta entered the bedchamber.

The first thing she saw was the gown thrown across a chair. Silver taffeta: Anna's favourite colour, pale against a lurid crimson stain.

Until then, she hadn't wholly believed it. But now Geillis's betrayal hit Margareta like icy water.

Anna moaned. Immediately, Margareta moved towards the great bed and the other women parted for her: the awkwardly hovering Scotswomen; Vibeke, empty-handed, looking like a soldier who'd lost their sword. Anna lay curled in a ball, arms wrapped around the agony and emptiness of her belly. She looked tiny, doll-like, not the queen she'd begun to be. What did crowns or jewels matter in this room?

Margareta lay down next to Anna. There were no words that could make this right, none that would heal Anna's pain. Instead, Margareta kissed Anna's cheek, smoothed her hair, crooning a long-forgotten lullaby. A song for a child. For the baby who would never be born, and for the woman who was scarcely more than a child herself.

The shutters were nailed closed. Dark velvet hung across the windows. Only a pair of candles alleviated the gloom, one either side of the bed with its scarlet hangings. Margareta couldn't think of anywhere she'd get less rest; it would be like lying in a pool of blood.

'Two months,' she murmured, despairing. 'Without daylight.'

John stared around the chamber, equally appalled. 'The baby might come early. Leap up and down on the bed to encourage him.'

'I'd break it,' Margareta said bitterly.

'It might not be so bad.' John tentatively rubbed her shoulders. 'The quiet – the peace.'

'You think I'll ever be peaceful again? After what I did to Anna?' What Geillis had lured her into doing. How she wished she hadn't trusted her.

'Don't speak of that,' he warned, glancing at the maid laying a fire. 'Besides, it wasn't your fault.'

'As much mine as those women who never even met her. Or the earl who dreamed it all up. You know I'm to blame.' No doubt Sophia agreed. She'd written to let the queen know of Anna's miscarriage, and her own pregnancy, and been met with stony silence. If Sophia discovered what she'd done, she'd be cast out onto the street – and deservedly so.

'They used you.'

'I allowed myself to be used.' She shook her head bitterly.

'What good would blaming you do?' She knew he was trying to hide how much he did blame her. 'All we can do is make sure there's justice for Anna.'

'How? Trapped in here, what can I do?'

'Don't worry.' His face was grim. 'We're ready.'

He kissed her, a lingering farewell. Before she could ask – who, how – he was striding away, on business she couldn't help with and would only ruin if she tried. The doors closed behind him. The maid slid the bolts home, and Margareta was trapped, helpless in the darkness.

31

Even on a Sunday, there was work to be done. Hearths to be swept, water fetched from the well, yesterday's cold cuts laid out for the Setons to break their fast. Being out half the night helping Agnes with a breech birth hadn't helped; by the time the household set out for kirk, Geillis had been awake so long she was contemplating dozing off during the sermon.

When they reached the kirkyard, Mistress Katherine glanced back at them all, as always, ensuring they looked respectable, or at least clean and tidy. Her gaze lingered on Geillis, and her lips thinned. Resentment for Geillis assisting Agnes again? Or perhaps regret that she couldn't keep her promise of helping Geillis take revenge on her husband.

Seton turned, as if sensing Geillis's thoughts. But his eyes skimmed over her as if she were a speck of dirt, and he took his wife's arm, leading her inside.

As Geillis took her place beside Jeanie, she couldn't help squirming uneasily. Every time she'd set foot in a kirk since All Hallows' Eve, guilt had writhed in her belly. Two Sundays on, she still felt ashamed of what had been done – what she'd been part of – in a sanctified place. Even the crucifix was no comfort; the carved Christ only reminded her of the tiny manikins Bothwell had tossed on the flames.

'Repent then,' the minister cried, 'and turn to God, so your sins may be wiped out.'

If only, Geillis thought. My sins are too many to count. And I know I'll be forced to sin again. She thought of Wemyss's offer to meet at St Giles'. How could she sully yet another kirk? How could she ask Margareta's husband to save her when Geillis had betrayed Margareta so cruelly?

Jeanie's head drooped onto Geillis's shoulder. How Geillis envied her innocence, her peaceful sleep, while Geillis sat, aching with weariness, listening to a man preach about an absolution she'd never find.

Rain had fallen while the service dragged on. By the time they left the kirk, the paths were pitted with brown puddles. Shoulders hunched against the weather, wishing she'd been awake enough to don Margareta's gloves, Geillis didn't notice they'd reached the crossroads until she heard Agnes speak.

'Come, Geillis. We need to see Mistress Hughes again.'

The breech birth. Geillis unthinkingly moved towards Agnes.

'Hold.'

She'd never heard Seton speak so authoritatively. Surprised, Geillis halted, a few feet from where Agnes waited with Blossom.

Seton smiled. 'You won't be visiting anyone.'

Agnes snorted. 'I haven't time for this. Making sure a woman doesn't bleed to death is more important than your nonsense.'

'But far more important,' Seton said silkily, 'is punishing witches.'

Gasps rustled among the servants. Before anyone could speak, hoofbeats approached from the Haddington road. Riders dressed in black rounded the bend, led by the sheriff of Haddington.

'Master Seton,' the sheriff said. 'As arranged. Where are they?'

His smile full of satisfied spite, Seton pointed at Agnes and Geillis. 'Take them.'

The sheriff gestured to his men, who dismounted and moved towards the women. 'Agnes Sampson, Geillis Duncan, I arrest you in the name of His Grace King James, on suspicion of high treason, conspiracy to murder, and witchcraft.'

As they dragged her towards the waiting horses, the final word beat inside Geillis's skull, a hammer about to shatter all that she was, leaving only the echoing damnation: *witchcraft*.

PART III

We have scotch'd the snake, not kill'd it;
She'll close, and be herself, whilst our poor malice
Remains in danger of her former tooth.
'Macbeth'

32

There were rats in Haddington tolbooth. Geillis could hear them scrabbling in the stones. Last night she'd jolted awake, convinced one was creeping past her cheek, only to discover it was her own arm, crushed beneath her weight as she slept. She'd tried to stretch, but there were only so many positions she could twist into with her wrists chained, and by morning every muscle throbbed.

How long had she been here? A week? Longer? There were no windows to tell her it was day or night, only stretches of time when the air grew colder. All she knew was that more prisoners kept arriving, and with more prisoners came more filth, and more rats.

At first it had just been Geillis and Agnes. Geillis had been shaking, convinced the guards would pass every word to the sheriff. Meanwhile Agnes simply sat cross-legged and closed her eyes, infuriatingly calm; she'd been here before.

'Stop fidgeting,' she'd barked. 'No need to fret. Just wait.'

But as time passed, and other prisoners started arriving, she'd stopped rebuking Geillis, and Geillis suspected some of the noises she'd taken for rats were Agnes gnawing her nails.

Bessie had been next. Then some women Geillis remembered from the Fiery Hills and the kirkyard: Janet Stratton, some Stobies and Linkups. But no Euphame MacCalzean, no Barbara Napier. Was their money keeping an arrest at bay?

'Grierson's been arrested,' Janet told them through a split lip; she hadn't gone with the sheriff's men quietly. 'They're hunting Fian.'

'Will he have gone to Bothwell?' Bessie asked, looking between them all frantically. 'Surely Bothwell won't let him be caught?'

'He'll have to if you keep blurting out his name,' Agnes snapped. 'He's promised to reward us – but not if we betray him. So keep silent. Never, ever mention his name, or he'll abandon you to whatever fate they have in mind for us. Understand?'

Ilsa's fate. The flames. Geillis could only echo the others' words.

'Yes, Agnes.'

Since then, hardly anyone had spoken. Too fearful, perhaps, or too exhausted – it was impossible to rest with accusations of witchcraft hanging over them.

Claws skittered past Geillis's ankles and she jerked away. She'd never liked the Setons' kitchen cat, but now she longed for his company.

Suddenly the cell door swung open and the sheriff strode in.

'On your feet, all of you. You're changing lodgings.'

They were herded onto a cart and lashed to the railings, forced to stand like livestock. Rain turned the wood slick and made adjusting their feet treacherous. Once Bessie slipped, cracking her kneecap so loudly Geillis thought the cart had split in two. But their guards barely noticed, and Bessie's sobs dwindled to plaintive sniffs.

The Edinburgh road had never seemed so long. Geillis's soaked dress felt more water than wool, and rain spooled down her cheeks faster than she could blink, plastering her hair against her skull. There were tiny puddles in the jut of her collarbones, the hollows between her knuckles, and she was too numb to dislodge them.

Worse than the cold were the people they passed. Some hissed under their breath; some crossed themselves, for fear made everyone turn to old beliefs for comfort, even popish superstition. Others spat scornfully at the cart. A gobbet of phlegm landed on Geillis's arm, and she watched in frozen disbelief as it slid down her sleeve, leaving a glistening slug trail behind.

'Devil's whores!'

'Burning's too good for you!'

And the worst words, muttered by women who looked away quickly afterwards: 'May God forgive you.'

In Edinburgh, the cries grew louder. More people spat. Small boys hurled clods that spattered against the cart. Geillis heard Bessie choking; she'd probably been hit in the face, but Geillis was too weary to turn, let alone commiserate. Filth covered her dress; she smelled dung and wanted to weep in humiliation.

The cart passed Holyrood Palace and swung onto the Canongate, creaking uphill over the cobbles. In the distance, Geillis could just make out the rain-lashed castle, gripping the crag like a great eagle. Were they heading to its dungeons? A bell tolled, and she jumped as if it were an explosion.

It was St Giles'. The kirk where Wemyss had suggested meeting. At the thought of him, Geillis's wrist rubbed against Margareta's ring, still sewn into her cuff. Her one hope.

They'd stopped. The guards dragged them off the cart, leaving their wrists bound. Trying to swipe the rain off her face with the ropes, Geillis peered up at the building before them. Grey walls reached up towards a sky that suddenly seemed less grey, less cold in comparison. Slit windows pierced the stone, narrow as sneers; most were muzzled by iron bars. The tolbooth.

'Welcome home,' a guard said, shoving Geillis forward. 'You'll not be leaving for a while.'

It was worse than Haddington. When she first saw the chains in their cell, Geillis had almost been pleased: shackles for ankles, not wrists. But before long, she cursed herself for a fool. The iron's grip was cold; every time she moved her feet, ice seeped into her legs. Whenever someone stirred, the clanking scraped along everyone else's ears like fingernails. A gutter ran through the middle of the cell, but their chains were just short enough that whenever anyone squatted to piss, half their waste soaked the stones. After one day, the air was fetid; by the third, Geillis had given up trying to breathe through her mouth; this latest defeat made her shrivel inside.

St Giles' was a stone's throw away, and its bells wouldn't let them forget the passing days. Once again, Geillis wished she'd gone to meet

Wemyss. Whatever he might have asked would have been better than being in this cell, where rain drove through broken shutters. If the wind was south-easterly, Geillis had to shrink into a ball to avoid being drenched; if it was north-westerly, Bessie huddled and shivered.

No one slept. They weren't allowed. As soon as darkness fell, guards marched in, brandishing torches in their faces, so close Geillis smelt her hair singe. If anyone dropped off and their breathing changed, the guards dashed water over their heads. At least, Geillis hoped it was water. How could she tell when the whole cell stank?

'Do they mean to drive us mad?' Bessie wailed after three sleepless nights.

Agnes had glared at her. 'That's exactly what they intend.'

Was it working? Bessie wept in her corner. Geillis had bitten her lips so raw she couldn't sip water without tasting blood too. But Agnes sat, spine straight as a willow wand, eyes blazing with anger.

By the fourth day, Geillis was so exhausted she could scarcely see. Every noise hurt her head; even moving her fingers felt like lifting rocks.

'They want to break us,' Agnes said quietly beside her. 'Are you as fragile as they believe, Geillis? Or made of sterner stuff?'

Why was she asking Geillis questions? How could she not be too drained to speak? But then Geillis heard footsteps approaching, and realization glimmered.

They were about to be interrogated. The guards had waited until the women were feverish with sleeplessness, shivering, aching, tearful. As close to breaking point as possible.

The doors opened.

'Geillis Duncan. Come with us.'

Every step hurt. She'd longed for the shackles to be removed, but now they were gone she could feel the sores where they'd bitten her flesh. They'd held her feet slightly pointed for days; now, every time her foot flattened against the floor, splinters of pain shot up her shins. Forced upstairs, she gasped in agony as her toes hit each tread. By the time they thrust her through a door, her lower body was on fire, and it took her a moment to recognize who was waiting for her.

'You!'

Her thighs clenched with old horror; even after days of rats and filth, her skin crawled with revulsion at the sight of him.

Seton sat before the fire, picking at his fingernails with a knifepoint. 'Oh, yes,' he agreed, calmer than she'd seen him in months. 'Geillis Duncan, you are accused of witchcraft. How do you plead?'

'Not—' She halted. There was no one else there. The only furniture, apart from Seton's chair, was a long, low table. 'Am I on trial? Shouldn't there be a jury? Shouldn't this wait until the assizes?'

'See how much she knows of the law?' Seton said to the guards. 'No woman should know as much – unless she has cause to find out.'

A guard sniggered. Once, Geillis might have yearned to hit him, but the effort of hating someone other than Seton seemed impossible now.

Seton rose and stalked towards her. 'There will be trials,' he said softly. 'I've ridden as far as the borders, tracking conspirators. Yesterday, I captured a friend of yours. John Fian.'

Geillis shook her head. 'We're not friends.'

'But you know him. Much the same thing.'

'Knowing someone's name can't be evidence against me!'

'Wrong, I'm afraid,' he said. 'But I seek a different kind of evidence today. I seek proof that you're a witch.'

'I am no witch!'

He ran the knifepoint along her cheek. 'Exactly what a witch would say.' He turned to the guards. 'Strip her.'

'No!' She tried to wrench away – but even if she hadn't been at her weakest, she'd have been no match for the guards. One gripped her wrists while the other yanked at her laces, tugging and tearing until once again she was forced to stand naked before Seton. The guard gripping her wrists met her eyes then, very deliberately, dropped his to her breasts, then lower – then leered.

Geillis spat in his face.

Next moment she was gasping in pain as the guards dragged her by the hair and shoved her onto the table before lashing her wrists and ankles to the table legs.

'Shave her.'

She hadn't wept until now. But as her hair was sliced away, even the greasy, matted tangles it had become, Geillis couldn't stop tears falling. No use struggling anymore, not when the guards held a blade to her scalp and scraped her hair to a rough stubble. Even when they slipped, drawing blood – and they slipped often – Geillis didn't struggle. She stifled sobs, but she lay still. When Seton said, 'And the hair below,' she lay even stiller, her salt tears stinging on fresh cuts as they ran down past her ears to the table.

The guards finished. Despite not having been in a chamber with a lit fire for over a week, Geillis had never felt colder. Her shorn head and body felt as exposed as moors in midwinter.

Seton stood beside her head. 'Now, Geillis, I'm going to test you for the devil's mark.'

She'd heard of this test – pricking freckles and moles and nipples to see if they bled, or if the accused felt no pain. But she'd never considered how many marks there were on a single limb, let alone her body. Her face was still freckled from summer. There were four moles on her left arm, and six on her right. What of her shoulders, or her back? How many times would Seton prick her?

Steel glinted near her eyes and she gasped in horror. She'd imagined a tiny needle, the sort Mistress Katherine used for fine sewing. But this was the length of a hand, and wielded by a man who despised her.

He pricked her face first. Even when it hurt to cry out because she was bleeding from a dozen wounds, Geillis couldn't stop moaning. When he moved down to her arms, he drove the needle even deeper, skewering her flesh, and she hadn't known she could make such noises. Her armpits were next, then her chest; Seton stabbed each of her breasts with a vindictive snarl, and she shrieked. By the time he moved down to her belly and her hips, her raw lips had broken open again, and her mouth filled with blood; once he'd reached her feet her throat was ragged with screaming. Finally they untied her, and she wept with relief – but then they flipped her over and the pricking began again, working up her legs to her buttocks, back, shoulders, already bloodied scalp.

'Nothing,' one of the guards said, voice quavering with nausea. 'Should we take her back to the cell?'

Please. The quiet cell, where no hands would touch her, was the most beautiful prospect imaginable.

Seton snorted. 'I'm not done with her yet. Where else would the devil mark his whores, but in their most secret places?'

She barely had time to be horrified before they flung her onto her back again. She tried to clamp her legs together, but the guards wrenched them apart. Seton stalked from the head of the table to lean over her. Geillis tried to brace herself. And then he drove the needle into her flesh.

She was lying on the floor before the fire. Everywhere was agony. When she tried to move, her new scabs cracked like scales. Had she fainted? How else had she got from the table to the floor? Who had dragged her clothes over her unresisting limbs?

'You're awake.'

Seton's voice. She tried to scrabble away, but agony exploded between her legs and she moaned helplessly.

'Poor Geillis.' Seton's boots appeared in front of her, crusted with mud; Fian must have led him quite a chase. 'What a terrible time you've had.' He crouched down. 'If only you'd had the sense to serve me better, you might yet have been free.'

She hauled herself up to sitting. 'You accused me.'

'You betrayed me,' he retorted. 'You let the Sampson woman murder my daughter. Even afterwards, you refused to stay away from her. And then your behaviour with Bothwell ... Geillis, you have only yourself to blame.'

She shook her head, forcing her thoughts past the fog of pain. 'But you're on Bothwell's side. If he's incriminated, you are too!'

'Allegiances change. Besides, who would accuse me? You? After I've been so assiduous?' Seton smiled and drew something out from his doublet. She saw metal and jerked away; his smile widened. 'Do you know what this is, Geillis?'

She shook her head, not wanting to know.

He took her hand, terrifyingly gentle. 'They call them pilliwinks, or thumbikins. Such silly names for something so … damaging.' He slipped the device around her thumb. 'You might not think it now. Look how small it is! Look what a fraction of you a thumb is! And yet, I'm told, our hands are among the most sensitive parts of our bodies. And, of course, the most useful. Whatever would a girl like you do with crushed thumbs?' Slowly, he wound the screws, until the vice pressed close.

Geillis swallowed. 'What do you want?'

Seton turned the screws once more. Her thumbnail pinched her own flesh. Blood throbbed against metal. 'I want you to serve me now, Geillis. You will never mention my dealings with Bothwell, not to anyone. They never took place, understand?'

'Yes.'

'Let's practise, shall we? Just to make sure.' He tightened the screw and she gasped, trying to twist her hand away, but that only made the pain worse. 'How were you first persuaded to join the witches?'

'No—' She broke off, panting in agony.

'Oh, Geillis,' he crooned. 'I know you don't wish to name anyone. That's very kind. But what harm can it do to give up the names of those already accused? They damned themselves long ago. No one could blame you for their fates.'

But she'd blame herself. That was worse.

'Come, Geillis. You know the name I want to hear. If you give me her name, I won't tighten the screws again.'

'Please,' she whispered. 'Stop, please.'

'A name, Geillis. One name, that's all.'

He knew the name. She was already here. This wasn't about the name; it was about Seton's mastery over Geillis.

'Why be loyal to that creature? Would you even be here if not for her?'

How many times had Geillis asked herself the same question? Agnes had placed her in harm's way. Agnes had lured her into Bothwell's schemes. Geillis had been raped, arrested, pricked, all because of Agnes, Agnes.

The screw turned. Geillis screamed. And in the midst of her screaming, a name tumbled out.

'Agnes! Agnes Sampson.'

Alone in the cell, Geillis couldn't stop shivering. It wasn't the icy wind skirling through the bars; it was the thought of Seton. Not the blundering, posturing man she'd worked for, struggling to govern himself, let alone his household, but a newly empowered man. Who had given him that power?

Clearly not Bothwell. He didn't trust Seton, and why would Seton have arranged Geillis and Agnes's arrests if he were truly working for Bothwell?

St Giles's bells tolled and Geillis flinched. If only she'd taken Wemyss up on his offer. She cradled her injured hand close to her chest; even the brush of thin wool on broken skin made her cry out, and through her cuff Margareta's ring felt like yet another torture device. If she'd met Wemyss, Seton might not have had yet another opportunity to hurt her.

If not Bothwell, then who? Seton would be too terrified to betray the earl unless for someone more powerful. His kin might have royal blood, but they were sparrows beside Bothwell's hawk. Only one person stood above Bothwell.

Seton now served the king. Which meant King James had condoned, perhaps even ordered Geillis's arrest.

Geillis leaned back against damp stone; its chill bled through her shorn scalp. How had they ever believed they could fight against these forces?

The door opened and Bessie staggered in. Cuts on her shaved scalp had turned her forehead crimson, then mingled with tears, leaving grisly stripes on her cheeks. Her wrists and neck were covered with wounds: she'd been pricked too.

The guards fastened Bessie's shackles and stalked out. Bessie turned her face to the wall and wept. Geillis had no comfort to offer her.

Where was Agnes? What had been done to her – and how much more because of Geillis's betrayal?

Janet Stratton returned next, limp and whimpering feverishly. Then the Linkups and Stobies, all shorn, all bloodstained, none of them willing to meet anyone's eyes.

Agnes was last to be brought back. Purple bruises circled her skull like a horrible garland, blossoming from a ring of scarlet rope burns. They'd bound a knotted rope about her head and tightened its ends with every question. Agnes must have felt as if her skull were about to shatter, driving bone into brain.

The guards closed the door, leaving them in the gloom with their injuries and shame.

Agnes spoke. 'Did you follow my instructions?'

Stark white faces turned to her, eyes huge beneath shorn scalps. No one spoke.

'Answer me,' Agnes hissed. 'Did anyone mention his name?'

Geillis had – but Seton already knew of Bothwell's involvement and had his own reasons for keeping it concealed. One by one, the women shook their heads.

Agnes nodded; one eye twitched sharply, telling Geillis how much that gesture hurt. 'Good. Then—'

'Good?' Bessie cried, voice cracking with tears. 'How is any of this *good*? We've been humiliated, tortured—'

'Which is illegal,' Agnes pointed out. 'Testimonies cannot be extracted through torture, especially not from women.'

'What about witches?' Geillis asked. 'No one cares what's done to a witch, as long as it gets rid of her.'

'If the law's being ignored,' Agnes continued, 'then whoever's orchestrating this believes they're above the law.'

Geillis watched realization dawn on the others.

'Then …' Bessie hesitated. 'The king ordered our arrests? But how could he even know our names? Did someone betray us?'

Geillis swallowed; a wound on her throat pinched. She hadn't been that traitor. Did that lessen her betrayal now?

'That isn't important now,' Agnes said. 'What matters is what we do next.'

'We're in jail,' Geillis pointed out bitterly. 'We can't do anything.'

Agnes shook her head. 'Bothwell gave us a task. We can still carry it out, even from this tolbooth. If we do, he'll reward us. Remember – I've been arrested on charges of witchcraft twice before, and each time he ensured my freedom. He'll do the same for all of us. Trust me.'

Geillis frowned. 'What – should we shriek about cursed bloodlines so loudly they hear us in the marketplace?'

'He wanted us to spread fear.' Agnes leaned forward, barely wincing now. 'The only thing that frightens men more than witchcraft is a woman they cannot control. They want us to confess to witchcraft? We shall not. Do you hear me? We will not confess.'

33

Margareta hadn't felt so lost since she first arrived at the Danish court as a child. She'd still received no word from Sophia, but, returning from her confinement in early January after almost two months shut away, everything else seemed to have changed. The fashionable ruff shapes, the popular madrigals. And far more significant things.

Geillis had been arrested. She'd heard the news when her waters had broken – when the midwife, the *wrong* midwife, had entered, and in spite of herself, Margareta had longed for Geillis's gentle hands, her warm reassurance. Even if it had been a lie all along. Only when little Johnny had finally emerged, red-faced, round, perfect, had Margareta truly acknowledged her greatest fear: that Geillis's betrayal had not only killed Anna's child, but damaged Margareta's. Yet Johnny was safe, and in the midst of her overwhelming new love, she'd found herself bewildered by the gratitude she felt towards the Scottish apprentice.

Johnny's father, meanwhile, brought news of another ruinous change.

'How could this happen?'

John was rocking the cradle, having dismissed the nursemaid, restraining himself from pushing too hard. Frustration coiled in his clenching fists. 'I did everything I could.'

Margareta wanted to hit him, to bellow her rage. The cradle between them was both a well of tenderness and an infuriating obstacle. 'You were brawling on the Canongate!'

'I was attacked on the Canongate,' he corrected her. 'Lennox struck me with his sword. He could have taken my head off, by the way, if that concerns you at all.'

'He'd have had to strike hard,' she snapped, 'since your skin's so damnably thick. What in God's name had you done to provoke him?'

John sighed. 'He accused me of being too friendly with Bothwell. Said I needed to think carefully about which nobles I crawled to. As if anyone could crawl to that child Lennox. So I said I'd listen to anyone ahead of his puling nonsense. At which point he drew his sword.'

'In front of the king.'

'Yes.'

'You were fighting in front of the king.'

'I was attacked in front of the king,' he retorted. 'And the king's punished me for it.'

'And me, apparently!'

'At least we aren't banished,' he offered. 'James sent Lennox away to await royal forgiveness.'

'No,' she said grimly, unable to stop tears breaking loose. 'We've just had our marriage declared invalid and our newborn son a bastard. How lenient.'

'Margareta ...' He rounded the cradle and wrapped her in his arms; she didn't have the strength to resist. 'I'm sorry. Furious, resentful, still certain of my own innocence – but also sorry.'

She dashed her knuckles over her eyes. 'Does James think himself God now? He cannot declare marriages invalid on a whim!'

John shook his head apologetically. 'Evidently he can. He says since our marriage didn't take place in Scotland, or with my father's consent, or James's, it's not valid in his kingdom.'

'Your father's consent?' She pounced on this. 'Won't he speak up?'

'My father hasn't been to court since I was a boy. Hates spending money. Asking the king for favours is an expense he can't – or won't – stretch to.'

'Can't we just get married again?'

'Only with James's consent.'

Tears threatened again; she bit her lips. 'He'll hardly grant that now!'

John hesitated. 'Actually …'

She heard his tone shift. 'What now?'

'He says he'll give permission. If I serve him.'

'You're already serving him!'

'This is how kings work.' John laced his fingers through hers. 'Binding men to them, tighter and tighter. Promises given, rewards dangled just out of reach, new conditions imposed.'

'Tell me.'

John sighed. 'I must help interrogate the accused witches. And assist with … drawing out their confessions. But that could take months – there are so many of them.'

It seemed wrong to ask while gazing down on their son, as if it might somehow taint little Johnny, making him grow up cruel, or frightened, or obsessed with witchcraft. But she had to know. 'How many?'

'So far? More than twenty. They haven't finished rounding up suspects yet.'

'Are any …' She'd been about to ask if any were guilty, but she couldn't bear dwelling on the answer to that question. 'Have any confessed?'

'Not yet.'

'Yet?'

John stepped away from the cradle, as if he too worried that saying such things around their son would defile the very air he breathed. 'They're torturing the accused. All of them.'

His words came back to her. 'Drawing out their confessions?'

He nodded. 'For our son's sake, I must break James's own law and torture prisoners. And whatever pain it causes me will be nothing to what I must inflict on them.'

This was the price of their marriage. A dowry steeped in blood. 'What will be done to them?'

John drew in a breath before rushing out a list. 'Pricking, thumbscrews, forcing them to go without sleep, binding their heads in knotted
ropes … and worse.'

She gaped, imagining Geillis's bruised and bloodied body, her
exhausted eyes. 'What could be worse?'

His voice was grim. 'They call it the witch's bridle.'

Geillis was dragged from the cell in the middle of the night. They
hauled her by the arms, too fast for her sore-cracked feet to keep up,
but every time she stumbled they only marched faster through the
dark labyrinth of the tolbooth.

Where were they taking her? They'd taken Agnes three nights ago;
no one knew where. Trial, another gaol – or worse? When Geillis
asked, the guard laughed. 'You'll find out soon enough. If I were you,
I'd enjoy my last moments of not knowing.'

Every time Geillis heard more footsteps than usual outside, she
thought it was the mob rushing to Agnes's execution, not merely
market day or a service at St Giles'. Whenever she smelled woodsmoke
or roasting meat, she was convinced it was Agnes's pyre, Agnes's
flesh.

The guards paused outside a door and knocked. When it opened,
Geillis's knees almost gave way with relief.

It was Wemyss. Wemyss, who'd offered her help. But now when
he looked at her, his eyes were as severe as his black garb. He knew
what she'd done with the herbs – and he despised her for it.

'Thank you, gentlemen.' He steered Geillis inside.

Two torches flickered above a desk, their jagged flames the only
light in the room. Seated in their glow was another man whose grizzled beard and grim face made him appear chiselled from stone.

'Mistress Duncan, this is Chancellor Maitland.'

Should she have heard of him? Had she heard and forgotten?
Names, people, places – anything before the cells seemed as churned
up as a water barrel after laundry day.

Maitland nodded. 'Thank you for joining us.'

As if she'd been invited to dinner. Were they about to bring out roasted peacock?

'I hope you will aid us,' Maitland continued. 'We seek information.'

Wemyss moved to stand behind Maitland, arms folded. Something about his lowered brows, his thinned lips … he didn't want to be here.

'Now then,' Maitland said, shuffling papers. 'I've been told you have some skill with herbs. That does sound useful.'

His voice was almost kindly.

'Sickness is rife in January,' Maitland said. 'What would you recommend for a cough?'

No danger in telling him that, surely? 'Ginger. Steeped in hot water. Some honey for the soreness. Or a syrup of mallow roots.'

'How helpful,' Maitland said. 'And who told you that?'

Geillis wavered. 'I can't remember.'

'I doubt that. If you can remember herbal remedies, you can remember a name.'

'My mother.' Bridget was dead; naming her was harmless.

'Really?'

'Yes.'

Maitland sighed. He set his quill back in the inkpot and folded his hands. 'Geillis, I find lies offensive. And I always find out who has lied to me, and then I am so very disappointed. Now, I know you are lying. Shall I tell you how?'

She didn't dare speak.

'Your mother died almost two years ago,' Maitland stated. 'During her lifetime, no one summoned you to their sickbeds. But since then, many have sought you, haven't they?'

'Yes.'

'So your knowledge of remedies must have improved. Unless you summoned up your mother's ghost, someone else must have taught you. Who?'

Geillis hesitated.

Maitland leaned forward. 'Was it Agnes Sampson?'

They already knew. Wemyss had seen Agnes on All Hallows' Eve. What harm lay in giving them a name they already had?

'Yes.'

'And where did she get her knowledge?'

'I don't know. Perhaps her mother ...'

'Perhaps,' Maitland conceded. 'But not all of it. We believe some of Mistress Sampson's knowledge was unnatural. Ungodly. Did you ever believe that, Geillis?'

'She just knew a lot about herbs.'

'So she only ever used her skills to heal the sick?'

She thought of the wax figures, the whistling. 'Only to help people.'

Maitland eyed her thoughtfully. He already knew, she realized. He just wanted to hear what lies she would tell.

'I know you're afraid,' Maitland said gently. 'I know someone's frightened you. And I do not believe that person was Agnes Sampson. I'm not asking you to hurt your friend, but to help her. I believe Agnes has been led astray by someone very powerful. She is a victim, not a villain. All I need from you is that person's name. Then I can let Agnes go.'

'Let her go?' Back to Tranent? Were they about to be released?

'And you with her, of course. Otherwise you'll have to share her suffering. And she has suffered a great deal. Even before she came here. Did she never tell you?'

'Tell me what?'

'About her child, of course.'

Geillis froze. What child? She knew Agnes had been a mother – but she'd never dared ask what had become of her children. She thought of the chamber in Agnes's house, the one she wouldn't offer Geillis.

'Now, I've only heard rumours,' Maitland continued. 'It would be helpful if you could tell me the truth – about the child's death, about his father ...'

Geillis heard a low groan from the shadows behind her. She'd heard such noises before. The kind women made after a labour had lasted several days and still no child had emerged. You only made such noises if you were exhausted, body and mind, and had been in pain for so long you couldn't remember what not being in pain was like.

'Wemyss, show Geillis how Agnes has suffered.'

Face blank, Wemyss removed a torch from its bracket. He took Geillis's arm and she wanted to shake him off – whatever he was about to show her, she didn't want to see – but he was too strong and she didn't dare. They moved into the darkness. Wemyss lifted the torch, and Geillis forced herself to look.

Agnes's wrists were chained above her head, and another chain around her waist clamped her against the wall. She was naked, and Geillis wanted to cry at how shameful this was for Agnes, to have her slack body exposed, her pale, drooping breasts, the silver scars on her belly where children – and whose children? – had stretched her flesh taut, and the newer scars, the pricking scars. But the shame wasn't the worst part. The worst part was the bridle.

It was an iron muzzle nailed to the wall. One strap went over Agnes's skull from jawline to jawline; the other encircled her face, pinning her mouth open. A bridle-bit clamped her tongue down, so tight even swallowing water would lacerate her tongue. Blood stained Agnes's face everywhere metal touched flesh, some scabbing over, some fresh scarlet. Her mouth was stretched into a gruesome smile, making her resemble a wild beast lifting its head from a kill.

'Agnes,' Geillis whispered, lifting a hand to reach for her.

But Agnes grunted a sharp rebuke: she didn't want pity. The effort sent iron slicing into her flesh and she groaned in agony.

It had been Agnes who insisted they keep silent about Bothwell, who insisted it would be worth it – and Agnes who appeared willing to endure more pain than any of them to ensure Bothwell wasn't named. If Geillis named him now, it would be a betrayal. But if she didn't?

'Some call it the scold's bridle,' Maitland said. 'But it is also known, rather aptly, as the witch's bridle.'

Were all men obsessed with torture implements? What malevolence made them delight in women's suffering?

'I imagine you would not wish to wear one, Geillis.'

'No.' The word slipped out before she could help herself and she clenched her tortured hand. The thumb hadn't healed; she suspected it never would – it was crooked, the split nail black and protruding at strange angles.

'Then give me a name, Geillis. A single name, and I can release Agnes.'

Bothwell. One word, and Maitland would give them what Bothwell hadn't: freedom.

'Who was it?'

If she didn't give them a name, she'd share Agnes's fate. Stripped naked, pinned to the wall for days, bleeding with every breath, silenced and shamed.

'It's just a name, Geillis. That's all.'

Like Seton had said. *One name, that's all.* And she'd screamed out Agnes's. He'd said it would make no difference – but here was Agnes, tortured beyond belief. She couldn't betray her again. Because it wasn't Agnes's fault, never had been. Men like Seton and Maitland were to blame.

Yet they wouldn't give up if she stayed silent. Would it be Bessie next? Would she resist longer than Geillis? If she didn't, what would be the point of Geillis suffering?

'Was it a man?'

'Yes,' she breathed.

Agnes blinked at her. How could such a small gesture convey such disgust?

'And his name?'

She gave them one. A man already captured: the schoolmaster whose feet danced faster than flames. 'John Fian.'

Maitland was silent. Wemyss looked back at him. Then Maitland sighed in disappointment.

'Take them back to the cell.'

'No!' Geillis twisted in Wemyss's grip. 'You said we could go free!'

'But you lied,' Maitland said calmly. 'So it's only fair that I've lied too. Guards! I am done with the prisoners.' As the door opened, his eyes travelled over Geillis, slow and cold as a pike gliding through dark reeds. 'For now.'

*   *   *

Ahead, the guards dragging Agnes were jeering, deliberately elbowing her bloodied head, treading on her hem, and Agnes's every moan cut Geillis. This was her fault. And whatever they did to Fian next would be her fault too.

'Keep moving.' Wemyss jerked her arm, forcing her to stumble.

'Please,' she whispered, 'please. Help us—'

'Why?' He stopped so suddenly her arm was yanked back, and she gasped in pain. 'Why in God's name should I help you? You and Agnes tricked my wife and murdered the queen's child – *you*. I'm already helping you enough by keeping that quiet.'

She flinched at his accusation as if it were boiling oil in her eyes. 'Then I'm grateful—'

'I'm not doing it for you, you fool. I'm doing it for Margareta.'

'You're not the only one keeping quiet for her.'

'Is that a threat?' His eyes glittered dangerously and she recoiled.

'No! But … I haven't betrayed her. Not in the way you think.'

'Haven't betrayed her? You endangered her – endangered our child and killed another! So let me tell you what I think, Geillis.' He said her name as if discarding soiled linen. 'Every time you mention a name, one of your friends gets hurt, and it's me that has to do it. Eventually, I'll be ordered to hurt you, and they won't stop at one thumb. So why not end it all now by giving them the one name they really want?'

Bothwell.

'You don't understand,' she said miserably. 'I can't. The only thing I can do is stay silent.'

He shook his head in disgust. 'If only you had. For John Fian's sake.'

He thrust her onwards, and as she stumbled through the dank corridors, her hopes felt as crushed as her hand. Neither Wemyss nor Margareta would save her. And she would never dare – or deserve – to ask for their help again.

Every time John returned from the tolbooth he looked like a soldier staggering away from the battlefield. He kept his back straight, his stride long – until their bedchamber door closed behind him and he sank down wherever he stopped: the bed, a chair, even the rushes.

Margareta hated seeing him like this. He'd always been strong, always able to suggest solutions. Now, he ground his knuckles against his eyes as if scouring away what he'd seen.

'Would you like wine?' she offered helplessly, bouncing Johnny on her knee. 'Or food?'

John looked up, unseeing. 'No.'

'To sleep? I could get a tisane …' But procuring herbs was the last thing she ought to suggest, and she fell silent.

Slowly, John said, 'I should like … to hold my son.'

She hesitated, then rose and placed Johnny into his arms. Resuming her seat by the fire, she watched them on the hearthrug. Johnny's tiny frown, the way he tilted his head as though listening intently, how his eyes widened in surprise – all these were John, and yet Johnny, at eight weeks old, was less than the length of his father's arm. Johnny rooted curiously at John's chest; realizing there was no prospect of milk, he nuzzled in for a nap. As the child's eyelids fluttered, John's face softened.

'You're worth it all, little man,' he murmured. 'If what I do today keeps you safe tomorrow, it's a price I'll pay a thousand times.'

Margareta wasn't sure she wanted to ask. 'How high was the price today?'

'Higher than before. Yet still not high enough.'

'They won't confess?'

'Not to witchcraft, or to Bothwell.'

'Even under torture?'

'Not even then.' He kissed Johnny's head. 'Today we put the boots on John Fian.'

'Boots?'

John grimaced. 'We encased his legs in wood. Then drove wedges in, and with every wedge a question – who was at the Fiery Hills, who at North Berwick, what did you do there? Yet all Fian's admitted is that he was out after dark because he hoped to lie with the women.'

'How can he continue withholding the truth?' Margareta breathed, horrified.

John shrugged. 'Perhaps it *is* the truth. At first, maybe he just hoped to seduce one of them.' He lifted one of Johnny's tiny hands and watched the baby's fingers unfurl to clamp around his. 'I've never seen anything like this, Margareta. The sight of torture implements is usually enough to spill anyone's secrets. But this group will admit nothing.'

Margareta bit her lip. 'Has it occurred to you that the majority might have nothing to confess?'

'You mean they might be innocent?' He sighed. 'Dozens of times. When I heard Fian's flesh splitting. When we clamped the bridle on Agnes Sampson. When I saw Geillis Duncan's ruined hand. How could they endure that and still refuse to change their stories?'

Geillis, who had betrayed Margareta and killed Anna's baby. Yet no treachery could justify torture. And she was still the Geillis whose herbs had kept Johnny safe, who'd promised her silence would keep Margareta safe – and who still had Margareta's ring. Silence couldn't explain that away if it was discovered. She swallowed, too loudly. 'Their stories could be true.'

'Or something else terrifies them far more than torture.'

'Bothwell?'

He nodded grimly. 'We need them to name him. If they don't, it will all have been for nothing.'

'But you all know! You, Maitland, James – you're all certain Bothwell's behind this. Why torture these people just to get information you already have?'

'It's not enough,' John said bleakly. 'We have no evidence. Witchcraft doesn't leave traces – there are no bloodstained weapons or footprints. Only words – and no one will talk.'

'And yet people are being brutalized every day. If there's no evidence against Bothwell, surely there's none against Geillis and Agnes either.'

John closed his eyes. 'It's different.'

'How? How is it different?'

'Because Bothwell's an earl.' He looked up at her. 'Arresting school-masters and midwives is one thing. But to arrest the most powerful noble in Scotland, who half the kingdom seems to think should be king? Without testimonies condemning him, we cannot move against Bothwell.' He pressed his cheek against Johnny's downy hair. 'They must name him. Or else they'll keep being tortured … and I must help torture them.'

Margareta hadn't spoken alone with Anna since returning to court. There'd been no opportunity, she told herself, and knew this wasn't true. There had been as many opportunities as ever – helping Anna dress, walking in the gardens, brushing her hair before bed. But Margareta hadn't taken them. How could you say to your queen, your friend, that it was your fault she lost her baby? Especially now Margareta's own baby thrived.

She was ashamed. Every day she stayed silent, her shame spread like a plague rash.

In the end, it was Anna who spoke first.

Anna and her ladies were walking in Holyrood's gardens, pattens crunching on snow. Draped in white, the plants were almost unrecognizable: rose bushes became pale statues, while the frozen fountain seemed like a fallen moon. The distant summit of Arthur's Seat was a blued smudge against snow-bearing clouds.

'We might almost be at home,' Anna said wistfully.

A servant approached, bearing a tray of hot cider. Taking one, Anna nodded to Margareta; while the other ladies stood sipping cider and stamping their feet, the two of them moved away.

'You miss home?' Margareta asked, trying to feel her way into what Anna wanted to discuss.

Anna let the cider's steam envelop her face. 'It was a simpler time. All I had to worry about were ribbons and sleeves. Whereas here … I'm only permitted to speak of ribbons and sleeves, but my true worries are far deeper.'

Margareta watched cloves swirl in her cup. 'How have relations been with the king?'

Anna sighed. 'They have *been*, at least. But …'

'But?'

'He's hardly enthusiastic. Or regular. He visits my bed less than once a fortnight, and last time it coincided with my courses, so we simply bade each other goodnight. So stupid.'

'Stupid?'

Anna flicked irritably at a rose bough, sending snow scattering. 'I have so few chances as it is, and he wastes one by coming on the wrong day! If he truly wished me to conceive again, he could at least put some effort into counting!' She laughed bitterly. 'I tell you, Margareta, sometimes I do nothing but. I count the days since my last courses, then the days since James last visited and how many until my next courses and on which day I might permit myself to hope. Sometimes I go too far and count the weeks and months until a baby might be born, and the possible saints' days that could share the prince's day of birth. And then … then I bleed again, or spend the night alone again, and I wish the numbers in my head were insects that I might crush them.'

'Oh, Anna.' Margareta wanted to embrace her, but they both kept their hands clasped tight around their cups, gripping warmth like a talisman.

'And then I count up the times I took that woman's herbs,' Anna continued. 'And I wonder if I killed my own child.'

Margareta froze.

Anna's eyelashes were wet. 'Was it my fault, Margareta?'

'No!' Cider spilt as Margareta touched Anna's shoulder. 'If it was anyone's fault, it was mine – I gave you those herbs. If not for me, you might never have heard of Agnes Sampson.'

'So it was the herbs.' Anna nodded bleakly. 'The physicians told me my body might have been at fault, or it was something I ate, or too much dancing. The minister said I should have prayed harder. But if it was Agnes Sampson, then … it was still my fault, but she was more to blame than me.'

'Anna, you cannot blame yourself. Blame me – I met the woman, you never did. I didn't question her enough; I didn't even ask what the herbs were before giving them to you.'

'You trusted her.'

Had she trusted Agnes? She'd wanted to – because if she could trust Agnes and Geillis, she could trust Ilsa too. All had proved treacherous. 'Yes. You were so desperate, and I wanted to help you – and the herbs she gave me never …'

'Never did your child any harm,' Anna finished. 'A fine little boy, isn't he? All dark curls and chuckles. I wonder, would my child have been dark or fair?'

Margareta deserved to feel the stab of these blades. After all, Anna felt them every day. 'Anna, I am so very, very sorry.'

'As am I.'

'If you wish me to leave your service—'

'Why would I wish that?'

'Because …' Margareta's frown mirrored Anna's. 'It was my fault you lost your baby. You should despise me.'

'But I begged you to help me,' Anna pointed out. 'I drank her herbs. I asked you for more. I don't want to punish *you*, Margareta. I want to see Agnes Sampson punished.'

The viciousness in Anna's voice chilled Margareta. 'What will you do?'

'I told James about the herbs. When I said Agnes's name, he was furious – but not with me, or even you. He knows who she is. So he's decided to take over her interrogation.' Anna smiled. It was Sophia's smile: the cruelty only a queen could summon. 'We shall watch as the witch suffers.'

34

They were burning a witch on Castle Hill. Geillis could smell it. First the wood smoke, reminding her of coming home to her mother's stew after helping her father mend nets. Then another smell, a stench horribly like roasting pork.

It was Fian. They'd heard him being taken out of the tolbooth, the clank of guards, a thump of something heavy hitting the ground, and a man's cry.

'Please,' Fian had said, his pompousness reduced to an imploring whine.

'What's the matter?' a guard had laughed. 'Can't you walk?'

She'd pressed her head against the stone, willing Fian to speak with his old imperiousness. But he hadn't said a word. Eventually, another guard had said, 'Crowd's waiting. If he can't walk, tie him to the hurdle.'

They couldn't see out of the high window, but Geillis had pictured it: Fian strapped to the wooden board, screaming as they bound his ruined legs. What had they done to leave him so crippled? She didn't dare imagine – and yet, hearing Fian's moans as they dragged him over the cobbles, she could imagine only too well. Would they have done it anyway? Or was it her fault?

'Do you think he confessed?' Bessie whispered. She was twisted like Geillis, her palms flat against the wall as if she hoped to push them aside and flee. 'You can't be executed unless you confess. Can you?'

You also couldn't be tortured under Scottish law, but Geillis's maimed thumb proved how little that mattered. Either Maitland's men had tortured a full confession out of Fian, or they'd wrung out enough to condemn him. Truth or lies, she doubted they cared.

Could he have mentioned Bothwell? Agnes hadn't been in a cell with him; she hadn't ordered him to keep silent about the earl. She glanced over at Agnes, trying not to flinch at the wounds on the older woman's face. Since the guards had flung her back in the cell, Agnes had barely spoken; Geillis didn't know whether it was the pain in Agnes's body or mind keeping her so quiet.

But now Agnes forced her lips apart; blood ran down her chin. 'Bothwell will keep us safe.'

Geillis stared. Before she could speak, a great roar erupted up the hill.

'They must have lit the fire,' Bessie observed. She might have been talking about a baker preparing the day's loaves. Perhaps it was easier to pretend that was all it was.

But then the smells came, and there could be no more pretending.

'No screams,' Bessie said, still talking the awfulness away. 'That's a mercy at least.'

'Mercy?' Geillis repeated. 'They're burning him!'

'But they've strangled him first.'

Was that all the mercy any of them could hope for? Geillis watched the snow drifting between the bars at the window. After a while, some of the flakes changed, became papery, powdery, and they didn't melt when they touched the ground. Staring at Fian's ashes, Geillis thought, Bothwell didn't keep him safe. And she'd named Fian rather than Bothwell. Had she protected the wrong man?

She turned to face Agnes. When her eyes met Geillis's, they raged – with fever, or stubbornness?

'Agnes,' Geillis whispered, 'how can you still believe in Bothwell?'

Her lips parted; blood oozed. 'Old habits … die hard.'

Geillis bit her own lip, hesitant, imagining. 'But what's he done to earn your loyalty?'

Agnes stared past Geillis at the white flakes. 'He had it from the moment I met him. Ten years ago – the only time in my life I behaved like a moonstruck girl.' She paused: to swallow blood, or weighing up how much to reveal? 'I was gathering herbs in winter, digging beneath the snow when I saw him fall from his horse. I ran to help, and he laughed at the sight of me emerging through the birches. "Are you a dryad come to seduce me?" he asked, and if any other man had uttered such foolishness, I'd have scolded until the air turned blue. But from him … We looked at each other, and I knew we both intended to seduce the other, even though he had a sprained wrist and I was ten years older than him and fifty times poorer.'

'You were his lover?' Was this why they had all ended up in the tolbooth: because Agnes had once loved Bothwell?

Her smile was bloodstained, pitiful. 'He was mine. Three nights, he stayed with me. My cottage became a barrow from an old tale, a world outside the world. We drank blackberry wine and lay on his fur cloak before the fire, the marks of our teeth and nails glowing on our skin. And then the moon waned, and he returned to his countess.'

'Did you bear his child?'

Had she been staring so long that her eyes were watering? Or was Agnes – fearsome, stoic Agnes – on the brink of tears? 'I called him Francis, for his father. I never thought he'd receive more than a name – I asked for no more. But then he came for his son. He promised he'd raise him to be a fine lord. I think he even believed his own words. So I … I let my Francis go.'

'What happened to him?'

'He went to Stirling. Tradition demands royal bastards are raised there, and Bothwell always did believe he was good enough to be king. And our son was better than any royal child.' Agnes swallowed, wincing at broken skin and memories. 'But then the sweat struck.'

A chill wormed down Geillis's back. There had only ever been one ending to Agnes's tale.

'Bothwell came for me. He knew if anyone could save Francis, I could. We rode through the night to reach Stirling – only the guards wouldn't let me in.'

'But you were with Bothwell!'

'One man's orders have always outweighed Bothwell's.'

'King James?'

Agnes's eyes sparked with tears and fury. 'It was barely a year after he'd executed his last regent, and the new power had gone where it always does: to a man's head. He refused to let me see my son. Royal physicians only, he'd decreed. No dirty, ignorant peasant women, who bring more diseases than they cure. Bothwell was furious. "If you won't let Agnes go to my boy, I'll bring my boy to her," he snapped, shoving the guards aside and running to our son. But he was too late. He brought Francis out to me, and his skin was already cold. My beautiful boy, dead because of James Stuart's selfish fears.'

Geillis remembered asking Agnes if she might live with her, the sudden closure of Agnes's face as she'd said that spare chamber was being kept for ... and then nothing. They hadn't spoken of it since; too obsessed with her own pain, she hadn't considered that Agnes was wracked with agony – and had been for years. Geillis folded her ruined hand around Agnes's. 'No wonder you hate him so.'

'He deserves to be punished.' Venom shook her voice. 'And I will see it done.'

'Then ...' Understanding dawned. 'That's why you wanted to be the one to poison James's child.'

Agnes nodded. 'After we met Ilsa, I demanded Bothwell explain why he'd chosen you. He knew what James had done. He knew what I wanted. But he insisted that if I were involved, James would recognize my name – our link – and know I meant his bride harm.'

'Except you helped me anyway.'

'Well, you needed my help.' An echo of Agnes's old causticness. 'I've never disobeyed Bothwell in anything. Except this. And I don't regret it. I want James to know what I've done.' Agnes's smile glittered scarlet. 'Before I'm finished with him, I will make sure he never forgets my name.'

The palace buzzed like a plague pit, whispers seething faster than insects. A witch trial, here in Holyrood: one of the evil hags who sought to murder the royal couple would be brought to justice!

'If she doesn't escape first,' Elline whispered as they left morning prayers on the day of the trial. 'I heard she could sail out to sea in a sieve – what prison cell could hold her?'

'It has held her for two months,' Vibeke pointed out. 'Besides, how could anyone sail in a sieve?'

'Witchcraft,' Elline breathed, relishing the scandalous word. 'Isn't it obvious?'

Vibeke sniffed. 'If she's really a witch, why hasn't she escaped?'

Sensible questions – but not sensible to ask them aloud.

'No need to defend her,' Margareta said quietly, letting Vibeke hear her warning. 'She'll have the chance to defend herself at her trial.'

Vibeke thinned her lips grimly. 'Will she? I think the king's already signed her death warrant.'

Margareta suspected Vibeke was right. Who would listen to Agnes's protestations of innocence? Certainly not James, who despised witches and women, and believed this one had tried to wipe out his bloodline. Anna's pregnancy had never been officially announced; to charge Agnes with its termination would have brought scandal into the very throne room. Margareta didn't know which was more dangerous: Agnes free to poison other pregnant women, or Agnes condemned – making everyone who'd ever sought her advice guilty by association.

But when the guards brought Agnes into court, all such thoughts vanished. Margareta bit back a gasp; the sharp rustle of breath and hands around the courtroom proved others hadn't managed to stifle their shock.

John had told her about the bridle. She'd known Agnes had been tortured. But hearing words and seeing their consequences were worlds apart. All Margareta had pictured was a horse bridle – uncomfortable, but not painful.

Wounds ran from ear to ear and from crown to nape, crusted with dried blood, hideous against her shorn, pale scalp; dozens of smaller cuts pocked Agnes's face and neck. Worst of all was the damage around her mouth. Everything from nose to chin was scraped red-raw, crosshatched with scratches. Her lips were ragged strips of meat.

Either side of her mouth stretched a raw, glistening wound, a horrible rictus grin sliced into her flesh.

She murdered Anna's child. You cannot pity her.

But she'd also saved hundreds more. Agnes could have saved hundreds in the years to come. Instead, she was on trial for crimes no one could prove.

The guards led Agnes to the dock and clamped her wrist irons to the railings. They remained either side of her, as if an injured, bound woman twice their age might suddenly try to outrun them.

Beside Margareta, Anna twisted the rings round her fingers, as if she wished Agnes's face were in her grasp. Rubies sparked, and Margareta suddenly thought, *Geillis.* She'd promised to keep Margareta safe – but if Geillis had been tortured anywhere near as cruelly as Agnes, why would she keep that promise for long? She'd already betrayed Margareta once: why not twice?

Slowly, Margareta placed her quivering hand atop Anna's – not for comfort, but as a reminder. They couldn't lose composure, not here.

From the gallery where the ladies sat, the chamber seemed arrayed like a battlefield: jurors to the left of a platform where the king, Maitland, and the prosecutors sat. To the right, the spectating nobles, including John, seated near Bothwell. The earl's eyes barely flickered as they passed over Agnes, who stood between the lines of men, about to be trampled by their charge.

The prosecutor rose – a tall, red-haired man Margareta had only ever seen whispering into Maitland's ear or awaiting the chancellor's quiet instructions.

'Agnes Sampson of Nether Keith, you are called before this court to answer charges of witchcraft and high treason. You stand accused of the following crimes. Item one, that you had foreknowledge of the death of William Markeston. Item two, that you used witchcraft in the attempted healing of the cripple John Thomson. Item three, that you used incantations to heal John Peiny. Item four …'

And so it went on. Dozens of people whose sicknesses Agnes had cured, whose childbeds she'd eased, whose deaths she'd made more comfortable. People who'd sought Agnes out above all others, believing she could save them. Like the man who'd called Johanna to his wife.

Margareta dug her nails into her palm. She couldn't think about her mother now.

'Item forty-one, making a wax figure of John Moscrop, father-in-law to Euphame MacCalzean at the said Euphame's desire, for the destruction of John Moscrop. Item forty-two, putting a powder made of men's corpses under Euphame MacCalzean's bed for the slaking of her grinding pains. Item forty-three ...'

Euphame MacCalzean. Margareta remembered the proud, well-dressed woman in Barbara Napier's house, who'd barely acknowledged Agnes's presence. Had she denounced Agnes? Surely not: these crimes incriminated her too – supposedly murdering her father-in-law, using ground corpses to ease childbed pains. Was it only Euphame MacCalzean's money that kept her safe? Or was she in the tolbooth too?

Was Margareta safe? She'd visited Barbara and Euphame – if they were implicated; if Margareta had been seen ... And the ring, the gloves she'd given to Geillis. She dug her nails into her palms, struggling not to run her fingers along her hair, her face, every place Agnes's blood had been shed.

'Item forty-eight, sailing out of North Berwick to a ship where you and your company raised an evil wind. Item forty-nine, convening at Ormiston with the intent of destroying David Seton, but the wrack lighting on his daughter. Item fifty, meeting with the devil at North Berwick kirk. Item fifty-one, preparing a wax figure for Barbara Napier to avenge herself on a man who had done her great wrong, believed to be Archibald Douglas, late Earl of Angus. Item fifty-two, enchanting a ring belonging to Barbara Napier that she might allure the heart of Lady Jean Angus.'

And now Barbara. Were these accusations true? Did they need to be? Margareta didn't dare move her face even a hair's breadth, as if the bridle were already clamping her.

'Item fifty-three, for being a notorious witch and user of sorceries, abusing the poor simple people, drawing them away from God's mercy and to the service of the devil, your master. How do you plead?'

Agnes's voice grated with painful effort. 'Where would you like me to begin?'

'Then you concede that some – perhaps all – of these charges are true?'

Agnes sighed. 'I knew William Markeston would die. Men who've been trampled by horses and had their bellies sliced open by ploughs usually do, especially if their masters finish ploughing the field before calling a healer. As for John Peiny, I sang while he lay sick – it helped him sleep.'

'What manner of song? The devil's music?'

'A mixture of hymns and folk ditties, I imagine.'

'Then you do not *know*?'

Agnes fixed him with a glare. 'I sat up with him from dusk until cockcrow – two winters ago. Strangely enough, I can't recall the precise order of songs.'

'Do you often have lapses of memory? Can we trust any of your recollections?'

'As much as anyone else's.' Her voice was bitter, as if Agnes knew – whatever she said – she was doomed.

'You would have us believe your mind equal to a man's?' The prosecutor looked round the chamber, letting earls, lairds, the king, all meet his eyes, then burst out laughing.

When the mirth ebbed away, Agnes said quietly, 'No, I would not wish that.'

How many men realized they'd just been insulted? Margareta found John's face, forced laughter still contorting his lips. Near him, Bothwell's eyes narrowed above a smirk. He understood. But then he knew Agnes better than other men.

'I'm glad to hear it,' the prosecutor said, sober again. 'Now—'

'As am I.'

Everyone turned towards the dais at James's voice – more out of surprise than respect. He sat slightly hunched, as if to make himself as small a target as possible for the assassins he always believed were lurking. Only the ermine edging his doublet marked him as royal. Yet as he leaned forward, something changed. His wavering eyes steadied; his curved spine no longer seemed craven, but the posture of a calm, confident man.

'Agnes Sampson,' James said, taking the measure of the woman in the dock as he named her. 'I have not summoned you into my palace to hear about commoners' ailments. Those charges merely provide a testament to your character. What truly interests me are your crimes against our sovereign person.'

Agnes merely blinked at him, unfathomably patient.

James matched her for composure. 'Do you wish me ill, Mistress Sampson?'

She regarded him coolly. 'Why would I? We've never met.'

James laughed. 'If all men thought thus, no king could ever have been harmed. You haven't met me, true, but you may have met someone you think might be a fitter king. Someone you know intimately, perhaps.'

Margareta watched Bothwell. He didn't even twitch – but did his jaw just clench?

'If that is what interests you,' Agnes said, 'your lawyers haven't carried out their tasks very well.' There was a strange note of triumph in her voice – as if James knowing of her connection with Bothwell were somehow a victory. 'I'm not charged with meeting powerful men. Few of those mentioned are capable of ruling a farm, let alone a kingdom.'

'So why do you want me dead?'

'Have you proof I do?'

A vein throbbed at James's temple. He hadn't envisaged this, Margareta knew. James had never given a public performance that matched those he managed in private – or in his mind – and the prospect of being outwitted by a woman, a lowly midwife, clearly infuriated him.

'The storm,' James spat. 'September before last, you conjured storms that raged between here and Denmark. You raised more when I crossed the North Sea to Oslo, and more again when I returned to Scotland last April. You sought my death – do you deny it?'

'Entirely.'

James stared. 'What?'

'How could I have raised such storms? Why would I want you dead? A dead king without an heir would mean civil war. Nether Keith is close enough to the border that we know what war does to crops, how it wounds women and children as much as soldiers. Why would that tempt me?'

But that isn't a denial, Margareta thought.

'What of North Berwick?' James renewed his attack. 'Your convention on All Hallows' Eve?'

Seeping blood rendered Agnes's condescending smile gruesome. 'You may find our country traditions strange. But All Hallows' gatherings are popular ways of fending off whatever restless spirits might walk that night.'

'I see.' James stroked the ermine at his neck. 'I suppose you had traditional music too, and old-fashioned dances.'

'Yes.'

'And traditional food – baked apples, roast chestnuts?'

'Yes.'

'And traditional entertainments? Acrobats, dwarves – or wax figures thrown onto the flames?'

Agnes twitched. 'I don't recall seeing any such figures.'

'Another lapse of memory?' James said, dripping false sympathy. 'As you said, we all suffer them from time to time.'

'Indeed. You, for instance, seem to have forgotten you have a wife.'

Gasps seethed around the courtroom. Few troubled to hide their whispers as they stared at James, the vein in his forehead pulsing faster than any galliard, and then up at Anna in the gallery.

James glared at Agnes. 'You stand there, accused of the worst crimes imaginable, and dare pass judgement on me?'

'I have judged you,' Agnes said, 'and found you wanting.'

'I am your king!'

'She's your queen,' Agnes pointed out. 'Yet you didn't mention her. You mentioned Denmark, and Oslo. You mentioned your return to Scotland, and how you thought the storms had been sent to kill you. But you neglected to mention your wife. As you've neglected her ever since you were wed.'

More gasps – and a snort of laughter. Margareta couldn't see who emitted it – definitely not Bothwell, whose face remained rigid with studied calm. Some younger man, as reckless as he was beardless? A jaded laird, weary of concealing his contempt?

James was scarlet with fury. 'You know nothing of my marriage.'

Agnes laughed coldly. 'Wrong, James Stuart. I know what you said on your wedding night.'

'Witchery,' someone hissed.

'She called him James Stuart,' another whispered.

Margareta stole a glance at Anna. The tiniest spot of pink in her cheek was the only sign of discomfort. Where was this going? Rumours of favourites were one thing – but saying Lindsay's name in his wedding bed spoke of something deeper than mere lust. Of a softness. And any softness was a target.

James lifted his chin, as if to stop it trembling. 'Prove it.'

Agnes arched an eyebrow. 'You wish me to declare your words before everyone? Very well. You said—'

'No!' James was almost purple now. 'Repeat them only to me.'

'Then you'll have to come over here.' Agnes jangled her chains. 'Or you could release me?'

James's lips thinned. Stiffly he rose, shoving his chair aside, and stepped down from the platform. He stalked across to Agnes, scowling at the guards, who drew back hurriedly.

Agnes leaned forward and whispered. Only two other people in the chamber knew what she was saying.

Alexander.

I told her that, Margareta thought. In Barbara Napier's house, I gave her a weapon to wield against the king, against Anna.

But Agnes was giving them a reason to kill her. And if they asked how she knew, would Agnes give Margareta up? There was no reason for Agnes to protect her – only Geillis had made that promise, and Geillis had lied to her. And what did promises matter when metal bit flesh?

Murmurs seethed like wasps: courtiers wondering what Agnes could be saying, how she could know, what it meant if she did speak true. Margareta almost wished Agnes had shouted the words defiantly, like a mad fishwife. James letting her whisper only proved he had something to hide.

His back was rigid. Thrusting himself away from Agnes, he stormed across the chamber, not meeting anyone's eyes. Margareta stole a glance at Alexander Lindsay: the king's lover was staring at James, face contorted in silent concern. Perhaps he didn't want their affair dissected in a courtroom – or maybe he simply loved James and didn't wish to see him humiliated.

He reached his chair but didn't sit down. Grinding his teeth, James pressed his fists against the table. 'Agnes Sampson has spoken words only I and Queen Anna could possibly have known. This is all the evidence needed to prove her a witch. I call upon the dempster to pass sentence.'

The dempster rose. 'Agnes Sampson, you have been found guilty of witchcraft. For this crime, you will be taken to Edinburgh Castle and there bound to a stake and strangled until you are dead, and thereafter your body will be burned to ashes.'

She saw Bothwell's mouth twist: was that anger or pain? But not enough for him to speak up in his ally's defence.

James sneered. 'Be grateful we have granted you mercy.'

Agnes's lip curled. 'If this is your idea of mercy, there are many who would make a better king than you.'

James leaned forward, striving for menace. 'Care to name them? I might even permit you some of your herbs to numb your pain – and believe me, the guards will make your death painful.'

Agnes smiled. 'Every single Scot.'

The court erupted. Gasps, roars, accusations: all exploded in a wild cacophony. Above it all, Margareta heard James's rage-wracked howl. 'Take her away! Burn her! Burn her!'

Once again, they heard the crowd baying, the guards clanking. But this time they heard nothing from the condemned prisoner.

No matter that Geillis hadn't slept in days, or that her ankles were a red mass of sores. She hauled herself up and stood in the grey light slipping through the window. Behind her, chains rattled as the others rose.

'She'll have kept silent,' Bessie said. 'They won't have broken her.'

Geillis said, 'No one could break Agnes.' As well try to tame the sea. They'd bloodied her and beaten her, tortured her for days, dragged her before the king to face trial. The only way to control Agnes was to kill her.

Sometimes silence was a blessing – like when they heard no screams from Castle Hill. Sometimes silence was agony – like when they all stood staring at the barred window as the smell of burning crept into the tolbooth and the snow that was not snow began to fall.

35

They didn't dare say it outside their chamber. But when the door was locked, darkness fallen and their son sleeping, Margareta and John faced one another.

'He's lost control.'

'He's losing his mind.'

John poured two large cups of wine and they both sank into chairs before the fire.

'He's sent more witch hunters out. He's even authorized them to pursue anyone over the border.'

'Can he do that? Won't Queen Elizabeth be angry?'

'Furious, I expect. Risking the wrath of the woman who executed his mother, whose throne he longs to inherit – it's …' John stopped.

Margareta prodded the fire, coaxing flames into life. 'It's madness. The king's obsessed to the point of madness.'

It had been two months since Agnes Sampson was burned on Castle Hill. Eight had been burned in Haddington, more in Dalkeith and Dumfries. At least fifty were imprisoned awaiting trial. And still no one had named Bothwell. Nor had anyone named Margareta. Geillis hadn't spoken. But now Agnes, their clear leader, was dead, would Geillis's fears wrest Margareta's name from her lips?

James's humiliation at Agnes's hands hadn't deterred him. Rather than worrying another witch trial might shame him further, he'd flung himself into the witch-hunt. He visited the tolbooth nearly every day. According to John, sometimes he merely watched the prisoners for hours, as if they might suddenly conjure up the devil in their cells, condemning themselves before James's very eyes. On other occasions, he observed while Maitland supervised the torture of new prisoners, commenting on the efficacy of particular methods. The boots he disparaged, remarking that a man might still ride after wearing them, and they would only be truly effective if they encased the whole limb rather than just up to the knee. Thumbscrews, however, he approved of, noting that despite their apparent simplicity, they distressed the accused far more, as if people were fonder of their hands than their feet. When John told her, Margareta had felt sickened.

'Have I told you his latest conceit?' John shook his head disgustedly. 'He's writing a book.'

'What?'

'Inspired by Nils Hemmingsen and Tycho Brahe. If ordinary men, as he called them, can pen treatises on witchcraft, how much more fitting that a king should write one. After all, Queen Elizabeth's poetry is highly regarded, and her father wrote a well-respected treatise on faith.'

Margareta raised her eyebrows. 'Does he think Queen Elizabeth will be impressed? There's a world of difference between poetry and ranting about witchcraft.'

'And in the calibre of their minds.' John grimaced. 'James believes these witch-hunts will prove how great he can be – how powerful, how masterful. Soon Scotland will see he's God's representative on earth and anyone working against him is doing the devil's bidding.' He stared into his wine. 'I fear Scotland will believe precisely the opposite.'

'Exactly what Bothwell wanted,' Margareta pointed out. 'For everyone to believe God's forsaken James. He's playing into Bothwell's hands.'

John nodded. 'But he won't see it. He's too blinkered to realize if he carries on like this, he might as well place the crown on Bothwell's head. And Bothwell's plan will have succeeded.'

'Geillis Duncan! On your feet!'

She blinked, surprised. She'd been dozing, face on her knees so the guards wouldn't see and yank her up by her hair. Shouting was almost polite by their standards.

Geillis pulled herself up, hardly noticing the stiffness – wincing at every movement was normal now. But it wasn't normal for the guards to unlock her shackles and drag her out of the cell. They hadn't interrogated her since Agnes's death, nor questioned any of them for what she assumed were months, having heard people emerging from St Giles' talking about Palm Sunday.

Why now?

The guards stopped outside a door Geillis recognized. Behind it was the chamber with the iron bridle nailed to the wall. She clamped her muscles against the sudden loosening in her bowels: she would not betray how terrified she was.

'Enter.'

The guards dragged her in and chained her to the wall. She struggled as the bridle brushed her cheek – but they didn't put her in it, nor strip her as Agnes had been stripped. They simply fastened irons about her wrists, and left.

She wasn't alone. But the voice commanding them to enter had come from the shadows, and she squinted. A winter in gloom hadn't given her the ability to see through darkness; if anything, her eyesight had worsened. Who was there?

A flint sparked. Moments later, a torch flared, revealing a dark-haired man seated at the desk. His beard was patchy, ragged; as she watched, he tugged at it, yanking a knot out rather than unpicking it. His eyes bulged slightly, making him look both startled and repulsed. Metal glinted at his throat: he wore armour under his doublet. She'd had metal pressed against her flesh for months – why would anyone choose that scraping coldness, the sores?

Suddenly, she recognized him. She'd seen him once before, on the Leith docks, that gorget glinting in the light as he stepped past Bothwell onto the gangplank.

'Your Grace,' she said, curtseying immediately. Her chains rattled and she tried to still them, not wanting him to think she mocked him.

'You are the witch known as Geillis Duncan?'

She caught the *yes* before it tumbled out. 'I'm Geillis Duncan.'

'And you have been charged with witchcraft – ergo, you are a witch.'

'No!' She flinched at her own shrillness. 'A charge isn't a conviction. I haven't even had a trial – I've only been accused.'

'I see.' He tilted his head pensively, and she cursed herself for putting the thought of a trial in his head. 'Let you insist on your distinctions then. After all, our words do matter.'

'They do.' Was it safe to agree with him? What exactly was she agreeing to?

'Especially those words that endure after we are gone.'

Was he threatening her? Geillis's lips parted, but she couldn't choose words, not after his.

But he was smiling. A kind, almost fatherly smile as his jewelled fingers tapped the papers before him. 'I am writing a book, Geillis.'

'A book?' The only books she'd ever seen were Bibles and hymnals, and the gold-tooled spines she'd had to dust in Seton's house, never removed from the shelves. Books were gleaming, sacred things, treasure troves of wisdom. It hadn't occurred to her that living people wrote them.

'*Daemonology*, I plan to call it,' he said proudly. 'A dialogue between two philosophers in the Socratic style. More entertaining than merely laying out my own creed, don't you think?'

She had no idea what he was talking about. 'Yes, Your Grace.'

He smiled. His boyish pleasure at her approval startled her: was it really so rare that anyone complimented him? Shouldn't his court be bursting with people eager to flatter their monarch?

But perhaps such adulation was directed elsewhere. At Bothwell.

'I need your help, Geillis.'

'My help?'

'Precisely. You see, I must expose the most pernicious elements of witchcraft prior to arguing against them. I will need to describe means of identifying witches, of interrogating them, in order to justify their fates.'

Who exactly did he need to justify himself to? Surely the king could do whatever he wished?

'And I believe you can provide this information.'

Did he think her a complete fool? She'd be denouncing herself: she might as well show him a freckle and declare it the devil's mark.

'I doubt I know any more than you,' she objected, dipping her head submissively. 'You're the king, surely one of the most learned men in Christendom. I'm a lowly servant.'

'Such modesty,' he said coolly. 'But in this area your knowledge far outstrips mine. If only there was a way to make you share it ...'

His eyes drifted to the bridle. Geillis's bowels clenched again.

'My life,' she blurted out.

'Your life?'

'I'll tell you what I know,' Geillis said quickly, 'in exchange for my life.'

He arched his eyebrows. 'You look to bargain with me? A lowly servant girl offering terms to an anointed king?'

'Kings aren't above bargaining.' She tried to straighten up defiantly, as Agnes would have done, and her cheek jarred against the bridle. 'Just because I barter for eggs and you for terms with Denmark.'

'You appear to be comparing my wife and her dowry to eggs.' His amusement was edged with quiet anger.

'Why not? They're both things we were willing to pay for.' She gabbled on, fear making her bold. 'I want to live, and you want to know what I know. Why shouldn't we strike a bargain?'

'You're my subject,' he pointed out. 'You should obey your sovereign.'

'But you haven't ordered me, Your Grace. You've asked me. If you wished to treat me as a subject, you'd have commanded. Instead you asked. That was truly gracious.'

His eyes were hooded in thought. She barely dared breathe.

'Very well, Geillis Duncan. You may keep your life – for as long as you prove useful.'

Margareta held the note at arm's length, as if it might burst into flames. 'An invitation? But why?'

John glanced around before steering Margareta into a deserted corridor. 'My best guess is that Bothwell wants to know what I know.'

'But why invite me?'

'You know Anna,' John pointed out. 'I imagine he'll ask me the latest news from the tolbooth and ask you about Anna's womb.'

Margareta crumpled the note. 'So, if we accept this invitation—'

'From an earl to a laird's son – we cannot refuse.'

She hated to admit it. 'What are we to tell him?'

John looked worried. 'He won't be fooled by lies. We must tell him the truth.'

'The truth! John, the truth is that Bothwell's acolytes gave me herbs that poisoned Anna's baby – that my milk-sister was burned for witchcraft! The truth would see us both dead.'

'But Bothwell would be just as endangered if the prisoners spoke up. He wants to know if he's safe.'

'None of us are safe!' Margareta gnawed her knuckles. 'What if James finds out you've passed information to his enemy?'

'He commanded me to spy on Bothwell. He involved me in the interrogations so Bothwell might think me more valuable.' John eyed a nearby portrait of one of James's ancestors, as if itching to slash it to ribbons. 'I must give Bothwell enough information to convince him of my loyalty – and hold enough back that I can convince James of my loyalty too.'

She touched his hand. 'And where does your loyalty lie?'

He stared at her, then pulled her into a rough embrace. 'I scarcely know anymore.'

What had Margareta expected of Bothwell, away from the bear pit of the court? A bared ruthlessness, claws unsheathed, every smile a snarl. Pride, certainly, for he sought to take James's place and wouldn't trouble to hide his ambitions without James's allies watching. Elegance – since James so clearly lacked any, his rivals sought to outdo him in that regard even more. But she hadn't expected warmth.

Bothwell greeted Margareta and John effusively, kissing her cheek and clapping John on the shoulder, before ushering them into plushly upholstered chairs and pouring malmsey.

'Come now, you must be exhausted. When our eldest was a baby, my countess tired merely crossing a garden!' Bothwell winked conspiratorially at John. 'Despite employing an army of wet nurses and cradle-rockers – and Latin tutors before the boy could even pronounce

"Mama". Every time she produces a child, I contemplate taking up highway robbery – and with our next baby due in autumn, I must dig out my pistols.'

Yet another child, Margareta thought. The birth would remind everyone in Scotland that Anna's belly had never rounded with an heir.

'We could be partners,' John suggested. 'You demand they stand and deliver, and I'll ambush from behind.'

Bothwell grinned at Margareta. 'However we obtain it, and however much we acquire, you and my countess shall manage to spend it!'

He spoke of his wife so lightly, mocking her lavishness. Lady Bothwell rarely came to court, as if Bothwell refused to have her serving Anna, curtseying to the woman she would supplant if he got his way. Perhaps she was merely resting: a first pregnancy was taxing enough, let alone a fourth. Or did her absence speak of something else? Fear? Guilt? Margareta wondered whether being married to Bothwell was as pleasant as the earl was pretending – or whether the countess, like everyone else, was a pawn in his schemes.

Throughout supper, his levity continued. Mirth and merriment, smiles and kindness with every dish. Bothwell told John about a nest of falcons in the Pentland Hills: 'Less than a day's ride, and we'll bring back half a dozen prime hunters. Two for us, and you can sell the others for me and keep a cut of the profits – and we'll have a grand day hunting!'

Full-bellied and wine-warmed, Margareta watched the servants clear the food away and set up the table for games. Part of her was horrified at how much she was enjoying herself. They weren't supposed to like Bothwell; they were meant to spy on him. For Anna's safety, they had to make sure Bothwell failed. And yet …

He was far better company than James. Witty and generous, he led conversations without clamping a fist around them. He made offers of patronage you wanted to accept, not because they might bring advancement, but because you wanted to be closer to him, basking in his glory and hoping he might even offer you true friendship one day.

This, she realized, was the most dangerous thing about Bothwell. He was seductive. He made you want him to win, want to help him win. No wonder John felt so adrift. Even Margareta was starting to wonder where her loyalty should lie.

'So tell me,' Bothwell said, dealing cards for primero as if handing out forbidden sweets, 'what entertainments does Anna have planned for the end of Lent? Plenty of feasts and dancing, I hope!'

'As do most of her ladies,' Margareta agreed, picking up her cards.

'Not you?'

'Women of my height struggle to find willing dance partners.'

Bothwell smiled. 'You've found at least one willing partner here – we'll dance a galliard so fast the rest of the court will look like sluggards. And will Anna be leading the dances?'

'Nothing short of a broken ankle would stop her.'

'Nothing?' Bothwell eyed her thoughtfully as she cast aside the two of spades. 'There's no condition might prevent her?'

What harm could telling him do? Anna's empty womb wasn't a secret anyone could keep for long – by Easter it would be clear she hadn't conceived before Lent's enforced abstinence, and every month thereafter would continue to make it clear there would be no forthcoming heir.

Margareta laid down the five of clubs and took a new card without registering what it was. 'None.'

'I wonder how she endures it,' Bothwell said, sounding so sympathetic Margareta almost believed him. 'Catherine de' Medici was married for eleven years without producing an heir. They say she placed cow dung on her private parts to aid conception.'

'Then I'm not surprised it took eleven years,' Wemyss quipped. 'King Henri must have thought he was lying with a beast.'

'Of course, poor Anna isn't the problem,' Bothwell sighed.

Poor Anna? Compassion from the man who would wear her husband's crown? Margareta schooled herself not to look at John, not to reveal how suspicious this made her.

'I'm surprised she isn't seeking a solution,' Bothwell continued. 'Women have, in the past. Even queens. There are people who could help Anna if she asked in the right places.'

So that was it. He wanted Anna's desperation to drive her into the so-called witches' arms – he wanted Margareta to return to Barbara Napier, not to kill more of Anna's unborn children, but to implicate Anna and shame James. Surely he knew that Margareta had already implicated herself. Had he contrived Margareta's guilt in order to bind herself and Wemyss closer to him?

John laid his own card down with a snap. 'But some of those people currently dwell in the tolbooth. I doubt Queen Anna would wish to be seen consorting with suchlike.'

Bothwell laughed. 'Ah, but she doesn't need to be seen.'

No – because Margareta would go on her behalf. And then what? Arrest. Torture. Even flames. She needed air – needed to haul in a breath without proving she was imagining smoke. She couldn't show Bothwell how frightened she truly was.

Bothwell picked up a card. 'Speaking of the tolbooth, how went your session today?'

'Unproductive,' John said. 'No confessions, no new information. Maitland left in such a temper, I thought he'd break his toes kicking the walls.'

'I can imagine – the old fool.' Bothwell topped up their wine glasses, though none were empty. 'So no one's succumbed to questioning? Or to … other methods?'

John shook his head. 'Either they have formidable strength – or they fear something worse than pain.'

Like Bothwell's wrath, Margareta thought.

'But Maitland thinks one could be broken,' John continued. 'Robert Grierson. He's a big man – Maitland reasons that such a man rarely came off worst in a fight and will therefore be more susceptible to pain.'

'Or Maitland's jealous of his stature,' Bothwell gibed. 'Small men often delight in greater men's suffering, and Maitland is small in so many ways.' He sipped his wine. 'What does he hope to hear?'

John shuffled his cards as if his mind were on the game. 'A name. Both he and the king are convinced there was a leader.'

'They executed the ringleaders,' Bothwell said lightly, as though this were meaningless gossip. 'That Sampson woman and the schoolmaster – Fian, was it?'

Margareta caught Bothwell's eye, and for a moment she thought she saw that same expression she'd seen in the courtroom: rage and pain. But now hardened into a frightening resolve. Had Agnes's death touched him so deeply?

'True,' John said. 'But this conspiracy was so vast – the accused hail from such wide-flung places. A midwife and schoolmaster cannot possibly have organized them all. Maitland wants to know who the true ringleader was.'

'The devil, surely,' Bothwell said offhandedly. 'These are witch trials we speak of – I doubt the devil's constrained by how far a horse can trot in a day.'

'But Maitland seeks to accuse a man.'

Bothwell laid down a card. 'Namely me. He hopes someone will accuse me.'

With justification, Margareta thought. And yet he spoke as if he'd been insulted.

John sipped his wine. 'Perhaps, my lord, the best way to stop your name being dragged into this is to ensure someone else's name is dragged in first.'

Bothwell lifted an eyebrow in feigned surprise. 'Accusing the innocent?'

'Preferably not. There are powerful people who haven't yet been accused.'

Like me? Margareta stared at her cards, hiding her confusion. Was John searching for a name? Or seeking to incriminate someone else – to draw eyes away from his own wife?

'Indeed,' Bothwell said thoughtfully. 'Remind me, Wemyss, wasn't Agnes Sampson convicted of helping Euphame MacCalzean and Barbara Napier gain revenge?'

Her cards fluttered; Margareta clenched them tightly, not daring to look up.

'She was,' John said, his indifferent tone hiding his caution. 'One for a property dispute, I believe, and the other for being assaulted by Archibald Douglas.'

'So their stories go,' Bothwell said coolly. 'Of course, if one were to probe deeper, one might find vindictive women. Disobedient women. Ones who say too much to the wrong people.'

Too much about what? If Euphame and Barbara fell, would Margareta be pulled down with them?

'Perhaps it's time,' Bothwell continued, 'for those women to be confronted with their sins. Those investigating might recall that Mistress Napier is kin to the Earl of Angus. Rumour has it she helped poison the old man.' He paused – and did he wink? 'I never did like the Douglases. If there was one witch among them, perhaps there were others.'

So Barbara was merely a means of slandering the Douglas name? And if any Douglases were convicted of witchcraft, their property would be forfeit – property in the borders, adjacent to Bothwell's own lands.

'Perhaps.' John nodded. 'And the MacCalzean woman?'

'Few women are more suited to wearing bridles.' His bitterness startled Margareta, and she wondered then: what had Barbara and Euphame said about Agnes? Was Bothwell taking revenge on them for betraying the dead woman? 'The man attempting to take her property on his wife's behalf was David Seton. No doubt you recall the name.'

'Of course,' John said. 'The first woman accused was in his household – Geillis Duncan.'

Geillis, who still had Margareta's ring; Barbara and Euphame who'd met with Margareta. Her lungs tightened.

'Agnes was convicted of targeting Seton. Perhaps at Euphame MacCalzean's instigation?'

Perhaps – such an offhand word. Bothwell tossed insinuations carelessly as if scattering hemlock into wine.

John wet his lips. 'I'll be sure to mention it.'

In the quiet, Bothwell laid down a card and pulled up another. 'Good work,' he said softly. 'Excellent work.'

Margareta discarded the five of diamonds and drew up the king of spades. That made two kings: potentially a winning hand. But she was surrounded by people who knew the rules of the game far better than she, and who didn't care if they broke them or how devastating a loss might be for others. This was not a game Margareta wanted to play. The odds were stacked against her.

36

Each time he summoned her, Geillis couldn't help thinking a king should have better things to do.

'So,' he asked, quill poised, 'how would a witch heal the sick?'

Geillis sipped the water he always placed beside her, a strange courtesy. Anything to delay answering, to compose her response. 'Surely healing is doing God's will? How can you accuse someone of the devil's work for taking away sickness?'

He eyed her testily. 'That's a physician's task.'

'What if people cannot afford a physician's service or live too far away from one? Would you tell a mother not to give her feverish child camomile because I'm not a physician?'

'Certainly not.'

'But how can it be witchcraft if you permit it – you, God's voice on earth? How can it be witchcraft to use plants God created to help the people he put here?'

'Interesting,' he said, scribbling.

How had it come to this? Philosophizing with a king, when six months ago she'd been sweeping hearths? And other things besides – but she wouldn't confess to those. She couldn't refuse to answer his questions, but she didn't have to spill her soul in response to them.

'Is it the intention then,' he mused, jotting away, 'or the act itself? Can we call one person a witch for the same act that makes us call another a healer? Or must the whole be weighed together? One well-intentioned deed cannot outweigh a lifetime of the devil's work.'

He often thought aloud. Geillis used such times to stretch, trying to roll her shoulders or rotate her hips without rattling her chains. Eventually, he'd address her again.

'Have you ever danced?'

'Danced?' She was thrown – how could this follow what had gone before?

'Yes – jigs and reels, that sort of thing.'

She shook her head. 'Hardly ever. Even harvest celebrations were more about food than dancing. We'd be too tired – bringing in the hay is exhausting.'

'So you never danced in a kirkyard?'

She stiffened. Admitting that would be one step away from admitting who she'd seen there, and then he'd ask about the Fiery Hills and Inchkeith and Lucy Seton. He'd been lulling her into a false sense of security with his moralizing quibbles – and now he struck.

'Never, Your Grace.'

'Then why did you ride to North Berwick? Several witnesses saw you there.'

Easier to name Geillis than Bothwell. Had it been Agnes or Fian, before they died? Bessie? Grierson?

'I played music for the dancers. But I never danced.'

'More hidden talents!' He laughed, suddenly derisive. 'What can a servant girl play – the lute? Virginals?'

'Pipes,' she said defiantly. 'And the mouth harp. My father taught me.'

'Did he indeed? And what tunes did you play?'

'I—' She couldn't remember. She'd just played, desperate to keep the terror at bay. 'Just old country tunes.'

'Could you play them again?'

'Your Grace?'

He leaned forward. 'Play for me now.'

'I've no instruments,' she protested.

'I have them here.' He reached into a sack of black velvet, so dark she hadn't seen it in the gloom, and drew out her pipes and harp.

'Those are mine,' she breathed. 'How did—'

'Your former employer was only too happy to oblige.'

Of course. She could imagine Seton raking through her few possessions, pawing over things she'd kept private, just as he'd once pawed
at her body. And finding Margareta's gloves among them. Had Mistress
Katherine claimed them – or was Seton holding them back, waiting
to use them against Geillis? If she didn't burn for a witch, she could
hang for a thief. Those men who'd tried to sell jewels from the wrecked
ship – they'd died for their greed. She could feel the weight of
Margareta's ring in her cuff, and it felt more like a millstone than an
anchor; every time they chained her up, she yanked her cuff down,
pretending to be flinching from the irons, not terrified they'd find
evidence to condemn her. Or Margareta.

'Prisoners' possessions are always forfeit,' the king reminded her.
'Really, these now belong to me.'

A battered set of pipes and a mouth harp, played to make a little
girl laugh at animal noises: all she had left of her father. And now
King James, who had troupes of minstrels at his beck and call, had
taken them for his.

'I should like you to play for me as you played on All Hallows' Eve.'

'Why?' she blurted out, hastily adding, 'Your Grace, why?'

He smiled. 'Because you're lying to me, Geillis Duncan. You're
hiding something. You say you played at the convention in the kirkyard – therefore you must be a skilled musician. But does your music
praise God, or the devil?'

He took up the instruments and crossed the chamber. The firelight
flickered on the metal beneath his clothes; if not for that gorget, she
could have stabbed his throat. She hated him enough that she could
have pierced his flesh with her father's pipes. He was goading her like
a dancing bear, making her writhe away from hot blades, calling her
pain entertainment.

'Which will it be?' he asked softly. 'Pipes or harp?'

Not the harp. Its sounds would be too easy to slander as the devil's
music.

Choosing the pipes was like taking a parent's hand. The smooth
wood beneath her fingertips, its grain familiar as lines and calluses
on a palm. But her ruined thumb couldn't grip them anymore, so she

had to wedge her palm awkwardly against the pipes, and her parents were long gone; there was no hand for her to hold.

She played 'Western Wind'. She played 'Summer is a-coming in'. Old tunes, familiar, harmless tunes – and all the while King James's eyes scoured her face as if he might peel away her skin to see the lies beneath.

'Stop,' he said at last. 'Enough.'

She didn't want him to take the pipes away. Couldn't he leave her something of her own beyond the reeking clothes she'd worn since November? But he took them, and her hands felt weak and useless, as if they were all that could have kept her from drowning, and now the waters were closing above her head.

'So,' the king said quietly, 'you are a woman of many skills, Geillis Duncan. I wonder – how skilful are you when it comes to resisting pain?'

He was going to torture her. Or, more likely, he'd watch another man do it for him, his eyes blazing with vindictive pleasure. Back in the cell, Geillis curled her left hand into a loose fist, cradling it against her chest.

Now her thumb was more gnarled than an old woman's. The knuckle would never bend again. It should have been splinted, daubed with comfrey paste and wrapped in lime-stiffened bandages, then kept in a sling. That was what Agnes would have done. Instead, she'd torn a strip from her shift and tied her thumb to her forefinger as best she could, using only her right hand. Then she'd lain awake, the throbbing of her own blood reminding her that to live was to suffer.

And that had only been one digit. Not even a limb. They'd used the boots on Fian. All the damage to her thumb, magnified a hundred times. Geillis flexed her feet, feeling the irons chafe against her scarred ankles, imagining wood encasing her legs, and then tightening. Would bone split before wood? When they drove the wedges in, did splinters lead the way, impaling flesh, a pain you would think agonizing until your bones began to creak, and you discovered you knew nothing of true agony?

How strong *was* Geillis when it came to resisting pain? She'd screamed Agnes's name to Seton – what would she scream to King James? What would anyone scream? She glanced around the cell at the grey husks of her fellow prisoners. They couldn't all hold out forever. The promise of rewards from Bothwell grew ever fainter; Bessie might believe Bothwell truly was the devil and would torture her for eternity if she betrayed him, but surely the fear of punishment from him was dwindling compared to the fear of torture here and now. Without Agnes, who was left to urge their silence?

Sooner or later, someone would talk. Then what would become of those who'd kept silent? Geillis's fingers strayed to the ring again. Could it be enough to bribe a guard?

A sudden commotion burst out in the corridor. Raised voices, footsteps, the sounds of a struggle. The prisoners turned, slow with stiffness and surprise, to stare at the cell door.

'Unhand me, you fool!'

Geillis recognized that voice. Cold, imperious: it was Euphame MacCalzean.

'You cannot possibly put us in there!'

That voice, shriller, more frantic – Barbara Napier.

The door swung open and the guards thrust the women inside. They stared, aghast, and Geillis flinched, remembering how repulsive the cell had become. The stones were splashed with their waste, which the guards never completely scoured away. Rat droppings were half-buried in old, damp clumps of straw. As for the prisoners, their shaved hair was growing back raggedly, some streaked white where the razors had left scars. Everyone's clothes shivered with lice. They were a foul sight, Geillis knew – but when they were all equally mired in filth they could pretend it away. Now, confronted with well-dressed, clean women, shame flooded back.

But neither was as impeccably attired as Geillis remembered. Euphame's hat was askew, a pin swinging over one ear on a loose strand of hair. Barbara's sleeve was only half-tied on, and ribbons flapped like unravelling fishing nets.

'This is impossible,' Euphame protested. 'Do you not know who we are? I have influential friends – you'll be punished for this!'

The guard holding her laughed. 'These are the king's orders. Who do you think will save you – that fat walrus of a husband you left chewing his supper? Or the kin you tried to murder with witchcraft?'

Euphame flailed for words. 'I never … You don't understand—'

'Of course not,' the guard said, falsely agreeable. 'That's because I'm not a witch.' He shoved her forward and she stumbled, hands flying out to catch herself. Geillis heard wet straw squelching. Euphame stared at her hands in horror as the guard fastened Agnes's old shackles over her white lawn stockings.

Behind her, Barbara was weeping. 'I can reward you!' she insisted. 'I'll give you coin – I'll double your wages. Just give me a cell of my own, not this … this cesspit! I beg you, please!'

'I beg you, please!' the guard mimicked in a high voice. He dragged her over to an empty set of shackles and thrust her to her knees. 'How about you beg each of us in turn?'

Old fear leeched the blood from Barbara's face. She'd been raped, Geillis remembered: Archibald Douglas had assaulted her, and birthing his baby had nearly killed Barbara. What would she do to avoid that pain again? As for Euphame, no man would ever have spoken thus to her. She knew nothing of lewdness, of men who grabbed at your body with hot, clumsy fingers. How little would it take for her to talk?

How much better might it prove for Geillis if she offered her version of events first?

As this thought bit at her mind, somewhere in the tolbooth a man began to scream.

Margareta shot bolt upright as John staggered into their bedchamber. She glanced at the door leading to the wet nurse's room with a flash of anxiety. But then all her attention was seized by John.

Moonlight seeped between the curtains, revealing his face: bone-pale and blood-spattered.

'Dear God – what's happened?' She flung the covers aside and ran to him.

'It's not mine,' he said, stumbling as if drunk – and yet there was no wine on his breath.

'Then – whose?' Visions chased through her mind – cutpurses in a dark alley, royal soldiers accusing him of being Bothwell's man,

Bothwell's allies accusing him of betraying their master to the false king.

'Robert Grierson's dead. And I helped kill him.'

John sagged as if a blade had ripped his flesh. Somehow, Margareta managed to drag him over to the bed and lean him back against the pillows. She poured him a cup of wine and, after a brief hesitation, one for herself. When she pressed the drink into his hand, she thought his trembling would spill it. But then he took a sip and his hand steadied.

'What happened?'

He stared into the depths of his cup. 'We went too far.'

'You were ordered to go too far.'

'And I didn't question it.' He shook his head, disgusted at himself. 'Maitland said *more*, and I said nothing. The king said *harder*, and I said nothing.'

'How could you have said anything?' She touched his cheek. 'They'd have asked why. They'd have asked whose side you were really on. You had to stay silent.'

'Grierson didn't.' John turned aside from her touch. 'He could have stopped us if he'd given up the name we wanted.'

'Bothwell?'

John nodded. 'But he didn't. He'd been tortured for days. They – we – racked him until his bones were wrenched from their sockets. His legs and arms weren't limbs anymore, just twisted sacks of blood and bone. He couldn't even crawl. It was like seeing a newborn baby try to move – yet he was even more helpless.' He looked towards the wet nurse's room, horror carving hollows beneath his eyes. 'Then Maitland bade me fetch red-hot pliers and skewers.'

Margareta couldn't bear to hear it – and yet she sensed John had to say it.

'Maitland asked the questions,' John continued. 'Each time Grierson refused to answer, I drove a skewer beneath his fingernails. If he still refused, I ripped the nail away with the pliers. And he did refuse. Ten nails, and not a single word.' He shook his head in sickened awe. 'I've never seen such strength. He was a huge man, Grierson. He'd have outwrestled us all – he could probably have fought off James and Maitland at once. Even in chains, bleeding and broken, we couldn't defeat him.'

'Did Maitland make you kill him?'

'No.' John's mouth twisted bitterly. 'Neither he nor James would give up. After the pliers failed, he tried the boots. When they failed, he ordered me to put Grierson in the bridle. You saw what it did to Agnes Sampson. Even if prisoners hold completely still, it slices their flesh open. But Grierson … as soon as the bolts closed, he began flinging his head from side to side. Maitland thought he'd gone mad. James thought him possessed.'

'What did you think?'

John was silent for a moment. 'I think he saw a way out. There was something in his eyes – a glimmer of hope, not madness.'

'Hope?'

'That it might end.' He gave a long, shuddering sigh. 'Grierson choked to death on his own blood. He *chose* to.'

Margareta set her wine down, suddenly sickened by its colour. 'Then …' She hesitated. 'It isn't your fault. You didn't kill him.'

John laughed bitterly. 'I obeyed Maitland and James without question.'

'The chancellor and the king! That's no choice at all!'

'Bothwell chose not to obey them.'

'You can't possibly think he's in the right!' She reached for his hand, but it lay flat and unresponsive in his lap. 'John – you don't truly believe that.'

'Don't I? James has tortured his subjects, broken his own laws, and for what? Petty vengeance and superstition bordering on insanity. People have *died* again and again because his pride was hurt.'

'You think Bothwell would have behaved any differently? The hold he has over those prisoners – he must have terrified them to make them stay silent for so long. He might believe he'd make a better king, but he'd be as brutal as any of them in the end!'

'As brutal as Sophia?' There was a new savageness in his eyes. 'We've been working for Anna at her mother's command, but is Sophia a better master than James or Bothwell?'

Margareta shook her head. 'Queen Sophia hasn't—'

'They burn witches in Denmark too,' John snapped. 'They burned your mother and sister. Do you imagine Sophia wept for them? Do you think Anna would weep? Because I think they're just as ruthless as the Scots you look down on.'

'I don't—'

'You do. You believe you're serving a better person. But just because Anna's fair-haired and wears pretty gowns, it doesn't change who she is. She's royal. Cruelty's in their blood.'

Margareta bit the inside of her cheek. It isn't him, she told herself. These aren't his words – this is pain and anger and guilt speaking.

'Ask yourself this,' John said. 'Since Ilsa died, has Sophia once written to you? Because she hasn't responded to me. Not when James declared our Johnny a bastard, not even when her own daughter lost her baby. We've all been cut loose. She won't protect us anymore – we must protect ourselves.'

Blood stung. She'd bitten too deeply, and now she tasted her own blood – and remembered Ilsa's words. 'My sister once told me witchcraft was in my blood. That I'd never be able to escape it.'

John's lip curled. 'She was right. Look at us now.'

'No.' Margareta shook her head stubbornly. 'I didn't choose witchcraft. Not because I thought I was better than Ilsa or any of those prisoners. Nor because I think I've chosen a better master than Ilsa did. I chose not to turn to witchcraft for *me*. Because I don't want it. I don't want treason or conspiracies. I want a life with you, with our son.'

'Ah, Margareta,' John said grimly. 'That's exactly what you cannot have.'

'Why not? We could leave court, go to your father's lands – we could live there quietly—'

'Too late,' he said simply. 'It was too late when I was born a laird's son. It was too late when Sophia charged you to guard her daughter. We're part of this, Margareta, and the only way out is the path Grierson chose.'

37

There was blood on the floor. In the firelight, it seemed merely a different shade of darkness, but Geillis knew better. No one had scrubbed the stones: they wanted the stains to remain.

Grierson had died here. The king had described his death as if describing the weather. Gruff, blustering Robert Grierson, who tossed a hay bale onto one shoulder at harvest time while others heaved and sweated in pairs. He'd died in the chains she wore now, choking to death in the witch's bridle that nudged coldly against her shoulder.

Geillis didn't want to die. She didn't want to die for a man who would never consider dying for her, to choke to death on words that might save her.

The king tapped his quill. 'Now then, Geillis. How can we distinguish between an ordinary cat and a witch's familiar?'

She could have described the malevolent ginger creature in Seton's kitchen, whose spite was entirely feline and nothing to do with the devil. She could have repeated the rumour that Agnes had drowned a cat in the sea to curse a man.

Instead, Geillis said, 'I'd rather talk about something else, Your Grace.'

His eyebrows arched. 'You think you can decree what we discuss?'

'Today I can.'

He'd betrayed them all. Agnes had believed in him, and he'd abandoned her. Geillis owed him nothing, and how could his threats touch her in this tolbooth?

'I want to talk about the Earl of Bothwell.'

His eyes gleamed. 'Then I want to listen.'

* * *

Spring had reached Scotland: the parkland beneath Arthur's Seat was golden with wildflowers, and returning birds darted across a blue sky. It was a beautiful day for riding. Margareta should have been enjoying herself. But since Grierson's death and Euphame and Barbara's arrests, she'd struggled to enjoy anything.

Was anyone else at court distressed? She watched the other riders critically. The king had spent the afternoon racing his earls and laughing with Alexander Lindsay. Yet James was so terrified of witchcraft he'd overseen nigh on a hundred arrests and dozens of deaths, trusting his councillors so little he'd insisted on taking over many interrogations.

'How can he smile?' she whispered to John as they rode past the lake.

John's face was stiff from feigning smiles. 'How can he not? How can we not?'

He was right. Appearing worried let your enemies know they'd frightened you, and that was half the battle lost. James had to ride out boldly whenever he longed to hide in a guarded tower.

'Smile, Margareta,' John said quietly. 'Someone's always watching.'

'But I'm nobody!'

He shook his head impatiently. 'When will you accept it? Anyone who watches Anna watches you. Anyone who watches Bothwell watches me – and if they watch me, they're also watching you. We have to be on our guard.' He grinned, as if she'd shared a fine jest, then called to Lindsay, 'See the deer tracks in that clearing? There's a stag worth hunting!'

As he pushed his horse away, Margareta pasted a smile across her face. But it was like wearing one of Anna's cast-off gowns: it didn't fit, and its brightness attracted too many eyes. How many had she already caught? Had anyone seen her visiting Barbara's house?

'Are you unwell, Margareta?' Anna nudged her palfrey alongside Margareta's, her dove-grey riding habit and the palfrey's matching coat making them look more like a centaur than woman and beast: something magical, superior. Someone worthy of service? Margareta tried not to think about John's angry words. Anna was not Sophia.

'No – just worried about little Johnny,' she invented hastily. 'He had a touch of colic this morning, but the nurse says he'll be well, that she's rarely seen such a healthy boy.'

Anna's face clouded over. 'You are blessed. You should appreciate your blessings.'

'I do! I didn't mean—'

'Did you hear about Bothwell's daughter?' Anna stared resolutely ahead; Margareta knew she was trying not to cry. 'Her godmother, Queen Elizabeth, sent her a fine New Year's gift. A prayer book – embroidered by the queen's own hand.'

'If it's only just arrived, it's scarcely a great favour.'

Anna shook her head. 'Queen Elizabeth meant to send a message.'

'You cannot mean she supports Bothwell?'

'Her goddaughter's father? Why not?' Anna's voice quivered like a bowstring held too long. 'It should have been my child. She should have been their godmother, should have sent them gifts and promised them support, not Bothwell's brats!'

'Anna, it's a prayer book. It isn't an army, or any true declaration.'

'It's a sign,' Anna said hollowly. 'One sign after another – people want Bothwell and his dynasty to rule Scotland. They don't want a barren Danish girl.'

Margareta leaned as close to Anna as she could. 'You aren't barren! You aren't even afraid you are! Do you hear me? You are patience and grace; you are pious hope and gentle smiles. Besides, Queen Elizabeth, a woman famous for her barrenness, cannot frighten you into submission with spiteful messages! You are the anointed queen of Scotland, and you *will* be mother to the kingdom's heir!'

'How can I believe that?' Anna asked bleakly.

'You don't have to believe it. You just have to convince everyone else you do.'

As they rode on through dappled sunshine, Margareta couldn't help thinking how easy it was to give advice. Telling Anna to be brave and hopeful was almost as natural as breathing. Yet Margareta couldn't be either.

She'd spent most of her life telling Anna kind lies. Her embroidery was too delicate for silk, not so hastily finished it unravelled. No one had noticed her stumble in the dance; how could they when Anna's headdress was the most splendid ornament in the hall? Now here she was, lying again.

But telling Anna the truth would be cruel. Admitting the truth to herself was a wrench. Because sometimes Margareta did believe Bothwell would be a better ruler than James.

Ahead, Bothwell rode alongside the king, one hand on the reins, one at his hip, seeming to swagger even in the saddle. Who did Queen Elizabeth favour? Either or neither – the ageing queen was notorious for her refusal, once to produce an heir, now to choose one, toying with names like tossed knives. King James, Arbella Stuart, the Spanish Infanta. Was Francis Stewart, the assumed heir to Scotland, among her juggled names? If her throne might ultimately pass to the Scottish king, would she prefer Bothwell to James? Or did she just want James to believe that, the better to control her cousin?

John had once delighted in unravelling such knots, in the days when he delighted in anything. But she couldn't ask him, for he was swept up in the throng around James and Bothwell, close enough to both that even Margareta couldn't say who he rode behind.

As they clattered into Holyrood's courtyard, Margareta longed for her bedchamber, to sink her head into her hands behind closed doors. Grooms brought out mounting blocks for the ladies; men swung down nimbly, avoiding the hounds scampering underfoot. It was so busy, at first Margareta didn't notice the guards.

They were stationed around the courtyard, spines straight as their weapons. Now they moved, ignoring countesses' outraged gasps, earls' furious barks, as they closed in on their target.

Bothwell.

He realized too late: they'd already surrounded him, trapping some of his companions alongside him – including John.

'Francis Stewart,' the captain of the guard said. 'You are under arrest on suspicion of high treason and conspiring with witches.'

Bothwell's hand shot to his sword; his eyes flickered around the courtyard, assessing the odds, potential escape routes. His voice rang out, unfaltering. 'These charges have been laid by jealous knaves.'

Margareta saw James's shoulders stiffen.

John leaned forward and whispered in Bothwell's ear. Whatever he'd said, it made the earl's jaw set – and the sight made James turn on his heel and stride away, as if he didn't care to waste his time in the company of traitors. Did he number John among them now?

'This is the foulest conspiracy!' Bothwell shouted after James – and the tide of courtiers following him. 'Let anyone who believes these charges be damned as a liar and a fool!'

But anyone speaking against the charges would be damned. The guards clamped gauntleted hands around Bothwell's shoulders and dragged him away.

Not waiting for the mounting block, Margareta leapt down and ran to John. 'Why did you stand beside him? Don't you know how it looked?'

He glanced around the emptying courtyard, keeping his voice low. 'To whom – the king or Bothwell?'

'To us all! You whispered in his ear – a man arrested on the worst possible charges. Now everyone will think you're Bothwell's ally!'

'Including Bothwell.'

She stared. 'Don't you see how dangerous this is?'

He laughed mirthlessly. 'Believe me, Margareta, I know that all too well.'

'Then what, in heaven's name, are you doing?'

'Playing my role as best I can.' His eyes were grim. 'I was instructed to make Bothwell believe I'm helping him. If I stood by while he was dragged off to a dungeon, would he ever trust me again?'

'What of the king? Will he ever trust you again now?'

'I doubt James has ever trusted anyone.'

'Don't jest – not now, not about this!'

'I'm not jesting.' He gripped her hands. 'I told you: the only trust that really matters is that between us. Margareta, you must trust me.'

She searched his face, trying to read his allegiance in the creases below his eyes, the lines remembering long-ago laughter. But she couldn't. 'Then tell me what you said to Bothwell.'

He closed his eyes briefly, as if disappointed. 'I told him to pick his battles wisely.'

'What did you mean?'

'What do you think I meant? That he shouldn't try to fight his way free of a royal palace when surrounded by armed guards and many enemies!'

'But ...' She hesitated. Asking further questions would only exasperate him more. 'It sounds as though you anticipate battles ahead.'

'You know there must be.'

'And ... that you plan to support him in those battles.'

'Bothwell has to think that.'

'But if James thinks it too?' She shook her head in frustration and fear. 'This feud can only end with the destruction of either James or Bothwell – and theirs won't be the only lives lost or ruined. How many have already died for it?'

'You don't have to remind me!' he snapped. 'I saw Grierson die! His blood stained my hands!'

'What about your blood? Whose hands will that stain? John, aligning yourself with Bothwell is too dangerous!'

'No,' he said bleakly. 'To stop playing the game now – that would be too dangerous. We must keep going, Margareta. Blood will be shed. Lives will be lost. But we cannot stop now.'

38

Even in their cell, the women heard the news.

At first they heard the unmistakeable sound of armed men on cobbles and knew guards were approaching the tolbooth. Then the gossip began, swirling and hissing until it was as loud as a gale.

'Bothwell? Surely not!'

'An earl arrested? *That* earl?'

'Treason. Must be.'

'Or else …'

'Witchcraft?'

Or both, Geillis thought, gripping her knees so tight her knuckles whitened. She'd accused him of both.

'They can't have arrested him,' Bessie breathed, staring at the stones as if a gap might open up and reveal the truth.

The guards' footsteps passed by, heading uphill towards the castle. Out of respect, Geillis wondered, since an earl surely couldn't be confined in a mere tolbooth alongside peasants and petty criminals. Or were they sending him to Edinburgh Castle's iron-barred dungeons out of fear he'd escape?

As scandal seethed in the streets, Euphame spoke.

'Someone must have confessed.'

Geillis looked up. Euphame's eyes darted around the cell, suspicious of them all.

'Aye,' Bessie retorted, 'and recently too. Let me think – who's only recently been imprisoned?'

'You dare accuse me?' Euphame's old haughtiness reared up. 'You, a lowborn jade!'

'We've been here since December,' Bessie pointed out. 'You and your friend have only just arrived – and suddenly Bothwell's in irons?'

'Maybe it was Grierson.'

They all stared at Geillis.

'Grierson was tortured to death,' Geillis pointed out, building her lie as carefully as a house of cards. 'Maybe he confessed before he died.'

Blame the dead. Grierson, Fian, Agnes – wherever they were now, Geillis's words couldn't harm them.

There was silence. Euphame's haughty glare became thoughtful; Barbara regained a trace of colour.

'That's possible,' Euphame said slowly.

'It doesn't matter who mentioned Bothwell's name!' Barbara burst out. 'Now it's been spoken, we can save ourselves. We can simply blame him.'

Bessie shook her head. 'But Agnes said—'

'Agnes is dead,' Euphame snapped. 'Barbara's right. We could all save our own lives. Bothwell promised us places at his court. No doubt he made you promises too. But once a man's convicted of treason, everything he has is forfeit to the crown. Very soon, he'll have nothing left.'

'So he's doomed,' Bessie said. 'And we helped him – so what hope for us now?'

'We'll blame him,' Euphame said, ruthlessly pragmatic. 'Why not? Everyone would believe us – women led astray by the wicked earl, frightened into submission. That's the story the king wants to hear, so we might as well say it.'

'And then …' Bessie hesitated. 'Do you think they'll let us go?'

Euphame's lips thinned. 'They must. After all, we're innocent victims.'

None of them were innocent – and none guiltier than Geillis. She'd given up the names of those now dead; she'd named Bothwell as leader of a great conspiracy.

I'm not innocent, she thought. But I don't intend to become a victim.

'Besides,' Euphame continued, 'we can give them more names.' She met Geillis and Barbara's eyes. 'You met her. Queen Anna's lady-in-waiting.'

Margareta. The ring nudged against Geillis's wrist. Margareta was the last person who'd treated Geillis with any kindness – who'd believed Geillis deserved any. Wrongly, of course: Geillis had repaid her with deception.

'No.'

The word escaped before she could stop it – but she could stop other words. She had to.

'Why not?' Euphame demanded. 'Talking could keep us alive! Why not tell them the queen's own women are involved?'

'Because that makes their accusation true!' Geillis leaned forward. 'Think about it. If you tell them about the queen, you'll have to mention the herbs – and that's confessing to witchcraft. But if you just mention Bothwell, then it's nothing to do with witchcraft. It's just women asking for his help, and that's no crime.'

'We've done nothing wrong,' Barbara insisted, staring imploringly at Euphame. 'All those rumours about ships and dances in kirkyards – we never did any of that.'

Bessie grunted. 'Even if you did, doesn't make you a witch. Like you said, we're all victims.'

'And no one else has to join us,' Geillis said. 'Not the queen, or her ladies. They've done nothing more than the women Agnes and I helped every day, nothing more than you, Euphame, or you, Barbara. They just wanted healthy children.' She drew in a breath. 'Only one person deserves to be on trial. Agreed?'

One by one, the women all nodded.

They put Barbara on trial first. The weaker one, Geillis thought as the guards led her away; they heard Barbara sobbing along the corridor, and again when they brought her out of the tolbooth to escort her down to Holyrood. And then nothing.

Even the waiting was a form of torture. The not knowing. Every time a large group walked along the Canongate, the women in the cell winced, wondering if it was guards dragging Barbara to Castle Hill. An outbreak of laughter – were they jeering her? Or was it just ribaldry spilling out of a tavern?

St Giles' knelled the hours, again and again. Either Barbara had much to tell – or she was being cross-examined about many crimes. Had Geillis been wrong to assume she'd prove weak? When Barbara had first been flung in the cell, weeping and wailing, it had seemed impossible she could ever withstand questioning, let alone torture. But she had survived, though they hadn't tortured her yet, just shaved her head and pricked her. Geillis knew there was far worse.

But this was a woman who'd embroiled herself in a conspiracy to overthrow the king. She'd arranged the poisoning of the queen's unborn child. She'd survived rape and losing her position; she'd been determined to rise again. Maybe Barbara was far tougher than Geillis had imagined an Edinburgh gentlewoman could be.

Dusk had fallen. How long ago? She'd lost count of St Giles's bells. How much longer could a trial last? Geillis peered through the gloom: nearly everyone was dozing. Only Euphame's eyes gleamed, desperate and resolute: she wouldn't rest until she knew.

Then, footsteps outside. Would they go straight past the tolbooth? But no, the guards were entering – she heard the doors creak open, then slam. Was Barbara with them? Or had they come for another prisoner?

The footsteps grew closer. Closer.

Then Geillis heard a guard grunt, surprised: 'Lucky bitch only got herself acquitted, didn't she?'

Geillis met Euphame's shining eyes. If Barbara could be acquitted, was there hope for the rest of them?

'Acquitted?' James hissed, rising from his seat in the great hall. '*Acquitted?*'

Maitland bowed. 'That was the jury's decision, sire. Perhaps we might discuss this matter in a Privy Council meeting?'

James drove his fist against the table. 'I didn't arrange this woman's trial so a jury of fools could find her innocent!'

There was a sudden silence. Margareta glanced around furtively, trying to gauge the court's mood. Some were merely impatient, eyeing the dishes the pages had just brought out. Others relished this latest scandal with the cruelty of the uninvolved. But some were nervous, suspicious, appalled at the king's words.

Arrange, he'd said. An arranged trial, with the intention of arranging the verdict too: he'd openly declared he wanted Barbara Napier dead, and he didn't care whether she was innocent or guilty.

She'd always known justice held little sway in witchcraft trials. But for the king to say so aloud …

'Your Grace,' Maitland tried again, 'shall we withdraw?'

James's eyes almost burst out of his skull in outrage. Then he seemed to take in his surroundings: his watching court, his pale wife, and even, perhaps, the face of the man who wasn't there, yet whose presence always haunted him.

'Yes,' he muttered eventually, then, louder, 'We will dine in private with our most trusted councillors. Goodnight to all.'

He strode out, followed by Maitland, Lindsay, and several earls. Anna, marooned on the royal table, took a deep breath, then stood.

'My dear people, we have a feast to enjoy. I trust you will all rise to the occasion.' She gestured to the minstrels in the gallery and, as tunes swirled above the court, beckoned to Margareta. Leaving Anna's other ladies, she wove her way through the pages as they brought out the remaining dishes. Sinking into Lindsay's vacated seat, Margareta tried to smile as if she'd been summoned for companionship alone.

'Barbara Napier,' Anna said quietly, adjusting a platter so roast peacock concealed her face from the hall. 'I've heard this name.'

'Yes,' Margareta said, awkward with knowledge. No good trying to lie. Being caught in deceit would be worse than telling the truth. 'She is – was – an associate of Agnes Sampson.'

Anna shook her head tersely. 'They're all associated with that woman. What was this woman's part?'

Margareta hesitated. Barbara's part was Margareta's part. 'I met Agnes Sampson in her house.'

'So she is guilty?' Anna speared a piece of peacock on her knife but didn't eat. 'Then why has she been found innocent?'

'Nothing's been said about what happened to you.'

'The jury do not know?'

Margareta swallowed, trying to conceal her own dread from Anna. 'No one who knows about ... what was done ... could admit to it without condemning themselves. Keeping your name out of the trials is better for everyone.'

'But why has she been acquitted?'

'Perhaps there was no evidence.' Pray God there was none – and none against Margareta either. Or Anna – if Margareta had been seen buying herbs, it wouldn't be difficult to work out who for. Consulting witches was a crime even if you didn't know they were witches. Even if you'd believed you could trust them with your life – with the lives of unborn children.

'Evidence never troubled them before. Hearsay and rumour formed at least half the charges against the Sampson woman.'

She was right – and pointing out flaws Margareta had already spotted in her own arguments.

'Maybe fewer witnesses came forward. That is ... fewer were willing to come forward.'

Anna's eyes narrowed; it gave her an uncanny resemblance to her mother. 'Why? Because she's rich?'

Margareta nodded. 'It's the only difference I can see. She's well connected – she has Douglas kin.'

'But if she's tried again ...' Anna bit her lip. 'What if she admits meeting you? What if she suggests I'd given you permission – encouraged you even?'

How many times had Margareta reassured Anna? Now she saw her own terror turn Anna's eyes dark.

'We consulted witches,' Anna whispered. 'It doesn't matter how powerful you are. Gentlewomen, earls ... what if you're next? If they take you, who will stand up for me?'

She could have suggested James. Yet Margareta wondered: if Anna was implicated, would James prefer to be rid of her than spend any effort defending her? As for his wife's friend, there would be no salvation offered.

Within days of her acquittal, Barbara was dragged from her home to stand trial again – and this time brought back to the cell in chains.

'It was the king,' she said hollowly when Euphame pressed her for an explanation. 'He wouldn't accept the first verdict. Even though the same questions were asked and I gave the same answers, saying nothing of witchcraft, only of asking Bothwell for help, they all changed their minds.'

Of course they did, Geillis thought bitterly. It would take a brave man to cross a king twice.

'But why …' Euphame hesitated, a rare sight, then ploughed on. 'Why do you still live? Surely you won't be given a third trial?'

The ghost of a smile hovered on Barbara's lips. 'I pleaded my belly.'

Geillis looked from Barbara's handsome but lined face to her belly. It was rounded, true enough, but it always had been, and probably with good food and thickening years, not a baby.

Euphame spoke bluntly. 'They believed you?'

Barbara nodded. 'They cannot hurt me now, not without harming the child.'

'A child conceived in this tolbooth?'

Barbara hesitated – and Geillis understood. There was no child.

Impatience warred with pity in Euphame's voice. 'And in eight months' time? Or less? What then?'

Barbara's faint smile faded. 'I know it won't last. But perhaps all we need is more time. Every day we live, isn't there a chance this will all blow over?'

Geillis caught Euphame's eye, and she knew they were thinking the same thing. If King James had gone from merely interrogating suspects himself to overturning verdicts until they suited him, what hope could there possibly be?

They came for Euphame next. She left the cell with her shoulders straight, her chin high, never anything less than regally haughty – even with desperate tears silvering her eyes.

'Perhaps they'll acquit her too,' Bessie suggested in the aching quiet that always followed a fellow prisoner's departure, as if no one knew whether to settle back into blank-faced inactivity, or twitch with the fear that never wholly left.

Geillis sighed. 'After the king interfered with the last trial? I can't see a jury daring.'

'She could plead her belly,' Bessie said, desperation turning her huge eyes watery.

Geillis glanced over at the bloody rags piled next to Euphame's patch of straw. The guards always took ages to fetch water whenever the women bled; she suspected they enjoyed knowing the prisoners were waiting in discomfort and shame. 'They'd know she was lying.'

'I heard of a woman over Haddington way,' Bessie insisted, 'who bled every month, regular as any moon, and then suddenly dropped a child into the straw while she was milking the cow.'

Geillis had heard such stories too – but she'd heard many more about girls who wore loose shawls, who had their reasons to produce stained rags every month rather than admit the truth to themselves, or their parents, or husbands who'd been away at the wrong time. Let Bessie comfort herself with stories.

There was a sudden commotion outside. They recognized the sounds: they'd heard them for Fian, and again for Agnes. Was it Geillis's imagination, or was the baying wilder this time? Were the crowds more vicious because this time the accused was from Edinburgh? A woman who'd sneered at them, barged past them in the street, now receiving her comeuppance.

'Burn the witch!'

'Traitorous whore!'

The shouts were gleeful, vindictive. Even as the sounds of the guards died away, the roar of the crowd persisted, moving up the Canongate towards the Lawnmarket, chased by more howls as others joined the mob.

'They found her guilty,' Barbara breathed. 'Euphame, guilty.' She looked astonished that anyone had dared oppose Euphame in anything, let alone so grave a matter as a trial.

And they weren't wasting any time. Even if Euphame had tried pleading her belly, it had clearly been dismissed. They wanted her dead far more than they worried about the possibility of an innocent life being lost along the way.

A great cheer erupted from Castle Hill. Moments later, the smell of smoke, rough and thickened, as if the wood had been slightly damp, reached the tolbooth. The fire had been lit. Euphame was already dead.

And then the screams began.

They were gasps at first, indistinguishable from the crowd's roar. Then they grew louder, shriller, unmistakeable.

'She's being burned alive,' Bessie gasped.

'Why?' Barbara whispered, hunching into a ball, knowing only a lie separated her from Castle Hill. 'They showed the others mercy!'

Another scream rent the air. The noises were barely human now, wordless outpourings of agony as flesh blistered and melted, and even bones began to blacken.

'It's a message,' Geillis said bleakly. 'To Bothwell, and to all of us. No matter who you are, there will be no more mercy.'

39

Clouds hung low over Edinburgh, pressing down on the castle's highest towers, obscuring the summit of Arthur's Seat. Unseasonable weather for June. No wonder a shivering Elline claimed the smoke from Euphame MacCalzean's pyre still clung to the city, a cold, looming ghost.

'She laid a curse with her dying breath,' Elline whispered to those who'd listen. But if anyone asked who its target was, Elline fell silent. Even her zeal for gossip faded when she strayed too close to treason.

But they didn't need dark clouds to remind them of Euphame's end. They didn't even need to have witnessed it themselves: her screams could be heard across the city. Margareta, remembering Johanna's burning, knew someone had built Euphame's pyre with drawn-out suffering in mind. John, who'd witnessed the execution, looked a decade older than the man Margareta had danced with in Kronborg; the shadows in his eyes had thickened and the furrows around mouth and brows were carved deeper.

Everyone at court had been affected by the burning, though no one was foolhardy enough to reveal their revulsion to the king who'd ordered it. Some hadn't been horrified at all; rather, they'd nodded approvingly, even enjoyed the spectacle, as if a burning woman was as entertaining as dogfighting – more so, since witches deserved to suffer more than beasts. Margareta was relieved by the prospect of their summer sojourn at Falkland Palace; at least its stones wouldn't echo with screams.

Not like the stones in the tolbooth. Even from outside, the building looked forbidding; the night turned its walls iron-dark, its narrow windows as shadowy and stern as the visor slits of a warrior bearing down on her.

'Are you sure you want to do this?'

Euphame's burning had brought the flames ever closer to Margareta. She couldn't avoid the tolbooth any longer. Margareta looked up at John. 'I doubt anyone ever wants to enter here. But we have to know if I'm safe – and Anna too.'

If anyone understood, he did. He nodded and drew out a key. 'This is the guards' entrance – which no one watches. We won't be seen.'

They'd slipped out of Holyrood after dark in black cloaks, ducking into alleys, darting between shadows. It should have been almost impossible to see them approach the tolbooth – but if anyone were watching, Margareta and John would look far from innocent. Yet the risk of not coming, not knowing until it was too late, far outweighed the possibility of being watched on a dark night. She steadied a shiver as they entered the tolbooth.

Edinburgh's streets had been hushed, distant voices ruffling the quiet's edges. But the tolbooth's quiet was closer, darker. The voices Margareta heard as they moved through empty corridors were too close, only separated from her by stones and locked doors. There was no wine-softened laughter here, only mockery and hapless cries.

'I'll fetch her,' John said, unlocking a door and removing a torch from its bracket. 'Wait in here.'

Margareta took the torch and stepped inside. As the door closed behind her, she couldn't help flinching. She could have been dragged here – tortured here. Still might be. Geillis had only to say her name, and she would go from palace to cell in a heartbeat.

The chamber was sparse. Only a desk and chair. Of course, Margareta thought, it hadn't been furnished for comfort. Was there even a fireplace? She cast the torch about, searching.

There was a fireplace. At once, Margareta realized why it was there: to heat the devices hanging above it. Sickened, she jerked the torch away – and then she saw the bridle.

The cell walls seemed to close in as she stared, until she almost felt stone and metal gouging into her flesh. She'd seen Agnes's face, heard

Grierson's agonies in John's words. Those horrors doubled now, the bridle glinting mere inches from her skin. How had Geillis kept Margareta's name back, knowing the bridle was here?

'Lady Margareta?'

There it was: her name on the Scottish girl's lips. But not an accusation, only a soft marvelling. Margareta turned to see Geillis entering the chamber and John closing the door on them both to keep watch outside. A stench beyond staleness, beyond mere dirt, clogged the room. Imagining the squalor Geillis had endured for months, Margareta wanted to weep.

'I never thought to see you again,' Geillis said. 'Or at least …'

'Only in one circumstance.'

'Yes.' She took a step closer, grunting as if with pain; as she moved into the torchlight, Margareta gasped. Always thin, Geillis looked gaunt now, her skin stretched taut over jutting bones, her eye sockets sunken craters. Her once abundant red hair barely grew past her ears and was streaked white from old wounds; scars pitted her face like the ravages of smallpox. No disease had done this. It had been human hands. Margareta felt sick at the thought.

'Boy or girl?'

Margareta stared. 'Boy. Johnny, for his father. But how can you care about such things when you've been treated so cruelly?'

Geillis shrugged; Margareta thought her collarbone would break her skin open. 'Once a midwife, always a midwife. How was your childbed, in the end?'

'Horrible. She insisted I lie down when I wanted to stand, and she kept declaring I had no idea what a painful labour was unless my baby came shoulder-first like hers had.'

Geillis's eyebrows arched; several scars plucked a cobweb across her forehead. 'Some have to belittle others' pain to feel powerful.'

Margareta hid her shame by turning to set the torch in a bracket. 'No one could dismiss yours.'

'I didn't mean you.'

'Why?' Margareta burst out. 'Why have you spared me? I've done nothing to deserve it!'

Geillis almost smiled. 'That's why. You've done nothing.'

'But – surely there are other innocents in this tolbooth? You had my ring; Euphame and Barbara met me – it would have been so easy to name me!'

'You sound almost as if you wished it.'

'I can't imagine what you've suffered. I won't insult you by suggesting I could have withstood it.' Margareta shook her head. 'Ilsa was right – I know nothing of your world.'

'You still speak of her. Most people would deny ever having known a burned witch.'

'I daren't speak of her to anyone else.' Margareta pushed her hands through her hair in frustration at herself. She hesitated, steeling herself to dredge up the accusation. 'You knew what those herbs would do.'

The torchlight flickered, bloody against the stones.

'Yes.' Geillis lifted her chin. 'That's why I halved the dosage.'

'What?'

'I couldn't do it,' Geillis said quietly. 'I meant to save children, not kill them. Most herbs can heal or hurt depending on how much you take. I thought it would make a difference. But ...'

'But Anna lost her baby anyway.'

'I guessed as much when no bells rang to herald a new prince.' Geillis sighed. 'Witchcraft or no witchcraft, women lose children all the time. We pretend it doesn't happen, that we can't see the empty spaces they should have filled. But it always matters.' She stared at the shadows hiding the bridle. 'I never took up much space in the world. I doubt anyone will notice the gap I leave behind.'

'*I* will notice,' Margareta said fiercely. 'Every time I look at my son, every time I walk in the gardens, I will remember, and be grateful because you helped me when you had no cause.'

'Oh, I had cause.' Geillis met Margareta's eyes. 'I needed to remember who I once was. A girl who hoped to help others, to do good, not damage. And you were once kind to me.'

'Kind?'

Geillis nodded. 'You offered me a seat and a lemon cake. You gave me some gloves. Perhaps it meant nothing to you ... but for years, no one's cared about my comfort.' She swallowed. 'Your sister might not have thought you did anything to help anyone. But you have helped me.'

'I should have done more.'

Geillis gnawed at her cuff, pulling at loose threads; she shook her wrist and something fell into her palm. 'Here. You should take this back.'

Red and gold glowed: Margareta's ring.

'You kept it all this time?'

'Yes.' Geillis watched the flames flicker in the ruby. 'They dragged names out of me. I couldn't help myself. But every time, I told myself that if I only named people already imprisoned, it was all right. If I protected the innocent, I could still claim to be good. By keeping your ring secret, I kept you safe.'

'I didn't deserve such loyalty.'

Geillis attempted a wry smile. 'Who gets what they deserve?' Her smile vanished and her lips suddenly trembled. 'Margareta ... could you do something for me?'

She could have hesitated, could have worried what Geillis might ask. But then Ilsa would truly have been right about her. 'Of course.'

A tear worried at Geillis's lashes. 'The last time anyone held my hand was to crush my thumb. Even before ... when their third baby died, my parents stopped touching me. As if I reminded them of all the brothers and sisters I should have had. I doubt anyone will touch me kindly ever again.'

Margareta's hand closed over hers and she wrapped Geillis in her arms. 'I owe you my life, Geillis Duncan. The least I can do is hold you now.'

All the way back to Holyrood, Margareta gripped the ring; by the time they reached their chamber, cramp seared her fingers. Was she safe from burning now? What of her gloves – if Seton found them, could he trace them back to her?

Untying her cloak, she tiptoed across to listen at the nursemaid's door. 'Johnny's asleep. Let's to bed.'

'I'll join you later.' John remained by the door, his face set. 'I'm going to the castle.'

Margareta stared, aghast. 'To see him?'

'I have to.'

'You certainly do not!'

'Yes, I do,' he said simply. 'Just as you had to see Geillis.'

'You're sneaking in to visit the king's arch-enemy, and you speak as if you owed Bothwell a favour! Can't you see how this will look?'

'That's exactly why I must see him – to appear loyal to him. I have to wear this mask as long as possible.'

He kissed her farewell – and then he was gone, leaving Margareta wondering if John even knew anymore where the mask ended and his own face began.

Glad as she was to be leaving Edinburgh, Margareta didn't relish the prospect of packing. She hadn't even begun her own; as twilight turned the palace grounds blue, she was dealing with Anna's jewellery. Every piece had to be found, cleaned, polished, inspected for missing stones or damaged clasps, dispatched for repairs if needed or wrapped in muslin and velvet, then placed reverentially in a mahogany coffer. Even by candlelight, Margareta's head ached from squinting at gold and silver filigree.

Around her, Anna's chambers were in upheaval. Elline was trying to pair up all the royal stockings, rummaging in chests and crawling under furniture in search of embroidered lawn and constantly crashing into Vibeke, on her own hunt for gloves. Beyond the chamber, Margareta could hear the familiar chaos of preparations: stewards barking at pages; lairds berating stable lads. Meanwhile Anna flicked through sketches for masque costumes, a chewed fingernail revealing her now constant anxiety, heedless of how the discarded sketches wafted across the room every time a lady passed, necessitating a frantic scrabble to retrieve them before they fluttered out of the endlessly opening doors.

It was so chaotic, no one noticed the bells.

At first, they were a distant tinkling, and Margareta rubbed her temples, her headache worsening. Then the ringing grew louder, closer, an urgent clanging no one could ignore.

Elline sat back on her heels, a stocking limp in one hand. 'What *is* that?'

'Alarum bells,' Vibeke said, peering out at the darkness. 'Maybe there's plague in the city.'

'But there's plague every summer,' Margareta said. A ruby brooch grew slippery in her tensed hands. 'They didn't ring a bell last year.'

'Are we under attack?' Anna asked. 'Who would dare attack the palace?'

The only man bold enough was locked in the castle cells. Unless … could there be a mob at the gates? Margareta had heard of apprentices growing restless in hot summers, rioting in the streets – but never out of the blue. Might Euphame MacCalzean's friends be seeking revenge for her terrible end? Yet no one had spoken out for her while she lived; why speak for her now?

Footsteps were approaching. Not the sedate steps that ordinarily approached a queen's chamber. These footsteps hurried, clattered – and then John burst through the doors, dishevelled and wild-eyed.

'It's Bothwell, Your Grace. He's escaped.'

The courtyard seethed, a tumult of horses and carts, hounds and men, as two groups tried to prepare for departure in one space: the royal progress and James's army. Impossible to move without stumbling into armed men or tripping over abandoned chests. Despite the chaos, it was an excellent place for a private conversation.

'How could he have escaped?' Margareta demanded in a whisper. 'Of all prisoners, surely he was the most closely guarded?'

John tightened his horse's saddle. 'Prisons are only as good as their guards are trustworthy.'

'He had help?'

'The captain of the guard is gone too. It looks as if they simply walked out together.'

'What – strolled out of Edinburgh Castle, unseen, unchallenged?'

'Would you challenge your captain if you were a guard?'

'But surely …' She hesitated, unwilling to admit her suspicions. 'He cannot have escaped long before you reached the castle. Didn't you see him?'

'Dozens of alleys lead off Castle Hill,' John pointed out. 'Easy for them to disappear down one. Besides, the hour was late.'

'Yes,' she said quietly. 'Later still by the time you returned to Holyrood.'

He shot her a sharp look. 'By the time I'd led a search of the castle and raised an alarm – yes, it was later.'

'But—'

'I told you,' he said, taking her hand. '*Trust me*. Everything I do is for you and Johnny now.'

Horns blasted. Around them, men were mounting horses, adjusting weapons, bidding farewells.

John pressed her hand gently. 'I must go.'

She couldn't bring herself to ask the question she truly wanted to ask. 'How long will you be gone?'

John shook his head. 'Hard to say. It's believed Bothwell fled to his estates in Kelso. A day to the borders, and then who knows? The search, the fight if he's found …'

Hooves clattered. The army was leaving, James at its head. No time to ask questions, or to be anything other than the dutiful wife. John swung into the saddle and leaned down for Margareta's kiss. Suddenly the army was gone, and the only people left in the courtyard were women, servants, or old men.

Anna ascended the mounting block, June sunlight gilding her hair like a coronet. Her voice was nightingale-clear. 'Our duty lies at Falkland Palace. Let us depart.'

No one would have guessed that her husband had just ridden out to hunt their arch-enemy. Nor that the tolbooth was still full of people who'd tried to kill her and her unborn child, or that the ashes of other ill-wishers had been buried at crossroads. All anyone could say of Anna now was that she looked like a queen.

* * *

They rode north, through dappled-green forests and across heather-purpled moors. With every hoofbeat, the questions surrounding Margareta's mind tightened like thumbscrews.

Why had John returned so late? Why to Anna's chamber rather than straight to the king? Love for Margareta? Loyalty to Anna or duty to Sophia? Or had he been deliberately avoiding James?

John knew more than he'd told her. That had always been the case, but where before it had been infuriating, now it was frightening.

It is believed Bothwell fled to Kelso. Did that mean someone had laid a false trail?

It looks as though they simply walked out together. Someone had made it look that way. And he'd said *as though*. He knew it to be false.

Trust me. Everything I do is for you and Johnny now.

She'd doubted that once, but no longer. Now, her doubts were of a different sort.

What if John had decided that their best interests couldn't rest on James and Anna's shoulders? What if the double agent's allegiances had changed?

What if John was now Bothwell's man?

A fly was crawling across her leg. Geillis watched it as if the sores that had lured it belonged to someone else. Better to feel detached from her body: whatever was done to it would matter less. Whatever had already been done could become irrelevant.

The leg the fly crawled across, for instance. There were dozens of tiny scars from Seton driving the needle deep. Beneath the shackles, half-crusted scabs oozed pus over the purple, taut flesh that had somehow avoided chafing enough to heal. Every morning one hip cried out with stiffness, but she'd grown almost deaf to it, barely noticing the stones' cold rigidity anymore. What did it matter? She'd scarcely thought about her leg before; it had just been something that helped her walk, ride, crouch. She'd knelt to sweep hearths; she'd stretched up to reach clay jars of flour when making bread. Useful, but never loved. Like Geillis herself.

It's the silence, Geillis told herself. That's what's making you maudlin.

That, and what she heard when no other noise drowned it out: Euphame's screams.

Everyone had been quieter since that day. Gone were Bessie's mewls, Barbara's sobs. Instead, silence bore down on them. What was there to say?

Even the alarum bells hadn't made them feel better. So Bothwell had saved his own skin. Meanwhile, they all festered in the tolbooth. Not waiting, for waiting implied expectation, even hopes or fears. Merely enduring.

Outside, a trumpet blasted. Some proclamation at the Mercat Cross outside St Giles'. Probably a disgruntled alderman complaining about noise after dark. Geillis watched the fly approach a different sore.

'In the name of His Grace King James the Sixth these indictments are brought against Francis Stewart, Earl of Bothwell.'

She jerked. Dislodged, the fly buzzed upwards, spinning irritably.

'Such is his malicious and ungodly nature that, after committing sundry slaughters and other odious crimes, he has taken up arms against His Grace's person on many occasions. He has consulted with necromancers and witches, both within and without Scotland, for bereaving His Grace of life. He has escaped ward and committed treason against the crown. Henceforth, the said earl is declared rebel and traitor, and all his estates are forfeit.'

Barbara stirred. 'So much for a reward.'

'All followers of the earl are ordered to leave Edinburgh forthwith and declared likewise rebels. The earl's factor, Ninian Chirnside. The steward ...'

Geillis remembered Chirnside's hand clamping around her jaw. If she'd been glad of anyone's punishment this last year, she was glad of his.

And then another name caught her attention. A name she'd once, with girlish blindness, associated with hope.

'Lord John Wemyss.'

40

There was no loneliness colder than being a traitor's wife.

Yet Margareta still walked free. James had taken Bothwell's pregnant wife and their children hostage, warding them in Aberdeen, far away from the border forests of Dalkeith and from Bothwell's estates in Caithness, the last places Bothwell had reportedly been sighted – at opposite ends of Scotland; Margareta doubted that was accidental, and she had to wonder whether John had helped spread some of these rumours.

It is believed Bothwell fled to Kelso. Because John let James and his army believe it? She'd wondered at the time and had grown even more suspicious after the Mercat Cross proclamation. Had John sent the army on a wild goose chase to Bothwell's border estates, knowing the earl had gone north? Once the pursuit was on, had John slipped away to wherever Bothwell was truly hiding?

Where else could John have gone? He'd left James's army, unnoticed until they were taking possession of Bothwell's estates, and disappeared. Either he'd pledged allegiance to Bothwell, or he was alone in a country where he was a hunted man.

Or he was dead.

He was a double agent, she knew that. His role was to convince both sides of his loyalty. He'd helped Bothwell escape, and that condemned him in James's eyes. He'd ridden out with the king's army, interrogated and tortured the king's prisoners – would that condemn him in Bothwell's eyes too? Trying to convince two sides would ultimately only convince both you were disloyal, and if either side decided John was a traitor, there was only one punishment.

Meanwhile she was a hostage without cell or shackles. She gripped her son close every moment she could, terrified he would be taken from her, and ached every time his smiles and frowns echoed his absent father's. She hadn't realized until now just how much she loved John – and it was too late. Too late if he was dead; too late if he was a traitor, since declaring your love for a traitor was itself tantamount to treachery. And too late to tell the one person she needed to tell.

Falkland was deserted. Dust motes hovered, listless in white bars of light. Mirrors gaped dully, reflecting only unlit chambers.

In the emptiness, Margareta's footsteps knelled like driven nails. They'd all ridden out hunting without her. Ordinarily she'd have been first to Anna's side, but the sidelong stares, the hissing behind hands, the cold gaps everyone left around her had made her reluctant to rush to her duties. She'd dawdled, even contemplated not leaving her bed at all, before dragging herself into gown and ruff, and marching into the gauntlet of royal corridors – only to find them empty.

A page trotted past, glancing at Margareta over the bolt of scarlet silk he was ferrying somewhere, and the sly judgement in his eyes decided her. She'd wait in Anna's chambers. Even their silence would be preferable to feeling the servants' eyes weigh her, measure her, and doubtless find her wanting. Gritting her teeth, she strode on, savagely thrusting her heels against the wooden floors, taking bittersweet pleasure in the harsh noise. But once inside Anna's rooms, she couldn't continue – it felt as much a violation as scratching Anna's face. Instead, Margareta slowly approached what should have been her usual seat, next to Anna's. There was a basket of half-finished embroidery: not hers, not anymore. But now that she was here …

She'd almost finished a cutwork scarf by the time footsteps approached. Her needle faltered – she'd hoped to stitch her nerves smooth, but they frayed with expectation.

Anna's ladies burst in, an effervescent bubbling of laughter, silk, gossip, and lace. Once, it had bubbled around Margareta, bearing her along with it; now it hit her like hailstones. Each woman's eyes fell on Margareta. Elline let out a nervous laugh, which Vibeke's jab cut short.

But Anna's response hurt most. She stared at Margareta as if she were a stranger.

'You are bold to show your face here, Lady Margareta.'

Margareta swallowed; she heard the gulp echo. 'I could no longer bear to be out of your presence.'

Anna's lip curled. 'Once more, you prove that you are not the woman I thought you were. She was never a sycophant.'

'She was never anything but loyal to you.'

'How dare you use that word to me now?'

'Because I have given my life over to you!' Margareta cried. 'All that I am, all that I do – it is loyalty to *you*! In the name of all my years of loyalty, I beg you to hear me speak!'

Anna's stillness spread through the chamber, freezing everyone in its grip. Without taking her eyes off Margareta, she said, 'Leave us.'

For a moment no one moved, unsure who was targeted by the words.

'I said leave us!'

Anna's command snapped like a whip and her ladies fled before it, leaving Margareta alone with the queen.

Silence eddied, Anna and Margareta at its centre like two islands. Margareta's throat felt dry; she wanted to swallow but couldn't bear the thought of the sound rupturing the chamber again.

'Well?' Anna raised an eyebrow. 'You asked me to hear you, yet you are not speaking.'

'I …' How could Margareta convince her? 'I need you to know – to understand – I would never betray you. I never have, and never will.'

'You are a traitor's wife.'

So she was John's wife now, when it suited the king and queen to condemn her for it? Margareta thrust her anger down. 'I am his wife because your mother commanded it.'

That eyebrow again: no sickle could be sharper. 'So you deny you are happily married? You deny loving him?'

Margareta shook her head. 'I cannot deny that – but I am far from happy! He's betrayed my trust too. I didn't know he was Bothwell's man – I thought that a feint to discover Bothwell's plans.'

'You thought you could trust a spy. A double agent.'

'I—'

'Understandable, I suppose. After all, I made the same mistake with you.'

'Anna!'

'Do not call me that!' Anna's eyes seethed like blue flames. 'You have no right to address me as a friend, as if you cared for me.'

'I have always cared for you!'

'Liar!' Anna spun on her heel and strode to the window, as far away from Margareta as possible. 'You were made my companion so my mother could use you to watch me. You were forced into a space that never fitted you, and you've always chafed against it.'

'That isn't true.' And yet hadn't Margareta always felt out of place among Anna's ladies? Her doubt must have shown in her face, for Anna's head jerked back in a harsh laugh.

'Oh, but it is. You resent your position. You despise us.'

Who was this *us* now? Once, it had meant Anna and Margareta, but now? Was it her husband, her adopted kingdom – anyone but Margareta?

'And you worked with Bothwell to hurt us.'

'I did not—'

'Don't try to deceive me! Who met with the Sampson witch? Who gave me herbs to kill my child while her own traitor's whelp thrived?'

Her words struck Margareta like a whip. It would do no good to offer Geillis's confession: Anna wouldn't want to believe it. All it would take was a word from the queen, and Margareta would burn on Castle Hill. And if Anna were the one to offer up Margareta as a sacrifice, Anna might be safer.

'Small wonder,' Anna continued, 'your lover conspired to help Bothwell escape – is even now scourging the land.'

'I swear, I didn't know!'

'Don't claim innocence!' Anna gave that harsh laugh again; it was like seeing a swan spit tar. 'You've always thought me a fool, you and my mother. A simple girl whose head contains only ribbons and lace. Everyone wants me to be a delicate princess, a creature from a faery tale, all gossamer and light – but no one who lives and breathes can be that. I have ridden out storms, defied the devil's schemes and witches' arts; I've seen my life's hope bleed away, and I am no child anymore! I am the Queen of Scotland, and I will be respected!'

'You will always have my respect.'

'And you have lost mine forever.' There was no laughter in Anna's voice now. 'Consider yourself fortunate, Lady Margareta, that I allow you to remain at court. That I do not bring charges of witchcraft against you. After all, I have more than enough with which to condemn you, and it wouldn't be the first time your family has been tainted with such charges.'

She knew. Realization swept over Margareta, ice-cold. Anna knew not only about Euphame and Barbara but about Ilsa, perhaps about Johanna too. Perhaps she'd always known, and Margareta and Sophia had been too arrogant to imagine she could know anything at all.

'Anna, I—'

'I told you – do not call me that.' The queen turned away. 'I believe your duties will take you elsewhere today, Lady Margareta.'

41

On good days, Geillis wondered whether they had been forgotten. No one had been interrogated for over two months – and without interrogations, there could be no further trials, and no executions. Being ignored was the greatest safety they could wish for. Besides, they'd all been wrung dry. Months of fractured sleep and pain and fear had squeezed every piece of information out of them; surely no one had any secrets remaining.

But on the bad days Geillis knew with every fibre of her being, every fragile bone and inch of unburnt skin, that the delay was designed to break them. Each day the rats crawled over their shins, and their hearts faltered with every approaching footstep, they all grew more brittle. Bitten lips became bloodier; already-matted hair tugged and torn. On such days she couldn't forget that bloodshed was like wine. People desired it, thought it glorious, daring, exciting. Then they sipped and wanted more. They drank and drank, growing ever more raucous, not knowing when to stop. Things broke, some irreparably. Afterwards, they felt sick and vowed abstinence. But they always forgot. Always came back for more.

'Water. Please, give us water.'

Bessie, pleading at the end of her chains, voice rasping with weakness. Once, Geillis had envied Bessie's singing, how melodies soared like swallows from her lips.

'You won't get any,' Geillis sighed. 'Unless it comes from a well in a plague-riddled part of town.'

Plague. The word ought to have held more fear. No doubt everyone else who heard it shrank away, clutching children's hands tighter, narrowing their eyes at once-liked neighbours. It had made the king and his court flee Edinburgh for Falkland's clearer air. But Geillis only wondered if dying of plague would be preferable to burning.

Bessie ignored her. 'Water,' she croaked again. 'More water, I beg you.'

'Hell's teeth!' The cell door swung open and the guards burst in, one brandishing a torch snatched from its brazier. He thrust it at Bessie's face and she fell back, whimpering. 'Keep on whining and I'll burn you alive before you can stand trial!'

The other guard snorted. 'Waste of a good torch.'

The guard rammed his boot against Bessie's ribs. 'Die of thirst for all I care, witch – but don't whine about it!'

Suddenly the rumpus within the cell was interrupted by one outside. The guards dropped Bessie and rushed to the window; unchained, a man could just see out of it.

'What's happening?'

'Where's it coming from? Sounds close.'

Glass smashed; a dog barked, setting others off. Men were shouting, rough, angry bellows of people determined to fight.

'Maitland! Come out, you coward!'

Was that Bothwell's voice? It couldn't be. Geillis struggled to sit upright, straining towards the window.

'Bothwell!' one of the guards breathed. 'Thought he was in Dalkeith.'

'Kelso, wasn't it?'

'What's he doing here?'

'Looking for a brawl, obviously.'

'But …' The guard shook his head. 'He must know the court's not here – there's no flags over Holyrood. What's he playing at?'

'He's drunk,' the other guard sighed as more glass shattered. 'Glad I'm not charged with keeping the peace out there – sooner a pack of whinging women than Bothwell spoiling for a fight.'

'He's an idiot. Coming here in the open, with barely two dozen men – what sort of fool does that when there's a price on his head?'

Geillis frowned. Even drunk – if he was – Bothwell was no fool. He wouldn't enter Edinburgh, risking capture, unless he wanted something.

'A crown for anyone who brings me Maitland!' Bothwell yelled. 'Two crowns if they knock his hat off!'

Laughter clattered up the Canongate – no longer just men, but the higher, softer laughs of women and children, joining in the mockery.

That was it, Geillis realized. Bothwell wasn't here to fight Chancellor Maitland, the king's right hand, able to summon many more troops than Bothwell's rebels. Bothwell was here to mock Maitland and the monarch he represented. Who would remember Maitland's absence today? None. Instead, they'd all tell stories about his cowardice. About how formidable a foe Bothwell must be.

'Come on, Francis,' another man called. His voice was familiar; Geillis struggled to place it. 'They'll not come out to face you. We're wasting our time.'

'Not at all,' Bothwell countered. 'We're near Edinburgh's finest taverns – let's drink our fill!'

'Be thankful we're not watching the city tonight,' one of the guards muttered.

'Is anyone? Nobody's trying to stop him.'

They wouldn't dare, Geillis thought. With the king away, who would stand up for James against the Earl of Bothwell? He'd escaped James's custody: the witch-hunt intended to drag Bothwell down had failed to hold him. If he couldn't be stopped by a king, what chance did commoners have?

Had Geillis betrayed him too soon?

'They're going,' the shorter guard observed, sounding relieved. He turned away from the window as if to leave – but then stiffened. He grabbed his partner's torch. 'Look. Is that what I think it is?'

In the harsh brightness was Barbara, her back hunched against the guards. Her face hung heavy with bleakness: the face of a woman who knew she was doomed. Spreading across her skirts was a dark, unmistakeable stain. Either the baby was lost – or there had never been a baby to lose. The stain might as well have been a signature on a warrant.

They burned Barbara on the last day that felt like summer. Was it still August? It might have been September, even October. Geillis had long ago lost track of days. All she knew was that a sun shaft left a red streak on her exposed calf while Barbara's body burned. The next day, rain spat a chill into the cell and pecked at her clothes, and the next day, and the next, until winter winds whistled against the chains around Geillis and Bessie's ankles – and the shackles hanging empty on the walls. Agnes. Euphame. Barbara. All gone to Castle Hill.

The cell door clanged open, and four guards strode in.

Bessie whimpered as two guards released her shackles and dragged her upright. Geillis hunched lower, hoping the other two would go past to Janet or the Linkups – but they came straight for her.

'Not today,' Geillis murmured, wincing as the releasing irons scraped her sores. 'It can't be today.'

She wasn't ready. Shouldn't there be some new charge? She couldn't have done anything to be charged with in this cell – surely there was no reason to put her on trial?

Her legs barely supported her as they marched her out of the cell, their hands clamped around her elbows, wrenching her onward when she stumbled. They didn't care that her ankles struck stone, or that loose floorboards raked her bare feet.

Where were the guards taking them? And why?

Only once had they been interrogated simultaneously: last winter, when they'd first come to the tolbooth. Their interrogators didn't want them sharing stories. Whatever lies Bessie told couldn't save them unless Geillis spun the same falsehoods.

Which left one choice: to tell the truth. And yet the truth would condemn them all.

They'd reached a door. One guard knocked, then pushed it open into darkness. Geillis recoiled as if it were an opening coffin and she about to be buried alive. The guards hauled her in, her flailing limbs no hindrance.

Maitland rose as if greeting a worthy guest perfumed with bergamot, not a woman reeking of the cells. 'Mistress Duncan.'

Why was he being polite? He was Lord Chancellor – he could have called her whore, hag, jezebel, and she couldn't have retorted.

'My lord,' she managed, her guardedness emerging as a tremor.

'Please,' he said, gesturing to a chair placed before the desk. She'd never had a chair before. Only chains, only standing until her very bones seemed to carve through the soles of her feet, until dangling from iron almost seemed appealing. But he had invited her to sit, and so she must sit, and there would be a price to pay for such comfort.

'Leave us.'

They sent the guards away when they were about to turn screws. Geillis hunched lower, as if her own body could somehow shield her.

'Now,' Maitland said, the softness in his voice rustling like a silk skirt through the gutter, 'might I offer you some refreshment? Water? Ale? Wine?'

'Why?'

'I am told you have been suffering from thirst.'

'That was Bessie, not me!'

'You are not thirsty?'

'No – I mean, yes! But I never complained!'

'Why not? Why have you never complained, Geillis Duncan, through all of your suffering?' His gentleness terrified her. 'Do you fear no one will listen?' He came closer, perching on the desk. His fingers, soft as babies' cheeks, cupped her chin. But their grip clamped and pinched: the fingers of a man who always wore gloves to do his dirty work. 'But I am here to listen now.'

She tried to lean away; it was impossible. 'I've told you everything I know.'

'I doubt that. You've always seemed remarkably intelligent for your station. I believe you have answered our questions with commendable honesty – and so we must beg your forgiveness. We have been remiss in not asking you the right questions. Questions which might allow you to demonstrate just how much knowledge you possess.'

'I don't understand.'

'I think you do. We asked you about Agnes Sampson and Euphame MacCalzean. We asked you about the Earl of Bothwell. But there are many people we have not yet questioned you about.'

'No.' She surprised herself with the strength in her voice. 'I won't speak of anyone else. I don't want anyone else being hurt.'

'Now, I don't think that's true.' He smiled kindly. 'As I said, you are an intelligent woman. You understand no one truly wishes to hurt another without good reason. Which you have.'

'What good reason?' She gave a croak of a laugh. 'I know I won't leave this tolbooth alive. The only reward you could tempt me with is the one you won't offer me.'

'You are not so naive.' He lifted her hand, caressed the ruined thumb. 'There are many ways to die. Swiftly, painlessly, peacefully. Or … his way.'

'Whose?'

He smiled again. 'Enter.'

The door swung open. Stepping inside, his face crueller than ever in the torchlight, was David Seton.

'You can either be of service,' Maitland purred, 'or I shall give you to him. And he will take great pleasure in making you cooperate.'

Seton's lips parted, as if to pant, and she remembered that breath, hot and fast on her neck. Her entire body wanted to flail, every tiny scar stinging as if torn open. He'd hurt her even more, find new ways to hurt her, and she would scream until she died. She knew what it was like for a woman to die screaming – she'd heard Euphame die, and it hadn't been quick.

She hated herself for saying it. 'What do you want from me?'

Seton looked both triumphantly amused and disappointed, like a cat toying with a mouse that had given up trying to escape.

Maitland smiled. 'You need only listen to some names and tell me what they mean to you.'

And what would it mean for those named? Death? Or merely imprisonment? Perhaps even exile. She tried to believe it wasn't the first, and knew she was deceiving herself.

She had no choice. She nodded.

Maitland gave another smile and gestured to Seton. 'Be a good man and act as scribe.'

Geillis found little to smile about these days. But Seton's disgruntled scowl as he remembered he must obey the chancellor and thus be obedient in front of Geillis: perhaps she could smile about this later.

'Lord Home,' Maitland said abruptly. 'Alexander, the Lord Warden.'

Geillis shook her head. 'I've never heard of him.'

'The Earl of Errol, Francis Hay.'

'No.'

'The Master of Glamis, Patrick Lyon.'

'No.'

Seton gave a snort. 'My lord, this girl's a practised liar. You cannot trust a word she says.'

'Thank you, Seton,' Maitland said coolly. 'I make my own decisions about whose word to trust.'

'But—'

'Enough.' He didn't raise his voice. He was Lord Chancellor of Scotland; every word he uttered was a threat.

Seton picked up the quill again. 'Yes, my lord.'

'Now, Geillis,' Maitland cajoled, 'try to remember. These are not good men. Not your friends, not worth your kindness. They have ruined themselves with their foolishness, greed, and hostility. They rampage through civilized streets, breaking the peace and threatening other men. It would be right and just for you to tell the truth about them.'

'I am,' she whispered, almost wishing she had something to tell him so he would stop purring at her. It was like talking to King James – both men veered between stroking your head and clamping you in irons. They wanted to win you over, knead your secrets out of you like knots from tired muscles – and yet they couldn't help lashing out. Did their power make them afraid? Or their terror make them deadly? Either way, men's fear was a world apart from women's fear. 'I'm sorry – I don't know those men.'

He sighed. 'Very well.' He began to move away, then suddenly turned back. 'Perhaps this one will awaken a memory. The Laird of Logie's son. John Wemyss.'

Her jaw dropped. 'But he spied for the king!'

Maitland smiled. Seton dipped his quill in ink expectantly.

'Now then, Geillis,' Maitland said softly. 'Tell me everything you know about John Wemyss.'

Bessie hadn't met him. Only Geillis. Wemyss's fate lay in her hands.

Protect Margareta, she thought. You promised. But Seton and Maitland were watching her, two carrion crows smelling blood. Had she strength left to keep her promise?

42

Margareta had spent most of her life watching Anna. But she'd watched without seeing. Anna was sinew, not silk; steel, not starlight. How could Margareta not have understood it before?

Watching the masque Anna had organized, Margareta was struck again by her shrewdness. It was the tale of Theseus and the Minotaur: a hero served faithfully by a beautiful princess, slaying a wicked beast in a dark labyrinth so that all bowed down before him. Anna, in silver-spangled taffeta, played Ariadne, and the pretty Duke of Lennox played Theseus – and was it an accident that Theseus wore the same colours as James, or that his cloak was embroidered with lions and unicorns, the royal emblems of Scotland? Anna didn't need to sit on Privy Council meetings to influence her husband, or his court. She praised James with a dance and warned his courtiers with music, and only fools would have failed to read her message.

Margareta had certainly read it. She hadn't been invited to dance in the masque.

Margareta took a gulp of wine – or tried: she was surprised to find her glass emptied. Trying not to cough on the sudden inrush of air, she set the glass down, hoping simultaneously that the pages would refill it swiftly, and that they wouldn't notice for a while. It would be her third glass – no, her fourth – and the masque was only just finishing. As if there weren't already enough scornful, suspicious glances flung her way; the last thing she needed was to be derided as a drunkard as well as a traitor's wife. Of course, Gabriel Vinstar had been a drunkard. Perhaps it was in her blood. Just like the witchcraft she'd imbibed at Johanna's breast.

With a flourish of glimmering skirts and cascading lutes, the masque concluded. Half a beat behind everyone else, Margareta joined in the applause; on the flower-strewn stage, Anna drank it all in. Who clapped loudest, longest, least? How they responded to the queen's masque spoke of how they responded to the king and queen. Which meant Margareta, determined not to finish too soon, continued a moment too long, and suddenly all eyes were on her. Flushing, she ducked her head, horribly aware that everyone would assume both wine and shame were to blame. She didn't know which was worse.

Perhaps she should go to John's father in Fife after all. She might not be welcome there, but at least there wouldn't be so many people watching her.

The dancers were moving past her, slipping into seats in prestigious positions. She didn't look up; she'd watched the daily skirmish often enough as Anna's ladies fought for a seat far away from Margareta, battling to make their distaste more ostentatious than anyone else's. Eventually they were all jostled into position, and Margareta heard a familiar grunt as Elline slumped down beside her. Perhaps dancing had exhausted her: Elline usually fought harder.

Elline gave an elaborate sigh as plates of food arrived. Margareta eyed a platter of beef swimming in a burgundy sauce; it would stain Elline's peony-pink costume spectacularly.

'Did you see that Douglas woman shoving me?' Elline complained loudly. 'Arms like hams – I could hardly fight back.'

Further up the table, the Scottish ladies scowled and spoke soothingly to the poor plump Douglas in question.

'Still, I suppose someone has to sit here.'

Exasperation goaded Margareta into a retort. 'Must you insult everyone at this table?'

'Only those who deserve it,' Elline snapped. Then she dropped to a whisper. 'I have to. They mustn't think I sat here on purpose.'

Hope flared. 'Then you forgive me?'

Elline gave her a pitying look. 'I was commanded, Margareta. Believe me, I'd rather dine elsewhere. Even grizzled, gouty lechers are more appealing than traitors.'

'Elline, I'm not—'

'I won't listen until Anna listens – if she ever does.' Elline made a performance of selecting pieces of salmon and not passing the platter to Margareta, but placing it back on the table with a clatter.

'Then why are you here?'

'Because the king wishes to speak with you.'

Margareta dropped the salmon she'd just speared. 'King James?'

'Be rather hard for King Christian,' Elline muttered. 'Tomorrow, at dawn.'

White mist swam across the gardens, shrouding bare rose bushes and smudging the distant Lomond hills into shadowy breaths. As dew dampened her hems, Margareta wondered if James had known it would be misty, if he'd chosen this time and place for its secrecy. If he were a woman, such foreknowledge would be enough to charge him with witchcraft.

Shaking the dangerous thought from her head, Margareta stepped beneath the glistening branches of a great oak. Pale tendrils of light wormed between the brown leaves; it was like being inside a rotting apple.

James, unaccompanied, awaited her by the trunk. 'Lady Margareta.'

She curtseyed. 'Your Grace.'

'Rise,' he said, gesturing curtly, as if he distrusted even her deference.

'You asked to see me, sire?'

He nodded once, looking her up and down. What did he see? Grey pouches beneath her eyes, a poorly starched ruff – none of the best laundrywomen cared for her clothes now – and a front-lacing gown; weary of her maid's barely concealed disgust, she'd taken to dressing herself. As for James, the lines around his mouth and eyes had tightened and multiplied, making him look both wearier and manlier: lines etched by shouldering responsibility, rather than shrugging it aside to a regent.

'Do you know,' James said, watching the oak branches behind her lift in a breeze that reached them a breath later, 'I've always liked autumn above any other time of year.'

His performed nonchalance disturbed her; he couldn't have summoned her here to discuss the seasons. 'A beautiful time, sire. Especially in the first light of day.'

'A time of change,' James said, as if she hadn't spoken. 'Or so everyone supposes. But as the gaudy flowers fall away, the stems remain. Leaves are shed, but the tree stands tall. Not so much a change as a realization that glamour is mere frippery, and strength lasts. Autumn is the season for remembering where power truly lies.'

She'd hardly expected warmth. But the chill that rippled through her shocked her with its force.

James ran a hand along a low-hanging branch, his gloved fingers like some great spider creeping up on the leaves. With a brittle snap, he broke off a twig and eyed it almost pityingly. 'So many people in my kingdom want to think me stupid. Their fathers and uncles helped depose my mother, after all, and how convenient for them if I were just as weak. He's a coward, they say. A baby when he took the throne, and still no stronger than a boy. He lets pretty youths dictate policy rather than good sense – oh, I've heard it all.'

Ought Margareta to deny such things were said? But that would be a lie, and he'd know it.

'What they don't realize,' James said, 'is that it suits me to let such rumours scuttle about. If unpopular policies are blamed on Lindsay, so much the better for me. If men assume I have no more wit than a child, how much easier outfoxing them becomes. I know my kingdom, Lady Margareta, and I know my court. I have ruled all my life, and I intend to rule and to live much longer.'

'Long life to Your Grace,' she murmured. It sounded too much like a toast, and she had no cup to raise.

He acknowledged her words with a careless waft of the dead leaves. 'Already a longer life than many hoped. You've heard, naturally, of the would-be assassins who placed a pistol to my mother's swollen belly. Of my father's murder, and the murders since: three of my regents – my uncle, my grandfather, the Earl of Mar. I executed the fourth. You see, Lady Margareta? I have lasted. Others … haven't.' His hand tightened and the leaves crumpled; rusty scraps fell to earth. 'It will be so again. Bothwell's cut from the same cloth as his uncle, and look where that man's ambitions got him. Exile, imprisonment, and death in a Danish gaol. We didn't even hear of it in Scotland for months, and I doubt anyone cared, much less shed a tear.' He turned to face her. 'This rebellion will fail. So I ask you now, do you wish to be on the winning side?'

She wet her lips. 'I have always been loyal to Queen Anna, sire. That loyalty is yours too.'

'But Wemyss? Did you not vow to be faithful unto him in your little Danish ceremony?'

The wedding he chose to ignore. Trying to hide her anger, she searched for an answer. 'God set you above all others in Scotland, sire – above all Scotsmen.'

His quiet hum might have been a mirthless laugh. 'Perhaps you should remind Wemyss of that fact, Lady Margareta.'

'He doesn't need reminding!' she burst out. 'He was commanded to gain Bothwell's trust!'

'Lady Margareta,' he repeated slowly, 'perhaps you should remind Wemyss of that fact.'

She understood. 'But how? I haven't seen him since Bothwell escaped Edinburgh.'

'Interesting, is it not, what people claim not to have seen? There's a girl in the tolbooth who denies knowing you – and yet she saw your husband in North Berwick. Acting in my interest, she says. But her former employer insists she's a liar, so what to believe?'

Geillis. She'd kept her promise to Margareta – but what tortures had wrung John's name out of her? And how long before Margareta was named too? 'Sire, I swear. I haven't seen him.'

'But you will see him now,' he stated, his words steady as an incoming tide. 'Otherwise, that girl in the tolbooth might have her other thumb crushed. And then she might remember seeing you at a certain house. Giving you herbs. I wonder what you could have done with those herbs.' He met Margareta's eyes. 'It would be so easy for me to have you killed. But easier still for you to do my bidding and meet with your husband.'

Sweat trickled down her spine. 'I don't know where he is.'

'You do not need to. A message will be sent in your name, and a meeting will take place.'

Margareta looked away – but all she saw were dead leaves crushed beneath trees or still futilely clinging to branches. 'You wish me to be the bait. For my husband to walk into a trap.'

'No,' he said, and he'd never sounded more regal. 'I intend to catch a far bigger fish than John Wemyss.'

Was this how John felt? This straining discomfort, this wanting to writhe away from her own flesh, as if the skin on her back had become clammy seaweed. Waiting for her husband in a Stirling taproom, Margareta hunched forward, trying not to let her chair touch her shoulder blades. She'd never felt so guilty.

But he'd deserted her, betrayed her trust, hadn't he? Why should she feel ashamed of luring him here under false pretences? Was it the nature of the pretence? James and Maitland had deliberated over what ruse would be drastic enough to drag John out of hiding. Finally, Maitland had said, 'Tell him your son is gravely ill.' Margareta had recoiled: imagining it felt like tempting fate. Writing the words, passing them to Maitland – who'd given the letter to a man who knew a man who knew where Bothwell was – had felt like blasphemy. Even now, she wanted to dash outside, saddle a horse – any horse – and gallop back to Falkland Palace to check Johnny was well. Surely divine punishments were meted out to those who pretended their children were sick.

Or perhaps she felt so guilty because she longed to be reunited with her husband, whatever the circumstances. Because she loved a traitor.

Drunken voices reverberated against the floorboards. Margareta eyed the jug of wine on the table. She'd already had a glass; it wouldn't do for John to arrive and find the jug emptied. Besides, for all that she craved its velvety richness, the prospect made her nauseous. Maybe it was the smell – spilt ale, horse droppings in the yard, the greasy stew she'd seen downstairs. Or maybe, once again, it was guilt.

Footsteps on the stairs, and a knock at the door. Instinctively her right hand jerked towards the wine jug, and she clamped it beneath her left.

'Come in.'

John stepped inside. She'd risen before she could think, and gripped the edge of the table to stop herself running into his arms. He was the same. His beard thicker, longer, flecked with road-dust, his face browned from a summer without the certainty of any bed for the night. But he was still her husband.

And she didn't know whose side he was on.

'Margareta,' he said, and her name sounded like stolen hippocras on his lips, as if he wanted to drink her in and dared not. 'Is Johnny here? Is he – tell me I'm not too late.'

'No.' She swallowed. 'Johnny was never ill.'

'Never ill?' John blinked. 'Have you gone mad?'

She bridled at his sharpness. 'You're offended that I've lied to you? I thought such behaviour was acceptable in our marriage now.'

'Lying about our son's health could never be acceptable!' He strode across the room and seized her shoulders. 'God's wounds, Margareta, what's wrong with you?'

'You left me!' She wrenched out of his grasp, shoving him away. 'You've no idea what I've endured these past months, while you and Bothwell have been carousing round Edinburgh and scampering in and out of forests like Robin Hood and his blasted merry men!'

'You think we've been *entertaining* ourselves?' He laughed in disbelief. 'Margareta, we're outlaws. The price on our heads would feed a castle for months. I'm convinced every farmer we pass will tell the king our whereabouts. I don't know where I'll sleep from one night to the next; if I'll awake with a knife at my throat.'

'Then perhaps you shouldn't have left! You chose to turn traitor – this is the price you pay.'

'I didn't choose this!' He reached for her again, but the fury in her face halted him. 'Margareta, you were there, you heard James command me to spy on Bothwell.'

'*Spying* is a far cry from helping Bothwell escape his cell.'

'Bothwell wouldn't have been convinced by anything less! I had to help him, or my subterfuge would have been ruined.'

'But if you'd only left him there, all this would be over!'

'So he'd have become a martyr? No. He has to be Scotland's enemy, not her hero, or James and Anna will never be safe.'

Margareta's fingers were shaking. She thrust her hands into her sleeves, twisting lace between her nails. 'If you could only know how much I'd like to believe you.'

'Then believe me, Margareta!' He came closer, lifting a hand towards her cheek. 'Believe me. I am not the traitor they say I am.'

He touched her skin; warmth bloomed beneath his fingertips. She yearned to lean into his touch. 'It's too late.'

'Don't say that.'

'What would you have me say? That I'll trust you without question? I'll love you blindly, even if you lead us over a precipice? I cannot.'

He stiffened. 'What do you mean? You ... don't love me?'

She flinched at his baldness; the movement thrust air between them. His hand hovered.

'I don't trust you,' she said quietly. 'And you cannot have my love without my trust.'

'Then let me prove myself worthy!' His body was taut, as if chafing against invisible restraints. 'Is there nothing I can do?'

Margareta turned away. He couldn't see her face as she opened the trap's jaws. 'You can give Bothwell up.'

'I was never Bothwell's man!'

'Tell him ...' She caught sight of her reflection in the window. Avoiding her own gaze, she said, 'The court will spend Christmas at Holyrood. An excellent opportunity for anyone wishing to harm the chancellor or seize the king.'

She could feel his eyes on her. 'How would Bothwell gain access to a royal palace?'

'The king's doctor, Nasmyth, is willing to let him in.'

'A sudden conversion. Why would he give his loyalty to Bothwell?'

Margareta shook her head. 'I don't know exactly. Only that something will happen in December which might give Nasmyth cause to turn against the king.'

'And will Nasmyth's actions lead to a promotion or an execution?'

'Who knows where any of this will lead?'

'Where might it lead for us?'

Not to the flames. That was all she dared hope.

She turned around and met his eyes. 'This is the only way back for you. To King James ... and to me. Decide, John. Double agent or not, where your loyalty really lies.'

The coastal path to Tranent was too flat. Where the rest of Scotland plunged and reared into mountains, or ended in cliffs concealing rocky coves and white bays – as if the whole land were complicit in keeping secrets – this route was painfully exposed: there wasn't a moment when she couldn't see Arthur's Seat if she looked over her shoulder.

As she rode, Margareta tried to tell herself that the flatness would make it harder for anyone to follow her. The court was travelling back to Edinburgh today. They'd be much slower, and she'd had almost a day's head start, coming from Stirling rather than Falkland. She could be back at Holyrood before anyone fathomed where she'd gone – or that she'd gone at all.

Or so she prayed. Because if she was seen riding to the Setons' house, what possible explanation could she give that wouldn't condemn her?

There was a sharp tang to the air in Prestonpans: salt, blood, coal – a smoky, oddly familiar smell. As she saw the sign for Tranent, she realized: it reminded her of Geillis. Her red hair, the only gown Margareta had ever seen her wear – they'd borne this scent. Until she'd been thrown into the tolbooth because of the people Margareta had come seeking.

The Setons' house was four times the size of anything else in Tranent, though Margareta could see instantly why the Setons had been lured by Bothwell's promises of riches and power; large houses were always smaller than someone else's house. But for all its size, it had an air of neglect. Several tiles had fallen from the roof and still lay there, their red fragments ground into the earth by passing feet. Only one of the four chimneys belched smoke, while the roses around the porch drooped over the front door, bare black stems trailing at eye level for anyone who entered. Perhaps no one did.

'Can I help you?'

Margareta fought to control herself; she couldn't appear afraid. She didn't wheel her horse, merely inclined her head to inspect the woman who had just entered the courtyard. Her eye sockets were purple gouges; lines crosshatched her pale face like a fraying fishing net. Her velvet gown hung loose across her chest. She had the look of a woman who'd always been slender, but something had reduced her to gauntness.

'King's business,' Margareta said coolly. 'I wish to speak to Mistress Seton.'

The woman went even paler. 'Is it about David ... or about Geillis?'

'You are Katherine Seton?'

'Yes, but ...' Katherine hesitated. 'Has David been torturing people without permission again? I warned him he wasn't clever enough to hide things from Chancellor Maitland.'

'Not this time,' Margareta said, revulsion curdling, not only at David Seton's apparent cruelty, but his wife's willingness to disavow him. 'I wish to inspect Geillis Duncan's possessions.'

'David already handed over the pipes and harp.'

'There was nothing else?'

Katherine hesitated. Her grey eyes ran over Margareta, as if a long-dormant intelligence were flickering back to life. 'Not that David knew of.' She glanced around the deserted courtyard. 'Come.'

Margareta dismounted; for want of a groom, she tied her horse to the gatepost and followed Katherine inside, ducking the stray rose thorns. Katherine led her through darkened corridors and upstairs; Margareta noticed handprints in the dust coating the banisters. Katherine reached into her pocket for a brass key and unlocked a door.

It was a bedchamber. Although it smelled as stale as the rest of the house, it was far tidier. A childishly stitched sampler hung above a neatly made bed where a doll rested on the pillow.

'No one else comes here now,' Katherine said, and Margareta heard grief echo in her voice. 'So it seemed the best place ...'

She knelt by the bed, and for a moment Margareta wondered if she were about to pray. But instead, Katherine reached past the bedcovers and drew out a leather bag.

'This was hers. I kept it because ...' Katherine bit her lip. 'Well. Her cures worked. Until, that is, they didn't. And ...' She gnawed again. 'Bad enough that David root through everything she owned, pretending he sought wax manikins or hag-stones. But you're a woman. You understand. A woman has to have certain things at certain times, and for a man to grab them in his clumsy, meaty fingers or trample them underfoot ...' She shook her head. 'He'd done enough to her already. He gloated about it – as if I'd be proud of him!'

Margareta took the bag. It was soft with wear, but the strings had been tied neatly and the stitches running along one seam were tiny; the bag had been cared for. Carefully too, she opened it. The knots came loose easily, as if they'd been chosen for speed.

'Of course, everyone's disgusted with him,' Katherine said, with bleak resignation. 'More than half the servants have left. And our neighbours ... Strangely, people don't want to work for a man who has his own servants arrested. Or befriend a man who betrays those he's dined with.'

Inside the bag were paper twists of herbs, some bound with different types of grass. Margareta knew nothing of herbs, but she was certain Geillis had grouped them thoughtfully. There'd be a cluster for childbirth, one for fevers, another for headaches. There were folded rags too, along with a homespun girdle. Margareta had a similar girdle, though hers was fine linen, and she understood what Katherine had meant: not only was it awful to think of David Seton finding this and leering, then crumpling it, but the idea of Geillis having been forced to go without this for all her time in the tolbooth was horrible.

And then, beneath the girdle, her fingers touched kidskin.

'As for those,' Katherine said, 'I had no intention of letting David find them either.'

Don't freeze, Margareta ordered herself. Slowly, she drew out her gloves, desperate for her fingers not to tremble.

'I didn't know whose they were,' Katherine continued. 'Barbara's, Euphame's, or some other woman's. But I was determined not to let them be connected to Geillis – or Geillis be connected to them. I may not have been able to save them – or whoever these gloves belong to. But I will not contribute to their deaths.'

Margareta found her voice. 'Why should you care?'

'Because it was my fault. My maddened grief that made me lash out at Agnes Sampson – the very woman who helped give Lucy life.' Katherine's fingers touched the blankets, taut with the strain of not trembling. 'She is dead because of me. Dozens are dead because I loosed David's leash and the king seized hold of it.' Katherine met her eyes. 'I failed to protect Geillis. I will not cause anyone else's downfall.' She held Margareta's gaze, and in that moment Margareta was certain Katherine knew why she'd come, knew who the gloves belonged to.

'Euphame and Barbara dined in my house. They were once my friends, Euphame my kin by marriage – and yet I did nothing to defend them. I couldn't stop their burning,' Katherine said. 'Or whichever poor soul David says will burn this week. But I did not cause it. And that is as much innocence as I can hope for now.'

There was such pain in her voice: the pain of loss and of clinging onto dignity at all costs. Then Margareta registered what she'd said, and horror clenched in her belly.

Something will happen in December.

She had to get back to Edinburgh.

43

'Up! On your feet!'

They were dragged upright before they could resist. Geillis gasped as her irons bit fresh blood from her ankles; Bessie cried out, similarly hurt. But there was no time to nurse their injuries; the guards hauled them out of the cell.

Not Seton. Don't give me to Seton, not now.

But she wasn't marched towards the dark cell where the witch's bridle hung. Instead, the guards led her to the door – and out of the tolbooth.

Sunlight struck her face like boiling oil. She tried to twist away, but the guards gripped her too tightly. Ahead of her, Bessie gave a shrill cry. 'Please, you cannot!'

They hadn't turned downhill, towards Holyrood and a trial. They were being marched up, to Castle Hill.

'No,' Geillis breathed.

The Canongate thrashed with bodies, a tide pushing them inexorably upwards. People came to tavern doors to see what was happening, and each one joined the mob driving towards the castle. Men leered close, broken teeth and foul breath looming over Geillis; pinch-faced women spat at her feet. Small boys darted close, daring each other: 'Touch her skirts! Nip her arm!'

'She'll turn you into a frog!'

'She'll hex your mam!'

She won't, Geillis thought. She never could. Poultices and tisanes, that's all she would ever have given them. And the unfairness struck her again. She'd only started learning to be a midwife because her mother had died, because she'd been desperate. Look where trying to heal others had brought her.

The guards hauled her onwards. Her wasted calves screamed out at the slopes; her numb feet cracked against cobbles, and she saw blood burst out of her toes but could no longer feel them. If only her whole body could become so numb.

The castle reared up like a vast gargoyle, the spiked wings of its towers and ramparts hooked around the crag that overlooked the city. Below the gates, guards kept the crowds at bay from a cleared square. At the square's centre were two pyres, a stake rising out of each like the masts of a ghost ship.

Her guts turned to seawater. This was where she would die. This was the hour.

The guards parted; the women were thrust through. Now Geillis saw the wooden platform behind the pyres, and the black-robed man ascending it.

Chancellor Maitland raised a hand. The crowd's baying simmered to a hiss.

'These women,' he declared, his voice ringing out across the hill, perhaps even the whole city, all the way to the firth where the *Margaret* had sunk so long ago, 'have been found guilty of witchcraft and of gross treason against His Grace King James. For these crimes, they are sentenced to die.'

He paused. Waited. When the muttering became a cheer, he nodded, as if in approval, and raised his hand for quiet. 'Do the prisoners have any last words?'

Bessie flung herself forward, but the guards yanked her back. 'I don't want to die!' she howled. 'I never meant any harm! Please, I don't want to die!'

One of the guards rolled his eyes and cuffed her across the mouth. Coughing blood, Bessie subsided into sobs.

'We haven't had a trial!' Bessie wailed. 'This isn't fair!'

'It is the king's will,' Maitland said calmly. 'Therefore it is also God's will.'

Did Geillis imagine it, or was the crowd shifting, muttering? Were the stares no longer of hatred and fear, but pity?

They were all looking at her expectantly. Waiting for her last words.

Cold air kissed Geillis's neck, and she thought of the witch's bridle. She'd never been gripped by its iron, and yet it had still controlled her. Every time she'd spoken, its screws had wrenched the words out of her; its bands had wrought them into shapes she'd never meant to create, and people had bled and died for what terror of the bridle had driven her to say.

But she wouldn't have to wear it now.

If my silence can save you, it will. But what good was silence now? It was time for Geillis to speak.

Quietly, she said, 'It was all a lie.'

'What?' She'd startled the word out of Maitland; his frown deepened as if he wanted to call it back.

'I lied,' Geillis said, louder, clearer. 'When I was asked for names, I gave up Euphame MacCalzean and Barbara Napier. But I lied.'

Gasps rippled around the hill; the muttering spread like a bloodstain. *Your words are your only weapons,* Bothwell had told her, *and you must learn to wield them if you wish to survive.* She was wielding them now – but not for her own survival. For Margareta's.

'They weren't witches,' Geillis said. 'They were frightened women hoping to ease their childbed, to keep their own property, to regain their stolen positions. This isn't justice – this is vengeance and spite, and scores of Scots have died for it.'

She saw people frowning, jeers hovering on their lips. Some whispered to their neighbours; others spat scornfully.

Above her, Maitland narrowed his eyes. 'The last words you'll say before meeting your maker – and you chose yet more falsehoods. For shame, Geillis Duncan.'

All for show, she thought. This was a performance dressed up as justice – and her part was nearly done.

The guards shoved her forward, gripping her elbows as if they feared she'd run. But there was nowhere to go except up five wooden steps to the top of the pyre. Her hands were roughly bound behind the stake. She grunted as more ropes yanked her body against it, and it suddenly struck her as foolish to care about this pain, this breathlessness, when there was so much worse to come. A smile twitched at the corner of her lips. How Agnes would have liked that, smiling on your own pyre.

On her left, Bessie was shrieking, her sobs breaking out like splinters. But Geillis chose quiet now. Not a silencing, not a hand over her mouth or a blade over her head, but a choice, not to say what men wanted her to say. She had spoken and finally been listened to. She could sense that in the crowd. If they believed her, Margareta would be safe, for if Euphame and Barbara had been innocent, there was nothing to incriminate her. Whatever Wemyss might have done, Geillis couldn't protect him, didn't know enough to try. But her words might have saved Margareta. She turned away from Bessie's yells – and recognized a face in the crowd.

Margareta. Despite the risks, she'd come to bear witness. Her eyes met Geillis's, and she clasped her hands as if in prayer. Hands gloved in kidskin. Katherine Seton must have returned them to her. She hadn't been able to protect Geillis, but she'd protected Geillis's secret, knowing someone, somewhere would be harmed by it. Sudden gratitude swelled in Geillis – and even pity for the grief-hollowed woman in Tranent. There were worse fates, Geillis thought, than to die at the stake.

Seton would never touch her again. Only the flames, burning away every mark he'd left on her skin, until her ashes were pale as snow.

'King James,' Maitland said, somewhere behind her, 'has granted these women mercy.'

Liar, Geillis thought. And something bubbled up inside her, as she realized the chancellor was silencing her because she needed silencing. Because her words were powerful after all, and he feared what she could scream out for all Edinburgh to hear.

The torchbearers remained still. Geillis heard heavy feet climbing the steps behind her. Bessie cried out – but her wail was cut short. The rope came around Geillis's neck, and when the guard began to twist it tight, Geillis closed her eyes and felt only relief.

44

Margareta owed Geillis her life. And there was no way to repay the debt. All she'd been able to do was watch – watch as she had been unable to watch Ilsa, letting a dying woman know that not everyone in the crowd despised her. That someone in the crowd even loved her. When she'd heard Geillis's words, she'd wanted to weep but had to hide the tears Geillis deserved.

Even three weeks after Geillis's death, Margareta grimaced whenever the smell of roasting meat writhed out of Holyrood's kitchens. Whenever she donned a necklace, Margareta shivered as cold stones closed around her neck. She'd seen Anna constantly loosening her pearls, as if she too were desperate to avoid constriction, even if those pearls could have bought a hundred guards to help her escape. But there was nowhere for Anna or Margareta to go.

Margareta rubbed her ankles together as she watched cloud shadows prowl across the floor of Holyrood Abbey. It was quiet here, only the murmur of rain beyond the walls and the gentle echoes of far-off voices. But she wasn't here for refuge.

'You are early.'

She turned, curtseying. 'I had nowhere else to be, Your Grace.'

King James grunted cynically as he joined her below the vast window. 'Hardly. You're my wife's lady-in-waiting – I would hate for you to grow lax in your duties.'

She was so tired of hearing threats dressed up in courtesy, like hemlock in jewelled goblets. Why pretend? 'I've done everything Queen Anna's asked of me, sire.'

'Apart from help her bear a child.'

Margareta reeled at his bluntness. How much did he know? 'Not for want of trying, sire.'

He grunted again – with impatience? Grief? Margareta didn't trust herself to guess. Nor could she read his face as he ran gloved fingertips along the nearest tomb. 'My father lies here. What was left of him, at any rate.'

She'd heard Henry Stuart had been murdered, but she hadn't expected such crudeness from his son. 'My condolences, sire,' she offered hesitantly.

James snorted. 'Never knew the man. Can't say I'm entirely sorry – half-rotted with French pox by the time he died, I gather. Probably no nose to speak of. I sometimes wonder how such diseases affect the body after death. Will his corpse be more rotted than Davy Rizzio's over there, though their deaths were less than a year apart?'

Was he trying to shock her? Or was this, too, some kind of threat? When she'd first met James, she'd thought he was desperate to make others laugh, but perhaps he'd been laughing at them all along.

'Wasn't Rizzio your mother's secretary?'

'Or lover.' James shrugged. 'Depends who you listen to. Some men claim he was my father. Others insist Rizzio could never have fathered a child, for the same reason they doubt I ever will.' He touched the stone again. 'Agnes Sampson and Geillis Duncan, of course, have no tombs at all. I sometimes wish they did.'

'Sire?'

He twisted his lips in a strange smile. 'Best not, I know. Turn away for a moment and a tomb becomes a shrine. But the thought of them in the air I breathe, the water I drink … it sickens me.'

'Do you regret their deaths?' It was a bold question, too bold – yet he didn't admonish her.

'Not their deaths. They had to die, and what are a few women compared to the kingdom's safety?'

A few women? Well over ninety, and several men too, dismissed as nothing.

'However, I should like to forget them. And I cannot do that until Bothwell is defeated. How goes our plan?'

'I think Bothwell believes in Doctor Nasmyth's conversion.' And why not? Executing people without a trial hardly inspired loyalty. 'He's more confident of support than before. I gather Geillis Duncan's final words helped make that more convincing.' The gibe on Geillis's behalf felt like a stab with a blunt knife: it would never drive home.

'A little too convincing – I could have done without her sowing such doubt.'

In his mind too? Margareta didn't dare ask. 'Bothwell's instructed Nasmyth to look out for a sign, and that will be the night he attacks.'

'What manner of sign?'

'I don't know, sire.'

'Then I suggest you find out.'

'Even Nasmyth doesn't know,' she protested. 'He was told he'd be warned on the day, and the sign would be unmistakeable. Perhaps you ought—'

'You think to instruct me now?' He regarded her coldly. 'Remember, it is I that instructs you. And you will follow my instructions if you wish to remain useful. You've seen what happens to those who lose their value. They all go to Castle Hill in the end. Even mothers. Have you ever wondered what becomes of the children witches and traitors leave behind?'

Johnny. Her baby. What would become of a child left behind if his mother burned and his father was executed? At best he'd be shunned by day and would shiver alone after dark, too frightened of his nightmares to sleep; at worst … She couldn't let that happen. 'I am yours to command, Your Grace.'

'Then find out what the sign will be.' He turned to go. 'And for God's sake, patch up your quarrel with my wife. You'll be far more useful in her confidence than outside it.'

Once, gaining Anna's confidence had been as easy as breathing. Anna had taken Margareta's advice on everything, from trivialities like ribbons and ruffs, to more serious matters, like when Anna's first monthly had arrived. But now?

Margareta approached Anna's chambers with trepidation. She half-expected the guards to send her away, but they let her in without comment. They seemed distracted – and when the doors opened, Margareta realized they'd been eavesdropping.

Anna's chambers were in disarray. Half-finished masque costumes were scattered about, gowns swooning over chairs, headdresses askew on the rushes, while crumpled sheet music littered the tables. Anna's ladies hovered, hands and voices fluttering helplessly. No one seemed to have noticed Margareta.

'Why not try this brooch instead?' Vibeke suggested.

'I think it's already splendid,' Elline put in.

Anna, prowling like an enraged wolf, rounded on them. 'Idiots! Can't you see it's hopeless?'

Margareta took in Anna's garb: a Grecian robe made of turquoise silk, currently fastened with three different belts – gold brocade, teal velvet, ivory stitched with pearls. A silver cloak hung from her shoulders, clasped by two elaborate golden brooches, its vast train coiling round Anna with every spin. As Margareta watched, Anna turned again and almost tumbled over. Furious, she yanked at the cloak.

'You'll tear the silk!' Elline yelped.

'Enough,' Margareta sighed. Striding across the chamber, she caught Anna's hands and stilled them before unclasping the brooches. Over her shoulder, she said briskly, 'Vibeke, this is no fit state for the queen's chambers. Elline, camomile tea and honey cakes, quickly. Lady Douglas, a tune on the virginals.'

None of them refused. She might be a traitor's mistress, but she was also, apparently, the only woman capable of organizing chaos.

'Come,' Margareta said to Anna. 'Let's sit by the fire, and you can tell me all about it.'

Anna let herself be led to a chair. Once, Margareta had misread her acquiescence as simplicity, her placid exterior as passivity. She wouldn't make that error again.

'Tell me, Anna. What vexes you?'

Anna gestured at the mess. 'I wanted to put on a masque for Christmas. But it's all wrong.'

'Why? We can put it right.'

Anna sighed. 'Any masquing seems wholly inappropriate. Dressing up as rivers and sea nymphs – ridiculous.'

'Nonsense. You've always organized splendid masques.'

'Women are dead!' Anna hissed. 'Almost a hundred! I should be dressing up as a hangman, not a goddess!'

Elline arrived with a tray before Margareta could reply. Taking it, Margareta dismissed Elline with the eyebrow arch she'd used since childhood; Elline went, pulling the face she'd practised for just as long. Margareta pressed a cup into Anna's hands. 'None of this is your fault, Anna.'

'It was my failure to reach Scotland that started all this.' Anna closed her eyes, letting the steam from her tea envelop her face, as if imagining herself on a pyre. 'And now it transpires those women died for a lie.'

'You mean Geillis Duncan's last words?'

Anna nodded. 'She denied everything. *Everything.*' Anna leaned closer. 'Don't you see? People confess their sins at the last, they don't concoct new lies. Geillis was about to meet her maker. She didn't scream to save herself – she spoke calmly to rescue other women's reputations. She confessed to lying, not witchcraft. And if she wasn't a witch, how can we believe any of the others were?'

Margareta needed to tread carefully. 'Then … you no longer believe Agnes Sampson conspired to murder your child?'

'Not unless her ghost still walks.' Anna looked away. 'You wouldn't know … I think only Vibeke realized. Perhaps not even her.'

'You mean there were others?'

Anna nodded. 'Once. Perhaps twice – I don't know. There was blood the second time, but there's blood every month …'

'Oh, Anna.' Margareta reached for her hands, and Anna let her. 'I wish I'd been with you.'

Anna gave a rough shrug; Margareta had scarcely ever seen a more heartbreaking gesture. 'You couldn't have changed what happened. Maybe no one could. Maybe it wasn't the herbs that pushed the child out of my womb. Maybe it was me.'

'Anna, you can't blame yourself.'

'But if it wasn't witchcraft, then women have died because my body failed to keep a baby alive. How is that anything other than my fault?'

Margareta squeezed Anna's hands. 'If men executed women every time another woman lost a child, no children could ever be born again. What men have done in Scotland and Denmark this year and last is none of your doing. You are not to blame, Anna.'

'Then who is?'

She could have said *Your husband*. She could have said *Maitland*. But she had to say, 'It all comes back to Bothwell. He is wholly to blame.'

Anna tossed her silver hair back. 'And your beloved along with him.'

Margareta met her gaze. 'You know better than to believe that.'

Anna laughed sharply. 'A few gentle words, and you think I'll be soothed into believing your lies again?'

'I think anger makes us believe many things. But when we see clearly again, we realize they weren't all true.'

'And what have you realized? Aren't you angry with him?'

'Furious.' Margareta gave a bitter smile. 'But only for the position in which the game he's playing has put his family. I don't believe he's Bothwell's man.'

'Do you believe he's my husband's?'

Margareta hesitated.

Anna pounced. 'So you admit he's a traitor?'

'No!' Margareta knew better than to reach for her hands again. 'I know he doesn't put King James's interests first – because he tries to put mine first. And that means yours. You are my queen, Anna. You have been since we were children, and you always will be.'

Anna was silent. Then she gestured at her gown. 'Well then. How do you suggest I remedy this wretched costume?'

As they picked their way towards the end of Advent, Margareta grew tetchy with fasting and anxiety. The attack hadn't come. She'd sent Johnny and his nurse to John's grudging father in Fife for safety, and his absence throbbed like a missing limb. She'd tried to send word to

John, but the messenger had returned with her scroll still sealed, saying the camp had been abandoned and not even a rumour to trace the rebels. When she passed Nasmyth in a corridor, he'd been no wiser.

'I haven't heard anything,' he'd hissed, eyes shooting sideways like a frightened rabbit. 'I've no idea what sign to look for, and I can hardly unlock the door every night!'

He twitched so much he was practically hopping; Margareta couldn't imagine a less suitable agent. However well James was paying him, no coins could shine bright enough to chase away the darkness conspirators dwelled in, nor make a pillow soft enough to sleep on.

She couldn't remember the last time she'd slept well. She might have won back Anna's confidence by saying John put her interests first. John might have told her so himself – but that didn't mean she believed him.

Advent ended. Christmas was celebrated. And there was no sign. Had Bothwell seen Holyrood dangled like bait before him and suspected a trap? Had John tried too hard to convince Bothwell to attack – and only succeeded in betraying himself?

Snow fell like ash over Edinburgh; when Margareta peered out of the window in Anna's chambers, she could barely see Holyrood's walls, let alone the city beyond. How could anyone travel in this, still less attack a palace?

Behind her, silver plate clinked, and she turned to see the table laid for supper. A quiet one for once. After the strained Christmas festivities, where everyone had strived to prove their merriment to James, Margareta was relieved to be away from the great hall. Only Elline looked disappointed as they all took their seats; perhaps she considered her new hairstyle wasted on a female audience, who ignored her tossed curls.

'I thought perhaps a game of riddles after supper,' Vibeke said as a platter of some roast bird or another was passed around: there'd been so many the past few days Margareta couldn't have told duck from goose if they'd paraded before her fully feathered. 'I heard an excellent one from Chancellor Maitland.'

'Oh, I'm too weary for riddles,' Elline complained. 'Besides, you always win.'

'I'm surprised you're eager for games, Vibeke,' Anna said archly. 'Didn't you lose your favourite brooch at dice last week?'

'*My* favourite brooch,' Margareta chipped in. 'Which Vibeke had only won the day before by insisting I reroll my winning throw.'

'You dropped the dice on the rushes!' Vibeke retorted, grinning. 'Blame your own clumsiness, not my respect for rules.'

They all laughed. Margareta had missed this: their easy chatter, slipping into Danish – like collapsing into cushions after a long ride. No one had called her a traitor's whore for weeks. Perhaps forgiveness was too much to hope for, but maybe forgetfulness was possible. She picked up a piece of meat: partridge, she decided.

Gunshots rang out.

The meat tumbled from her knife. Vibeke gripped Margareta's arm so hard she could feel which fingernail was broken. No one dared breathe. Perhaps it was only an overzealous guard, mistaking a fox's shadow for a threat.

A volley of bullets tore through the air. Somewhere a man screamed.

'Dear God,' Anna breathed. 'Are we under attack?'

She doesn't know, Margareta realized. James hasn't told her – and neither have I.

Margareta rose. Her breath caught in her chest. Slowly, she edged towards the window and peered out.

Shadows crept across the courtyard through falling snow. Gunpowder flashed and one of the shadows fell with a cry. But the dark mass was still so vast she could barely see the white of the courtyard beneath them. How many men did Bothwell have? Enough? The word slipped into her mind, stealthy as a cat, and she suddenly wondered if part of her wanted him to have enough men to achieve his goal – because that might bring John back.

Powder flashed – and Margareta flung herself down just in time: the glass shattered. Shards rained down, stabbing her cheeks, her shoulders. Gasping in terror, Margareta scrambled away, not caring about the fragments cutting her palms.

'We have to hide!' Elline screamed. Like the others, she'd dived to the floor; now she crawled to Anna's side and plucked at her sleeves.

Anna shook her head. 'If we aren't safe here, we won't be any safer for hiding under a bed.'

'But—'

'Enough.' Anna stood up. 'I'd rather be taken on my feet than hiding under furniture. I am a queen, not a quivering girl.'

Until then, Margareta hadn't believed Bothwell would hurt Anna. James, yes. Maitland, in a heartbeat. But now she knew: Anna wouldn't be safe in Bothwell's hands. None of them would.

Slowly, Margareta rose and, on trembling legs, went to stand beside her queen. Anna's hand found hers; Margareta didn't know whose grip was tightest. A sliver of glass pierced Margareta's finger; if it was stabbing Anna too, neither of them cared.

More gunshots broke out. They were inside now, explosions ripping through the palace corridors. Margareta stared at the door, its oak all that stood between them and bullets. Vibeke darted forward and shot the bolts, then leapt back as if the metal had burned her skin.

'The guards will stand firm,' Margareta insisted.

'How many are outside tonight?' Anna asked, voice bowstring taut.

Margareta swallowed. 'I counted six.'

Elline sobbed. Vibeke gulped.

'Six strong Scots,' Margareta said, fighting to sound calm. 'With halberds, pistols, and stout hearts. We are well protected.'

But Bothwell might have sixty, or six hundred men, for all she knew. Halberds couldn't block bullets, and Bothwell's men only needed to aim true six times.

She heard the clash of metal. Footsteps: some running, others stumbling. Thumps that might have been bodies on stairs. Glass breaking, men screaming. And a cry, over and over: 'Justice! Justice! À Bothwell!'

'God above,' Vibeke gasped.

'Don't,' Anna snapped, and Margareta didn't know whether she was warning against panic or prayer.

Bullets fired. Too loud, too close. Another scream, and there was no denying it now: the invaders were on the other side of the door. Anna's hand was clammy with sweat, or was it Margareta's? Men were yelling, grunting, moaning, the wordless noises of battle: aggression and pain and desperation. A body slammed against the door and their cries were all drowned by the man's unearthly howl. No one could make that noise and live.

Let it not be John.

Swords rang against swords, cold percussion shot through with the gasp of metal sliding into flesh. Who was winning, guards or raiders?

'Stand firm,' Anna whispered. 'No matter what happens.'

The fighting stopped. Margareta felt a rush of relief – and then she realized what it meant. Someone had won. And someone had lost.

A fumble of metal. Swearing. Then a snapped command. A hush fell. Only the ragged sounds of heavy breathing and quiet groans growing ever quieter. The kind of groans you wished would end and hoped would continue forever because of what it would mean if they stopped.

'Have they gone?' Elline whispered.

No one answered her. They didn't dare hope. Margareta didn't know what to hope for.

Suddenly the door shook. Another blow, and the nearest paintings trembled, and the walls coughed up stone dust. Elline screamed, and her shrieks grew louder with every strike. The door buckled. Splinters jutted, pale and brittle as straw. Vibeke was weeping. Anna's breath snagged in her throat. Margareta's gasp was as shrill as nails on slate.

Wood split. The door gaped; through a jagged wound of wood and iron, she saw masked men dressed in black, their hats rammed low. Was one John? She couldn't tell.

The hinges creaked, bent, and broke. The wreckage of the door crashed inwards. Smoke belched in after it, a mixture of dust and gunpowder – and fire. Sweet Jesus, the palace was burning. Panic rose like bile: she didn't want to burn to death.

A man stepped through, wielding a pistol and a sword. His voice was rough with bloodlust and smoke. 'Where's James Stuart?'

Anna drew herself up. 'The king is not here.'

The man moved closer. 'If you're lying, girl, you'll regret it.'

Was that James Douglas's voice? The bastard son of Scotland's last regent – if he was involved, how many other nobles had been swayed by Bothwell's cause? Had Geillis's execution, two women dying without trial, been the final straw?

Anna's grip on Margareta's hand tightened – not with fear, but steely rage. 'I am the Queen of Scotland, and you a rogue too ashamed to show your face. How dare you enter my chambers uninvited and then accuse me of deceit?'

The man lifted his weapons, brandishing a threat. 'Where's your husband?'

He wouldn't dare, Margareta told herself. He wouldn't dare strike the queen.

But his gun wasn't aimed at Anna. It was aimed at Elline. Sobbing, terrified Elline.

Anna's face sagged. 'He isn't here, I swear. I haven't seen him for hours.'

The gun jerked closer to Elline's head; she whimpered.

'Please,' Anna said quietly. 'Don't hurt her. We don't know where James is.'

She hadn't called him the king. As if she didn't want to antagonize the rebels – or didn't know whether he'd still be king by morning.

Douglas glared at Anna, then Margareta, raking their faces for the flicker of a lie. Margareta didn't dare blink. Her throat crackled with cries crushed into silence.

Then the gun moved. Elline collapsed. It took Margareta a moment to realize there had been no shot. Instead, Douglas was leaving – they were spared.

'Affleck,' Douglas barked, 'stand guard. The rest of you, with me. James and Maitland are cowering somewhere in this palace. Let's smoke them out!'

The men outside followed Douglas down the corridor. Affleck moved to block the doorway.

'Thank God,' Vibeke whispered.

'Don't thank Him yet,' Anna ordered. 'Elline, come sit by the fire. Vibeke, bring wine.'

Margareta stared at the rebels' receding backs. One of them might be John. Unless he'd already fallen?

She had to find him.

She was running before she'd thought to run. Her outflung arms hit Affleck's back. Caught off balance, he stumbled, leaving her a passage through to the gallery, and she darted past.

'Stop! Don't make me shoot!'

But she couldn't turn back now. She ran on, almost tripping over a moaning guard.

'Stop!'

She leapt over a fallen bust, skidded on shards of stone and stumbled – just as Affleck fired. The noise roared behind her, and she didn't have time to scream. She felt the bullet raze past, smelt gunpowder and singed hair. But no blood. No pain. He had to reload, and she had to find John. She ran through the next door and out into the stairwell.

It was pitch-black. Someone had torn the torches out of their braziers and stamped them out. Margareta edged forward, feeling blindly for the treads as she descended.

Downstairs the fight continued, the retorts of pistols and clash of blades beating like a heart: incessant, roaring with blood. Emerging into the hall, she could make out dark shapes on the floor. They weren't moving. Barely breathing, Margareta crouched beside them. Her fingers touched skin. Smooth, hairless: a boy. The other wore a beard – as did John. Did this man have a scar through his left eyebrow? She searched – and her fingertips met blood, sticky and still warm. But no scar. Her own relief repulsed her: how could she be gladdened by these corpses? And yet she was. No point pretending otherwise. She left the dead men, following the sound of fighting. It was coming from one of the towers. Had they found James there?

Or had he been waiting for them? How much easier, after all, to defend a tower than the king's bedchamber?

She didn't have time to think about that. Margareta hurried through abandoned rooms where eerie light penetrated the shadows, revealing half-eaten meals, overturned card tables, spilt wine mingling with bloodstains. Everyone had fled. Where? As far away from the king as they could – or to barricade themselves in with him?

Ahead, the noise grew louder. She could hear shouting now: 'À Bothwell! À Bothwell!'

'For the king!'

'Come out, you coward! Stop hiding behind Maitland's skirts!'

That was Bothwell's goading roar. So he still lived. And how many of his men?

She'd reached the foot of the tower, and she clutched the banister, staring up. The torches still flared here, hurling sharp red into the blackness. A man screamed; she heard the slumping thuds of a body falling downstairs. It didn't appear before her. Did that mean he'd got up – or that he couldn't?

Suddenly, the noise doubled. Men yelling, swords colliding. Whatever doors had kept James safe were open.

And then guns fired. Howl shattered wounded howl. Another volley: more screams. Then Bothwell: 'You craven bastard, Maitland! You haven't the balls to face me blade to blade!'

Guns fired again. Bothwell swore as more men yelled in pain.

'Give it up, Francis!'

John! He was alive, unhurt – or at least well enough to speak.

'Come on!'

Bothwell roared with rage, then yelled, 'Retreat! Dash out the torches behind us!'

Footsteps flooded downwards, frantic, stumbling. Men emerged from the tower, faces wild and red with sweat and blood. One careened towards her, clutching his belly; another man caught him and they staggered away together. Another ran past, a ragged gash splitting his brow. Douglas again, his right arm limp, his left still brandishing a pistol. More men dashing past, none of them the one she wanted to see.

And then he was there, leaping down the last three stairs and running.

'John!'

He turned, horror staining his face. 'Margareta, you shouldn't be here!'

'I had to see you!'

He glanced back at the stairs just as Bothwell appeared. His cheek had been laid open, but he looked exhilarated by the fight.

'What are you doing, Wemyss? Run!' He glanced at Margareta and laughed. 'Now's not the time for swiving, my lad!'

'I'll follow you,' John told him.

Bothwell slapped him on the back. 'Don't get yourself killed for a kiss. You know where to meet.'

As the earl dashed away, John looked back at the stairs. No footsteps.

'They'll fire on us rather than give chase,' he spat. 'Francis was right – cowards, the lot of them.'

'John—'

'You should go back to Anna,' he said roughly. 'Stay safe.'

'I'm not going.'

Emotions warred across his face. Then he growled and grabbed her hand. 'Have we just discovered which of us is most stubborn? Come on then!'

They ran, out into the snowy courtyard, past the crumpled bodies of royal guards, through the gates, and into Edinburgh's streets. Gunshots peppered the air. Ahead of them a man shrieked and fell, his blood seeping across the snow. A bullet rang against the cobbles at Margareta's feet and she screamed. John pulled her close, half-dragging her at his pace. The cobbles were slick, their every step a toss of the dice that might land anywhere. They were on the Canongate now, buildings looming over them, black hulks against the ashen clouds. Behind them guns fired again, but no one screamed. They were out of range now, snow falling too fast for anyone to aim true.

'This way!' John pulled her into a side passage. Suddenly the cobbles pitched steeply downwards, and Margareta clutched at John, biting back a cry. Carefully, they edged downwards and out of the alley.

They emerged on the frozen shore of Nor Loch: a vast veil of ice spreading away. Behind them the crags sheared up, the castle's silhouette jutting out against the sky. Snow drifted across the loch on a bitter breeze. Margareta shivered, suddenly aware how poorly she was dressed. Her satin slippers were soaked, her toes numb. She had no cloak; snow-flakes caught on her bare shoulders, glittering briefly before melting, each one pricking the chill deeper into her skin.

'You're cold,' John said, exasperation tinged with affection. 'Here.' He wrapped his cloak around her, pulling her close. 'What were you thinking?'

She wanted nothing more than to close her eyes and relax into his embrace – but when had she ever done so? Always there had been fear and frustration. 'I wanted to see you!'

'Enough to risk bullets? I'm flattered, but—'

She lifted her head and met his gaze. 'You said everything you do is for Johnny and me. How much more have you risked, and how many times?'

'Until you're safe and we're officially married – not enough.' He kissed her, and she remembered their first embrace on a storm-wracked ship. Once again, their kiss was seized amidst danger and all the more precious for it. 'But let the risk be mine, not yours.'

'That's hardly fair,' she protested. 'If you wanted to be certain of my safety, why didn't you warn me? You were supposed to tell Nasmyth the sign!'

He frowned. 'What are you talking about? I did.'

'But no word came to us! If I'd known—'

'You'd have warned Anna – and you'd all have barricaded yourselves in a tower.'

His meaning sunk in. 'Then – James knew, but chose not to tell us? He protected himself, but not his wife?'

'Perhaps he thinks she'll be more useful as a martyr than a wife. Are you surprised?'

'I wish I was.'

'The whole of Scotland wishes James were other than he is, in myriad ways.'

His tone set her on edge. 'You talk as if you'd truly turned to Bothwell's side.'

'Margareta ... I can't deny I've been tempted. These past months, hearing Bothwell talk, seeing him act ... I know he'd make a strong king – but only as the witch's bridle is strong. I've seen dozens die at the stake for his schemes, and God knows how many in this raid. He's just as careless with other people's lives as James.'

'So whose side are you on?'

'Ours,' he said simply. 'I want us to survive – and so both James and Bothwell must believe I'm theirs until the final moment, when one of them claims victory.'

She touched his face. Cold as she was, her palm melted the snow-flakes on his beard. 'This will be the death of you, John. You cannot convince them both forever.'

He laid his hand over hers. 'Then we have to hope one of them loses before I do.'

'How can you live with such a thin hope?'

'Is it thin?' He smiled wryly. 'I've survived so far.'

'So far!' she echoed bitterly.

'And I will survive this,' he said firmly. 'I will live, and I will come back to you.'

His kiss was the only warmth on that frozen shore. The snow billowed white between them and the shadows.

John rested his cheek on her forehead. 'I must go.'

Margareta closed her eyes. 'I could go with you.'

'Dressed like that? You can't become an outlaw in satin slippers.' His laughter turned to grey smoke on the night air.

And then he stiffened. 'Hide. Now!'

She was almost too numb to move, but he hauled her into a gap between the rocks, thrusting her into a crouch.

'John, what—'

But he was darting away, crashing along the shore – and then she grasped why he was being so loud. Because other noises were approaching.

'There!'

'Catch him!'

She pressed herself back against cold rock. A shot rang out and she stifled a scream against her knuckles. *Let them have missed. Dear*

God, let them have missed. Then the sounds of fighting, fists against flesh, feet against ribs.

'Well, well. We'd hoped to catch Bothwell, but look what's washed up on this shore.'

Maitland. He'd left their tower bolthole in pursuit of the rebels. And now the man who'd ordered John to put Grierson in the boots, the bridle, had John surrounded.

'Trying to prove you're a man after all, Maitland?' John laughed – how could he laugh now? 'You of all people know this isn't wise.'

'Master Wemyss,' Maitland sighed, 'you're under arrest. Advising others about wisdom is … at best, unwise.'

'Arresting me won't help your cause. Let me go.'

'Where's your cloak, Wemyss?'

Margareta froze. Her breath came too fast, in white rags. She yanked the cloak high. They couldn't find her. It was already disastrous enough. But if they were both caught, what would become of Johnny?

'Covered a body with it,' John said lightly. 'Sentimental, I know.'

'And you so famed for cynicism. Has fathering that charming child of yours altered your behaviour?'

Her tears were falling freely now. Maitland was threatening her baby, and all she could do was weep into John's cloak.

'But perhaps you weren't expecting the snow to fall again,' Maitland continued. 'Convenient, wasn't it? A snowstorm, concealing Bothwell's escape, almost concealing yours. Some might wonder whether it was wholly natural. Or whether, perhaps, a traitor's lover might have conjured it.'

Her belly clenched. He suspected her. Had he seen her on Castle Hill? Had he heard Geillis's final words and realized who she'd been protecting – and decided to punish Margareta regardless?

'Come with us, Wemyss,' Maitland said softly. 'Or I might see what else has washed up on this shore.'

There was silence. Then John said, 'Tolbooth or castle?'

Maitland chuckled. 'Neither. His Grace wishes to keep you close.'

They were gone, shadows in the white swirls, and the snow closed up behind them.

45

She couldn't get warm. She'd staggered back into Holyrood, half-frozen, having abandoned John's cloak on one of the bodies in the courtyard – at least that ruse would hold true. Then she'd marched up to the first guards she'd seen and imperiously demanded they protect the queen's chambers. Horribly aware how her absence would look to Anna, she'd steeled herself for questions – but she'd found Anna, Elline, and Vibeke all collapsed in Anna's bed, exhausted and tear-stained. When Vibeke stirred, Margareta had whispered, 'I brought guards. We're safe now.' She prayed the explanation would seem satisfactory.

But even wrapped in Anna's ermine-lined covers, with the fire banked and Elline's snoring body alongside hers, Margareta still shivered.

She'd heard the vindictive triumph in Maitland's voice; she knew what he did with prisoners. John was at the mercy of a butcher. And not only John. His words came back to her. *Perhaps James thinks she'd be more useful as a martyr than as a wife.*

Anna dead at Bothwell's hands, her starlight hair spread around her limp body, her white throat slashed: a vision that would unite Scotland and rally all of Christendom against Bothwell. A deposed monarch was one thing, a kidnapped puppet monarch hardly unusual in Scotland. Queens had been killed before, of course: James's mother and two English consorts had been beheaded. But a queen slaughtered by rebels? That would be a heinous crime. And an innocent martyred wife would look far better for James than a wife whose ladies had consulted witches.

She'd always tried to talk Anna out of her fears. But now Margareta didn't know how to reassure her. James had left her unprotected in an act of cold calculation.

Margareta stared helplessly at the shadows. Armed men hadn't been able to fight James. How could one Danish woman – a traitor's wife, kin to witches – oppose a king? He was going to execute John, let Anna die, and without them protecting her, Margareta would burn on Castle Hill.

Witchcraft is in your blood, Margareta. You cannot deny it.

Would the taint never wash away? Nearly all the accused witches in the tolbooth had been burned or tortured to death. Those who had died in the cells had been buried by darkness in unsanctified earth; no gravestones marked their remains. Those who had burned were gone, their ashes taken by the wind. And yet Margareta couldn't forget them. She imagined their ashes lurking between the stones of Edinburgh Castle, floating on dark ripples across Nor Loch. Fragments of Geillis and all the others, carried across Scotland by winds from the North Sea. The very air Margareta breathed was witchcraft. The water she drank, the earth she walked. And, always, her blood, her very self. Just as Ilsa had prophesied, she would never escape it.

Margareta had always thought her friendship with Anna would save her. But Geillis and Agnes had believed that of Bothwell, and he hadn't saved them. However much more she meant to Anna than those women had to Bothwell, what could Anna truly do? In the end, only men's words counted.

James's words mattered most of all. Somehow, Margareta had to make him say the ones that would keep her, John, Anna, and Scotland safe. Only the king could stay an execution.

By morning, gallows had been erected at the Mercat Cross. By noon, the bodies of nine rebels were creaking; by dusk the snowflakes no longer melted on their flesh.

None of them were John. Not yet. They were common men, poor men. Like Geillis: following Bothwell out of fear and desperation, believing he would reward them and keep them safe. He'd failed on both counts.

'I heard they used the boots on Affleck today,' Vibeke said quietly as they tried to sew while glaziers worked on the broken windows in Anna's chambers, wrapped in furs against the winds whistling through the gaps. 'I danced with him once, you know. At the wedding celebrations.'

'He won't be dancing again,' Elline sniffed. 'I'd like to see that Douglas in the boots, the one who tried to shoot me.'

Margareta stared at her embroidery, unable to sew. Affleck had tried to shoot *her* and capture the king: she ought to despise him. But how could she, when John might suffer the same fate any day – any moment?

'Perhaps,' Anna said, 'we should be giving thanks for our deliverance, rather than delighting in the torment of others.'

Margareta risked a glance at Anna. Did she know how close she'd come to death – or that her husband had allowed her would-be murderers into her chambers?

There was a knock at the door and a page sidled in. Margareta was struck by the strangeness: the ruined door hung off its hinges, and yet pages still knocked on the splintered wood.

But his words obliterated any further observations.

'Lady Margareta, Chancellor Maitland wishes to see you.'

He was waiting for her in the cloistered courtyard, wearing black, as ever; against the softly falling snow, he looked out of place, like charred earth in a village, reminding everyone of what had once been, and what violence had wrested it away. Or what violence was yet to come. How long had he been waiting for an opportunity to attack Margareta?

'You look well, my lady,' he said as she approached. 'I feared you'd be abed with a fever – hours in the snow can be debilitating even to the strongest. Women, of course, are all the more susceptible.'

Beneath her cloak, every hair was raised. 'Thank you for your concern, but I've always had a resilient constitution.'

'So I've noticed.' He eyed her up and down. 'I suspect you could walk through a plague pit and come out unscathed. One might wonder whence your remarkable abilities derive. And whether you've ever used them for aught more sinister than your own health.'

She swallowed. 'As well ask how Alexander Lindsay always wins races, or how the Duke of Lennox's face grew so pretty. God blesses us all in different ways.'

'Was it a blessing that made your lover so dexterous a liar?'

Evasion was exhausting and terrifying; she tried to counter-attack. 'Hasn't King James told you? He lies for the royal cause.'

'Ah, but which one?' Maitland smiled coldly. 'Your mistress? Her mother? Or the man who would usurp the throne?'

'Why are you asking me?' she snapped. 'Does your wife know your every thought?'

'Because I would like you to ask Wemyss,' Maitland said. 'Whether he wishes to prove himself loyal – or burn as a witch.'

She'd dreaded hanging, torture. But not burning. Not that worst of deaths. 'He's no witch!'

Maitland smiled again. 'They're building a pyre on Castle Hill as we speak. Shall I order a second pyre so you and your lover can burn together?'

'What do you want?' she hissed. 'What do you want from me?'

'You are a threat,' he said simply. 'You lead the queen astray, and your lover is an outlaw who imperils the king. You are the earth I will scorch to leave Bothwell isolated and defeated, and if that means the ashes stray into Holyrood itself, so be it. Unless you and Wemyss convince me of your loyalty, I will watch you burn until your very bones turn black.'

Maitland had turned the palace into a prison. He led her to a disused chamber on the top floor, guarded by two armed men. Just as one turned the key, Maitland said, 'Remember, Lady Margareta. Come out with a solution to the threat of Bothwell – or not at all.'

Margareta gritted her teeth. How could she and John devise a solution neither the king nor his chancellor had ever found? She could already feel the flames tasting her skin.

Inside, leaning against a pile of rolled tapestries, filth-matted hair hanging over a bloodied nose and a black eye, was John. As soon as he saw her, he struggled to his feet, manacled wrists clanking. 'Margareta – you shouldn't be here—'

She cut him off with a kiss, clutching fiercely at his hair, shoulders, waist – all unburned, all whole. But for how long?

John broke their kiss long enough to ask, 'Is Johnny well?'

'Yes.' Margareta kissed him again, trying to sate herself before they talked, as talk they must. 'He's with your father. Every time he causes any mischief, I get a letter saying how like you he is.'

'Intrepid and dashing, I assume.'

'I'm sure you were a terrible child.'

'And I've only got worse.'

'Quite.'

They smiled – and as if that were a reminder that they shouldn't be cheerful, their smiles vanished.

'Maitland sent me.'

'Christ's wounds.' John rubbed his unshaven jaw, wincing. 'I'd hoped he hadn't seen you. Is this his revenge for my mocking him?'

'Revenge, or ruthlessness.' She shook her head. 'All I know is he wants Bothwell destroyed, and he'll happily burn us if it will so much as scald Bothwell.'

'He threatened burning?' John paled at the thought. 'Margareta, I won't let him harm you. He can do what he likes with me, but I'll do anything to stop you suffering the same fate as your mother and sister. And Geillis.'

'What can you do?' she whispered. 'You're a prisoner. He's going to burn us on Castle Hill. Johnny will be orphaned and Maitland will call it justice!'

'Justice!' John spat. 'There hasn't been justice in Scotland since James's mother returned from France to rule. Princes, regents, earls are murdered in the streets, while women burn for knowing of healing herbs.'

'And Bothwell has let them,' Margareta pointed out. 'Geillis and Agnes thought Bothwell would save them – now they're ashes on the wind. And we'll join them, unless …' But she couldn't finish – because what could they do? How could they possibly defeat the most powerful noble in Scotland?

'You don't need to persuade me that Bothwell would be no better than James.' John grimaced. 'I've been outlawed with the man for months. Oh, he talks well, and he certainly believes his own legend – but I doubt I could name a dozen people who ever received the rewards Bothwell promised them. The only promises he keeps are his threats. His kingdom would be brutal.'

'The kingdom's already brutal.'

'But the king is not.'

'Have you forgotten what they suffered in the tolbooth? Geillis, Grierson—'

'What a king orders and what a king does are different – they have to be.' John gritted his teeth. 'There's no denying James commands violence. But he takes care to keep his own hands clean while Maitland and Lennox look cruel or foolish. Bothwell, however, when men displease him, he beats them bloody. I saw him bite a man's ear off in a brawl. He's savage. A good fighter – but wars end, and kings must rule afterwards. No, he cannot save Scotland.'

'Then who?'

'James.'

Margareta stared. 'But you've always said the opposite. You speak of James with scorn – sometimes I think you despise him.'

'I despise his choices, not James himself,' John countered. 'For all his faults, he is the rightful king, and he's the only man who might one day unite Scotland and England. Queen Elizabeth cannot live forever, and James is her nearest blood relative. If he doesn't win this war with Bothwell, the chaos engulfing Scotland will spread to England and the whole island will drown in blood.'

'Can James prevent that?'

'James has weathered storms all his life,' John pointed out. 'He's a survivor. To have survived assassins, conspiracies, witches ... he cannot truly be the weak fool Bothwell believes him.' His bloodied face was grim. 'I need to see James.'

* * *

Inside Anna's desecrated chambers a troupe of acrobats was performing, hoping to gain Anna's approval to entertain the court. Joining Anna's ladies on cushions, Margareta watched as a slender boy sprang onto a man's upheld palms, then rose into a graceful handstand. Would Anna and her ladies watch somersaults and cartwheels while John and Margareta climbed the steps to their pyre?

'We need a higher ceiling,' Vibeke observed. 'He'll stub his toes on the beams.'

'I'm aching just watching them,' Elline sighed.

Anna met Margareta's eyes. Quietly, she said, 'Perhaps there are better contortionists locked up in the palace.'

'Surely the best still walk free.' Margareta dropped her voice even lower. 'I need to talk to you.'

Anna gave her an assessing look, then rose, saying to the acrobats, 'Report to my steward when you've finished – provided you can keep my ladies entertained.'

They moved away to the repaired window, gasps of admiration rippling behind them at the next bizarre position. Outside, the setting sun cast copper flames over the snow.

'I suppose this is about Wemyss,' Anna said coolly.

'In part.' Margareta wet her lips. 'But it's also about you.'

Anna stiffened. 'Me?'

Margareta nodded. 'You were right. Maitland and James were willing to sacrifice you if it meant they could defeat Bothwell. They knew he'd attack Holyrood – and they left you unprotected. We must act. And I need your help.'

Anna stared at the snow as the sunset began to gutter into blue dusk. 'All my life people have thought me stupid. Frivolous. As if coherent thoughts cannot run through a fair head. It ought to be gratifying to find myself proven right. And yet … I almost wish I was that girl. Anna the fool, dancing past disaster in a pretty gown. I think she would be far happier than me.'

'Better to be wise and safe, however sad, than ignorant and imperilled.'

'I'm imperilled anyway.'

'That's why you must help me!' Margareta said urgently.

'I'm listening.'

'If you can arrange to see James alone – if I can bring John to him when no other advisers are there to interrupt – then he can save us.'

'How?'

Margareta hesitated, reluctant to confess that she didn't know the whole of John's plan. 'Anna, please trust me.'

'Trust you?' Anna's eyes widened incredulously. 'You're asking me to say nothing as you help a prisoner escape. You want us to be alone with a man who attacked the palace. How do you know Wemyss doesn't intend to assassinate James – or me?'

'How can any of us know another's intent for certain?' She took Anna's hand. 'But after everything that's happened, I do trust John. And I'm asking you to trust me.'

Anna regarded her with that winter-coloured gaze. 'Of all the women who serve me, I have more reasons to distrust you than any other.' She laid her other hand atop Margareta's. 'But despite that, I trust you the most.'

Sometimes boldness was the only way to get what you wanted. Anna, who had never before uttered so brazen a request, sent a message inviting James to her chambers that night, promising 'some news we have long desired to hear'. Meanwhile Margareta approached the room where John was locked up, brandishing a letter bearing Anna's seal, smudged enough that it resembled James's.

'The king demands an audience with the prisoner.'

The guards frowned. 'Chancellor Maitland said—'

Margareta gave him a cold glare. 'The hour is late – will you force your king to wait?'

Royal guards knew the consequences of angering the king. 'Very well.' He unlocked the door and stepped inside. She heard a key turn, then John grunting in pain swiftly followed by relief. He emerged, rolling his shoulders and rubbing chafed wrists, his bruised eye now a lurid purple, his moustache crusted with blood from his nose.

She must have looked horrified, for his mouth twitched in a weary, laconic attempt at a smile. 'Believe me, I could have looked far worse.'

She thought of Geillis and the others. They had to succeed tonight: she couldn't bear the thought of Maitland setting the boots to John's flesh.

'Come,' she said, striving to keep any feeling from her voice. 'The king and queen await.'

The guard shoved John in the back and John swore obligingly: they had to keep up the pretence that he didn't wish to be brought before the king he'd betrayed.

Every step they took through the palace thrummed another heartbeat through Margareta, all six feet battering a pulse against her ribs. What if they met someone? Maitland, his black robes indistinguishable from the shadows. Lennox, hot-tempered at the best of times. She'd be found out, and then it would be her wrists rubbed raw by shackles, the bridle swinging closer. And the pyres would be built.

Outside Anna's chamber, Margareta turned to the guard. 'You may wait here.'

Did he hear her voice crack as she tried to pull it back from shrillness? But he didn't know her well enough to realize the hitch in her words was anything other than a Danish accent. The guard merely nodded and took up a protective stance before the door – and Margareta led an escaped prisoner into the queen's bedchamber.

Anna rose as they entered. She wore an embroidered robe over her nightgown, her silvery hair rippling over her shoulders: the picture of innocence. 'He hasn't come. What if he doesn't want to see me?'

'He will come,' Margareta insisted, the instinct to reassure Anna silencing her own flaring doubts.

'But—'

'We've enough to worry about,' John said, 'without agonizing over everything that hasn't happened yet.' His familiar wryness and irritating refusal to be afraid were almost reassuring.

Anna's breathing steadied. 'Well then, Master Wemyss, will you tell us your plan?'

Before he could reply, someone knocked on the door and they all jerked like shot deer. Margareta grabbed John's hand and dragged him aside, out of sight: even if James were alone, they couldn't risk him seeing John before he was inside.

'Come,' Anna called, moving to the table. She put a hand on the wine jug, but her fingers shook too much to pour.

James stepped inside. He was alone, thank heaven, and dressed, like Anna, in nightgown and rich robe; he might have been any royal husband making a conjugal visit. 'Good evening, wife,' he said, a hint of mockery lacing his words. 'I must confess, your rather cryptic message intrigued me.'

Anna's smile wavered. 'I hope you'll be pleased.'

He still hadn't seen Margareta or John. She hardly dared breathe. James tilted his head; she imagined a cynically raised eyebrow. 'You cannot mean to tell me you're with child. That would be miraculous.'

Anna swallowed. 'It isn't that. It's a solution. To the problem of the Earl of Bothwell.'

James laughed. 'So you have discovered what none of my councillors or soldiers could? Bravo, Anna!'

'No,' Anna said, a flicker of anger in her lips. 'But he has.' And she looked over James's shoulder.

James turned. 'You!' His hand flew to his hip – and found neither belt nor knife. 'What the devil is this?'

John raised empty hands. 'I mean you no harm, sire. I swear it.'

'You escape from a cell, lure me here under false pretences, and expect me to believe that?' James let out a tight laugh, rubbing his throat, and Margareta remembered the gorget he always wore. Was Anna's chamber the only room James ever entered without armour?

'Yes,' John said simply. 'After all, you have in your possession one of the two things I treasure most in the world.'

James glanced at Margareta. 'Such sentiment, Wemyss. I expected better of you.'

'Better than loyalty? Better than faith? I am here for no other reasons.'

James said nothing. Behind him, Anna said, 'Will you hear him out, husband?'

He rounded on her. 'You dare speak sweetly to me! You and that crow of a maid – you've both deceived me! I should send you back to Denmark with nothing but the clothes on your backs!'

Anna flinched. 'James, please!'

Margareta said, 'Once you've heard him speak, sire, you may think differently.'

James glared at her. Then he looked back at John and snapped, 'You realize I could call the guards at any moment? They would kill you instantly.'

John didn't back down. 'I know. That I'm here anyway should make you want to listen.'

James stared. Suddenly, he threw back his head and laughed. 'So be it! Let us all sit down together and drink fine malmsey! And when you're done talking … perhaps I will still have you killed.'

John inclined his head in grim acknowledgement. 'I've had the threat of death hanging over my head for months. I measure my days in stays of execution.'

And so they sat. Margareta poured four cups of wine, praying that the spilled drops would be the only dark stains in the chamber that night.

James lifted his cup to John. 'To your attempt to save your life.'

John raised his. 'To my endeavours to prove my loyalty.'

James looked expectantly at Anna and Margareta. 'Well? It would be churlish not to offer your own toasts.'

Anna lifted her cup. 'To our hopes for the future.'

Margareta followed suit. 'To the Queen of Scotland.'

James frowned. 'And the King of Scotland?'

'That depends on whether you decide to kill John.'

He snorted, both amused and angered. 'Then let us find out.'

They all drank deeply, as if the slow seep of malmsey might rein in the fear racing beneath their skin.

'Well then, Wemyss. Explain yourself.'

John set his cup down. 'Sire, you charged me with spying on Bothwell that I might discover how to thwart him. I believe I've done so.'

'Since I gave you that task, he's besieged my palace. Hardly a successful mission.'

'When you play a man at chess, you do not discover his strategy in the first move,' John countered.

'So what is Bothwell's strategy?'

'He wants to rule Scotland.'

'Is that it? Your penetrating insight into the earl's schemes?' James spat out a laugh. 'Forgive me if I don't shower you with castles and titles.'

'He wishes to do so legitimately.'

James frowned. 'What do you mean?'

John leaned forward. 'Bothwell doesn't wish to be a usurper. He wants to be Scotland's rightful ruler. He's never wanted to murder you. To kidnap you and force you to do his bidding, yes, but kill you? That was his uncle's mistake. He killed your father and raped your mother, and the lords all deserted him. Bothwell will not risk the nobility uniting against him. He wants them to choose him over you.'

James's face was dark and unreadable. 'God chooses kings, not dissenting Scotsmen.'

'God chose your mother,' John pointed out. 'Scotland chose you. All along, Bothwell has wanted you to destroy yourself, to be terrified either into submission or into behaving so rashly that Scotland turns away from you and raises Bothwell onto the throne.'

James drained his cup and held it out for Margareta to fill. 'So what do you suggest?'

John smiled. 'If he seeks to gain the throne by legitimate means, those are the means you must use to stop him.'

'I am the king,' James hissed. 'Everything I do is legitimate; everything I do is sanctioned by God!'

'If you hunt Bothwell down and slay him, common men won't see that as God's work, but as butchery.'

'Why should I care what common men think?'

'Because you've presided over hundreds of commoners' deaths. Bothwell hasn't. They'll think of him as their champion. They'll want him to defeat you.'

'Then more of them will die on Castle Hill.'

John shook his head. 'More bloodshed isn't the answer. What's needed is the king's justice.'

James narrowed his eyes. 'I begin to think your vision of justice differs significantly from mine.'

'My vision is of Bothwell defeated. Not on the field of battle – but in the courts of law.'

James's face didn't change – and yet his interest was piqued. 'Go on.'

'Bothwell prides himself on his lineage,' John said. 'He's the highest noble in the land, and he wants everyone to know it. So you must strip that away from him. You've already declared him an outlaw, but you must go further. Strip him of his titles. Make his lands forfeit. And then ... exile him.'

'Exile him? On what charge?'

'Witchcraft.' John's eyes might have been torches, so fiercely did they burn. 'He must stand trial.'

'Ah.' James tossed back his wine. 'There we have a problem. All the witnesses are dead.'

'I'm not.'

Margareta's throat tightened; she struggled to swallow her wine. Even mentioning his survival would put the opposite thought in James's head. John was dancing on thin ice.

'And what would you contribute to this trial?'

'I saw him,' John said softly. 'I saw the Earl of Bothwell at the convention in North Berwick on All Hallows' Eve. He was dressed as the devil and commanded the women since condemned as witches. You know this. But I am the only surviving witness. And Bothwell wasn't the only Scottish noble there that night. Only I can give you their names.'

'So you wish to bargain with me?' James's eyebrows lifted. 'Me, your sovereign?'

John met his gaze. 'I do.'

'And your terms?'

'A royal pardon. Permission to marry Margareta.'

'You understand, of course, that as your sovereign, I could simply command you?'

John said, 'I haven't finished.'

James's purple-stained lips twisted in a snarl. 'You dare speak thus to me?'

'My final demand is that Queen Anna's safety be guaranteed.'

'You go too far!' James shot to his feet, dashing his cup to the floor. 'Remember who you are, John Wemyss. You're the son of a minor laird, with lands even cattle scorn, and you dare suggest the King of Scotland cannot look after his wife! Men like you cannot speak thus to princes!'

'What about prince to prince?'

James turned to Margareta, scorn contorting his face further. 'Is arrogance contagious? Do you think yourself so lofty now?'

'No,' Margareta said, 'but Queen Sophia might.' She drew out the letter John had given her and held it up so James could see Sophia's seal, trying to forget the words John had said as he handed it over: *In case I don't get out of this cell alive.*

James's eyes darted between them all. 'A conspiracy,' he whispered hoarsely. 'You're all conspiring against me—'

'We never wished to pit ourselves against you,' Anna said. 'Only to remind you of our loyalty – and of yours.'

'You impugn my loyalty!' James seethed with outrage.

'You abandoned me,' Anna said. 'You left me with scarcely a handful of men to protect me whilst barricading yourself in the most secure tower. Was that loyal? My mother does not think so.'

'Your mother is no longer a queen—'

'She is the king's mother, and Christian is just fourteen.' Anna took a sip of wine; Margareta wondered if it were to disguise her nerves. 'You struck a bargain with them when you married me. You made a vow before God – once in Denmark, and once in Scotland – to protect me. We expect you to uphold your vows.'

James turned his glare on Margareta and held out a hand as if laying a knife to her throat. 'Give me the letter.'

Margareta handed it over, straining to keep her hand steady. Watching James break the seal, fear pierced her core. She had no idea whether Sophia had written what John hoped. He'd told her all about the danger Anna was in – but what if Sophia dismissed him and Margareta as unimportant? What if, like James, she had no interest in keeping them safe, let alone rewarding them?

'She threatens me,' James said, icy with rage. 'She vows to take back my wife's dowry through court or violence, to blacken my name throughout Christendom, and unite every power from France to the Russias against me, unless I treat her daughter as she sees fit. And she also demands that I respect the marriage of her kinswoman to her loyal servant and allow them to sanctify their union in Scotland.' He looked up. 'How dare she? How dare you all?'

It was not the response they'd envisaged. Margareta didn't know where to look – at the king, or Anna's aghast face, or John, his hands flat on the tabletop, as if suddenly aware he held no weapons.

James tossed the letter into the fireplace. 'What do you take me for? A gutless, brainless boy-king? Or a feckless trifler who keeps faith with no one?'

'You haven't kept faith with any of us!' The words bolted from Margareta's lips like frightened horses.

'Haven't I?' James pointed at her. 'You I promised to keep from stake or cell, and are you not alive and free?' He pointed at John. 'You I promised a wife and a pardon – when you had earned them. Bothwell is free, so have you earned them? You remain alive, so have you had any sign that you will not earn them anon?' He turned to Anna. 'And as for you …'

Anna braced herself, her white hands folding into her lap like a cornered hare laying back her ears.

'I have made you a queen.' James shook his head. 'Is a country not enough for you?'

Anna swallowed. 'I want … I need a child.'

'For what? To raise him up as my rival?' James turned away, leaning on the mantelpiece. 'When you lost that baby, I grieved, as any man would. But I was also relieved. And that relief has rendered me reluctant to visit your bed ever since. Do you know what my cousin Elizabeth says when her Privy Council demand she name an heir? "Think you I could love my own winding sheet?" I was my mother's, the shroud that wrapped up her reign and made it ready for burial. I have not tried to beget an heir as best I could, because part of me doesn't wish to give the nobles an inch of cloth with which to smother me.'

'But I thought you preferred—' Margareta bit back her words.

James turned, a bitter smile on his lips. 'Preferred what? Men? So goes the rumour. But why must there be a preference at all?'

Better brazen than craven; they were already deep in trouble. 'On your wedding night …'

James snorted. 'I doubt I'm the first man to drink too much at his own wedding and say things less than wholly appropriate. Whatever I feel for Alexander, I know my duty. So let it be understood that I am fit to sire an heir, as and when I wish to. Without requiring herbs.'

Margareta bowed her head, thankful that the deference hid her flaming cheeks.

'Then when will you wish to?' Anna rose. 'Husband, when?'

'When Bothwell's defeated.'

'But don't you see?' She took a step towards him. 'This is the way. Just as Wemyss said, Bothwell will be defeated when his legitimacy is gone and ours is established beyond question. That is best achieved with an heir. When a prince is your nearest kin, your own beloved son, then Bothwell is pushed further from the throne, and you will have gained a loyal follower. Boys love no one so well as their fathers.'

'I didn't love mine,' he pointed out.

'You had no chance. Perhaps that makes you despise his memory more.' Anna reached out and took his hand. 'We will secure Scotland together. Our children will inherit two kingdoms, Scotland and England.'

John caught Margareta's eye, both horribly aware that they were out of place. Were they also out of luck?

'Master Wemyss,' James said. 'What am I to do with you?'

He stood, head high. 'What you will, sire. I am your faithful servant.'

'Indeed? Here I was, thinking you an escaped prisoner.'

The silence stretched, to the point of pain.

'Or perhaps,' James said, 'you are a brave young gallant, aided by your lover. A romantic tale worthy of celebration by every makar in Scotland.'

Was he taunting them? Or threatening them again?

But James's smile was no longer malicious. 'Perhaps my enemies are right and I am a vacillating, whimsical fool. But I find myself in merciful humour tonight. Besides, if you're to gather more evidence against Bothwell, you'll hardly be useful in a cell – or on a pyre.'

Margareta winced. John was torn between frowning and smiling. 'Do you mean to set me free?'

'Certainly not.' James let his words knell a moment, then chuckled. 'You're escaping, remember. The most brazen escape in a hundred years – out of the queen's bedchamber window. You'll gallop out of Holyrood on the king's own horse, with your lover riding pillion, and I shall be so amused by your derring-do that I shall pardon you.'

'Sire,' John said, pushing the habitual cynicism out of his voice to make way for genuine humility, 'I am more grateful than I can say—'

'I found you amusing,' James interrupted. 'Tell Bothwell that. Tell him I laughed. That I found *him* laughable.'

Not so much mercy as a calculated swipe: one that seemed a blundering miss until the blade struck home.

'Well?' James cocked a brow. 'What are you waiting for? There's the window, Master Wemyss. I believe the recent attack left some holes in the stones that will serve for footholds. Lady Margareta, best you steal the chestnut mare – the grey is like to bite you. You may leave my wife and me alone.'

Half-dazed, Margareta turned for the door and John moved towards the window.

'But remember this,' James said. 'You owe me your lives. All of you. And in my kingdom everyone must pay their debts.'

* * *

Leith Harbour was hushed. Only the cats were awake, soft shadows prowling hopefully round the lobster pots. Moonlight rippled across the sea, plucking silver lines like lute strings. As John pulled the horse up at the edge of the bluff overlooking the harbour, Margareta shook her head at the sea's calmness.

'Do you remember when we first tried to cross? The storms that drove us back – I'd never seen such violent winds.'

John rested his cheek against her hair. 'I remember you trying to dash across the decks – I had to save you from drowning.'

'You didn't—'

'I've no doubt you could have saved yourself,' he said, kissing her earlobe.

Margareta was silent a moment. Then, 'Have we saved ourselves?'

She felt his grimace as his jaw moved against her head. 'No one in Scotland is entirely safe. We've been saved by James – he won't let us forget that. But we have his protection, for as long as he chooses to extend it.'

'Even against allegations of witchcraft?'

'You still fear that?'

She thought of Castle Hill, of the pyre that might so easily have been theirs. 'I will always fear it. Nearly a hundred Scots were burned in a year. The danger hasn't gone.'

'No.' He pulled her closer against his chest. 'As long as men are afraid, there will be people accused of witchcraft.'

'You think it was just fear? That those storms were natural, that Agnes Sampson was just a woman with some herbs and a strange manner? That the dead were all innocent?' *That Geillis, now ash discarded at an unnamed crossroad, did not deserve to die?* The injustice hurt too much to voice.

'I think many people have been executed who didn't deserve it. But the only person whose opinion counts is the one who wears a crown.'

She stared out to sea. Somewhere beyond the moonlit waves lay Denmark, and the square in Helsingør where Ilsa and Johanna had died. They could go back. But Denmark was no haven, and Margareta's place was with Anna. 'That cannot be just.'

'No. But it's the world we live in. One day we must all face a king's justice, whether it be some mortal ruler or the king in the life to come.'

'You sound so bleak.'

'Our world is bleak.' He touched her chin, turning her to face him. 'All that lights the darkness is this.' He kissed her, and that kiss was deep fear, and need, and somewhere in the touch of two bodies, there was also hope.

Epilogue

The boy toddled between rosebushes, clapping his fat little hands always a beat behind the butterflies he couldn't catch. His chuckles cantered ahead of the spring breeze up to Stirling's walls, where Margareta rested her elbows on warm stone and watched the young prince. Henry, they'd christened him, perhaps in homage to the English queen's father, an attempt to flatter her into naming an heir at last – or perhaps James endeavouring to exorcise the ghost of that last Henry Stuart, his murdered father.

Even in the spring sunshine, she couldn't forget the dead. Geillis, Ilsa, Johanna, Agnes. All the others whose names she didn't know and no one would remember. But many of the nobles wandering in the castle gardens were haunted by memories of the man who'd nearly destroyed their king.

Exiled. The word was a sigh of relief. Bothwell was gone at last. It had taken years, but James had built higher walls with laws and trials and royal decrees than those of any castle, and Bothwell had been unable to breach them. John's evidence had done its work. Bothwell's erstwhile supporters now vehemently pretended they had been no such thing, to little avail. There was nothing left in Scotland for Bothwell now. Like his uncle before him, he'd fled overseas.

And what of her fate? Margareta knew where it lay: with the pale-haired woman laughing as her son wobbled towards her, a woman no longer accused of barrenness. And, of course, with the man at Anna's side. The sunlight flinched against the metal at James's throat; he still wore armour – not only that made of steel but also the studied flippancy with which he spoke in public to a wistfully resigned Alexander. Margareta and John were as safe as James chose to make them – and James would never believe himself safe. He would always see witchery in a storm, familiars where others saw cats. No crown could defend a man against invisible weapons.

'Mama!'

Johnny crashed into her legs, his sturdy body warm against hers as he held up his latest treasure for her inspection: a bird's eggshell, veined with sky-blue. 'Look!'

'The prettiest egg I ever did see,' she said, kissing his forehead. 'Aren't you clever to find it?'

Her husband joined her on the wall, resting one hand across hers while tousling Johnny's hair with the other. His fingers were ink-stained: letters for overseas, she supposed. He would never stop being James's spy. At night the knowledge still kept her from sleep. 'I smelled lemon cakes. Shall we go down?'

Margareta smiled up at him, remembering what a simple lemon cake had meant to a girl long ago. 'In a moment. Let's be alone here a little while longer.'

There would always be the court, with its intrigues and perils. But for now there was sunshine on skin, the scent of opening roses in the air, a kiss on a castle wall, and she remembered how to delight in being alive.

Historical Note

Much of this novel takes place in the gaps left by historical records; however, there are some occasions where I have deliberately deviated from the known facts. The timeline of Bothwell's rebellion against James VI has been condensed here: he made several attacks on royal palaces between 1591 and his trial in 1593. John Wemyss's escape from royal custody was from Dalkeith Palace rather than Holyrood, in August 1592, a breakout immortalised in the ballad 'The Laird O' Logie'. I have also altered some characters' names to avoid confusion: Katrine Skinkell and Hanna Kroas are here called Elline and Vibeke, and Ana Koldings has become Erna.

The North Berwick witch trials represented one of the most brutal periods in Scottish history. More than 100 individuals, mostly women, from the East Lothian area were accused of witchcraft. Many were imprisoned and tortured; it's likely some died of their wounds. The exact number of those executed as witches remains unknown.

Witchcraft was a capital offence in Scotland between 1563 and 1736. Some sources suggest as many as 6,000 people were accused of witchcraft in this period; recently, the Survey of Scottish Witchcraft have identified 3,837 Scottish people who were accused, of whom 84% were women. Around 67% were killed. Per capita, Scotland executed four times as many so-called witches than the average figure for any other European country, and three times as many as their English counterparts.

In March 2022, on International Women's Day, Nicola Sturgeon officially apologised on behalf of the Scottish government to those accused of witchcraft. The Witches of Scotland campaign continues to seek a national memorial for these victims.

Acknowledgments

Despite imagining these acknowledgements many times in my daydreams (along with my Desert Island Discs playlist and Strictly Movie Week routine), when it came to actually writing them, I had no idea where to start. However, it seems sensible to begin at the beginning. So the first mention must go to 11UEn1, class of 2018 (one of the loveliest groups I've ever had the privilege to teach!), who may or may not have noticed me zoning out after reading Tracy Borman's article about James VI's witchcraft obsession. If you know nothing about Act 1 Scene 3 of 'Macbeth', it's because I came up with the idea for this book when I was meant to be telling you all about the witches' prophecies. Sorry!

I am forever indebted to New Writing North, and the peerless support they offer to writers in the North of England. Winning a Northern Writers Award in 2014, and the Arvon Award in 2020, not only provided me with practical support to write, but also made me feel validated as a writer long before I was able to be published. Particular thanks go to Anna Disley and Will Mackie at New Writing North, along with Chris Mullin, who judged the 2014 Awards, and Andrew Kidd at Arvon.

To all the writers and publishing folk who have offered me constructive criticism and encouragement in various workshops over the years, particularly Anna Freeman, Emma Darwin, Margaret Elphinstone, Anne McLeod, and Anna Woodford. To Imogen Robertson, for her openness, warmth, and sage advice. To Chloe Timms, for organising the Zoom writers' group, an invaluably supportive and welcoming community, and, during termtime, the main reason I manage to write anything at all. To Thorne Ryan, for so generously giving up her time to share her insights into how to make 'The Burnings' a far better, more streamlined book.

To Anne Williams, my wonderful agent, for her patience, wisdom, and support; it's been a long journey to publication and I am so grateful to have had you by my side.

To Daisy Watt, my fantastic editor, for her enthusiasm and perception, and for always making me feel as though my edits were actually improvements rather than the rambling nonsense I secretly suspected them to be!

To Sarah Dronfield for her astute copyedits; I'm sorry for all the inappropriate colons.

To Genevieve Pegg, Megan Jones, Alice Murphy-Pyle, and the whole team at HarperNorth: thank you for your support and for welcoming me into the fold.

To my parents, who never took us on holiday without visiting an abundance of castles and stately homes: my Tudor obsession definitely owes much to our Warwick and Kenilworth adventures. Especially my mum, for encouraging my love of Shakespeare, books, and writing. My late grandparents, for always saying they would love to read the never-finished 'novels' I spent my childhood writing; I wish they could have held this one.

To Team Kelsey, for always being so encouraging and enthusiastic about my writing, and for never saying you thought the new member of your family was thoroughly odd despite me always being surgically attached to either a novel or a notebook.

To my friends, for being generally awesome and the best support network I could have.

To my beloved English department, past and present: the most creative, empathetic, witty, industrious, and supportive group of people I could ever hope to work with. If I can't spend my days writing in a seaside cottage, I'm glad I get to spend them with you lot.

Erin and Oliver have been no help whatsoever, unless I count the pram/sling naps where I thought through knotty plot problems, but they do make the non-writing parts of life more entertaining! I hope they grow up to love stories and history as much as I do.

And last, but certainly not least, to Tom, who I genuinely could not have done this without – you are wonderful, and not just at building bookshelves.

For more unmissable reads,
sign up to the HarperNorth newsletter at
www.harpernorth.co.uk

or find us on Twitter at
@HarperNorthUK

Harper
North